When i Found You

Catherine Ryan Hyde

BLACK SWAN

TRANSWORLD PUBLISHERS
61–63 Uxbridge Road, London W5 5SA
A Random House Group Company
www.rbooks.co.uk

WHEN I FOUND YOU
A BLACK SWAN BOOK: 9780552775724

First publication in Great Britain
Black Swan edition published 2009

Copyright © Catherine Ryan Hyde 2009

Addresses for Random House Group Ltd companies outside the UK
can be found at: www.randomhouse.co.uk
The Random House Group Ltd Reg. No. 954009

The Random House Group Limited supports The Forest Stewardship
Council (FSC), the leading international forest certification organisation.
All our titles that are printed on Greenpeace approved FSC certified paper
carry the FSC logo. Our paper procurement policy can be found at
www.rbooks.co.uk/environment

Typeset in 11/15pt Giovanni Book by
Falcon Oast Graphic Art Ltd

I   G1 8EX.

For Harvey

Part One

Nathan McCann

The Day He Found You in the Woods

Nathan McCann stood in his dark kitchen, a good two hours before dawn. He flipped on the overhead light, halfway hoping to see the coffeemaker all set up with water and grounds and waiting to be plugged in and set to percolating. Instead he saw the filter basket lying empty in the dish drain, looking abandoned and bare.

Why he always expected otherwise, he wasn't sure. It had been years since Flora set up coffee for him on these early mornings. Decades since she rose early with him to serve fried eggs and orange juice and toast.

Quietly, so as not to wake her, he took a box of oat flake cereal down from the cupboard, then stood in the cold rush of air from the icebox and poured skim milk into a yellow plastic bowl.

You don't have to be so quiet, he thought to himself. Flora was in her bedroom at the far end of the hall with the door closed. But he *was* quiet, always had been in such situations, and felt unlikely to change his pattern now.

As he sat down at the cool Formica table to eat his cereal, he heard Sadie, his curly-coated retriever, awake and ready to go, excited by the prospect of a light on in the house before sunrise. He sat listening to the periodic ringing of the chain-link of her kennel run as she jumped up and hit it with her front paws. Born and bred for just such a morning as this, Sadie recognized a good duck-hunt at its first visible or audible indication.

He often wished he could bring her into the house with him, Sadie who gave so readily of her time and attention. But Flora would have none of it.

Nathan stood in the cool autumn dark, a moment before sunrise, his shotgun angled up across his shoulder.

He insisted that Sadie obey him.

He called her name again, cross with her for forcing him to break the morning stillness, the very reason he had come. In the six years he'd owned the dog, she had never before refused to come when he called.

Remembering this, he shined his big lantern flashlight on her. In the brief instant before she squinted her eyes and turned her face from the light, he saw something, some look that would do for an explanation. In that instinctive way a man knows his dog and a dog knows her man, she had been able to say something to him. She was not defying his judgment, but asking him to consider, for a moment, her own.

'You must come,' she said by way of her expression. 'You must.'

For the first time in the six years he'd owned her, Nathan obeyed his dog. He came when she called him.

She stood under a tree, digging. But she was not digging in that frantic way dogs do, both front feet flying in rhythm. Instead she gently pushed leaves aside with her muzzle, and occasionally with one front paw.

He couldn't see around her, so he pulled her off by the collar.

'OK, girl. I'm here now. Let me see what you've got.'

He shined the light on the mound of fallen leaves. Jutting out from the pile was an unfathomably small – yet unmistakably human – foot.

'Dear God,' Nathan said, and set the flashlight down.

He scooped underneath the lump with both gloved hands at once, lifted the child up to him, blew leaves off its face. It was wrapped in a sweater – a regular adult-sized sweater – and wore a tiny, well-fitted, multi-colored knit cap. It could not have been more than a day or two old.

He felt he would know more if he could hold the flashlight and the child at the same time.

He pulled off one glove with his teeth and touched

the skin of its face. It felt cool against the backs of his fingers.

'What kind of person would do such a thing?' he said quietly. He looked up to the sky as if God were immediately available to answer that question.

The sky had gone light now, but just a trace. Dawn had not crested the hill but lay beyond the horizon somewhere, informally stating that it planned to come to stay.

He set the child gently on the bed of leaves and looked more closely with the flashlight. The child moved its lips and jaw sluggishly, a dry-mouthed gesture, as if mashing something against its palate, or, in any case, wishing it could.

'Dear God,' Nathan said again.

He had not until that moment considered the possibility that the child might be alive.

He left his shotgun in the nest of leaves, because he needed both hands to steady the child's body against his, hold the head firmly to his chest. He and his dog sprinted for the station wagon.

Behind them, dawn broke across the lake. Ducks flew unmolested. Forgotten.

At the hospital, two emergency-room workers sprang into rapid, jerky motion when they saw what Nathan held. They set the infant on a cart, a speck in the middle of an ocean, and unwrapped the sweater. A boy, Nathan saw. A boy still wearing his umbilical cord, a badge of innocence.

As they ran, rolling the cart alongside, a doctor caught up and pulled off the knit cap. It fell to the linoleum floor unnoticed. Nathan picked it up, stowed it in a zippered pocket of his hunting vest. It was so small, that cap; it wouldn't cover Nathan's palm.

He moved as close to the door of the examining room as he felt would be allowed.

He heard the doctor say, 'Throw him out in the woods on an October night, then give him a nice warm sweater and a little hand-knit hat to hold in his body heat. Now that's ambivalence.'

Nathan walked down the hall and bought a cup of hot coffee from a vending machine. It was indeed hot, but that's all that could be said for it.

He stood for several minutes in front of the coffee machine, gazing into its shiny metal face as if looking at a television set, or out a window. Or into a mirror. Because, in fact, he could see a vague, slightly distorted reflection of himself there.

Nathan was not a man given to eyeing himself for extended moments in mirrors. Shaving was one thing, but to look into his own eyes would cause him to demur, much the way he would if looking into the eyes of another. But the image was just ill-defined enough to cause him no stress or embarrassment.

So he stood for a moment, sipping the dreadful coffee, allowing himself to take in the evidence of his own sentience. Feeling, in a way he could not have explained, that some history was being shaped, the importance of which could not be fully estimated.

Something had been set in motion, he allowed himself to think, that could never, and perhaps should never, be reversed.

When he had finished the coffee, he rinsed out the cup at the water fountain and refilled it with fresh water.

He walked back out to the station wagon to offer Sadie a drink.

Twenty or thirty minutes later the doctor came out of that room.

'Doctor,' Nathan called, and ran down the hall. The doctor looked blank, as if he could not recall where he'd seen Nathan before. 'I'm the man who found that baby in the woods.'

'Ah, yes,' the doctor said. 'So you are. Can you stay a few minutes? The police will want to speak with you. If you have to go, please leave your phone number at the desk. I'm sure you understand. They'll want all the details they can get. To try to find who did this thing.'

'How is the boy?'

'What kind of shape is he in? Bad shape. Will he survive? Maybe. I don't promise, but he's a fighter.

Sometimes they're stronger than you can imagine at that age.'

'I want to adopt that boy,' Nathan said.

He felt more than a little bit stunned to hear himself say those words.

First of all, he had not really known this to be the case. At least, not in words. Not in an identifiable sense. It was as if he had told the doctor and himself in one broad stroke. And, secondly, it was unlike him to share his thoughts easily with others, especially if he had not had sufficient time to mull them over, grow accustomed to them.

It seemed this was a morning of unlimited firsts.

'If he survives, you mean.'

'Yes,' Nathan said. Already stung by the gravity of the warning. 'If he survives.'

'I'm sorry,' the doctor said. 'Adoption would not be my department.'

He told the story in earnest detail to the two policemen when they arrived and took his statement, careful to stress that the real hero was sitting out in the back seat of his station wagon.

'Baby'd be dead if it wasn't for you,' the more vocal of the two policemen said. He was a tall, broad-shouldered man, the type who seemed to rely more on brawn than intellect to guide him through this life. Normally Nathan would have been intimidated and repelled by such a man, law officer or not. So it raised a strange and conflicted set of emotions when the policeman spoke to him as a hero.

'And Sadie,' Nathan said. 'My dog. She's a curly-coated retriever. She's a remarkable animal.'

'Right. Look. We know you've got stuff to do, but we need you to show us the exact crime scene.'

'No inconvenience,' Nathan said. 'I was on my way back there now, to retrieve my shotgun.'

They began walking toward the hospital parking lot together.

'I want to adopt that boy,' Nathan said. Not so much to bare his soul, but in hopes of being steered in the right direction. He felt an unfamiliar sense of haste, as if something could slip away from him if he didn't hurry and pin it down.

'We couldn't tell you nothing about that,' the policeman replied.

Nathan wisely resisted the impulse to correct his grammar.

He would never have found the spot the first time without the help of his dog, as stated. That much was a given. Now he realized he likely could not find it again without her. Not for the sake of his shotgun, and not for the purposes of the law.

Initially he left her in the car, worried that she might in some way disturb the crime scene. Or that the policemen would somehow think she might.

It never occurred to him that he could not walk, in a direct line, back to the scene of such a momentous discovery.

For twenty minutes or so he walked around in a circle, noting that every tree looked very much like every other. He should have been paying better attention, he told himself. Perhaps even to say he berated himself would not have been stating it too strongly. He prided himself on the careful situational awareness of a hunter. But his routine had been destroyed earlier that morning, and everything had been changed. By the time he had realized the importance of noting and memorizing his surroundings he had been shocked into a state of being unable to do so.

And he was inordinately embarrassed about that, now.

And, in addition to feeling humiliated by the two officers who watched him fumble about lost, he also registered that his grandfather had given him that shotgun as a gift, and that it was irreplaceable.

'I'm sorry,' he said. 'I was so stunned to make the discovery. I guess I didn't properly note my surroundings.'

'Just take a deep breath and keep looking,' the larger, more vocal officer said.

'Maybe if I could get Sadie out of the car? She might go right to the spot.'

'Fine, get her,' he said. As if Nathan should have done so sooner.

She went right to the spot.

It took Nathan and the two officers a moment to catch up with her. And during that moment, Nathan worried terribly that she might disturb the crime scene. She might begin digging again. Although, he told himself, she had been digging at the crime scene already. But still he braced himself, needing her to behave perfectly in front of the police.

She didn't dig, or in any other way affect the pile of leaves. She just stood with her nose twitching, as if the earth under her feet might harbor an inexhaustible supply of abandoned newborns. And that another might be just about to surface.

Nathan caught up to her, and held her by the collar.

'Good girl,' he said, and picked up his priceless shotgun.

He stood looking around, memorizing his location. Searching for clues that would distinguish this tree from all other trees. That would allow him to find this place again. A bit like locking the barn door after the horse has been stolen, his brain told him. Something his grandfather had used to say.

He watched the officers marking off the area with crime-scene tape. And wondered, in a vague sort of way, why. It was a pile of leaves. What would it tell them? How would it help them find the person who had committed this terrible act? So far as Nathan could see, it had nothing to say.

'Where do you suppose she got a tiny knit cap the size of a newborn's head?' Nathan asked. Probably just to feel somehow connected to the moment again. 'After all, the baby was just a few hours old. I can't imagine that left much time for shopping.'

'I imagine she knitted it,' the quieter of the two officers said. 'Can't say for a fact, but it makes more sense.'

Another silent moment.

'If they find her, they won't give her custody of the child again. Will they?'

The bigger, more vocal officer seemed to be studiously ignoring him.

'I think she's made the point that she doesn't want it,' the quiet one said.

'If she changed her mind, I mean.'

'Well, she can change her mind all she wants. But she'll be in prison. For a very long time.'

Nathan felt heartened to hear that news.

'Maybe call the department of social services,' the more vocal cop said, correctly sensing where Nathan was headed with this. 'Now, if you don't mind, Mr McCann, we'll take it from here.'

Nathan made his way back to the car, slowly this time. Still holding Sadie's collar. And feeling a measure short of heroic.

*   *   *

'I want to adopt that boy,' Nathan said to his wife, Flora, over a late brunch. They sat at the kitchen table, Nathan smearing jam on his English muffin. He preferred butter, but was having to watch his waist.

'Don't be absurd,' Flora said. She sat with a cigarette high in the crook of her first two fingers, reading the paper. She had the gravelly voice of a drinking woman, which she was not.

Nathan sipped his coffee; it was hot and strong. He felt a pang of loss remembering there would be no roast duck for supper. 'Why is it absurd?'

'Neither one of us is very fond of kids. We made up our mind against them. Besides, we're hardly kids ourselves.'

'No, *you* made up your mind against them. You decided for both of us.'

Flora looked up from her paper for the first time. Peered at him through the smoke. 'I thought you said it was more than you wanted to take on in life.'

'This is different. This was meant to be.'

She took a puff of her cigarette, set it down on the ashtray, and regarded him briefly. 'Nathan,' she began. Nathan thought he heard a note of derision. Condescension, even. 'I've known you twenty-nine years, and you have never before said that anything was "meant to be".'

'Maybe in twenty-nine years nothing else came into that category.'

Still the harshness of her scrutiny. 'Why?'

'Why what?'

'Why what do you think? Why would you suddenly want to adopt the child of a perfect stranger? It makes no sense.'

He opened his mouth to answer, then stopped himself. You simply didn't say, to the person who has shared her life with you, that her company was not enough to fulfill you. The truth though it may be. It was unnecessarily hurtful, and not intended to serve the common good.

He took a different tack.

'I've just had this feeling. Since I found him. I can't describe it. But it's an emotion—'

She cut him off rudely. 'An emotion? That's unlike you.'

'My point, exactly,' Nathan said. 'And now that I have it, I don't want it to go away. I just don't feel willing to give it up again. To go back to the way things felt before.'

He stopped there, feeling he skated dangerously close to the judgment he had earlier decided against voicing.

A difficult pause.

Then Flora shook her head. 'Anyway, the kid probably has somebody. A mother. They could find the mother.'

'If they find her,' Nathan said evenly, 'they will put her in jail.'

'And then it could turn out he has some other kin that would take him.'

'Maybe,' Nathan said. 'We'll see. It just seems to me that when an infant is alone in the woods, slowly dying . . . then that child has . . . for all intents and purposes . . . no one.'

'I guess we'll see,' Flora said.

'Yes. I guess we'll see.'

Nothing more was said about it for the remainder of the day, though Nathan was sure he could feel its presence at each moment, and he wondered if Flora could, too. He glanced over at her often, but saw no signs of her being similarly haunted.

Nathan dined on a simple evening meal of chicken and dumplings. He praised Flora for her cooking of it, and it was a more than adequate meal. In fact, he might have enjoyed it a great deal if not for the sense that it could not replace the anticipated roast duck. It simply was not what he'd been set to receive.

After dinner, Flora retired to her room. She had a TV set in her bedroom, the only one in the house. Nathan despised the drone of television dialogue as background to his life.

It wasn't unusual for Flora to disappear right after dinner, but on this night Nathan was more than usually aware of it.

He sat on his bed across the hall, with his door open. Her bedroom door was closed, and as far as Nathan could hear, her TV had not been turned on yet. She must have been undressing for bed. Now and then he could see the vague shadow of feet cross the gap underneath her door. One of her floorboards tended to squeak when she crossed it, and she made no attempt to avoid it, as Nathan would have done.

For the first time in a very long time, years, Nathan felt tempted to knock on her door. Request that they spend a bit of time together. They could talk, or even play a game of cards. But before he could rise, he remembered her dismissive tone earlier in the day. No, the fact that he was feeling empty, he realized, did not mean in any way that Flora could, or would, help him fill that void.

He rose, and walked to the kitchen phone.

He called directory assistance, and asked for the number of the hospital.

He dialed, and got what sounded like a switchboard.

'Patient information, please,' he said.

'What is the name of the patient?' a cool woman's voice responded.

That disarmed him.

'Well. He doesn't have a name,' Nathan said. 'I wanted to learn the condition of an abandoned newborn I found this morning in the woods. I brought him to your hospital. John Doe is his name, I suppose. At the moment.'

'Are you family?'

'I'm the man who found him in the woods. What family would he have, then?'

'Then you're not blood family.'

'No. I'm not.'

'Then I'm afraid I can't release any information to you.'

'I see,' Nathan said. 'Will you please connect me with your emergency room?'

A pause, followed by what sounded like a sigh.

'Hold on. I'll connect you.'

A few seconds of silence. Nathan felt his molars pressing too tightly together along one side.

Then a click, and a brusque male voice on the line.

'ER.'

'Oh. Yes. I'm sorry to bother you,' Nathan said, wondering how he had started off on such disadvantaged footing. 'But I'm the man who brought in that baby this morning, and I was hoping to talk to the doctor who—'

'This is Dr Battaglia,' the voice said.

Nathan felt more than surprised. He had expected to leave a message which would not be returned until morning. 'My goodness, you work long shifts down there.'

'Ho,' the doctor said. 'You have no idea.'

'I tried to get some word on his condition without bothering you,' Nathan said. 'But they wouldn't tell me anything. They said I'm not blood family.'

'Yeah, they're like that. Swimming in their rules. Now, me, I guess I figure you're as close to family as that poor little beggar has got. So I'll tell you. He's still with us. Call back in the morning and talk to Dr Wilburn. I'll tell him you'll be calling. First twenty-four hours will be the most crucial. If the kid is still alive in the morning . . . mind you, it's no guarantee. There are no guarantees in this business. But if he's still kicking when you call in the morning, that'll be a very good sign.'

Nathan closed his door and lay, fully dressed, on the bed. Tomorrow he had a morning appointment with the recently widowed Mrs MacElroy. Helping her work out the financial details of her sad new life. That was inconvenient timing, but as soon as that meeting was over, he could begin to make his calls. Find out if the child had a social worker yet. Learn whom he should talk to, and how to proceed.

Then he chided himself for thinking of his meeting with the widow MacElroy as inconvenient. After all, her inconvenience was certainly greater than his. It wasn't like him to think so much of his own needs or place them above those of others.

He would have to watch that.

He listened to the occasional creak of Flora's squeaky board, and noticed it sounded lonely. Or maybe that was just him.

The Day He Lost You

Flora was asleep when he rose the next morning. Which meant there would be no coffee.

Never sure about the coffee situation, other than his role in drinking it, he felt hesitant to take on the job. It seemed better to make instant coffee for himself, even knowing it would be dreadful. That seemed preferable, somehow, to anticipating good coffee and then being disappointed by his own failure in that department.

The instant coffee was even more dreadful than he had imagined, though, because he didn't allow the water to boil fully.

He took two or three tentative sips, made a face, and poured it down the sink drain.

Then he called the hospital and spoke to Dr Wilburn. Deeply braced against potential tragedy.

'Ah, yes,' Wilburn said. 'I've been expecting your call.

Well, he's breathing. And that's good. Trouble is, we don't really like *the way* he's breathing. We're going to suction out his lungs and see if the situation improves. He's awfully young to survive pneumonia. If that's what's going on. But he's still kicking. What can I say? He's practically a miracle already. But complications are a definite possibility, and I'm afraid they're beginning to rear their ugly heads. Sorry to say he's not out of the woods yet.' A long pause, then a huge snort of laughter. 'Well, at least he is *literally*. Sorry. I know you probably think it's not very funny.'

'Thank you, doctor,' Nathan said. Not betraying his thoughts on the subject.

Then he rang off.

Mrs MacElroy usually offered him a cup of coffee, and when she did it was always superb. He made a wish that today would be one of those days.

'Oh, Nathan,' she said. The moment she opened the door. She'd only recently taken to calling him by his first name, since her husband's death, and he found it mildly unnerving. 'Tell me. Was it you?'

'Excuse me?'

She stepped back to allow him in.

She was a handsome woman, Nathan felt. More handsome than traditionally beautiful. About Nathan's age, she had a dignified way of dressing and carrying herself, and he admired that. None of this mincing about, pretending to be a woman half her age. She had some sense of decorum.

He stepped into her living room.

'I just had a feeling it might have been you. Just an intuitive feeling, I guess. Of course, you did tell me you were planning on going duck-hunting . . .'

Nathan briefly grieved his lack of morning coffee. The resulting absence of mental clarity certainly wasn't helping him now.

'I'm not sure I know what you're referring to, actually,' he said.

'Well, the headline in the paper this morning, of course. I know you must have seen it. Everybody's buzzing about it. Already I've gotten calls from my friend Elsie and my manicurist, and it's barely nine a.m. It isn't often something so momentous happens around here.'

'I'm guessing,' Nathan said, 'that the headline you're referring to was about the abandoned newborn. So then, yes. It was me.'

'Oh, Nathan. I just knew it.'

A cold feeling gripped his stomach. 'What else did the article say? I left the house this morning without benefit of coffee or the morning paper.'

'Oh, I have it around here somewhere. What did I do with it?'

She began to bustle. Or, at least, Nathan decided that bustling would be a good word to describe her actions. She wore a dark-navy shirtwaist dress, mid-calf length, with an attractive woven leather belt. As if she were going off to a front-office job in a good firm, rather than just opening the door for her bookkeeper. Her thick hair was pulled into a loose bun.

He sat on the couch, wishing she had caught his hint about the coffee. And also wishing the tight feeling in his stomach would ease.

'Did it say anything about custody? That is, did it indicate who would get custody? If the baby has family, I mean? That is, if his mother is never found.'

She had bustled off into the kitchen, but now her head appeared from around the door jamb. 'Oh, but she *was* found. I thought you knew. Now I know I grabbed it and took it to the phone with me when Elsie called. But I don't see— Oh, here it is.'

She hurried out into the living room again, extending a folded section of the morning paper in his direction. He accepted it, and dug into his suit coat pocket for his reading glasses. Noting that his hand trembled ever so slightly.

He skimmed as quickly as he could, in search of the most relevant information. The part that would settle his stomach. Or not.

The baby's eighteen-year-old mother, a Miss Lenora Bates, had been located. That comprised the bulk of the article. She had attempted to cross a state line with her boyfriend, Richard A. Ford, presumably the child's father, but had instead ended up in an emergency room, hemorrhaging. She and Ford had both been arrested, though not yet arraigned, and it was still under consideration, at the district attorney's office, what charges should be brought. She might face charges of reckless endangerment, or reckless disregard for human life. Or she might even be charged with attempted infanticide, or conspiracy to commit infanticide.

The article also said that the child, if and when he ever recovered enough to leave the hospital, would be given into the custodial care of his grandmother, Mrs Ertha Bates, mother of the troubled girl.

The news dropped into the waiting place in Nathan's stomach and found . . . nothing.

The sensation was similar to that of dropping a heavy object into a bottomless well, and then waiting for it to make a sound. The news made no sound. The feeling of aliveness that had opened in Nathan only twenty-four hours earlier, in front of the hospital coffee machine, closed. And that was all.

It was almost a comfort to have his familiar blankness back.

He glanced back down at the article.

In conclusion it noted that the infant had been found in the woods by a man on a duck-hunting outing with his dog.

Nathan folded up the paper, set it to rest on the end table near the couch, and sat a moment, digesting this new information.

He thought about lighting a cigarette. An open box of them sat on the coffee table. But he'd gone to the trouble to quit them several years ago, and didn't fancy going through all that again.

He shook the urge away.

Mrs MacElroy spoke, startling him. 'Why the woods? Why not a hospital or an orphanage?'

'I can't imagine,' Nathan said.

He made a mental notation: do a little research into how hard it would be to locate this Mrs Ertha Bates.

'Well, it certainly does make you the big hero.'

'Oh, I wouldn't say that.'

'Why, that child would be dead if it wasn't for you.'

'I suppose that's true.'

'They should have mentioned your name.'

'Oh, nonsense. It doesn't matter.'

'It does, too. It was a huge thing you did. You deserve credit.'

'I don't need credit. It was the same thing anybody would have done.'

'I keep thinking of my own son when he was just born. Thinking of him left to fend for himself out in that dark forest. It just makes my blood run cold.'

'I can't imagine how anyone could do such a thing,' Nathan said.

The conversation sounded and felt distant and removed to him, the way voices in the next room sound just before you drop off to sleep.

'May I get you a cup of coffee before we start?' she asked.

'Oh, yes,' Nathan said. 'Thank you. Coffee would be just the thing.'

When Nathan arrived home, Flora was sitting at the kitchen table, smoking a cigarette and eating three fried eggs, despite the fact that it was late for breakfast. Nearly eleven.

The article sat folded next to her plate.

'Please don't say it,' Nathan said.

'I told you that boy might have family.'

'I asked you not to say it.'

'Oh, is that what you wanted me not to say? How was I to know that? I'm not a mind-reader, you know.'

He ducked out of the kitchen again. Sat near the living room phone and picked up the local directory. It was the first and most obvious step in the task of seeing how hard it would be to locate Mrs Ertha Bates.

As it turned out, finding her was not destined to be difficult at all.

He noted her address in his appointment book.

He looked up to see Flora watching him from the kitchen doorway. He quickly put the appointment book away in his pocket again.

'What are you up to?' she asked.

'I'm not up to anything,' he said. 'I just needed to look

up an address. I just needed an address out of the phone book. That's all.'

She disappeared again, and he sat a moment, lost in thought.

Today? he wondered. No. Not today. Not for several days.

It would be unconscionable to discuss his situation with Mrs Bates until they knew for a fact whether the child would even survive.

He mixed up Sadie's midday meal – canned and kibbled dog food with a little broth – and carried it out to her run in the yard. He stood and watched her while she ate. Leaning on the chain-link and talking to her.

'So, I guess that was our little brush with fame, eh, girl?'

The comfortable crunching sound of her deliberate chewing.

'Eleanor MacElroy thinks I should have been mentioned in the paper by name. She thinks it was a great accomplishment. But all I did was look where you were looking. And I'd bet anything that even if they had mentioned my name they wouldn't have mentioned yours. But you wouldn't care, would you? You probably care less about credit than I do.'

She glanced up at him briefly between bites.

'Who knew that child had a grandmother willing to take him? Then why didn't that girl abandon her baby at its grandmother's house?'

She chewed the last kibble and licked the bowl with her wide tongue. Then she looked up at him thoughtfully, her head tilted to one side.

'Oh, so you don't understand it either, eh?'

Though he knew the dog was really curious about whether Nathan had anything besides lunch to offer her.

He felt a sudden pang of regret for not stopping to buy her a rawhide or some other nice treat. Something to reward her for what she had done.

Instead he let her out into the yard so he could throw the ball for her.

He ran a hand through the tight ringlet curls on her chocolate-colored neck.

'So why was I so sure how that was going to turn out, then?' he asked her.

But her eyes were fixed on the ball he had just picked up from its hiding place on top of the fence.

And a better question, Nathan thought. How could I have been so preposterously wrong?

But he didn't ask that one out loud.

Right through lunch he played ball with her. Almost until it was time for his afternoon appointments.

5 October 1960

The Day He Spoke His Piece For You

The home of Mrs Ertha Bates was kept tidy, but it was old. Autumn leaves had gathered in great piles on the roof, and in the rain gutter. Nathan stood at the curb, taking in his surroundings. Thinking she should sweep those off before the first snows threatened. Nathan certainly would have had them off by now, if this had been his house. But he supposed she had no one to do the work for her.

That tight feeling had returned to his stomach again. And he didn't enjoy it one bit. It was fear, plain and simple, and Nathan knew there was no point in denying or recasting it. His grandfather probably would have said that all men feel fear, but cowardly men deny it. Or perhaps he even *had* said that at some point.

But the truth was, Nathan did not ordinarily feel fear. This morning was only the second time in many decades. In as long as he could even remember. It seemed odd, and he wondered at the significance of it. It was as though only in the last few days had he had anything too important to risk losing.

The porch boards creaked and sagged under Nathan's weight.

He rapped on the front door, into which was set an arrangement of tear-drop-shaped glass panes forming a half circle.

A curtain slid aside, and part of a woman's face peered through.

Then the door opened, and the whole of the woman appeared. Nathan could only assume it was Mrs Ertha Bates.

She stood on the sill, did not invite him in. She was a woman perhaps his own age or a bit younger – forty-something – but old-looking, as though used too roughly, with graying hair, a faded-but-clean dress, and a plain white apron.

'Yes?' she said.

Nathan held his hat in front of him.

'I'm the man who found your baby grandson in the woods.'

'I see.'

'Is that all you have to say to me? "I see"?'

He immediately regretted speaking to her that way. Although he had not raised his voice or betrayed anger. Still, there was a rudeness, an effrontery, to his comments. It had just come out that way, unbidden. Because he had anticipated some specific reaction, and not received it. Somehow he had expected more.

'I can't know what to say to you,' she said, 'until I know more about what you've come to say to me.'

While they talked, her hands worked across that apron, smoothed and smoothed, as if trying to smooth away . . . what? Nathan wondered. Like all of us, probably only that which she was able to reach at the moment.

Of course, Nathan thought. She's afraid. Like me.

That knowledge put him more at ease.

State yourself to her, he thought. Quickly. While you're still sure of what you need to say.

'I wanted to adopt that boy.'

'So I heard.'

'But I didn't come to argue that.'

'Good,' she said. 'Because I am his flesh and blood.'

'Yes,' Nathan said. 'That is incontrovertible. Now let me tell you something else that also is. That boy would not exist if I had not been in just that place at just that moment. I'm not suggesting there was any special heroism involved, or that anyone else couldn't have done the same thing equally well. Only that it wasn't anyone else; it was me. No one can take that from me, any more than they can deny your claim by blood.'

There. That had been perfect. Just the way he'd

rehearsed it in his imagination for days. Smooth and definite.

'What do you want from me?' she asked, beginning to sound unnerved.

'Only this, and I think it's reasonable: sometime in the course of that boy's life, I want him to know me. I want you to bring him to me when he's grown. Or half-grown. That's up to you. And I want you to introduce me, and say to him, "This is the man who found you in the woods." That way he'll know me. I will exist for him.'

Ertha Bates stood silent a moment, smoothing.

Then she said, 'How would I find you?'

Nathan reached into his coat pocket and produced his business card. He'd been sure to have a supply along. And, in fact, he had even taken one out from its sterling-silver case, which had been a Christmas gift from Flora, so that he could produce it more easily. If asked.

Mrs Bates accepted the card without looking at it. It disappeared into one big apron pocket.

Her eyes found his directly.

'I'll have my hands full,' she said, 'with managing the information this child will hear as he grows. This is not the largest town in the world, and he will all too likely bump into those who know more about the story than I might think he's ready to hear at any given time. I don't plan to tell him – ever – sir, that his mother threw him out like yesterday's garbage. I don't think it would be mentally healthy for a child to entertain such a truth.'

'I have always felt,' Nathan said, 'that the truth is simply the truth. And perhaps does not exist for us to bend and revise. Or even filter to suit the feelings of those we love and want to protect.'

He watched her eyes, the change in her expression. She was leaving him, growing more distant. Closing to his requests.

Perhaps he had better take a more respectful tack. After all, this was not his grandson in question. It was hers. And she should be allowed to raise him using whatever methods and judgments she saw fit.

'Then again,' he said, 'it's really not my decision. Is it? You are the one to decide how he should be raised. So if I have a chance to meet the boy, I won't introduce any topics you might deem inappropriate.'

He continued to watch her face, but she betrayed little.

Nathan made a mental notation to commiserate with her situation. The way you would when speaking to someone who has lost a loved one. After all, her daughter was in jail. The whole town was speaking of the girl – this poor woman's girl – as though she were the devil incarnate. And Mrs Bates, at a rather inappropriate age, had been unexpectedly saddled with the care of an unhealthy infant.

The least he could do was express a message of condolence for her in this most difficult time.

Ertha Bates sighed deeply.

'All right, then,' she said. 'All right. As you say. When I think he's old enough to understand such a thing, I'll bring him around to see you.'

'Thank you.'

Nathan replaced his hat, turned, and took a few creaky steps. Then he looked over his shoulder, hoping she had not gone back inside.

She had not.

'Does the baby have a name yet?' Nathan asked. 'Have you picked out a name for the child?'

She drew his card out of her apron pocket and peered at it closely, as though her eyes were not good.

'Nathan,' she said, reading aloud. 'He has a name now, then.'

A flush of warmth came over his insides, washing away the tight knot of fear. At last. At last a healthy dose of the sort of feeling he had been pursuing.

'Thank you, Mrs Bates.'

Though he knew it was an old-fashioned, overly polite gesture, he tipped his hat to her before heading away.

'Thank *you*, sir,' she said, as he walked off her porch.

It was a huge statement, made all that much bigger by the way she spoke it. It caused the flush in his mid-section to glow more warmly. This is what had been missing in her greeting of him. And only now, as he walked off her porch, was she willing to deliver it.

Briefly, without much elaboration, but it was there. In that simple statement.

Thank *you*, sir.

Truth be told, Nathan had been anticipating gratitude. And, though delayed, it had eventually been delivered.

He turned back once more, realizing there was something he had forgotten to ask.

'Mrs Bates . . . Is your daughter . . . A knitter?'

She burst into a nervous little laugh.

'That is certainly not how I expected you to finish your sentence. I've had quite a few questions about my daughter in the last few days. Believe me. Most I won't even repeat. But not a single one went to her knitting abilities.'

'So she does knit?'

'Yes. In fact she does. Inherited it from me, I suppose. I'll have to bring her some yarn in prison. She'll have so much darned time on her hands.'

'Yes, ma'am. Well, I thank you for your time.'

Nathan turned and walked back to his car.

He had driven several blocks, replaying his parts of the conversation in his head, when he remembered with a start that he had forgotten his intention to express some type of condolence.

What had become of his manners of late? Why did everything seem to be shaken?

Nathan longed briefly for some aspect of life which had remained unchanged. But there was nothing as far as he could see.

The Day He Tried and Failed to Find Out Why

Nathan arrived shortly before eight a.m. at the county jail. An overweight, sulky woman with two small children already sat in the lobby, avoiding his eyes. Avoiding everyone's eyes. Other than she – them – he seemed to be the first to have shown up for visiting hours.

He logged himself in on a worn and dog-eared sheet carried over from yesterday's visitations. He signed his name, produced his driver's license – which he felt the officer behind the desk scrutinized too closely and for too long – and then filled in the name of the prisoner he was hoping to see.

Lenora Bates, he wrote in his careful script, hoping he was spelling her first name correctly.

The officer – if indeed he was some type of officer – took the clipboard which held the form out of Nathan's hands, turned it around. Began to read impassively. Then a deep frown unexpectedly furrowed into his brow.

'Have a seat,' he said. 'This will take several minutes.'

Meanwhile a female guard opened a door into the lobby, nodded at the woman with children, whom she seemed to know, and allowed them inside.

Nathan looked back at the officer behind the counter. Hopefully. To see if he could go in, too.

The man shook his head. 'You'll have to have a seat. As I say. This will take several minutes.'

'It didn't seem to take *her* several minutes,' Nathan said. Not combatively. Just in such a way as to invite explanation.

'I'm afraid your case will be more complicated. *Much* . . . more complicated.'

Nathan perched uncomfortably on the edge of the hard wooden bench the woman had just vacated. It was still warm from her bulk. Nathan had never understood how people could allow their bodies to get so large. Such a chaotic, uncontrolled existence.

Meanwhile the officer behind the desk picked up a phone and spoke into it quietly, in an obvious effort to keep his words from being overheard. But Nathan had always enjoyed unusually keen hearing.

'Ring up the watch commander. Tell him we need the coroner investigator over here.' A pause. Then, 'Father, I think.'

Nathan ran the single troublesome word around in his head. Coroner. No one had died in this case.

Had they?

With a jolt like a baseball bat to his stomach it struck him that the infant, Baby Nathan Bates, who had been doing so much better last time Nathan called to check on his status, might have died.

He jumped immediately to his feet, and the officer looked up, surprised.

'A payphone,' Nathan said hastily. 'Do you have a payphone here?'

'Yeah, there's one out front.'

He ran outside. The October air had taken on an even sharper nip. Nathan had been feeling in his bones that the first snow would fall soon.

He dug in his pocket for a dime, and called the emergency room of the hospital. He now held the number, memorized, in his head.

Dr Battaglia answered.

'This is Nathan McCann,' he said. Not even knowing what to say next. He could hear and feel his own pulse beating in his chest and neck and temples. It felt nearly impossible to breathe and talk at the same time.

'He's not here any more,' the doctor said. Sounding all too calm about it. 'Sorry to say this ends our correspondence, unless you find any more babies lying around in the future.'

Nathan saw the world grow brighter and more glaring

at the periphery of his vision. He worried he might pass out. He tried to speak, but no words materialized.

'Yeah,' the doctor continued, 'we handed him over to his grandma yesterday afternoon. Poor woman. She's probably nearly fifty and she won't get a good night's sleep for at least a year. Babies are for the young.'

Nathan very consciously filled his lungs with air. 'Then he's not . . . he's all right?'

'Yeah, he's doing great. Told you they could be strong little beggars. It's like God wanted 'em to get born and there's nothing going to stop them after that. He even had good color when I saw him last.'

'Oh. Well. Thank you, doctor. You've been very kind.'

Nathan made his way slowly back into the lobby of the county jail, the muscles in his thighs feeling loose and liquid, like runny jelly.

He took his spot again on the bench, where he waited, thinking very little, for well over twenty minutes.

'Detective Gross,' a small man said.

Nathan rose and shook his hand.

Detective Gross was a young man, or at least appeared to be so. He didn't look like he could be much over thirty, yet the hairline of his red head was surprisingly receded, giving his forehead a strange, angular look.

'If you'll follow me to my office. Sorry to say it's a pretty long walk from here.'

Nathan followed him outdoors, then into an adjacent building. Followed him down dingy halls with high windows that seemed not to have been cleaned for years. Followed him into a small office with a baseball-sized hole in one of its dirty window panes, casting a distinct beam of light at an angle across the room. Nathan took a seat on the other side of the detective's desk. He looked up at the window briefly, and thought of the recent bond measure to build a new jail. He had voted against it. Thinking himself far too overtaxed as it was.

He still had not spoken a word to this new man.

'This is always the very hardest moment in my job. Hate it, really. Nobody likes this. Not one bit. But I'm the investigator assigned to the coroner's division, and somebody has to do this, so here goes. I am dreadfully sorry to have to inform you that your daughter died sometime in the night last night.'

'Lenora?' Nathan asked. Confused.

'Yes. I'm afraid so.'

'Of . . . ?'

'Sepsis.'

'Related to her recent childbirth?'

'Yes. Exactly. Apparently it had been a difficult birth, with a lot of bleeding. Because she was so young, I guess, at least in part. Being barely eighteen, and very small . . .'

A long silence.

Then Nathan said, 'Don't you have medical care for your inmates? Oh, I don't mean that the way it sounds, only . . . Well, *don't* you? I mean, aren't you required by law to offer medical attention to any inmate who asks for it?'

'Ah, yes,' Gross said. 'And now you've just hit on it. Any inmate who *asks for it*. But we don't go around asking each one every day if she feels OK. The inmate has to speak up and let us know there's some problem. A raging infection with a high fever, for example. And your daughter never said a word.'

'My daughter. I think you must be confused. I have no children.'

The detective's face went blank. 'Lenora Bates was not your daughter?'

'No.'

'What was your relationship to the deceased?'

'None, really. I never met her. I'm just the man who found her baby in the woods.'

'So no relation to her family at all?'

'No, sir.'

'Oh, my. This *is* embarrassing. I shouldn't have given you any information at all. We haven't even had time to notify her next of kin yet. I'll have to have a firm talk with the guy who told me you were her father. He's put me in quite an awkward position.'

Oh, poor Mrs Bates, Nathan thought. Her daughter

dead, and here she didn't even know the news yet. And Nathan did. It seemed sad, somehow, that he should be feeling pity for her before she even knew she'd become a pitiable figure. Well, an *even more* pitiable figure.

'I never said anything to suggest I was her father, I assure you.'

'Well, bad assumption on his part, I guess. Maybe he figured nobody else would visit her. But it was highly unprofessional, let me tell you. You could help me out a great deal, Mr . . .'

'McCann.'

'. . . Mr McCann, if you could keep this under your hat for a couple of hours. The media will be all over this soon enough, but it's very important that her next of kin be notified properly before they hear it on the radio or read about it in the paper. I'm sure you understand.'

'I have far too much respect for poor Mrs Bates to allow such a thing to happen to her.'

'Thank you. Well, not to be rude, but I'd best get going on doing this difficult thing all over again. Can you find your way back to the parking lot?'

'I'm certain I can,' Nathan said, and rose to go.

'Mr McCann,' the detective said. Before Nathan could get out the door.

Nathan turned back. Watched a swirl of dust motes, stirred by his movement, fly in the beam of light from the broken window. Wondered what the detective would do for warmth when the snow began to fly.

'If you don't mind my asking, Mr McCann, what were you going to say to her?'

Nathan pulled on his leather gloves as they spoke. 'Say to her?'

'Yes. I just wondered – for purely personal reasons, mind you – about the purpose of your visit. I mean, here she did this unimaginable thing and left you to clean up from it, and I just wondered what you came to say to her.'

'Nothing, really. I had nothing to say to her. I was hoping she would have something to say to me.'

'Ah. I see. You wanted to know why. Why the woods? Why not a hospital? Or an orphanage? Why not put the kid in a basket and leave it on somebody's doorstep?'

'Yes, exactly.'

'Well, don't think you're the only one who wanted to know. Don't think she didn't hear the question plenty. From all the detectives who questioned her. And from the other inmates. Lots of the women in here are mothers. In fact, we had to keep her apart from the general population for her own safety. But we had no way to keep her so far apart that she couldn't hear the comments.'

'And what did she have to say in her own defense?'

'Nothing. Not a word.'

'She never spoke?'

'Not a word. So maybe she had a reason but wasn't saying. But my theory? My theory is that she didn't know the answer herself. World is full of people so troubled they don't even understand themselves. You could offer them a thousand dollars to explain their motivations, but they can't tell you what they don't know. And most of those miserable creatures find their way through here soon enough. So, I'm sorry, Mr McCann. If there was a reason, it died with her. But if you ask me, it's a question that never had an answer. Because there's just no explanation that makes a lick of sense.'

'I suppose you're right,' Nathan said. And stood mute for a moment. 'But she wasn't the only one in on it. There was the boyfriend as well. I wonder what he would say.'

'If you're willing to put up with another of my theories . . . Day before yesterday his mother came in and made bail. Mortgaged her house to make bail for the boy. Now, it's just a gut feeling, mind you. Call it a detective's intuition. But I'm hoping that poor woman has family to take her in when she loses that house. Because I saw the look in that boy's eyes on his way out the door. And I'd bet good money we're never going to see the whites of those scared eyes around here again.'

Nathan digested this news briefly. Inclined to accept the detective's instincts. Somehow the assessment felt right to him as well.

'Well, you'll be wanting to go see Mrs Bates . . .'

'Well, not *wanting* to, but . . .'

Gross rose and opened the door for Nathan, who found his way back to the parking lot on the first try.

At the corner drug store, Nathan found a dignified, appropriate card of condolence.

He paid for it, and took it to the post office.

There, with his good silver pen, in his best, most careful penmanship, he wrote in the card:

> Dear Mrs Bates,
> I am sorry for your loss. My thoughts are with you in this most difficult time.
> Very truly yours,
> Mr Nathan McCann

Then he sealed it into its envelope, addressed it to Mrs Ertha Bates, purchased a stamp, and sent it on its way.

2 October 1967

The Day He Watched You to See How You Had Grown

Seven years to the day after finding the infant boy in the woods, Nathan rose early on the pretext of going duck-hunting.

Because he had told Flora, perhaps even one time too many, that he was going hunting, he had to be careful of each detail. He had to remember to bring the shot-gun he did not intend to fire. He had to wear the proper pants and boots. To bring a heavy jacket he would only leave in the car.

Then, just on his way out of the house, he realized he had almost forgotten to take Sadie along.

Subterfuge had never been a talent of Nathan's, if for no other reason than lack of practice. But likely there were other reasons as well.

He had not devised this story to cover his tracks out

of dishonesty. It was more a matter of privacy. For once in his life, Nathan wanted to do something with complete privacy. He was not ashamed of his actions. He just wished to justify them to no one.

Well, that was not entirely true. He was a tiny bit ashamed.

Sadie began jumping straight up into the air as he approached her run, despite her advanced age, and Nathan's heart fell. How could he tell Sadie they were going hunting, and then not take her? He had never lied to her before. He had never let her down.

No, Nathan realized. He couldn't. He would not make a liar of himself after all these years. Not to his dog. Not to his wife. He would have to go hunting later in the morning. Even though it would be long after dawn. Even though conditions would be poor for hunting. He would likely come back every bit as empty-handed as he had that morning seven years earlier. But no matter. He would hunt.

But first he would drive to the Bates home. And wait quietly out front.

Autumn leaves lay gathered on the roof of the house just as surely as they had seven years before. Did they do this each year without intervention? Nathan wondered. Had she *ever* bothered to have the roof and gutters cleaned?

Still, the roof had not caved in. Even Nathan had to admit that.

It was after dawn when they appeared at the front door. But not much after. The light was still slanted and hazy when the door opened and Ertha Bates walked out on to the porch, a small, dark boy in tow.

She wore huge fuzzy yellow slippers and had her hair up in curlers. The boy wore a snowsuit that looked two sizes too big.

She looked astonishingly older, Nathan thought, and many pounds heavier. He was truly startled to see it. As if she had gone from her late forties to her late sixties in only seven years. Perhaps the care of a small child could do that to a person. Nathan briefly pondered what it might have done to him. But it didn't matter, really. His insides still ached and burned at the reminder that he had been robbed of the chance to try.

He didn't look at her long. He hadn't come to look at her. But the boy's back was turned toward him, to his dismay.

He seemed so tiny. Were all seven-year-olds so tiny? Nathan couldn't imagine they were. Maybe his poor start in life had stunted his growth in some way. Or maybe he was normal size for his age, and only looked small to Nathan. Maybe it was the sense of helplessness that made him seem so fragile.

Or maybe he just hadn't grown into that hand-me-down snowsuit.

Mrs Bates took him by the hand and walked him down the steps and out to the curb. Gave him a brown paper bag and walked back inside, leaving him alone to experience the second grade.

The boy stood at the curb, limply. Maybe sleepy, or maybe just bored. His breath appearing in great visible clouds. Now and then he wiped his nose on the back of one mitten.

Then he pulled off the mittens and unfolded the top of the paper bag, peering inside to see what he had been given.

Nathan thought of the baseball mitt he had dropped at the boy's house just two nights ago. For his seventh birthday. His hands looked so tiny. It had been a youth mitt, of course. And the man at the store had assured him a seven-year-old could enjoy it. With a great deal of room to grow, of course.

But now Nathan wondered if it was too big for the child even to use.

It always happened this way. Every birthday and every Christmas. Every time Nathan bought and delivered a present, helplessly guessing at what the child might want, he second-guessed himself with frustrating vigor. He had grown tired of it years ago, yet was still unclear as to how he could make it stop.

The boy looked less innocent and fragile from the front. But Nathan really wasn't parked close enough to see much. From where he sat he couldn't see the boy's face well enough to recognize him if he saw him again. And that had been the idea, Nathan supposed. To know him by sight if he ever crossed paths with the boy on the street.

Did he dare move his car a little closer? He certainly didn't want to be taken for any sort of child predator or stalker.

He looked briefly down at the ignition, unable to remember if he had left the keys hanging there. He had not. Before he could go into his pocket after them, he looked up to see the big yellow school bus pull up, blocking his view of the child.

Then it pulled away, leaving an empty curb.

So, that was it.

For seven years he had not allowed himself to do this. And he had promised himself he would never do it again. And now it was over.

And what had that accomplished? Nathan wondered.

Just a way of getting his hopes up high enough to be dashed again. But, hopes of what? Nathan wasn't even sure. Just chasing a vague idea of something that would fill him up inside. And proving himself wrong yet again.

He looked over the seat at Sadie, the older, grayer Sadie, who should have been retired by now, but who returned his gaze intensely. Hopefully.

'All right, girl,' he said. 'We'll go hunting.'

* * *

He came home shortly after eleven, empty-handed.

Flora looked up from her magazine. 'You never come home from a hunt without ducks,' she said.

'Today I did.'

'The only other time you came home with nothing was the day you found that baby.'

A long silence. Flora went back to her reading.

Just as Nathan thought she'd say no more about it, she spoke up again. 'Wait. Isn't this October second?'

'I think so. Why?'

'That was October second, too. Wasn't it?'

'Yes. I guess it was.'

'That's a coincidence.'

'Yes,' Nathan said. 'I suppose it is.'

'In the future, maybe you'll get smart and just stay home on October second,' Flora said.

'Yes,' Nathan said. 'I really hope I will.'

Part Two

Nathan Bates

2 September 1965

Feathers

Two years before that, on the afternoon before his first day of kindergarten, Nat Bates found a baby bird in the front yard. Under the maple tree.

It was almost too much to bear.

One new thing to accept, that was difficult and exhilarating and stressful and wonderful enough. But kindergarten *and* a baby bird was almost too much. Like something in his chest might burst, and then that would be the end of him.

At first he didn't even know what the tiny lump under the maple tree was. He knew only that it was alive. It didn't look like a bird. It didn't look like anything he had ever seen before. It had no feathers. It was no bigger than his palm. Pink. Bony, like the pictures he'd seen of dinosaurs, with the skin stretched over those bones looking strangely translucent and wrinkled.

It opened its beak as if demanding something from Nat. Something he was sure he didn't have.

He scooped it up in his hands and carried it in to Gamma.

'Oh, dear,' she said.

She didn't like animals in the house, Nat knew. But he felt he'd had no choice this time.

'What is it, Gamma?'

'It's a baby bird. It must've fallen out of the nest.'

'Maybe I could put it back.'

'Now, how are you going to get all the way up there?'

'I could climb up.'

'With a baby bird in one hand?'

'I could borrow a ladder from Mr Feldstein. If you could hold the ladder, I bet I could.'

'It's too late, anyway,' Gamma said. 'You touched it. You can't put a bird back in the nest once you've touched it. The mother won't feed it any more. Not once it smells like a human.'

Nat considered this for a time. Unwilling to accept any solution that ended badly for the bird he had touched.

'I guess *I'll* have to feed it, then.'

'Oh, Lord,' Gamma said. But she did not say no. Seeming to know from experience that he would not accept it as an answer.

Nat rinsed out an eyedropper in the bathroom sink

while Gamma went to fetch the heat lamp she used when her back went out.

They made the baby bird as comfortable as possible in an old hat box – which Gamma had been unhappy to give up – cushioned by a handful of Nat's white socks.

'His name is Feathers,' Nat said.

'You may not name him,' Gamma said. 'If you name him then he becomes a pet. And you'll want to keep him. And I don't like pets, and besides, you can't keep a wild bird, anyway. He'll either die or fly away. So you can't name him.'

'But I already did,' Nat said.

Gamma sighed deeply. 'Besides, that's a silly name for him. He doesn't even *have* feathers.'

'But that's just it,' Nat said.

'What's just it?'

'It's like a wish.'

Gamma just shook her head and went unhappily off to find something that could be fed through an eye-dropper to a bird.

She came in before bed to say, 'Stop looking at the bird and go to sleep.' In fact, she said it even before looking into his room. Leaving Nat to wonder if she could see through walls.

She'd often told him she had powers he could never understand. And certainly never foil.

'I was just checking on him.'

'You have school in the morning, so go to sleep.'

'I don't want him to die.'

'Well, they usually do die, so don't get too attached.'

Nat began to cry.

It was only partly the idea of the bird dying. More than that, it was a sense of too many new things to bear, and the feeling that something in his chest would burst because of it.

'Oh, dear, oh, dear. Don't cry, now. I didn't mean to make you cry. Just go to bed and we'll see.'

3 September 1965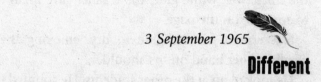

Different

Before Gamma left him at kindergarten, just as she was buttoning her big cloth coat and wrapping her neck in one of her many huge, hand-knit scarves, Nat said, 'Will you feed Feathers while I'm gone?'

'You can feed him when you get home. He doesn't need to eat every minute of every day.'

'But he didn't eat this morning. He wouldn't even open his mouth. Please, Gamma?'

'Oh, all right,' she said with a sigh. 'Now, you be good for a change.'

The teacher was very kind to him. And it was nice.

At first.

She was pretty, with brown hair that looked a touch red where the sun hit it. She wore lipstick, and a white dress covered with little bunches of red roses. She sat by the window in a burst of the morning sunlight, her arm draped around Nat's shoulder as he worked on his picture.

They had been given brushes and glue. And, after making a pattern on colored construction paper with the thick, wet, white glue, the teacher gave them glitter to sprinkle on the page.

Nat waited for the glue to dry, enjoying the soft weight of her hand on his shoulder.

He looked up at the other students. He counted them. He was a good counter. There were sixteen, besides himself.

He looked down at his paper again, imagining how it would look when the extra glitter could be shaken off.

'That's going to be beautiful, Nathan. You've done a good job.'

She likes me, Nat thought. He looked up at the other students again. Searching for a feeling. He couldn't quite put words to it. But some part of him was waiting for the teacher to go and put her arm around each of them, too.

She never did.

She likes me the best, Nat thought.

He looked up at her. She looked down into his eyes and smiled sadly. It made his stomach hurt.

It was the smile you get from a stranger at the department store when they see you've been crying, and they wish they could help. And it hurts them that they can't help. And all they can do is smile sadly to show that they wish you wouldn't be sad. But Nat hadn't been crying. And if he was sad, he didn't know it.

He filed the mystery away for later. Maybe much later.

Was there something inside him that was not there in the other sixteen as well?

The teacher told everyone to shake off the extra glitter and see how the pictures turned out.

'Now, you take these pictures home today and give them to your mothers,' she said. Her hand was still on Nat's shoulder. But now it felt heavier. Less comforting. She looked down at him. 'Nathan, you can take your picture home and give it to your grandmother,' she said.

Another arrow pointing, but at what, he was not sure.

Something was different in his case.

He folded the picture three times and slid it, as carefully as possible, into the pocket of his jeans.

When he arrived home, he ran straight to the hat box.

It was empty.

The heat lamp was turned off, and the white socks had been shuffled away, probably to the laundry hamper. Gamma liked things to go straight into the laundry hamper, and fast.

He found Gamma in the kitchen, heating up canned soup.

'Where's Feathers?'

'He flew away.'

'He was all better already?'

'Yes.'

'How could he get out of my room?'

'I opened the window for him. It's cruel to keep a wild bird when he wants to fly away.'

'You should have waited till I got home. So I could say goodbye.'

'Well, I'm sorry, honey.'

'He was mine. I'm mad because you didn't wait.'

'He wasn't yours. He was wild. You can't own a wild thing.'

'It still makes me mad.'

'I did what I thought best. Here, sit down, I have your lunch ready.'

Nat sat at the table. Fidgeted slightly as she tucked a paper napkin into the collar of his shirt like a bib. He almost never spilled on himself, but she got mad if he took it off. She said when he was old enough to do his own wash they could discuss it again.

She set a plate of soup in front of him, with Saltine crackers. It was tomato. Nat didn't like tomato. He liked chicken noodle, but almost never got it.

'How could he fly away without any feathers?'

'I don't know, but he did. Now eat your soup.'

Nat stirred it a few times as a stall tactic. Took a miniature sip. He had more questions, but had reached the end of Gamma's patience. She would yell at him if he brought it up again.

He took the glittery picture out of his jeans pocket. Unfolded it. Nearly half the glitter fell off on to the floor. He set it on the table, straightening it as best he could, while Gamma clucked at him with her tongue and went to fetch a broom from the pantry.

'My teacher said I should give this to you.'

Then he stuffed three crackers in his mouth all at once, causing Gamma to frown. He pulled out as many pieces as he could, so she wouldn't frown like that.

She leaned the broom against the stove and picked up his picture. 'It's a very nice picture,' she said. 'I'll put it up on the fridge.'

'What does it mean to be grand?' he asked, his mouth still full of half-chewed crackers.

'Don't talk with your mouth full like that. It's disgusting. Grand? Oh. Well, really it just means big. Like a grand ballroom. It just means it's very large. But most times it also means it's fancy and rich and very showy and such.'

She finished taping his picture to the fridge while she spoke, then began to sweep up the spilled glitter.

'What's grand about you?'

'About me?' she asked. And then brayed with laughter. 'Why, I would say nothing. Not a darned thing that I can see. Why would you ask an odd question like that, anyway? Who ever said I was grand?'

'Everybody,' Nat said.

'Everybody says I'm grand? Oh, nonsense. Eat your

soup.' Then, a moment later, 'Oh, wait. Do you mean everyone says I'm your grandmother?'

'Yes,' Nat said. 'That.'

'Oh, well, that's entirely different. That doesn't mean big or fancy or anything. It just means I'm your mother's mother.'

'You're not my mother?'

'Of course not. I'm your grandmother. You know that.'

Had he known that? He had probably heard the words.

'So my mother is . . .' But he had no ideas on how to finish.

'My daughter.'

'Oh.'

There was another huge question, waiting. It was right there. Yet he could not pin it down. In some ways it was so simple. As simple as, why don't we see her around here anywhere, ever? But even in its simplicity it was so heavy, so all-encompassing, that he could not bring himself to box it into those tiny words.

And, to make matters worse, Gamma's eyes had filled up with tears. They hadn't quite run down her face yet. But it was terrifyingly clear that they might, at any minute. And Nat sensed he was somehow to blame.

Gamma emptied the dust pan and settled back down at the table with him, swiping at her eyes with her huge fingers.

'Are you sure Feathers flew away?'

Gamma slapped the table hard with her palm, and Nat jumped a mile. 'Now I told you what happened, and I'll hear no more about it. Eat your soup.'

'I don't like tomato.'

'You don't have to like it,' she said, causing his hopes to momentarily rise. 'You just have to eat it.'

24 December 1967

Cold

On the eve of Nat's seventh Christmas, Gamma tucked him into bed early. As she always did on Christmas Eve.

The following morning was the only day of the year he could wake her no matter how 'ungodly' the hour. So she insisted they get an early start.

'Look,' Gamma said, pointing to the window. 'Looks like we'll have a white Christmas tomorrow.'

'I can't see,' Nat said.

He didn't want to get up and go to the window, because it was cold in his room. Gamma wasn't made of money, and saved on heating oil by keeping the house as cold as she could possibly stand. Which was colder than Nat could stand. He had just barely managed to gather enough of his own body heat under the covers to stop shivering, and he was not about to budge.

Gamma went to the window for him, and pulled the

curtain wide for him to see. Just small flakes, dry and sparse, swirling in the air outside.

'Will it stick?' he asked her.

'Can't say as I know. Just hold a good thought.'

But Nat didn't like snow, because it was all wrapped up in his mind with being cold, which he particularly didn't like. So he wasn't sure which way the good thought should go.

Gamma came back to the edge of his bed and sat, her great weight settling one side of his bed lower than the other and making the springs creak.

'Maybe my mother could come visit,' Nat said.

In the moment following the question, he saw and felt a clear reminder of why he never spoke such words out loud. The look on Gamma's face was something like what he imagined it might be if he had viciously slapped her without warning.

And, again, that horrible filling of her eyes. The tears that never seemed to break free.

'Where on earth did that come from?' she said.

'Well, only that it's Christmas.'

'It's been Christmas before, and you never said a thing like that.'

'But Jacob's father is visiting for Christmas.'

'Oh. I see. So that's what brought this on. Jacob's father. Well, Jacob's father and your mother are two entirely different cases.'

Maybe my *father* could come visit? That was his next

thought. And, also, why were they such different cases?

But the slapped look had passed away from Gamma's face, and the tears had been pulled back or swiped away, and Nat didn't want to risk seeing any of it again. Especially not if he was the cause of it.

It isn't nice to hurt other people, and if you absolutely must hurt someone, it's important that you never do it on Christmas Eve or on Christmas Day, or maybe even a day or two before or after that.

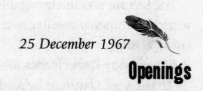

25 December 1967

Openings

In the morning, Nat ran downstairs wrapped in a blanket but still shivering. Gamma tried – but failed – to stay close on his heels.

'I guess I could put up the heat a little bit just for the special occasion,' she said.

But Nat knew it would take a long time to feel the change anyway, and he didn't want to wait.

'Let's just get to the opening.'

Gamma handed him two presents. 'These are from me,' she said. It was the first year she had admitted that his presents were from her. In previous years she'd claimed Santa brought them. But Nat, even in his child-like willingness to believe, could not help noticing that Santa's presents often looked a lot like Gamma's knitting.

The first present he opened was a pretty good one. A

fire truck. Made of metal and wood and painted bright red, it was about half as long as Nat was tall. And it had a real hose that pulled out, and a ladder that got longer and swung in whatever direction you wanted it to go.

'Thank you, Gamma,' he said.

The second was the inevitable knitting. A matched set with hat, mittens, sweater and scarf. Deep blue. A nice color, actually.

But nobody likes clothes for Christmas.

'Thank you, Gamma,' he said.

Then she went off in the closet and brought out the third box. It was big, and wrapped in gift paper he had never seen in this house. He felt himself begin to squirm deliciously. He wished he'd remembered to use the toilet before coming down. Not that he couldn't hold his bladder; he was not a baby and he certainly could. But now he would have to *think* about holding it.

'And this is from the man who found you in the woods,' Gamma said, setting the big box on his lap.

The last present from The Man, the one he'd gotten three months ago for his seventh birthday, had been a very good one, to say the least. A brand-new hand-stitched leather baseball mitt. It looked very expensive. It was nicer than anything any other boy on his block had. They all oohed and aahed when he showed it off to them. It was a little big for his hand; he'd had to practice gripping it just right from the inside. But he swore his hand had gotten bigger just in the past three months, because he could handle it much better now. Either that or he had finally gotten the grip right.

He tore wildly into the paper.

Inside was a box that claimed, by the writing on it, to be a chemistry set.

He frowned at it, unable to mask his disappointment.

'But I don't like chemistry,' he said.

'Well, he doesn't know that, dear. Because he doesn't know you.'

'Why does he give me presents if he doesn't know me?'

'Because he's the man who found you in the woods.'

'Oh,' Nat said.

He asked no more questions because he knew the answers wouldn't settle anything.

It was not news to him that many people in the world – the entire population of grown-ups, for example – behaved in ways he could not understand.

Jacob got to sleep over on the night following Christmas, because it was still vacation from school.

'Did you get anything good?' Jacob asked Nat, as soon as they'd gotten into his room and out of Gamma's range of hearing.

'I got this fire truck,' he said. And showed it to Jacob. 'From Ga— From my grandmother,' he corrected, realizing suddenly and for the first time that 'Gamma' sounded too babyish. 'Did you get anything better than this?'

'My father brought me a baseball with Joe DiMaggio's signature on it. But I don't think we can play baseball with it. It's too good. And it's in a plastic case. My mother says it's worth a lot of money but he only gave it to me because he feels guilty. Did you get anything else?'

'Clothes. I hate clothes.'

'Everybody hates clothes.'

'And this chemistry set.' Nat pulled it out from the closet, into the middle of his bedroom rug.

'That's a good one.'

'You think so? I hate chemistry.'

'Your grandmother gave you this? Wasn't she afraid you'd blow the place up?'

'No, it's from the man who found me in the woods.'

A silent moment. Nat had no idea he'd said anything confusing. But he watched Jacob try and fail to sort out what seemed like straightforward information.

'A man found you in the woods? What were you doing in the woods?'

'No. I wasn't. Not actually. I mean, I don't think so. He's just a man who gives presents. Isn't he?'

'I never heard of the guy.'

'You don't get presents from the man who found you in the woods?'

'I don't think so.'

'I thought everybody did.'

'Nobody I ever met. Except you. What else did he ever give you?'

'That's who I got the mitt from. He gives me something every birthday and every Christmas. He gave me an archery set. And binoculars. And he gave me an ant farm, but Gam— My grandmother wouldn't let me keep it.'

'Boy, I wish I did have one of those woods men. Let's see what we can make with this set.'

So they pulled out all the little test tubes and burners and bottles of various clear liquids.

Jacob decided they should try to make soap, because it was the very first project in the little booklet and seemed easiest. Nat went along, even though it sounded uninteresting, because he was pretty sure you couldn't blow up anything with soap.

They spilled a whole bottle of something medicinally smelly on Nat's bedroom rug in the process, but they did end up with a thick, bubbly liquid that they supposed was soap. It seemed not a very exciting conclusion to Nat, since they both avoided soap as much as possible and only washed when absolutely forced to do so.

'We could do another one,' Jacob said.

'Nah. I don't like chemistry.'

'What do you want to do, then?'

'I don't know.'

They lay on their backs crosswise on the bed for a few minutes, looking at the plastic stars on Nat's ceiling.

Then Nat said, 'I'll be right back.'

He padded downstairs, his bare feet freezing.

Gamma was sitting in her big upholstered easy chair, knitting. And watching a mushy black-and-white love-movie on TV.

'Who's the man who found me in the woods?'

Gamma sighed deeply. 'Well, you're just all full of questions lately. Aren't you? Now I'm going to miss my show. Well, you were going to ask sooner or later. So go ahead and turn down the volume and then come back.'

Nat ran to the TV and turned it down, wincing at the fact that a man and a woman were kissing on the screen.

Gamma's hands and knitting needles continued to fly as she talked.

'Every little boy or girl comes into the world like that,' she said. 'The stork brings you, and drops you in the woods. In a special secret hiding place. And for each little boy or girl, there's only one person in the whole world who knows how to find you. And that's the man who found you in the woods. So if anybody ever says anything to you about your being out lost in the woods, now you'll know what they mean.'

Her eyes remained glued to the story playing out silently on the screen.

'Jacob doesn't have a man.'

'Everybody has a man.'

'Jacob doesn't get presents from his man.'

'Well, then, you're the lucky one. Aren't you? Now run turn up the sound, hon. I'm missing the show.'

'You wanna trade for it?' Jacob asked. He didn't have to say he meant the chemistry set. They both knew what he meant.

Gamma had tucked them in and turned out the

lights. They had to keep their voices down so she wouldn't know they were awake. Because if she heard them she'd have to come back up and raise Cain.

'What've you got to trade?'

'My cat is about to have kittens. Trade you for a kitten. You can have your pick of the litter.'

'I should be so lucky. My grandmother would never let me keep a cat.'

'Not even in the garage?'

'She wouldn't even let me keep the ant farm in the garage. And it was all behind glass. Hey. Maybe I could pick out a kitten but it could live at your house.'

'Not a chance. My mom says every single one has to be gone in six weeks. I'm lucky I get to keep the mom cat. I had to cry.'

'What else have you got to trade?'

'A baseball bat. But it has a crack in it.'

'Can you hit a ball with it?'

'Yeah, but one of these times it'll pop right in half. Maybe not soon, though.'

'OK,' Nat said. 'Deal.'

And they shook on the trade.

4 January 1968

The issue

Next time he saw Jacob, it was the Monday after New Year's Day. The first day of the new semester of school.

Jacob walked the half-block to stand at the curb and wait for the school bus with Nat. As he often did, if there was enough time.

'The bat popped in half,' Nat said.

'Already? Oh. Well. I'll give you back the chemistry set if you want.'

'No, that's OK.'

They stood in silence for a minute or two, watching their breath puff out in great clouds and waiting for the bus as if it were a hangman's noose or a guillotine.

Then Jacob said, 'I asked my mother. And she said you really were left out in the woods.'

'I know,' Nat said. 'My grandmother told me. The day after Christmas.'

'Oh,' Jacob said.

That seemed to settle the issue between them well enough, so that it would not need to be raised again.

When Nat got home from school, Gamma was standing next to a packed suitcase in the living room. Already twisting a knit scarf around her neck.

'Where are you going?' Nat asked.

'Your Uncle Mick is in the hospital. His appendix burst. I have to take the bus to Akron to sit with his kids.'

'Where will I be?' he asked, hoping she would judge him old enough to stay at home by himself.

'I made arrangements with Jacob's mother. She's making that homemade chicken noodle soup you like so much for dinner. Now run quick and grab your toothbrush and a pair of pajamas, and anything else you think you'll need, and hurry over there right now. I have to go.'

Nat sighed, and trudged up the stairs to his room. He pulled his red pajamas out of the drawer, threw them on the bed, grabbed his toothbrush from the bathroom, threw it on top, then rolled up the whole mess, wedging it under his arm.

He liked Jacob's house well enough, but the situation made him feel he was being treated like a child – at nearly thirteen years old.

Gamma stood shifting from foot to foot at the bottom of the stairs.

'Can you possibly move any slower? You know I have to go.'

'Why can't *I* go? I like Uncle Mick.'

'Because you have school. And besides, you're too young to get into the hospital to see Uncle Mick, anyway. You'd only get to see his kids. And you don't particularly like his kids, if you recall. But that's not the main thing. The main thing is you are not going to miss even one day of school. Not with your miserable grades. Now here's a key to the house. I put it on a string so you won't lose it. So when you need to come home to get more clothes or whatever you'll be able to let yourself in.'

She hung it around his neck. Didn't even hand it to him and let him slip it on himself. Nat felt like a five-year-old holding still to have his mittens pinned to his snowsuit. It was putting him in an increasingly foul mood.

'So, is Uncle Mick going to be OK?'

Gamma's slapped look. A face full of horror. 'Well, of

course he is. How can you even ask such a question?'

How can I *not* ask it? Nat thought. How can *you* not ask such questions? But of course he kept those thoughts to himself.

'Oh, shit. Where's my cat?' Jacob asked.

'I don't know. Downstairs, I think.'

They were in bed, on lights-out. So neither was sure if they should move or not. And they spoke quietly.

'I have to get her in my room with the door closed. Otherwise my mom will throw her outside for the night. Especially when Janet is here.'

'Who's Janet?'

'Her girlfriend she yaks and gabs and gossips with for half the night.'

'I didn't know there was somebody here.'

'I'm not sure if she's here. I just know she's coming.'

'I'll go find the cat,' Nat said. Mostly because he liked the cat, and wanted an excuse to pick her up again. She always purred when he picked her up. He liked to hold her to his ear for a moment, listening to that soft motor. 'I can be quiet.'

He padded downstairs.

Sure enough, Jacob's mom had a girlfriend over. He could hear them talking in the kitchen as he searched the living room. He was able to gather that Janet had a gentleman friend. And that she was furious with him.

'Jacob, is that you?' The screechy sound of Jacob's mother's angry voice.

He hadn't been quiet enough.

'No, ma'am,' Nat said, sticking his head through the kitchen door. 'It's me. Nat.'

'Why aren't you in bed?'

'I was looking for Buttons.'

'Well, you better find her, too. Because if I find her first, she's going outside. Janet is allergic to cats.'

Nat wondered whether Janet's allergies explained the box of tissues on the table between them. Or whether Janet had been crying. Maybe it was both.

'You're Nat?' Janet asked. As if it made you very famous and distinguished to be Nat. As if Nat were a truly unusual and remarkable thing to be.

'Yes, ma'am.'

Janet turned to Jacob's mother. 'Is he—'

Jacob's mother shot her down with a look. A disapproving look and a slight shake of her head. As if to say, don't. As if to say, under no circumstances finish that sentence.

Silence.

'Am I what?' Nat asked. Rather bravely, he thought.

'Nothing, dear. Run find Buttons and then go back to bed.'

Nat backed out of the room. Walked very slowly to the bottom of the stairs, where he knew he would be shrouded in darkness.

There he sat. And listened.

'So, that's the boy.'

'Yes. That's him. Poor little bugger. I feel so sorry for him.'

'I don't blame you. Can you imagine? Your own mother. Trying to murder you.'

'Well, it wasn't murder. Exactly. Bad neglect, I suppose.'

'Are you kidding me? You must be kidding me! Bad neglect would be if she never changed his diapers. It was freezing cold out in those woods. It's a miracle he didn't die. Does he even know the whole story, do you think?'

'I don't know what he knows. His grandmother forbids everyone to talk about it. Jacob says he told him once, and that Nat said he knew, and didn't act like it was any big deal. Denial, maybe. Or maybe he was too young at the time to understand. Jacob says the kids at school sometimes make taunting remarks. And that four or five times Nat's gone home to his grandma and demanded to know what they mean.'

'How does Jacob even know that? Do they discuss it?'

'I think those were just the times he was right there. So you can imagine how often it must happen if he's overheard it four or five times in the six or seven years they've been friends.'

'What does his grandmother say?'

'She lies to him. Says the people who say such things are mistaken. Or that he misunderstood.'

'That's wrong, I think.'

'Well, what would you do? If you had a boy his age who had such a horrible thing like that in his past, what would you do? Would you tell him a thing so awful?'

A long silence.

'Whew. I don't know. I'm just glad I don't *have* to know.'

'Yeah. Me, too. Now get back to what you were saying about Geoffrey.'

Nat slipped out of Jacob's house, still in just pajamas and bare feet. Padded down the freezing sidewalk for half a block, to home. Opened the front door with the key around his neck.

Then he went upstairs to Gamma's bedroom, a room he had only three times entered, and began looking around to see what he could find.

He likely could not have put words to what he was looking for. But in his gut he felt there must be something. Pictures of his mother. Letters from her. There had to be something. And Gamma kept everything. She was not one to throw sentimental items in the trash. Or just about any items, for that matter.

He opened her dresser drawers but found only humiliating personal undergarments. He closed each drawer again, touching nothing, so Gamma would never have to know he had looked.

He looked on her closet shelves and found only shoes

and hats. Again, he left no evidence of his intrusion.

He looked under her bed and found a wooden cigar box.

He pulled it out. Brought it under the light. Opened it.

Inside were a few papers. Not nearly enough to fill the box. On the very top was a folded clipping from a newspaper. Yellowed with age.

Nat unfolded it.

It was the headline story, dated 3 October 1960. Two days after his birth. The headline read, in shockingly large, bold letters, 'ABANDONED NEWBORN FOUND IN WOODS BY LOCAL HUNTER'.

The jittery sensation that had haunted Nat's stomach since he'd stood in Jacob's kitchen was blasted away by the news. It felt good. It felt good to replace nervousness with shock. Because shock, at least in this moment, felt like nothing at all.

He had even stopped shivering from the cold.

He skimmed the article.

Lenora Bates. His mother's name was Lenora.

Richard A. Ford. His father's name was Richard A. Ford. So why wasn't his name Nathan Ford?

He had a mother and a father. Somewhere.

And on the night of his birth they had discarded him.

Were they still in prison? Or had they served their time and been released? And disappeared without so much as a word to him?

He scanned down to see about the man who found him. He wanted to memorize that name as well. But he was only referred to as 'a man on a duck-hunting outing with his dog'.

Nat started over and read the article word by word.

When he had finished reading he refolded it carefully and held it in his left hand while he slid the cigar box back under the bed with his right. Then he took the article with him to his room, where he packed a suitcase with only the most essential of his belongings. Jeans and underwear. Tee shirts. His baseball mitt. The article.

The phone rang, and it startled him.

He ran downstairs and picked up the phone.

'Hello?'

'Nat! Oh, thank God! We didn't know where you were.' Jacob's mom.

'I forgot something at home.'

'Are you coming back right now?'

'Yes. Right now.'

He hung up the phone and walked back upstairs, where he changed into jeans and warm socks and shoes. And a jacket he didn't like very well, because the one he did like had been left at Jacob's.

He let himself out, locked the front door carefully. Stopped at the curb and threw the key-on-a-string down the storm drain.

He chose a direction more or less by feel and began to walk.

* * *

It was unclear to Nat how long he had walked, or where he was headed. He knew only that the suitcase was heavy, and he had to keep transferring it from hand to hand.

He followed dark streets until they opened up on to the train yard. Which he assumed would also be deserted. Every place he had walked since leaving home had been deserted.

The entire world was asleep, he thought.

But not the train yard.

Here a huddle of four men stood around a fire built in an old oil barrel, warming their hands and laughing. A couple more men sat in an open freight wagon of a still train, their legs dangling and swinging over the edge.

They all looked up to mark Nat's arrival.

He walked closer. Liking the idea that someone lived here, and used the night for something other than sleeping.

'Well. Who do we have here?' one of the men asked.

Viewed up close, they looked poor. Their coats and beards were untended, to say the least.

'Nobody,' Nat said.

'Perfect,' the man said. 'You'll fit right in.'

Nat sat on the edge of a freight wagon, dangling his legs over the edge. Staring into the leaping flames of the fire.

Letting it hypnotize him. Burn all the thoughts out of his head.

He watched little lights swirl in the air above the oil barrel, thinking that some were sparks and some were fireflies, and that it was hard to tell them apart.

But no, it was too early in the season for fireflies. Or was it?

Maybe his eyes were playing tricks on him.

The old man sitting next to him was drinking whiskey straight from the bottle. He held the bottle out to Nat.

'Snort? It'll warm you up.'

'OK.'

He accepted the bottle. Wiped off the mouth of it with his sleeve. Pulled a swallow. Coughed. All the men were watching and they all laughed at him.

'Where do you go when you jump on a train?' Nat asked the old man.

'Anywhere I damn please,' the man said.

'That sounds good.'

'It has its advantages.'

Another younger man, standing warming his hands at the fire, said, 'Has its advantages for *us*. But maybe *you'd* best go home.'

Nat said nothing.

'Where's your family, boy?'

'Don't have any.'

'Well, what've you been doing up until now?'

Nat shrugged. 'Just living with a stranger, I guess.'

'Maybe a stranger is better than nothing at all.'

'I guess I used to think so,' Nat said. 'But I don't any more.'

21 March 1973

The World

When Nat woke again, the train was moving. The door to his freight wagon had been closed without his knowing it, and the train had departed. And there was no one else in the car except him.

Good, he thought.

He scooted over to the door. A crack about an inch or two wide allowed light in. And allowed him to see out. And he watched the world go by.

He saw mountains in the distance. He had never seen mountains before. And massive sheets of icicles hanging on rock faces. He saw fields of cows and sheep, and horses running in a big paddock with their tails raised like flags.

He saw the dankest, most depressed corners of cities. The junk yards and train yards and stacked cargo containers and chain-link fences and steel railroad bridges.

And then, the country again, with its barns and tractors and silos and irrigation ditches separating neatly tilled fields.

He watched for hours, which turned into watching all day. And never once felt bored. How could he be bored? It was the world. It had been here all along, but no one had invited – or allowed – him to see it. Did they think he didn't care about the world outside his miserable little city? Or was the world just like everything else? Just another secret to be kept from him?

His stomach felt empty and achy, but it seemed worth the sacrifice. No people. No school. No lies.

He would find food. He would beg it, or steal it, or work for it, but he'd find a bite somehow before the sun went down. That is, if this train ever stopped.

One way or another he would get by.

22 March 1973

Over

He woke in the pitch dark with a start. Still inside that freight wagon. Still unfed. Teeth chattering from the cold. His hip ached where it pressed against the cold metal floor. His mouth was dry, and he worked hard to wet his parched tongue with his own saliva.

He could hear the doors of train wagons being banged open. That's what woke him. And the noises were moving closer.

He wondered if there was still time to slip out and get away.

The huge cargo door slid open with a clang.

Nat squinted into a light. A light was being shined on him, and he threw a hand up in front of his eyes.

'OK, son,' a big male voice said. 'Your vagabond days are over. Grab your things and come with me.'

Nothing

'You scared the living daylights out of me!' The old woman shrieked the words too close to Nat's ear, making him wince. Then she raised her hand and struck him. Hard. Right across the ear, causing the inside parts of his ear to ache. 'And Jacob's mother. She was responsible for you. Do you know how scared she was?'

Another vicious smack, again on the same sore ear.

He looked up at the cops. As though they might be some help to him.

If Nat had smacked someone that hard, they would probably have arrested him all over again. Lectured him on how violence was wrong, and never solved anything.

But apparently grandsons were fair game.

The cops just raised their eyebrows at him and said nothing at all. But their looks seemed to say Nat deserved all that and more.

'And why? Because I left without you? Because you thought you should be allowed to come along? That is the most selfish behavior I ever heard of!'

Nat flinched. Guarded his ear with both hands. But she kept her hands at her sides this time.

'Is that why you did it?'

Nat said nothing.

'Answer me!'

Still Nat said nothing.

'What do you have to say for yourself, young man?'

'Nothing,' Nat said.

'You know, you're going to have to talk to me sooner or later,' she said on the long drive home.

She had estimated it would take her nineteen hours of driving to get back, and did Nat have any idea what all that gasoline would cost? Not to mention the wear and tear on the car?

He did not. Nor did he care.

'Sooner or later you'll have to say something.'

That's what you think, he thought.

'Why didn't you give them your name? If you'd told them your name I would have gotten the call yesterday. But no, you said nothing, and I had to wait another day while they matched you up with missing-child reports from all over the country. And poor Jacob's mother just about died a thousand deaths waiting. She felt so responsible for you. Why didn't you just tell the police who you were?'

Because, Nat thought, if I had wanted to get back to you I wouldn't have hopped a freight train to begin with.

'And then poor Mick's wife had to take two days off work to stay home with the kids because I had to come home and report you missing. And they can ill afford that cut in income. Especially now, with poor Mick in the hospital. You know, I'm beginning to think you're one of those selfish children who just always has to be the center of attention. Poor Mick doesn't even deserve my attention when his appendix bursts, because it always has to be all about Nat. Is that how it is, Nat? Because if that's how it is, I will not tolerate that. I will not raise some spoiled little child who feels he's the center of the entire solar system, and that we're all supposed to revolve around him like he was the sun. So, is that how it is with you?'

Nat said nothing.

'Why won't you speak for yourself?'

Because you don't listen, he thought.

'And now what am I supposed to do? They still need help at Mick's house, but now I don't dare leave you alone. Because I don't know if I can trust you. Well? Can I? Can I trust you?'

Nat said nothing.

'Well, it wouldn't even matter if you said I could. It

wouldn't help. Because I'd still never know if it were true. For all I know, you might just be lying.'

Imagine that, Nat thought. Imagine not knowing if the person you know best in the world is telling you the truth or lying to your face. But he didn't say any of that. Of course. He said nothing.

'Well, this is going to be a long drive,' she said.

Nineteen hours of this and I'll go crazy, Nat thought.

But she continued to talk. And he continued to ignore her. He just looked out the window and watched the world go by, in case he didn't get to see it again for a very long time. And for nineteen hours and more he said nothing.

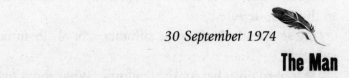

30 September 1974

The Man

'I hope you don't think I'm going to get all soft and break that promise I made to myself,' she said. 'Because I'm not. I said it and I meant it. No presents until you get your grades up above failing.'

He was lying on his back on the couch, watching TV. A show he didn't like. And pretending to ignore her. And pretending that receiving no gifts from her did not in any way hurt. She was standing over him, partially blocking his view. Railing at him. Which is why he was watching a show he didn't like. So it wouldn't bother him when she made him miss it.

He said nothing.

'You probably think I'll feel sorry for you tonight or in the morning. And that I'll run out and get something. But I won't. Because a promise is a promise.'

Nat said nothing.

'And I'm not restarting your allowance, either.'

Still nothing, though Nat felt as if he were *wanting* to say something. As if communication with her was vaguely possible and yet just beyond his grasp, all at the same time. As if, on the rare occasions he attempted to say something to her, the words hit a brick wall and fell to the floor defeated.

'You're already looking at summer school. In three subjects.'

He looked up at her for the first time. 'What about my present from The Man?'

She looked flustered for a moment. Then she said, 'Ah. It speaks.'

'Well? What about it?'

'Hmm. I hadn't thought about that. Well, you never like anything he gives you, anyway. So it's hardly a reward. That's between you and him, I suppose.'

'Has it come?'

'No. Why should it have?'

'Well, the mail's already been.'

'They don't come in the mail.'

This was miserable news to Nat, who had been counting heavily on getting a look at the return address. But he was careful not to frown or otherwise betray his thoughts.

'What do they come in?'

'They just show up on the porch in the morning.'

Which is similarly interesting, Nat thought. Because he took it to mean it would be delivered in person.

* * *

Nat sat up in the dark, in his room, on the padded window seat, looking out on to the street. On his lap lay the binoculars The Man had given him when he was six.

He watched the shadows of the maple tree sway on the far wall of his room. The street light out front threw spooky shadows, and a good strong wind was up that night. And it gave him something to watch. Because nothing happened on their street at night. No people. No cars. No nothing.

He could read the clock clearly, even though it was all the way over on the dresser. Its face glowed in the dark. And it ticked. The ticking had never bothered him before. But it bothered him tonight.

It was ten thirty.

Sometime in the next half hour he dozed off without meaning to.

He woke to the sound of a car door.

He jumped, and sat upright, his back stiff from the uncomfortable position. Across the street, a car was parked. An older station wagon, with its motor softly running. He couldn't see the color because of the darkness. And he couldn't see either the front or rear license plate because it was so directly across the street.

A man was walking across to his house, carrying a parcel.

He glanced at the clock. Five minutes after eleven.

He raised the binoculars and sighted through them.

Trying to get a good look at the man's face. But he was wearing a brimmed hat, and by now he was more or less directly below the window. He disappeared from view, too close to the house to be seen from Nat's vantage point. Then, a second later, he reappeared on his way back to the car. But now his back was turned.

He stepped back into his car, shifted into gear and drove.

Nat first tried to see the man's face, but it was too dark in the passenger compartment. Then he turned his binoculars to the license plate, but too late. He had only read the letters DCB when the car disappeared from sight.

Nat sat a minute, nursing his own frustration. That's not much progress, he thought. And he would only get two chances a year.

He tiptoed downstairs and out on to the front porch to retrieve his present. A medium-size box. He shook it a few times, but it only made a series of dull and not very telling thumps.

He carried it up to his room. Tore through the paper.

Boxing gloves.

And a punching bag of some sort, but not the kind Nat was familiar with. Not an inflatable speed bag that pops back and forth when you pummel it with both hands. It must be the big, heavy kind you hang from the ceiling. The kind that absorbs huge blows as if it were a person, a real opponent. But it was hard to tell, because it was only the leather and fabric shell of a bag. It wasn't filled with anything.

It had a chain at the top, presumably to hang it by.

Nat put on the gloves, not knowing how to lace them at his wrists.

'Well, old man,' he said aloud to the empty room. 'Now we might be on to something.'

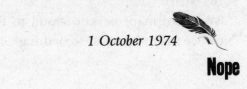

1 October 1974

Nope

On his way to math, Nat thought seriously about cutting class. He had the boxing gloves with him, in his book bag. And they were burning a hole.

The plan had been to bring them along and then go straight from school to the gym downtown. See if there was any way to get some instruction. Which seemed unlikely without money. But maybe he could just talk to somebody about them. Look at the way they laced theirs. Or the way their bag was filled.

On the way to math, he almost cut the rest of the afternoon's school and went straight to the gym. But he sagged inwardly, thinking how long he would have to listen to the old woman's railing. It didn't seem worth it.

He sighed, and went to class instead.

* * *

'OK. Take out a sheet of paper.' Nat's math teacher – whom Nat didn't like, and vice versa – always seemed gleeful when announcing tests. The whole class groaned, as if a single body with one voice. 'Now, this time you can't say I didn't warn you. I told you yesterday there would be a test.'

Nat briefly searched his memory. There was nothing there about a math test. He might not have been listening. Or he might just have forgotten. Or maybe it had something to do with the fact that he didn't care, not the tiniest little bit.

The teacher wrote the problems on the board. One through ten.

The minute the rest of the class began working on problem one, Nat craned his neck to pick up the answer from the paper of Sarah Gordon, just to his right. She was decent at math, and didn't block her answers with her arm like so many of the kids who sat near him.

The teacher whipped around and caught him immediately.

It felt almost like entrapment, Nat thought. Like the teacher turned away just long enough to let Nat Bates get himself into trouble, and then turned back just in time to gleefully nab him.

'Mr Bates. Front of the class.'

Nat sighed deeply. Hoisted his book bag. Trod heavily up to the blackboard.

'Principal's office. I trust you'll have no trouble

finding it with all your experience. Try following the rut you've worn into the hallway on your previous fifty trips. I'll call ahead, just in case you need a search party.'

Nat walked out of the classroom.

Some birthday, he thought. Why can't you get a day off from this hell on your birthday? It's only one day a year.

He trotted down the two flights of stairs. Along the dim and dingy hallway. Past the principal's office. Right out the front door.

As he trotted down the outside stairs in front of the school, he heard his name called.

'Mr Bates. Just where do you think you're going?'

It sounded like the assistant principal.

Without turning around, Nat waved goodbye.

'Can I help you, kid?'

'I don't know. I got these boxing gloves for my birthday. And I want to use them. But I don't know exactly how.'

The little man rolled his eyes.

He was weirdly short. Much shorter than Nathan. But probably twice his weight. Not fat, though. All muscle. Fifty-something maybe. He had a half-smoked cigar clenched between his molars, but it wasn't lit. His artificially dark reddish-orange hair was slicked back with a bizarre amount of hair cream, his jet-black shoes perfectly shined. Nat could see the reflection of the gym ceiling in their uppers.

The little man stood in a spill of light from the store-front gym windows, which also illuminated swirling dust.

'Jack, you got time for a kid who don't know nothing about nothing?'

Jack came out from the back room. He was younger, taller. Smooth-looking. Ladies'-man handsome. He had a big chip broken off the corner of a front tooth. Nat watched him approach. Actually stared as Jack approached, unable to take his eyes off the man's face. As if looking into a mirror that reflected not what Nat currently was, but what he wanted to become.

He reminded Nat of the often-imagined mental picture of his unknown father. The image of Richard A. Ford that he conjured up behind his closed eyelids.

'What, this kid?' he said.

He walked up to Nat and sized him up. Like Nat was a used car on a lot. A cheap one. Nat was less than a second away from turning on his heels to leave.

Then Jack smiled. 'Looks a little like Joey, huh? OK. Put on your gloves, kid. We'll see what you can do.'

Nat pulled his new gloves out of his book bag. Put them on and stepped into the ring with the laces still undone. The little man laced up both his and Jack's gloves, leaving him as unclear as ever about how he would later do that on his own.

'Hey. Nice gloves, kid. Where'd you say you got these?'

'They were a present.'

'Must've cost a pretty penny. These're the kind the

pros use. Somebody must think well of you to give you these.'

'Too bad it's nobody I know,' Nat muttered under his breath.

'What'd you say, kid?'

'Nothing.'

The little man ducked through the ropes and out of the ring.

Jack circled Nat a few times. Nat raised his hands in imitation of the way he had seen fighters box. He felt the sudden pressure of trying to impress an admired figure with no idea of how to proceed.

'No, no, no,' Jack said. 'You gotta keep 'em up. Up. Or you're gonna get killed. And think about your footwork, kid.'

Nat looked down and realized he was simply dragging his feet, circling, thinking of nothing but his gloved hands.

'Watch Jack's footwork,' the little man called out. 'When it comes to footwork, he's the king.'

Nat watched and imitated.

Jack threw a punch and it hit Nat square in the gut, knocking the breath out of him.

'OK, *Time*!' Jack called, giving Nat a moment to lean on the ropes and try to breathe. 'Boy, Little Manny, you weren't kidding when you said he knows nothing from nothing. Come here, kid. I'm gonna put you on this heavy bag.'

They ducked through the ropes together, and Jack led him up to a bag that looked a great deal like the one he now had at home. Except this one was filled.

'I got one like this,' Nat said. Trying to talk like someone who hadn't just been gut-punched. 'But it's just this outside part.'

'You gotta stuff 'em yourself. But that's good you got one. Cause you're gonna need the practice.'

'What do I stuff it with?'

'The ones we got here are stuffed with sawdust. Or sand. Or both. But don't try that at home, unless you really trust your ceiling. Old clothes works OK. Or you can stop at the dumpster behind that carpet store down the street. Get a bunch of old padding. You can roll that up around some old clothes or rags or whatever and then slide the whole thing inside. Now, step up to this bag here.'

He stood behind Nat for the first minute or two, correcting the position of his hands between each jab.

'Make you a deal,' Jack said. 'You go home and practice just like you're doing now – only don't forget that footwork – for a week. And then come back and maybe I'll get in the ring with you.'

Nat agreed, yet stayed for over two hours, working. Stealing glances at Jack. And feeling the warm sense of having been taken under somebody's wing. Someone he could relate to. Someone he could model himself after. A clear marker on the road to the man Nat suddenly wanted and needed to be.

When Nat got home with his big roll of discarded carpet padding, the old woman was nowhere to be seen.

Probably in a conference down at my school, he thought.

He stuffed the bag, then tried to figure out how to hang it.

Eventually he solved the problem by taking down the big hook that held the dining room chandelier and putting it up on one of the beams of his ceiling instead.

He pulled on his gloves and, leaving them untied, began to practice.

It felt good.

'What in heaven's name are you doing? And what is the chandelier doing lying on the dining room table?'

Too bad, Nat thought. The old woman is home.

He did not stop punching.

'Oh, good God! I can't take much more of this!' she screeched. 'You took the hook down from the chandelier for that? How are we supposed to eat dinner?'

'I'm not hungry,' Nat said. Still punching.

'I just came back from your school. The assistant principal called me.'

Nat said nothing. Just continued to punch.

'Did you leave school without permission?'

'Nope.'

'Excuse me? What did you say?'

'Nope.'

'So why does he say you did?'

Nat paused briefly. Looked at her for the first time. 'Maybe he was mistaken. Or maybe you just misunderstood.' Then he went back to striking the bag. Harder this time.

'So you were in school all afternoon.'

'Yup.'

'What class do you have right after math?'

'History.'

'And what did you study in history this afternoon?'

'The French Revolution,' he said, his voice broken and breathy with the exertion of his punches. 'Did you know that when Marie Antoinette said, "Then let them eat cake," she didn't mean cake like we eat, she meant this nasty crap that gets stuck on the pans when they bake bread? Did you know that? Kind of puts things in a whole new perspective. Doesn't it?'

A silence, during which he snuck a sideways look at the old woman's face.

'Well,' she said. 'Much as it really is nice to hear you string more than one sentence together . . . it's only been, what? A year or two since you've said that many words to me? Despite my pleasure over that, I think you're lying.'

'Nope,' Nat said.

She left the room.

Nat instinctively knew the trouble was not over, but he didn't let that interfere with his practice. He just kept jabbing for several minutes, feeling sweat roll down under the neckline of his tee shirt, tickling slightly. He liked the sound of his own puffing breath.

The old woman reappeared. He purposely did not look at her face.

'I called your history teacher at home. She informs me that you studied the French Revolution *last week*, and that today you were absent from class. I'm impressed you were even paying attention to the comments of Marie Antoinette. But it still means that you are a liar.'

Nat stopped punching. Stood with both gloved hands on the bag, leaning slightly. Panting. 'I guess it runs in the family,' he said.

The old woman lost her temper and charged at him. 'And this is going back!' She lunged for his heavy bag and tried to lift it down off its hook.

'No!' Nat said. 'No fucking way!'

'You do *not* use that language with me, young man!' she bellowed. And slapped him hard across the face. 'This present is going back.'

She grabbed for one of the gloves. Because it was unlaced, she managed to pull it off his hand. He tried to grab it back, but she turned away from him, and tucked it against her stomach, wrapping herself around the prize.

He lunged at her. Tried to grab them. But instead he only managed to slam into her with his shoulder. Hard. She banged into the wall and bounced off again, thudding into a sitting position on the floor.

Nat grabbed his glove back and stormed out of the house. Knowing he had just sacrificed the bag, but not knowing how to change that. Knowing only that the time had come to go.

He stopped halfway down the front steps. Looked back. It didn't seem likely that she should be hurt. Not really hurt. He could certainly run into the wall and fall down like that and be fine. But she was old, Gamma. Maybe he'd better go back in.

But she'd find a way to punish him for it. He knew she would.

He saw her face come to the window. Saw her place her hands against the glass, watching him go.

He turned and took the steps two at a time and ran.

He headed straight for the train yard, breaking into a sprint. Because he knew his only chance was to get there fast. He knew it was the first place they would look for him. His only hope of escape rested in getting there before the old woman called the police, and told them where to look, and they did.

He ran downhill a half-mile to the tracks, and jogged along them, hoping a train would come by. If he could hop on something moving, that would be much better.

He even stopped and put his ear to the rail, but he heard nothing.

When the narrow easement on each side of the tracks widened out to the train yard, he saw it was empty. There were no trains parked there. Not that a parked train would have helped him anyway, unless it was just about to get under way.

He shrank back into the bushes as he got closer. Wondering where the best place would be to hide. He pushed himself backwards into a stand of brush and crouched there, feeling the sharp tips of branches scratch his neck and back and scalp. He held very still and listened to the sound of his own breathing. It settled to normal for the first time in hours.

Dusk began to set in, offering the beginnings of a welcome cover.

He had no jacket. He would have to find some way to keep warm.

He closed his eyes. After a very long set of minutes – or it could even have been half an hour – he heard the rails buzz with an oncoming train. It was approaching from the other side of the train yard. He heard its welcoming whistle.

He didn't want to risk jumping it from his current location. Too narrow. Too little margin for error. He had never jumped a moving train, and he would likely only get one chance. And it was half-dark.

He tied the gloves together by the laces and hung them around his neck.

When he saw the big light on the front of the engine, he pushed out of the bushes and sprinted as fast as he could into the open train yard.

And was immediately met by two cops with their guns drawn.

'Nathan Bates?' one said. 'You are under arrest for assault.'

He stopped cold. What else could he do?

The train clattered past.

'I'm not Nathan Bates,' he said. When he could be heard again. 'You got the wrong guy.'

'Oh, do we? So, you're just some other kid the same age, in the same neighborhood, trying to jump a freight train with a pair of boxing gloves? OK. Tell you what. Come with us downtown. We'll see who you are. If you're not Nathan Bates, you can go. If you are, then you're under arrest for assault *and* making a false statement to an officer.'

They took the boxing gloves from him, cuffed his hands behind his back. Led him in the direction of a squad car parked on the adjacent street.

'So,' the other cop said. 'Any new thoughts on who you are?'

'I guess I'm Nathan Bates,' he said.

'It's a wonderful moment when these kids find themselves. Don't you think so, Ralph?'

2 October 1974

More Nothing

Nat woke on a hard wooden bench in a small, cold holding cell.

The door of the cell was open, and the two cops were standing in the open doorway, talking to each other in loudly exaggerated voices.

'So, tell me, Ralph . . . have you ever seen a kid rotten enough to assault his own grandmother and give her a concussion?'

His grandmother had a concussion? Was that true? He'd had no idea.

'No. I've seen some pretty rotten ones. But that takes the prize.'

'What would you do to your own kid if he did a thing like that?'

'No kid of mine ever would. I'd raise him up better than that. And he wouldn't dare.'

'Just theoretically, though. What would you do?'

'Well, if the grandmother would press charges, I'd lock his ass up in Juvenile Hall for a few years and that would teach him a lesson.'

'And if she wouldn't?'

'Then I'd have to teach him myself, I guess.'

Nathan pressed his eyes shut again. Waiting for it.

A few seconds later he felt himself lifted by the armpits. Pulled to his feet. His arms held tightly behind his back. He opened his eyes and looked into the face of one of them. Ralph. Betraying as little fear as possible. His shoulder joints were being painfully twisted, but he was careful not to complain or even let on.

'So, how does it feel to be helpless? Huh, boy? When somebody bigger and stronger is holding you like that, does it make you feel as helpless as, say . . . a little old lady?'

In truth, to be completely helpless – and then taunted about it – triggered a frightening burst of rage in Nat. It exploded up from his gut and overwhelmed him. But there wasn't much he could do about it.

He almost spit in the cop's face. He had begun to gather enough saliva to do so.

But no. He wouldn't. He would do nothing.

Let it be all them, he thought. All their fault. Don't even give them a good excuse.

Instead Nat shut down the inside of himself like a store at quitting time. Locked the door and hung out the sign. They could do whatever they wanted to him, and, other than physical pain, they could not make him feel anything about it at all.

'Oh, dear,' the old woman said when she looked up and saw his face.

She was standing at the desk arguing with an officer Nat hadn't seen yet. It seemed to take her a moment to get back to what they'd been arguing about. As if the sight of his face had knocked all other thoughts out of her head.

'Here's a question, then,' the officer behind the counter said. 'If you don't want to press charges, why'd you have us pick him up in the first place?'

'Well, I couldn't just let him run away,' she said.

'We're not your baby-sitters, ma'am.'

'No, I didn't mean it that way. You misunderstood me. I didn't mean that was the only reason. I just mean . . . Well, I was considering pressing charges, but I don't think it's the best thing for his situation in the long run.'

'It'd teach him a lesson.'

'Oh, would it? So then, the boys you let out of Juvenile Hall every day? You're saying they've learned their lessons, and they never get into any more trouble after that?'

Silence.

'Of course not,' the long-winded old bag continued. 'It just teaches them to be even more hardened criminals. Now, if you don't mind, my grandson and I are going to go home.'

'Fine. Good luck with him, ma'am. I'm sure you'll need it.'

She turned toward the door and walked quickly for a few steps, then stopped to look over her shoulder at Nat. 'Coming? Or do you like it here?'

Nat looked at the officer behind the desk. 'Do I get my boxing gloves back?' he asked. Quietly.

The officer pulled himself up straight and tall. 'In accordance with the laws regarding an inmate's property . . . the personal effects we confiscated when you were arrested have been turned over to your legal guardian. That is, as many of them as she chose to reclaim.'

Nat squeezed his eyes closed for a moment.

Then he turned and gingerly followed the old woman out to the car.

The light of morning violently assaulted his headache and made him wince. He wondered if he might vomit. Trying to control the impulse, he eased himself down in the passenger seat of the old woman's car.

Bending in the middle hurt more than he had anticipated.

She got into the driver's seat and started up the engine.

Nat was aware that the bad side of his face – the left side – was facing her.

Say something about my face, he thought.

She raised her hand to shift the car into gear, then stopped and put her hands in her lap again. Turned toward him and sat staring.

Say something about my face.

A long silence.

Then, 'Did you start a fight with those policemen?'

Nat said nothing.

More than halfway home, Nat finally opened his mouth. 'I didn't mean to hurt you,' he said.

The old lady never answered.

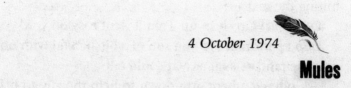

4 October 1974

Mules

Nat arrived at the gym about ten thirty in the morning. The little man was nowhere to be seen. Jack was in the ring, sparring with some guy who looked too old to be there. They didn't look up, probably didn't dare, so Nat just watched.

He leaned gingerly on a heavy bag, which swayed over and leaned against the dirty gym wall. And he watched Jack's footwork. And the way he held his hands, so that wherever the old guy tried to jab he just got Jack's gloves instead.

He watched for maybe five minutes, aching with admiration. The old guy never laid a glove on him.

When the old guy wore down and got tired, he made a mistake. And Nat saw it. Saw it before the guy even finished paying for it, which Nat thought was a good sign. He actually spotted what the guy did wrong. Where he left his opening.

Jack's right plowed through it like a freight train. Nat heard the two solid blows from across the room. The impact of Jack's gloved fist. And the older man's back hitting the mat.

'OK, *Time*! Go clean up, Fred. I went easy on you.'

'Don't patronize *me*, you son of a bitch.' Said with no genuine rancor as far as Nat could tell.

Jack offered a bent arm down to help the guy to his feet. Then he ducked through the ropes and headed in Nat's direction, removing his gloves as he walked. He had known Nat was there all along, Nat realized. He was just doing things one at a time.

He was wearing trunks only, no shirt. Nat glanced at the definition of his chest muscles. And his abs. Like a washboard, each section distinct and angular, as if he had been carved from clay. Nat knew he wanted that for himself. Wanted that body. That way of carrying himself in the world. Wanted Jack's life, if such a thing had been possible.

'Told you come back in a week. Wasn't that more like four or five days?' He caught sight of Nat's face and whistled softly. 'Man. Did you get the shit kicked out of you or what?' He grabbed hold of Nat's chin. Turned his face sideways for a better look. 'No wonder you wanna learn to fight. You should never let nobody do some shit like that to you.'

'What if it's a cop?'

'Oh. Well, that does get a little dicey, then. Doesn't it? Hey. Isn't this a school day?'

'I guess so.'

'Come to think, wasn't it a school day last time you were here?'

'I guess.'

'You just don't bother with school?'

'Not if I can help it.'

'Well. I guess I'm no truant officer. Where're your gloves, kid?'

'Don't have 'em.'

'You didn't bring 'em?'

'Don't have 'em. Period. At all.'

'They get ripped off or something?'

'Yeah. Something like that.'

'Man. Those sweet gloves. They were really primo. That sucks, kid.'

'Yeah. It really does. I don't have a bag any more, either.' A long pause. 'How much you think a pair of gloves like that costs?'

'More than you got, I bet. How much you got?'

'Nothing.' He had been living with a revoked allowance for nearly a year.

'Then I'd say they cost more than you got.'

'You got any work I could do around here?'

Jack laughed, a snort that sent a rush of air between his nearly closed lips. 'Like what?'

'Like someone to clean up or something? Mop the sweat off the floor?'

'That's Little Manny's job. Nope. Sorry, kid. Can't help you with the gloves.' Jack sighed. Worked his jaw as if chewing something tough between his molars. 'Tell you what, though. You may *not* take them home. Ever. I don't *ever* want to see any glove of mine walk out that door. But if you wanna practice here . . . you can take down a pair of them.' He pointed with a flip of his chin to the far wall, where half a dozen pairs of old gloves hung on hooks.

Nathan walked over to check them out.

He tried to find a pair that were in better condition than the others. But they were all the same. All horrible. Nathan guessed they must be twenty years old at least. Most of the brown color had been worn or scraped off the contact surfaces. Then they had been wrapped in duct tape to keep them from flying apart where the stitching had come unsewn at their seams.

He took down a pair at random, literally unable to see how any pair was better than any other.

'I know, I know.' Jack's voice from just behind his right shoulder. 'It's like having your Ferrari stole and then having to ride a mule. But if you wanna practice . . .'

'I do.'

He pulled on the gloves. Held out his hands so Jack could lace them for him.

Nat stepped up to the heavy bag and gave it one good

clean shot with his right. Pain exploded through his body. His jolted gut. The muscles all through his rib cage, his abdomen. The shock of the blow even made his head hurt.

He held still a minute, eyes pressed closed, forehead resting against the bag. Still holding it in both gloved fists.

He felt Jack's hand on his shoulder.

'Maybe in a couple days. When you get to feeling better.'

'I feel fine.'

He straightened up and hit the bag again.

And again. And again. And again. And again.

Jack was watching. So he could do anything.

Nat's miserable little city boasted only one mall. It was a good twenty-five minutes out into the suburbs. Nat had only been there once. When he was nine, and the old lady had dragged him along to go Christmas shopping. It was the year her sister died, and left her a pittance in extra cash. Since then, Christmas shopping had been less of a production.

Nat hitchhiked out there on a Friday morning. There was a sporting goods store out at the mall, or so he had heard. And Nat wanted to have a look at their boxing gloves.

He was standing in a rear aisle of the store when he saw them. They were in a heavy cardboard box, but the box was open in the front. Three-sided, like a presentation box.

The exact same gloves he'd been given, and then had taken from him.

He stopped cold and just looked at them for a long time. Then he reached a hand out to touch them.

It felt something like unexpectedly bumping into someone you loved on a busy street. Someone you thought was long gone. Or at least, Nat figured it would feel something like this. If there were anyone he loved.

They could literally have been the same ones. Well, no. That's not right, he thought. They couldn't be. Not literally. These were brand new. But the ones he'd lost were so new. There was just no way he could ever have told the two pairs apart.

He took the box down off the shelf and read the price tag. Almost thirty dollars. Nat swallowed hard. When he'd gotten an allowance, it was two dollars a week. Now it was nothing a week.

He was just about to put them back on the shelf.

He looked both ways. He was alone in that aisle. There was no one there to see what came next.

He pulled the gloves out of the heavy cardboard box, one at a time. Slid them into his book bag. Then he put the empty box on the shelf behind two others.

He swung the bag on to his shoulder and walked out the door into the mall. Reminding himself not to hurry.

Don't dawdle but don't hurry. Just act natural.

Wow, he thought. That was almost too easy.

He made a beeline for the down escalator. Just before

he arrived there, a uniformed man stepped in front of him. A very big man, wearing gray polyester and a self-satisfied expression.

'Mall security,' he said. 'You want to open up that bag? Show me what you got in there?'

Nat's first thought was to run. But he decided there was a better, smarter way. After all, just a couple of months ago he'd been walking around with an identical pair of gloves in his book bag. It didn't mean he'd done anything wrong.

'Just my boxing gloves,' he said. And opened the bag and let the guard peer inside.

'*Your* gloves.'

'Yes, sir. They were a present from— They're mine. I was just on my way back from the gym.'

The guy shot Nat a look he couldn't quite read. But it was not good news. That much was clear.

'Kid. You were being watched on a security monitor the whole time.'

'Oh,' Nat said.

The old woman sat behind the wheel of her ancient car, staring straight ahead. Nathan wondered when – even if – she would ever start it up and drive home.

'That's half my savings I just put up for your bail.'

'You'll get it back. I'm not going anywhere.'

'I can't take much more of this.'

'So you keep telling me.'

'I'm putting you on notice. Right now. If one more thing like this happens—'

Nat waited. But she never finished the sentence.

'Then *what*?'

'Don't start with me. I won't have this conversation with you.'

'No, really. Tell me. What will you do if I screw up one more time?'

No reply.

'I don't think you'll have much luck pitching me out in the woods by the lake. I'm older and smarter now. I'd probably find my own way out.'

She did not look at him. She looked forward, through the windshield. He waited for the slapped look to arrive. But she was far beyond the slapped look. Now she wore a look that said, 'I have armored myself against you, and you will never slap me again.'

She did not reply.

'Just your luck I wouldn't die this time, either,' he said quietly.

A pause, then she started the car, shifted it into gear and drove.

So began the first moment of a new era between them. The era when the old woman also said nothing.

In Nat's opinion, it was a huge stride in the right direction.

In the beginnings of that silence, he knew something. Clearly. Once you throw down that gauntlet of ultimatum, the one more thing will happen. Nat figured it probably wouldn't even matter much what it was. It would be the straw that broke her. And it had been defined. Prepared for. So it would happen.

It was only a matter of time.

Part Three

Nathan McCann

He Still Feels That Same Way Now

Nathan McCann answered the knock at his door to find an older woman standing on his stoop, accompanied by a sullen teenage boy. Hair hung into the boy's eyes; he looked away from Nathan as if he could establish the matter of his disdain just that simply. His skin was ravaged by teenage acne. He had one large fraying hole in the knee of his dirty blue jeans.

Nathan did not enjoy unannounced visits, nor did he initially connect with a memory of having seen these people before.

'Nathan McCann?' the woman asked.

'Yes.'

'Nathan McCann, this is Nathan Bates. The boy you found in the woods.'

A brief silence reigned.

Nathan looked more closely at the boy, who continued to avoid Nathan's eyes.

Nathan felt a pang of disappointment. As though part of him had known this moment would arrive, or a moment something like it, yet that part of him had expected more. Some sense of already-established bond or instant kinship. But no such bond could be seen, not anywhere from his door stoop to the horizon. The boy was simply a stranger. A sullen, unresponsive and unkempt one, at that. And there was no purpose in Nathan's denying it, even if it had been possible to do so.

Ertha Bates continued. 'I remember at the time you were keen to have this boy for your own. Very keen. As if you had always expected it would go just that way. And maybe even as though you assumed it would be a good thing, to have this young person in your life. You might have dodged a rude awakening on that score. Unless you're really brave enough to be wanting a second chance.

'So, tell me, Mr McCann, do you still feel that same way now? Because I am at my wits' end. I've had it, that's all I can say. That's all there is to it. I've had it. Each person has just a certain store of patience, and he has snapped mine in half. Just broken clean through it. And I will not live like this any more. This situation is completely outside my ability to cope. I raised five children on what I thought to be normal discipline, but if there's something this boy responds to, I haven't stumbled across it yet.

'You still want this boy, Mr McCann? You'd be doing me a great favor. And you'd be doing him a favor as well. I figure he'd be better off here than as a ward of the state, and that's his next stop, believe me.

'I was on my way to the police station right now to turn him over. Give up custody and let him be someone else's problem for a change. And then partway through the drive I thought of you. And first I thought, well, if I'm going to give up custody I have to at least keep that promise I made to you fifteen years ago. To bring him around to meet you. And then a voice in my head said, "Ask him if he still feels that same way now." Even though I really couldn't imagine why anyone would. How anyone could be that foolish. But the voice said to ask. So I'm asking. Because I'm sure he'd be better off here. That is, if you still feel that same way now.'

'Yes,' Nathan said. 'I still feel that same way now.'

The boy's eyes came up briefly when he said this, then flicked away again.

'Good. I have his things out in the car.'

'We'll help you carry them in,' Nathan said. 'Won't we, Nathan?'

Ertha Bates didn't linger. She did not appear to wish to discuss the issue further. There were no longing looks of regret. There was no sentimental goodbye. If she felt she would miss the boy she had raised as her own for fifteen years, she betrayed none of it.

As soon as they had unloaded the three suitcases and one laundry bag out on to the curb, she climbed back into her ancient brown sedan, accelerated with a faint screech of tires and drove away.

On the trips into the house with the boy's belongings, Nathan felt a pang of regret that Flora had not lived to see the day.

She'd teased him unmercifully for feeling it was meant to be.

'You can sleep in my wife's old room,' he said to the boy. 'What do you go by?'

'What?'

'What do they call you?'

'Oh. Nat.'

'Good,' Nathan said. 'That will avoid some confusion. Gradually we'll take my late wife's things out to the garage. You can make this room entirely yours.'

In the background, Nathan could hear Maggie barking sharply from the back yard. She could hear and smell that someone new was in the house, and would likely continue to bark until given the opportunity to investigate.

Nat stood with his shoulder on the door jamb. 'You two didn't even sleep together?'

Nathan dropped a suitcase and stood upright, his back poker-straight. He regarded the boy for a moment; the boy met his gaze unswervingly. Nathan felt the weight of importance of these early tests.

'It's not something I'd expect you to understand,' he said. 'But we loved each other in our way. Maybe it wasn't always the best way, but it was what we could manage.'

He purposely did not look to Nat's face for a reaction, because no reaction was welcome. He had said his piece, and it was nobody's business to question the matter further.

Instead he went around to the back door and let his dog come into the house. It was a luxury he'd allowed himself, and Maggie, often since Flora's death.

They walked together to Nat's new room.

Nat looked up, seeming stunned. 'Is that the dog?'

Maggie approached the boy with broad swings of her tail. She sniffed his offered hand for a moment, then gave it one good, enthusiastic lick. From the look on Nat's face, Nathan gathered the boy was not accustomed to warm greetings.

'No, it's not,' Nathan said, sorry to break the bad news to Nat, and also sorry, for his own sake, that it was not. 'No, Sadie is long gone. This is Maggie.'

'Oh, OK,' Nat said, and brushed the stunned look away.

Just as Nathan was leaving the room, the boy said,

'That's a coincidence. Huh? How we both have the same name.'

Nathan turned and studied the boy's face briefly. As far as he could see, there was no hint of teasing or sarcasm. At least, none that the boy made evident. Did he really believe it was coincidental? Had no one told him otherwise?

'It's not a coincidence. You were named after me.'

He watched the boy's face for some reaction. But apparently Nat knew the basics of assuming a poker face. He appeared to feel nothing, register nothing at all times. Though Nathan was not inclined to believe such an unlikely display. Not from this young man. Not from anyone.

'I was? Why?'

'Because I'm the man who found you in the woods,' Nathan said, not imagining that the situation could possibly need any more explaining than that.

'Oh,' Nat said. Then, just as Nathan turned to leave again, he added, 'I don't think you did me such a big favor, you know.'

Nathan stopped. Turned. More tests, he supposed. More histrionics of the type he didn't suffer lightly.

'Oh, don't you?'

'No. I don't.'

'Your life is not a big favor?'

'How do you know I even want it?'

'Every sane person wants his life.'

'Oh. So you think I'm insane?'

'No. I think you really do want it, and you're only saying you don't for effect.'

'What I'm saying,' he said, rising to a bit more anger now, his cheeks flushing slightly, 'is that I'd like to know what good my life is to me.'

'The value of your life is your own choosing,' Nathan said.

The boy stood with his chin held high, his back against the closet door. He said nothing for a brief moment, but Nathan could feel the words bounce off him unabsorbed. 'Is that even English, what you just said?'

Nathan pulled a deep breath. 'Were there any words in the sentence you don't understand?'

'Um. Let me see. The. Value. Life. Choosing. No, I guess I know them all. It's just what it's all supposed to add up to that I don't understand.'

'But you do recognize it as the English language.'

'Maybe one word at a time.'

'You know it's English.'

'English is supposed to mean something. That sentence didn't mean anything.'

'The fact that you don't grasp the meaning of something doesn't mean it has none.'

'So what am I supposed to do with a sentence like that? That means nothing to me?'

'Try filing it away for possible later use.'

'All right,' Nat said. 'But I'm telling you right now . . . that one's going to be in there waiting for a long time.'

At bedtime, Nathan rapped lightly before letting himself into the boy's room.

'What?' Nat said as Nathan pulled a chair to his bedside.

'I just came in to say goodnight.'

'Oh.'

Nathan took the photograph out of the pocket of his sweater and laid it on the edge of the boy's bed. 'That was Sadie,' he said. 'She was a curly-coated retriever. She was a remarkable animal. I miss her terribly. Maggie is a good dog, too. But that doesn't spare me from missing Sadie.'

Nat picked up the photo, studied it briefly.

Then he said, as if he had never registered the image on the old photograph, 'Why do I have to go to bed so early? It's barely eight o'clock. I can't go to sleep this early. I'm not a child, you know.'

But he looked like one. Very much so. He was small for nearly fifteen, and looked a bit helpless and lost, smothered in Flora's old bed sheets and flowered quilt. Nathan wondered if the boy could acknowledge his own terror. Even to himself.

'Because in the morning I'm going to wake you up very early and we're going to go hunting.'

'Hunting?'

'Yes. Duck-hunting. With Maggie.'

'I don't hunt.'

'Well, I'm suggesting you give it a try.'

'What time would I have to get up?'

'About four thirty.'

'No way. Forget it.'

'I'll be in to wake you. I'd like you to try it with me this one time.'

A medium-length, sulky silence. Then the boy's face changed. Only slightly. But perceptibly.

'Do you always go to that same place?'

He didn't have to elaborate. He didn't have to specify what same place. They both knew what he meant.

'Yes.'

'Could you show me the exact spot?'

'Yes.'

'OK. I'll go with you, then. This one time.'

Nathan picked up his photograph. Patted Nat on the knee through the covers. Reached for the light switch on his way out of the room.

Nat asked, as though not anxious to see him leave, 'Aren't you even going to ask me what I did to get thrown out of the house?'

'No. I thought it best to start fresh with each other. You'll have a birthday coming up next week. We'll celebrate.'

'Why do you remember my birthday after all this time?'

'How can I not remember your birthday? I found you

in the woods on October second, 1960. How could I forget a date like that? You were born the day before, October first. You'll be fifteen.'

'How am I supposed to live here? I don't even know you.' It seemed out of context with what Nathan had just told him, which Nathan supposed was why the boy said it. 'I don't even know this place. This is all completely strange to me. How am I even supposed to live here?'

Nathan sighed. 'A few minutes at a time, I suppose, at first. I won't pretend it's not a problem for you.'

'And you?' the boy asked, even more agitated. 'This is not a problem for you?'

'Not at all,' Nathan said. 'I'm happy to have you here with me.'

He turned out the light on his way out of the room.

He is Willing to Die to Make it Happen

'I can't believe you're stupid enough to give me a gun,' the boy said, trying to pull the huge flowered quilt back over his head. But Nathan had a good, tight hold of it. 'You certainly don't know me very well. I don't want to go duck-hunting. It's four o'clock in the goddamn morning. I want to go back to sleep.'

'There will be no swearing in this house,' Nathan said. 'And it's actually four forty-five. And I'm only asking that you try it with me this one time. If you don't like it I won't ask you to go again.'

'I shouldn't be forced to do things against my will.'

'You agreed last night that you would do this. I'm only asking you to remain true to your word.'

'Well, I don't remember *why* I said I'd do it.'

'Because you wanted me to show you the exact spot.'

'Oh.'

Nat sat up. Swung his legs over the side of the bed. Sat rubbing his eyes. Wearing only a short-sleeved tee shirt and faded boxers. Looking somewhat resigned, but a full measure short of cooperative.

Maggie, who had been spinning in circles around Nathan's knees, suddenly reared up on to her hind legs and kissed Nat on the nose. As if to say, why on earth would you want to stall at a time like this?

'What's she all wound up about?' the boy asked Nathan.

'She loves to go hunting.'

'Oh,' Nat said. 'Well. That makes one of us.'

Nat seemed quite content to walk away leaving the bed an unkempt mess. But Nathan ran through it with him, and they worked on it together. Nathan taught him to make hospital corners, he working on one side and Nat working on the other.

Nathan made a point to ignore the rolling of Nat's eyes.

Then Nathan attempted to bounce a quarter off the bed, with less than remarkable success.

The boy was sulky and quiet on the drive to the lake, but he showed something of himself by reaching back to scratch Maggie's head. At least, Nathan felt he was showing something from the inside of his recalcitrant bad-boy shell.

Maybe Nat didn't realize that he was allowing, and

displaying, a certain vulnerability by openly bonding with Nathan's dog.

Nathan made a mental notation: Ertha Bates had said if there was something this boy responded to she had not stumbled across it. But Nathan had discovered a chink in his armor already. Nat responded to dogs. He wondered if the Bates home had ever included pets. He didn't suppose it had.

He looked briefly over at Nat, who met his eyes defensively.

'What?'

'Nothing.'

Nat took his hand back from Maggie's head, sat facing forward, and sulked with his hands in his lap all the way to the lake.

Maggie leaned into the front seat, as far as she could get without breaking the rules, and even went so far as to let out a few quiet, thin whimpers in Nat's direction. But Nat stared out the window as if he hadn't heard.

'Check to see that the safety is on,' Nathan said as they unloaded the car in the dark. 'And then carry the weapon so it points at nothing. Up across your shoulder, or in the crook of your arm pointing forward and toward the ground.'

'But the safety is on.'

'With guns it's best to be double-safe.'

They began the hike to the lake, side by side, Maggie bounding ahead.

Nathan charted a path for them by flashlight.

The sky had just begun to lighten. In five or ten minutes they would be able to see their own steps, unaided, in the fallen leaves. It was the perfect time to go hunting. By the time they reached the lake the flashlight could be stowed away, and they could set up behind the blind using only available light. But it would not yet be dawn.

It was the time of morning that always made Nathan grateful for his own life.

'I wish you wouldn't make me ask,' the boy said after a short walk. 'I wish you would just tell me, and not put me through having to ask.'

'When we get there,' Nathan said, 'I'll show you the place.'

About a tenth of a mile later, Nathan said, pointing, 'Right over there. Under that tree.'

The boy walked over and stood looking down at a fresh blanket of the new season's leaves in the near-dark.

Nathan and Maggie waited, respectfully, until he was done. Nathan even resisted the temptation to feel impatient as the sky lightened. The experience was like that of watching a mourner at a funeral approach the open casket in dark silence.

It was not a moment one could rush.

Several minutes later, Nat turned and walked back to Nathan and the dog. Maggie jumped up and hit Nat in the chest with her paws. It was strictly outside of the rules and she knew it, but just in that moment she had been unable to contain her own exuberance. Nat said nothing. Nathan chose to let it go by.

Nathan expected the boy to renege on his hunting commitment. Now that he had gotten what he wanted. Nathan expected him to flip his middle finger and head back to the car.

Instead he followed Nathan and Maggie toward the lake, head slightly drooping. As if he were suddenly too tired to argue the matter further.

The lesson in hunting did not go well. In fact in time it broke down completely, with Nat leaping up in the air and waving his arms to purposely scare the ducks away.

'Fly away,' he shouted. 'Fly away, you idiots, or you're going to get shot.'

They did fly away, the reflection of their collective wings beating across the water.

Then he sat down behind the blind and waited to see what Nathan would do.

'The acting-out you've been used to doing,' Nathan said, 'will not be acceptable with me. While you're with me you will behave like a civilized person.'

'Great. You want me to shoot things. Very civilized.'

'Do you eat fowl?' Nathan asked.

'Do I eat what?'

'Are you a vegetarian?'

'No. I'm not.'

'Then, yes. It's civilized. What a man eats, he should be willing to kill. It's not absolutely necessary that he do so, but he should at least be willing to face the reality of it. To eat a chicken only if it comes from the market is the height of cowardice and denial. Someone still had to kill it.'

Nat rose and walked a few feet away. Kicked at the grass for a moment.

When Nathan looked up again, he found himself looking down the barrel of the boy's gun.

The gun was, of course, filled with light birdshot. And the boy was an inexperienced shooter. But still, it's hard to miss a substantial target with a shotgun. Plus the kick would raise the muzzle some, and a pellet through the eye could certainly prove fatal. So it was conceivable, though unlikely, that Nathan could be killed.

He weighed and juggled these factors as the boy spoke his piece.

'You can't civilize me,' Nat said. 'You can't make me stop swearing. Or learn to hunt. Or act like a gentleman, or be double-safe. I'll shoot you down before I let you make me into something I'm not.'

'I want you to be what you are,' Nathan said, 'only civilized. And the only way you can stop me is to shoot me dead, so if you're set on stopping me, then I suppose you'd best go ahead with that now.'

The boy's hands trembled on the shotgun for another moment before he let the muzzle drift slightly downward.

Nathan said, 'All you've probably needed all this time was someone who cared enough to insist you behave.'

And perhaps willing to die to make that happen, he thought.

The boy dropped the shotgun and ran away.

When Nathan and Maggie arrived back at the station wagon about two hours later, the boy was waiting for him inside. It pleased Nathan to see this, but he didn't make a fuss.

He placed his four ducks up front, in canvas sacks, two on the bench seat between them, two on the passenger floor near Nat's feet.

'I won't insist on this,' Nathan said, 'but it's a lot of work to clean and dress four ducks. I'd appreciate it if you'd help me.'

'Why did she do it?' Nat asked.

'I don't know,' Nathan said. 'I can't imagine.'

'Think how it makes me feel.'

'I have. Many times.'

'Then my grandmother abandons me.'

'Cry for yourself for the first of those two events,' Nathan said. 'You have that due you. But look hard at yourself about the second one. You did something to cause your grandmother to wash her hands of you. I just don't care to know what it was.'

'What do I have to do to make *you* wash your hands of me?'

'There's nothing you could do. I will never wash my hands of you.'

They rode the rest of the way home in silence.

Nat joined him in the garage for the cleaning and dressing. He wasn't willing to gut, but seemed able to pluck out the feathers.

'We'll put three in the freezer, and I'll roast one for our supper tonight. Have you ever had roast duck?'

'I don't think so.'

'You're in for a treat.'

They worked in silence a few minutes, then the boy asked, 'Do you know whatever happened to my mother, after they let her out of prison?'

Nathan froze in his movements, standing stock-still with a handful of entrails.

He remembered his promise to Mrs Bates. He had agreed not to raise any issues she might deem inappropriate. But Nathan hadn't raised this issue. The young man had raised it for him.

Besides, it struck him suddenly, Mrs Bates was out of the picture. She was no longer raising this boy as she saw fit; she had abdicated that position. Now it was all about how Nathan saw fit to raise a boy.

'What did your grandmother tell you on that score?'

'First she wouldn't tell me anything at all. And besides, if I asked she would start to cry. But last week I asked anyway, and she said my mother went off to California. That she was really busy trying to get some big career together, and so she never had time to write.' Then, with his hands still full of feathers, he looked up at Nathan. 'Are you just going to hold those disgusting guts for ever? I'd let go of that mess really quick if it was me.'

'Oh,' Nathan said. And put them on the newspapers he had arranged to wrap them in. 'In my opinion, she was wrong to tell you that.'

'Why?'

'Because it's not true.'

Nat looked up, quickly. Sharply. He dropped his half-feathered duck back on to its makeshift table with an audible thud.

Another chink in his armor, Nathan observed. He cares very much about the truth of this matter. And he is afraid to hear it. And also afraid not to hear it.

'What's the truth?'

'I'm sorry to have to tell you she died in prison. Just a handful of days after you were born. She had been bleeding. It had been a difficult birth. She developed sepsis.'

'Which is . . .'

'It's a serious infection that gets into your bloodstream.'

'And they didn't even help her?'

'She didn't let anybody know she needed help.'

'Oh.' The boy picked up the bird again. Resumed plucking its feathers. 'What about my father?'

'What about him?'

'I know his name. Richard A. Ford. Is he in jail?'

'No. He jumped bail. He's gone.'

'I could find him. Maybe I could live with him.'

Nathan heard the hopefulness in the young man's tone. Hated to dash it.

'The first is unlikely. He's hiding from prosecution. If the police haven't found him, it's unlikely that you will. But I think the second half of that proposition is even more troublesome.'

'Meaning what?'

'Meaning . . . they say the best way to judge what a man will do is by looking at what he's done in the past. He hasn't exactly shown himself to be the loving-father type so far. In fact, at the risk of hurting your feelings or offending you, I'd even go so far as to say that your biological father is not a father at all. There are certain human qualities involved in fathering. I'd say that he's more just a young man who accidentally got a girl pregnant. Look. Nat. You can try to find him. At some point in your life I'm sure you will. It's the kind of thing people feel compelled to do. Just promise me you'll be prepared for a disappointment.' A long silence, during which Nathan couldn't imagine this a fitting end to

such a conversation. 'I'm not sure why your grandmother didn't tell you the truth. I think she had this
idea that certain truths are not suitable for young
people. But I feel differently. I feel that the truth is
simply the truth. And that to shield someone from it is
only a manner of treating that person with a lack of
respect. I'm sure she didn't mean it that way, though.
I'm sure she was doing what she thought best.'

No reply.

'I'm sorry. I know these must be hard things for you
to hear.'

'Yes and no,' Nat said. He did not elaborate.

Nathan chose to leave him alone about it for a time.
In fact, for as much time as seemed warranted, however
long that turned out to be.

They sat down together to a roast duck supper with
applesauce and mashed potatoes.

Then they both stalled in a moment of strange
reverence prior to reaching for the food. As if the situation
at hand had stopped them cold, frozen them into the ice
of it, like the surface of a lake in the dead of winter.

Then Nathan broke his own promise to himself. He
asked, 'Are you sorry I told you? Or is it better to know?'

At first, no reply. Still no reaching for food.

Then Nat said, 'At least I know why she never wrote to
me. Never sent me a birthday present. Or a Christmas
present.'

'I did, though,' Nathan said. 'I hope they were always passed on to you.'

'Yeah, every birthday and every Christmas my grand-mother would give me a present, and she would say, "Here. This is from the man who found you in the woods."'

His voice sounded different, which caused Nathan to look up, but the boy was looking down at his plate, expressionless.

'I'm surprised she told you about me at all.'

'I think she thought if she kept saying that to me . . . from the time I was old enough to talk . . . I wouldn't think much about it if somebody else said it.'

'If she gave you a present from me every year on October first . . . then why did you act surprised that I still remember your birthday?'

The boy only shrugged.

'They may not have been the best, most appropriate gifts,' Nathan said. 'I don't know that I ever gave you what you wanted. Because I didn't have the advantage of knowing you. Knowing your likes and dislikes.'

'I don't think that's the important thing, though,' Nat said. 'I think the thing is, you never once forgot.'

'Well,' Nathan said, a bit embarrassed. 'Let's dig in, shall we?'

And he dished up the largest portion of duck on to Nat's plate.

Politely using his knife and fork, Nat took a tentative

bite of duck before even accepting the offered bowl of potatoes.

'This is good,' he said.

Nathan thought perhaps they had turned a corner. He expected that things might turn out all right between them after all.

25 September 1975

He Will Not Wash His Hands of You

The following day Nathan rose at seven, made coffee – which he'd grown quite adept at doing since Flora's death – and ate a quick breakfast, pouring boiling water on to Cream of Wheat.

Before leaving for the morning, he rapped lightly on Nat's closed bedroom door. He didn't open it, because he wanted the boy to feel he had some privacy. Especially in light of how much was changing for Nat, and how fast. But he did want to remind the boy that he would be gone all morning.

The night before, when he'd told Nat his schedule, Nathan had been under the distinct impression that the boy had been only half-listening. If indeed he had been listening at all.

'Nat, I'm on my way. I'll be gone all morning. As I told you last night. There are three kinds of cold cereal in the cupboard over the refrigerator.'

No response.

Part of Nathan felt sorely tempted to insist on some response. But he'd been doing so much insisting lately.

Later in the day he'd have to look into getting Nat registered for school in this new district, but after yesterday's early hunting morning, it seemed that the kindest thing Nathan could do was to go away and let him sleep in.

Nathan drove an hour and a half out of town to the rural kennel. The same kennel, run by the same breeder, that had produced Sadie and Maggie.

Sam, the breeder, greeted him at the door to the barn.

'How's the girl?' Sam asked.

'Maggie's fine. Thank you.'

'Glad to hear it. Scared me to see you. Didn't think you'd be needing another dog so soon.'

'It's not for myself,' Nathan said. 'I have a young man in my care now. Just barely fifteen. Seems there's not much he responds to. But he appears to like dogs. I know you specialize in fine hunting dogs, and that's not quite what this situation requires, but I thought you might know where I could find—'

'Boy, are you in luck,' Sam said. 'Got just the thing for you.'

He led Nathan over to a kennel cage in which lounged an adult curly-coated retriever and a half-grown pup that looked to be of indeterminate blood line. His coat was longer and straighter, making him look like a poorly-designed sheepdog. The liver color inherited from his mother was broken with patches of white. The hair on his face seemed to protrude in every direction at once.

'One of my best bitches got out and came home pregnant. Just my luck, had ten pups. You have any idea how hard it is to find homes for ten mutt pups? This little guy's the only one left. Five months.'

'What kind of a dog did she breed with?'

Nathan peered deeply into the dark, solid eyes of the adult curly-coated retriever, who steadily returned his gaze. She reminded Nathan of Sadie, which was not entirely surprising; she was likely a relative.

'No idea. But the people who took the other pups say they're pretty good dogs. Smart, with nice dispositions. I heard from three of the ones that took 'em, anyway. And none've come back.'

Sam opened the chain-link wire door of the cage. The pup came bounding out and jumped on Nathan, gnawing at his wrist as if it were a rawhide bone.

'Just needs someone to learn 'im some manners,' Sam said. 'Boy, this is kismet if you ask my opinion. Not an hour before you showed up here I was looking in that run and wondering what the hell I'm supposed to do with 'im.'

Nathan sat the pup down on the concrete barn floor

and looked into his eyes. He would be a handful for a time. But he would be Nat's handful. And his eyes reflected intelligence and sanity. Maybe he would take after his mother. Maybe the champion genes would be stronger somehow.

'What do you want for him?'

'He's a mutt. I want a good home for 'im. And I want 'im out of my hair. And that's all.'

On his way back through town, Nathan stopped at the bank, leaving the new pup in a carrier crate in the back of his car. He could hear the puppy yelping even as he stood in front of the teller's window.

He had just stepped out of the bank and was making his way down the leaf-covered sidewalk of Main Street when he heard a woman say his name.

'Nathan?'

Nathan turned.

It took him a moment to recognize her. In fact, she had to come several steps closer before he understood that it was Eleanor MacElroy.

'Eleanor,' he said, his pleasure at unexpectedly seeing her evident in his voice. And it was genuine. He did not assume a pleased tone just to be polite.

She hadn't changed much, Nathan noted. Oh, she had aged. But gracefully. Not as much as he had, it seemed. She had foregone the vain coloring of her hair that so many women of a certain age favored. Yet she had only a dusting of gray, mostly in the front-most strands of hair framing her forehead.

Nathan fully believed the theory that people, as they grow older, acquire the faces they truly deserve. In her case, it was no tragedy.

'Nathan, I haven't seen you in so many years. Twelve years, maybe. How are you? And how is Flora?'

Nathan didn't even need to offer an answer to her second question. Apparently the look on his face said it all.

'Oh, Nathan. I'm so sorry. How long ago?'

'Three years.'

'And have you married again?'

Nathan was more than surprised at the question. He was, in fact, quite thoroughly taken aback.

'Why, no. I haven't even thought of a thing like that. I'm not sure why you thought I would—'

'I guess I don't, either,' she interjected. 'After all, I've been widowed for fifteen years, and I haven't remarried. It's so good to see you, Nathan. Are you in a rush? Do you have a few moments? I'd just love to catch up and hear about your life. We could have a cup of coffee. Or, I guess it's almost lunchtime. Not quite, but . . . well, an early lunch.'

Nathan stood still in the flurry of his own thoughts.

Certain elements of this confusing conversation with Eleanor were clearing themselves. Coming out from hiding. But at the same time, he was involved in the weighing and measuring of how long he should be away. He actually would have enjoyed an early lunch with her. Very much. But he felt there might be a price to pay for leaving Nat alone too long.

And then there was the matter of the pup, howling now in the back of his car.

'I, uh . . .'

'Oh, never mind. I probably shouldn't have asked that.'

'No, it's not that at all, it's just—'

'I understand. Really I do.'

'No,' Nathan said. 'I don't think you do. I just can't get free right now, today. Not on this short notice. If I could just have a rain check . . .'

'Well. Of course. Dinner? At my house? I still remember how to cook. Or at least I think I do.'

'That would be wonderful. I'm still not much of a cook. I make an acceptable roast duck, but other than that I haven't had a decent home-cooked meal since . . .' He trailed off, somehow not wanting to say Flora's name.

'What night?'

'Well. Any night.'

'Tonight? Seven o'clock?'

Tonight. He would have to leave Nat alone again today. But he supposed that would be all right. So long as the situation came with advance warning. Besides, Nat would be busy with his new pup.

'Yes. I'd love to. Thank you. Tonight at seven would be perfect.'

When Nathan arrived home, he put the pup in the run with Maggie.

'Look after him,' he told her. Which she seemed already inclined to do.

Then he went inside to get Nat. But Nat was nowhere to be found.

Nathan opened the boy's bedroom door to find the bed neatly made.

Was it possible that he had made the bed of his own accord before leaving? And then, of course, the obvious question. Leaving for where?

Nathan walked to the bed and checked the corners of the sheets. Perfect on one side, sloppy on the other.

No, Nathan realized. Much as he longed to think otherwise, this bed had not been slept in since the previous morning, when he had taken Nat hunting.

Had he tucked Nat in last night? Come in to say goodnight? No, he had not. He had simply handed him a towel and a washcloth and said he'd see him in the morning. Aware as he was that the boy was surely feeling overwhelmed. And never thinking to doubt that his simple prediction would prove true. He found the washcloth and towel sitting still folded, unused and untouched, on the sink of Flora's old bathroom.

Nathan sat in the living room for a few moments,

quieting his mind and asking it to take a more organized tack.

The boy might have run away, home to his grandmother's house. After all, that was everything he had ever known. Nathan felt sure she would not take him in, but it was certainly possible that Nat would delude himself on that score. Could he have gone to classes at his same old school across town? Even though Nathan had not provided transportation or insisted? It seemed more than unlikely. No, likely he ran away. And not necessarily to his grandmother's house, either. More likely to parts unknown.

Nathan thought of calling the police, but two thoughts delayed him. One, he wondered if a teenager, particularly one prone to making trouble, might need to be missing for longer before the police would mix in. And, also, he felt he would have a hard time representing himself as the legal guardian.

He decided to check the attic and the basement. Not so much because he expected to find Nat in either place. It was more an organized act of research. If a suitcase had been taken, for example, that would say something.

Then he realized he hadn't checked Nat's closet and drawers. So he did that first. But none of the boy's belongings appeared to be missing. Which seemed to Nathan a very encouraging sign.

He walked down the basement stairs. Flipped on the light.

The door to his shotgun case – his locked shotgun case – stood wide open. On the floor in front of it lay his hacksaw, and a small pile of metal shavings. And, although Nathan owned three shotguns, the only one missing was – more than inconveniently – the priceless gift from his grandfather.

Was it possible that the boy had taken himself hunting? Maybe he had felt that bringing home a duck all on his own would earn Nathan's approval. But no, if he wanted Nathan to be proud of him, he would not have sawed through the lock on his gun rack. That's not the act of a young man seeking approval.

Nathan stood frozen, considering all of this, until the phone rang upstairs. It instantly formed a frosty core inside his gut. As if the ring itself contained bad news.

He vaulted up the stairs two at a time. Grabbed the phone off the kitchen wall.

It was Nat. Much to his relief, it was Nat.

'Where have you been?' Nat asked. 'I've been trying to call you all morning.'

'I told you I was going to be away all morning.'

'You did? When?'

'Last night.'

'Oh. I need your help.'

'What's the matter?'

'I'm in a little bit of trouble. And I need you to come bail me out.'

'Literally?'

'Yeah. Pretty much.'

'Where are you?'

'At Juvie Hall.'

Nathan sighed deeply. Well, at least he had been found. And would have to stay put. 'Where exactly is that?'

'I don't know. I didn't exactly drive here on my own, you know.'

'Is there an officer there with you?'

'Well, that's a pretty obvious one, isn't it? No, I'm all on the honor system. I could walk right out the door, but I'm just too honest to do it.'

'When a person is in your position,' Nathan said, 'it would behoove him to be polite to whomever he thinks can help.'

'Behoove? Whomever? That must be more of your English-as-a-foreign-language. Oops. You know what? Never mind. Forget I said that. In this case, I think I might actually see your point. I'm going to turn you over to one of these nice officers now. So they can tell you more about where I am.'

It seemed unfortunate to Nathan that all of the county offices were clustered together on to one campus in this town. Because, as it turned out, walking in the front door of Juvenile Hall involved using the exact same front door as one would use for either the men's or women's county jail. And Nathan did not enjoy his memories of the place. Not at all.

Despite two tries, no bond measure had been passed, and the place had deteriorated a great deal further in fifteen years. Nathan had voted in the affirmative twice since that first visit. But a two-thirds majority had been needed, and the measures had gone down to defeat just the same.

Nathan stepped up to the desk, only to be greeted by the same officer. It took him a moment to recognize the man. He was a good fifty pounds heavier. Much grayer and much balder. If only he could have retired, Nathan thought, before I had to come back here. He looked close enough to retirement age.

His name badge read Chas. A. Frawley.

The two men stood eyeing each other carefully.

It seemed impossible to Nathan that this man would remember him. Then again, he remembered the officer. After fifteen years. But it had been a disturbing episode for Nathan, and trauma tends to firmly cement memories in place. And, also, Nathan had the advantage of seeing the man in context.

'I know you. Don't I?' Frawley said.

'I'm not sure,' Nathan said, being – uncharacteristically – not entirely forthcoming.

'I never forget a face.'

'I've come to see Nathan Bates. The juvenile you arrested today.'

'Wait. I know. You're that guy who almost cost me my job. When that girl died in custody.'

So apparently Frawley had gathered his own trauma with which to cement the memory in place.

'I never said I was that girl's father.'

'You never said you weren't, either.'

'When you meet new people,' Nathan said evenly, 'do you make it a habit to tell them whose relative you are not?'

'This was a bit of a different—'

'I can't help feeling it's all water under the bridge after so many years. I'm here to see Nathan Bates.'

The officer snorted. Threw – literally threw – the clipboard with the sign-in sheet on to the counter in front of Nathan. It slid over and hit him lightly in the stomach at one corner.

'At least this one's alive and kicking,' Frawley said. 'And kicking. And kicking. And kicking. Little hellion, if you ask me.'

I didn't, Nathan thought. But he kept the sentiment to himself, feeling he was already on poor enough footing in this place.

'Can you please tell me what he's charged with?'

'Armed robbery.'

Nathan's jaw dropped, literally. He had to consciously remind himself to close his mouth. 'That's a very serious charge,' Nathan said.

'You're telling me. Tried to knock over a gas station with a shotgun. Lucky for him nobody got killed.'

'Maybe the gun wasn't loaded,' Nathan added.

Hearing the hopefulness of his own words. As if he could shape the truth with them.

Frawley snorted. 'It was more than loaded. It was discharged.'

'He *shot* somebody?'

'I only know what it says on this report. Weapon discharged. Gas-station owner injured. Nothing life-threatening. He was treated and released at the emergency room. Lucky for your boy. If he'd been badly hurt, you couldn't have even afforded the bail they'd've set. If he got bail at all. Wait till you hear how high they set bail as it is.'

'I don't need to hear that at all,' Nathan said. 'Because I have no intention of posting it. I just need to see him.'

'Good,' Nat said. 'You've come to post my bail.'

'No,' Nathan said. 'I'll come see you every visiting day. But I won't put up bond for you. Because I know you'll run away. You're going to stay in here until your trial, and then you'll go into the juvenile detention system and pay for what you did. I want you to tell me exactly what happened. I want to know how you could bring yourself to steal my shotgun and fire it at a perfectly innocent stranger.'

Nat's eyes registered genuine alarm. 'I didn't shoot anybody! Is that what they're saying? Then they're lying! Because I never shot anybody!'

'The man at the desk said the weapon was discharged. And that the gas-station owner was injured.'

'Will you at least let me tell you what happened?'

'Fine,' Nathan said. He crossed his arms against his chest. Leaned back, feeling the hard plastic of the chair press into his back. 'Tell me.'

'I'm just trying to get him to open the cash register. I'm holding the shotgun on him. And he reaches down to open the drawer. And then what does he do but pull a little pistol out of the drawer and fire it at me. I mean, who does that? Pulls a gun on a guy who's holding a loaded shotgun right in your face?'

'So you would have me believe it was all his fault? For trying to defend his business?'

'I didn't say that. Anyway, I threw myself out of the way. You know. So I wouldn't get shot. And I fell down. And the gun just sort of . . . went off.'

'So you did shoot him. Whether you meant to or not.'

'No! I didn't! I didn't hit him. I hit the cash register. And a piece of exploding cash register hit him in the cheek. I know that's what happened because I was still there when the cop helped him pull it out. He sort of sat on me until the cops came.'

A long silence. During which, at least, the boy had the wherewithal to appear humiliated.

'And if the round had hit him?'

'But it didn't.'

'If it had?'

'It was only birdshot.'

'Do you know what birdshot can do, fired at close

range? Right into someone's face? You could have killed that man. And it's really only by luck that you didn't. That the morning wasn't a complete and utter irreversible disaster is really not to your credit at all.'

Another long, embarrassed silence.

'I know,' Nat said. 'I've thought about it.'

'Well, you'll have time to think about it a lot more. You're probably here until you turn eighteen. Because I meant what I said about the bail. You are the one who did this, so you will have to be the one to pay.'

The boy said nothing for a long time. Then he said, 'You're right about one thing. I would have run out on the bail.'

'Why did you do this?' Nathan asked. 'Are you trying to get my attention?'

The boy shrugged. 'Everyone else does bad things. Why shouldn't I?'

'I don't. Lots of people don't.'

The boy sighed and brushed hair back out of his eyes. 'I believed you,' he said. 'I believed that as long as you were alive you'd never wash your hands of me. Never stop trying to civilize me. I was trying to get far away.'

'I see.'

'Wash your hands of me now?'

'No,' Nathan said.

Nathan had been home for several hours. He had fed Maggie and the pup in their run. Heated up a TV dinner for himself, hamburger patty with mashed potatoes. Eaten it in front of the news.

Then he brought Maggie and the nameless pup into the living room with him.

It wasn't until he turned off the TV and looked at the clock – noting that it was nearly eight o'clock – that he remembered.

He tried to look up Eleanor's number in the phone book, but it wasn't listed.

It took him several minutes, but he found her phone number in his old client records, in a banker's box in the garage.

When he got back inside, the pup was in the process of urinating against the corner of Nathan's couch.

Uttering mild, barely offensive curses, he first threw the pup back into the run, where the dog whimpered and yapped. Then he headed back to the garage for carpet and upholstery cleaner. But he stopped, knowing the phone call was more urgent. Which, considering Nathan's penchant for sanitation, made it unusually urgent.

She answered on the second ring.

'Oh, Eleanor,' he said. 'I am so sorry. In fact, I'm more than sorry. I'm downright ashamed.'

In the intervening silence, he could hear the puppy's heated complaints.

'I probably shouldn't have asked you,' she said.

'Eleanor. I've been a widower for three years. You've

been a widow for fifteen. There is nothing the slightest bit inappropriate about you asking me to dinner.'

'But when you didn't show up, I thought—'

'Well, you thought wrong,' he said. And told her, in about the three- or four-minute version, of the addition and then the subtraction of the boy he found in the woods. 'Have you ever had a day like that?' he asked. 'When something happens that's so huge it just erases everything that came before it?'

Silence on the line, during which Nathan believed she really was considering his question.

Then she said, 'I suppose the day Arthur had his heart attack was a day like that.'

A vivid memory reared into Nathan's consciousness. Opening Flora's door at eleven a.m. to see why she wasn't awake yet. He firmly pushed the image back down again.

'I'm sorry for what you must have thought,' he said. 'And I'm sorry because your dinner must have been ruined. And I don't suppose I'd blame you if you didn't think I was worth the second chance. But maybe I could take a rain check . . .'

At least this time he wouldn't have to worry that leaving Nat alone would amount to trouble. Because all the trouble in the world had already come to stay.

He Still Doesn't Really Know You

Several days later, on the boy's birthday, Nathan came to visit.

In fact, he had been to visit every day since Nat's incarceration. But on this day he made more of a production of the visit. He tried to make it special without being sad, as special occasions in tragic circumstances tend to be.

He brought a birthday cupcake – a whole cake seemed excessive under the circumstances – half a roast duck in foil in a paper grocery sack, a photograph of the still-unnamed pup, and a small wrapped gift.

He stepped through the front door of the county facility, silently mourning how familiar the place had become.

'Ah. You,' Officer Frawley said as Nathan signed in.

Nathan could still see his own name prominent on

the sign-in sheet among yesterday's visitors. There were only two, save himself.

'Yes,' Nathan said. 'Me.'

It was a veiled criticism of the kind of useless prattle Nathan despised. Any type of small talk was abhorrent to him. But the officer had no way of knowing that, so it had not been a rude comment, or at least could not have been perceived as such. In fact, Nathan assumed that to Frawley it sounded quite a normal thing to say.

'Any progress on the return of my shotgun?' Nathan asked. As he did each time he signed in.

'No, but it'll happen eventually. The wheels of evidence grind real slow. What's that in the wrapping paper? Not likely I can let you in with that. Unless you're willing to unwrap it. I pretty much have to visually inspect anything you bring inside. Are you willing to unwrap it?'

'I guess I can if I absolutely have to. But it's his birthday. I hate to ruin the surprise. I suppose I could wrap it again when you're done looking. If you have some tape I can borrow.'

'Hmm. Sorry. No tape. We use staples on everything. Let me take a closer look at that, then.'

Nathan handed it over.

It was small, light and soft. It was not in a box of any sort. Nathan hoped it would be obvious, just by feel, that it had no real potential to be dangerous.

'This is OK. I can make an exception for this. Couldn't

possibly hurt anyone, whatever it is. So, the little miscreant has a birthday today.'

'His name is Nat.'

The officer looked up at Nathan. Gauging. Measuring. It was clear from Nathan's voice that the man had overstepped a line. His interest seemed to be in learning how far.

'Right,' he said. 'My mistake.'

'Anyone can make a mistake,' Nathan said. Aware that much of his fate rested in the hands of prison employees for several years at least.

'No one else visits every day,' the officer said. 'Why is that?'

'I couldn't speak for anyone else.'

'Actually, I guess I meant, why are you so different?'

'I'm not sure I can speak to that, either,' Nathan said. 'I am the way I am. We all are the way we are and I'm not sure any of us really knows why.'

'I guess you got a point there,' Frawley said.

Nathan set the cupcake, the roast duck, the photograph and the gift on the wood table between Nat and himself.

Nat picked up the photo.

'What's this?'

'Your new dog.'

'You got me a dog for my birthday?'

'No. I got you a dog the day you got arrested. I just

hadn't gotten around to taking his picture until now.'

'Well, that makes more sense. Since you didn't know I wouldn't be around to meet him. Too bad about that. Are you going to take him back?'

'No.'

'You're keeping him for me?'

'If you want him.'

'Of course I want him. What's his name?'

'He doesn't have one. He's your dog, so you name him.'

Then the boy's eyes landed on the wrapped gift. The mystery of it clearly knocked all other thoughts out of his head. Even thoughts of dogs could not withstand the curiosity evoked by a wrapped gift.

'Open it now?' the boy asked.

The guard looked over Nat's shoulder to assure himself it was no more than Nathan had claimed.

'You may open it whenever you choose.'

The boy tore off the paper and stared at the gift. 'It looks like a tiny little cap,' he said, turning it over in his fingers.

'It is.'

The guard backed off to the corner of the room again.

'Who could wear a cap this small?'

'You, when you were only one day old.'

'You mean, I was wearing this?'

'That's right.'

'When you found me? I was wearing this? And what else?'

'You were wrapped in a sweater. A full-size adult sweater.'

Nathan tried to gauge the boy's reaction from his face. His eyes. To see if the gift pleased or displeased him. It had been clear to Nathan all along that the pendulum could swing either way.

And yet it was a risk he'd felt compelled to take.

But there was nothing in the young man's face by which Nathan could judge. It was something like trying to peer into a room while the shades are pulled down.

Nathan wondered briefly if life was hard for Nat in here. If the other young men were bigger. Tougher. But it was an unanswerable question, and one he could do nothing about, anyway. He considered it none of his business, and was certainly not about to ask.

'Now where did she get a cap this small, do you think?'

'My theory is that she knitted it. I know she was a knitter.'

Nat snorted. 'Right. Like my grandmother. Must run in the family. I never once had a hat or a scarf from the store. Or socks or mittens, for that matter. So, how did you get this? Wasn't it, like, evidence or something?'

'They took it off you in the emergency room and just threw it on the floor.'

'And you've kept it all this time? Why give it to me now?'

'I wanted you to know that she at least had some

ambivalence. She left you to die but part of her wanted you to live. She was trying to keep you warm.'

Nat sat back in his chair. Suddenly. Hitting the chair back with a thump. He twirled the tiny cap around his index finger a few times, then tossed it up in the air, caught it, and crushed it tightly in his palm.

'That's not a lot of consolation,' he said.

'No, but it's some. We don't always get much. I'm sorry if it's not a good gift. I still don't really know you. I don't know what kind of things you like.'

Nat's palm opened and he dropped the cap on to the table between them. Then he picked it up and smoothed it out. Reshaped it carefully. Set it back down, more gently this time. In fact, with an almost exaggerated gentleness.

'No, it's good,' the boy said. 'It's a good present.' He sat quietly for a minute, then added, 'The baseball mitt was good, too. I really liked that.'

'Good,' Nathan said. 'That's something.'

'And the ant farm, but my grandmother wouldn't let me keep it,' Nat said. 'And also . . .' But he never finished the thought. He picked up the photo of the mongrel pup. 'This is the best one ever. It sucks that I don't get to meet him.'

'You will.'

'And thanks for the roast duck. I've been hungry for it ever since that day we went hunting. Well. *You* went hunting.'

'You're welcome. I'm glad you like it as much as I do.'

'I have a question for you. But I know you probably don't know the answer. But I'm going to ask it anyway. Just to hear what you think.'

'All right.'

'Do you think it was something like suicide?'

'You mean your mother?'

'Yeah. My mother. So she's dying of this infection but she never tells anybody. She just lets it kill her.'

'It's crossed my mind.'

'Maybe she felt guilty.'

'I'm sure she did. I have no doubt of that. There's not one person I know of on the planet – not one person with a normal mind, that is – who could do a thing like that and not feel guilty. In fact, I think *that* . . .' Nathan pointed to the tiny cap, sitting between them on the plain, scarred wood table. 'I think that is reasonable evidence of her guilt. Right there. Which is why I brought it.'

They sat in silence for an unsettling length of time. Nathan resisted the temptation to interject any more of his thoughts. It seemed more respectful to leave the boy alone to think his own thoughts.

Which he seemed to be quite busy doing.

'Well. Good,' Nat said at last. 'She deserved to feel guilty.'

Whether or not she deserved to die from that guilt was a subject left unaddressed.

After a long, awkward silence, Nat spoke up suddenly, startling Nathan. 'I'm naming him Feathers.'

'Feathers?'

'That's right.'

'He doesn't exactly have feathers. He's more half wire-haired all over.'

'Well, of course he doesn't have feathers. He's not a bird, is he?'

'I meant feathers like the kind dogs have,' Nathan said. Nat's face remained puzzled. 'The long, flowing hair some dogs have on the backs of their legs. And on their chests. And tails. They're called feathers.'

'Oh. I didn't know that.'

'So, you're naming your dog Feathers because . . .'

Nat only shrugged. 'He just looks like a Feathers to me. So here's another question for you. Can a bird with no feathers fly?'

'No.'

'Not ever?'

'Not under any circumstance I know of.' Then, after a moment to sort his thoughts, 'No. That would be impossible. If you want a bird not to fly away, you clip its wing feathers. Without wing feathers it would be impossible for a bird to fly.'

'Right,' Nat said. 'That's pretty much what I thought.'

He Tries to Answer Why

Fortunately in some ways, and unfortunately in others, Nat had been sentenced to a juvenile detention facility more than two and a half hours from Nathan's home. The long drive was the discouraging factor. That and the fact that visitation was only allowed three times a week.

The good news to Nathan was that the place held no memories. And it held no one who harbored memories of him.

And several of the employees in the new facility were actually quite civil and kind. Like Roger, for example, the guard who supervised Nathan's visits. On some occasions, Roger actually spoke to Nathan. As if Nathan were a friend.

And since Roger was often the *only* one to speak to Nathan on such visits, his kindness felt extremely welcome.

*   *   *

As had so often been the case over the previous year, the boy said nearly nothing during that day's visit.

So, as had become Nathan's habit, he took out a book and began reading to Nat. It seemed the logical way to solve a dilemma. To miss a visiting day was not a viable option. Nor was talking in monologue form, as if to himself or to a wall. And he certainly could not control the responses of another. Especially not this other.

And they couldn't just stare at each other for an hour and a half.

Nathan guessed that perhaps Nat was having a hard time holding his own in this difficult environment. That perhaps he was learning he was not as tough as he'd previously thought. And that the situation was making him sullen. But Nat didn't seem to care to discuss the matter. And Nathan remained unwilling to pry.

On this day, he read to Nat from the ideas and opinions of Albert Einstein.

He read the section about our inherent social structure as humans. How our actions and desires are inextricably bound up with the existence of other human beings.

When he paused to turn a page, Nat made his only comment for the day.

He said, 'Thought this guy was supposed to be smart.'

'I think it's a matter of provable record that Einstein was smart,' Nathan said.

Nat only snorted.

Then, undeterred, Nathan continued to read from Einstein's writings until Roger signaled 'Time's Up' for the day.

Roger looked up and smiled as he buzzed Nathan through the security door.

'Think it helps to read to him like that?'

'Well,' Nathan said. 'I read somewhere that it helps to read to a patient in a coma. So, in comparison, I suppose my patient is more responsive than that.'

Roger laughed. A bit longer and harder than necessary.

Then he said, 'I'd say you're the patient one. Driving all this way. Three times a week. Just like clockwork. I could set my watch by you.'

'Does that seem remarkable?' Nathan asked.

'Oh, boy. You have no idea. Most of these kids, their parents probably live no more than twenty minutes from here, and they're lucky to get a few minutes a month. Or unlucky, as the case may be.'

'Somebody had to break the unfortunate parental stereotype,' Nathan said. 'I still don't think it seems all that remarkable.'

'It does when you consider he barely knew you three days before he got himself in custody.'

'No,' Nathan said. 'I've known him all his life.'

Roger lifted his eyebrows slightly. 'He's lying, then?'

'Not lying. He sees it differently than I do. But I'm not his father or grandfather.'

'I know. I heard about it. I know we're not supposed to know stuff like that, but word gets around. I'm not trying to invade your privacy, believe me. But I just wondered.'

Nathan could feel a sort of leaning-in on the part of this man, and realized quite suddenly that Roger had been burning to ask questions and make comments for some time. But he had been careful not to overstep his bounds, which Nathan respected. And which made Nathan kindly disposed toward answering.

Roger continued. 'It's just such an unusual situation. It's pretty rare when something like that even happens around here. So I'm just kind of curious about it, you know? But with no disrespect intended. It just makes you wonder about the ripples that go out from that one act. Is it because you saved his life? Because I heard once of some Eastern religion whose devotees believed if you save someone's life, you're for ever responsible for his soul. Or was that the American Indians?'

'No matter,' Nathan said. 'Since I don't believe a word of it, anyway.'

'Why, then?' Roger asked. He seemed sincerely curious. He appeared to hang on the dead air between the question and the answer. Nathan was willing to believe it was personal curiosity. He did not expect Roger to turn his reply into jailhouse gossip. He hoped he would not be disappointed. 'Why the remarkable commitment?'

'Why not?' Nathan asked. 'What else have I done with my life that's remarkable?'

Part Four

Nathan Bates

Roger came into his cell at the usual time, to say the usual thing. Or so Nat was sure.

He'd been napping. Without meaning to. He'd been drifting in and out of sleep. Dreaming about Jack. About working out in the gym with Jack. In the dream, Nat's chest and arm development matched Jack's exactly.

Nat lay on his back on his cot, careful not to get up, or sit up, or take any other action that might reflect caring.

It was such a regular event, each visiting day, that his two bad-tempered cellmates paid no attention. In fact, they focused a great deal of their attention into paying no attention. A hint of negativity hung in the air around each such occasion. Roger had several times said it was jealousy, which Nat could not imagine. Had he believed it, he would gladly have invited either of his cellmates to go sit at the table in his place. And, on their return, keep their mouths firmly shut about the thoughts of Ernest Hemingway on fishing, Albert Einstein on society, or President Carter on the fiscal realities of the country this year.

'You got visitors,' Roger said.

It was such a strange thing for him to say, such a thought out of place, that Nat honestly believed he had misspoken. He waited briefly for Roger to correct himself. To say he had meant *visitor*. Singular.

He never did.

'Visitors?'

'Yeah. You know what that is? It's like a visitor. Like you always get. Only in this case it's more than one.'

'Who?'

'Well, here's a thought on that. Raise your ass up off your cot, take it out into the visiting room, and then your eyes will tell you everything you need to know.'

Nat sighed deeply.

At least it wasn't two total strangers. At least it was only one.

Nat sat across the table from The Man and some woman he'd dragged along. Some woman the old guy's age. She smiled at Nat. He frowned and slumped deeper into his seat.

The old man seemed to need to break the silence.

'Nat, this is Eleanor. Eleanor, this is the young man I've told you so much about for so long. Nat.'

'What did you tell her about me?' Nat asked.

About this time Nat noticed that Roger the guard had stationed himself too closely by. He stood with his back against the wall, arms crossed, close enough to eavesdrop on the conversation. He stood in Nat's line of vision but behind his visitors, out of their sight.

Roger shook his head slightly at Nat's question.

Great, Nat thought. The rudeness police.

He slumped even further in his seat, and resolved to say nothing.

The old man went on talking for a good five minutes or so. It could have been longer. It certainly felt longer. He seemed to be the only person in the room willing to talk, and so he did. He went on about how he and this old woman had first met something like twenty years ago, and how they'd met again on the day Nat got arrested, and how they'd been seeing each other for a couple of years now, while Nat was away.

While he talked, Nat occasionally felt the old woman's eyes searching him. He was careful to look away. But it was hard to avoid her eyes and Roger's at the same time. And Roger seemed determined to make a point with his eyes, too.

Nat briefly wondered if turning eighteen would mean walking through the world without constantly being told what to do, what to say, what to think. Where to place your gaze.

Getting out of this hell hole wouldn't hurt those ends, either.

'So, we wanted you to be the very first to know,' he heard the old man say. Breaking through and interrupting his thoughts about freedom.

'Know what?' Nat asked. Literally not understanding if he had missed some part of the conversation or not.

'That Eleanor and I are getting married.'

A ringing silence.

'You're getting married?'

'Yes. We are.'

'*Why?*'

At the periphery of his vision, Nat saw Roger frown and shake his head. He also saw the old lady shift uncomfortably in her seat.

Nat looked up at the old man, who riveted him with his eyes.

'The same reason any two people get married. Because they love one another and enjoy each other's company. And because they've reached a point in their relationship where they know they're happier together than apart.'

Nat frowned and said nothing. Which created something of an awkward vacuum. Especially considering the visiting period had far more than an hour left to run.

*   *   *

'What the hell is your problem?' Roger asked as he marched Nat back down the hall to his cell block.

'Which of my many problems would that be?'

'That guy's given you everything. Saved your ass on the day you were born. Comes to see you every visiting day. Drives a five-hour round trip three times a week so you know you got one person cares enough for you—'

'I didn't ask him to—'

'I wasn't finished. How 'bout you just listen for a change? He's taking you in when you get sprung from here. Giving you a chance to start over. Now . . . would you like to explain to me why you would begrudge a man like that a little happiness from this life?'

Nathan just kept walking.

Roger stopped. Grabbed him by the back of his orange prison jumpsuit. Pulled him back and, rather gently for an unsupervised authority figure, Nat thought, placed his back against the peeling paint of the hallway wall.

'I think we were having a conversation,' Roger said, his face close.

Nat rolled his eyes. 'What was the damn question again?'

'Why *shouldn't* he get married?'

'I never said he shouldn't.'

'Why can't you be happy for him? Why you gotta give them a bad time?'

'It's just gross.'

'It's not gross. It's sweet.'

'They're old.'

'They're not that old.'

'They're like . . . over sixty. I think.'

'So?'

'So you don't think that's gross?'

'Lots of people get married when they're young, and then they're still married when they're sixty. And seventy. And eighty. Is that gross?'

'If you really stop to think about it, yeah.'

'Ah,' Roger said. 'I don't believe a word you say. You're not telling me the truth. And you're not telling yourself the truth. There's a reason why this bothers you. And you don't even know what it is yourself.'

'Like what?'

'Like maybe you're mad because he's getting some while you're holed up in here with a bunch of guys?'

'Oh, God. It just got even more gross. I don't want to think about them—'

'Or maybe you just want all his attention all the time.'

Nat actually thought about that for a minute. His grandmother had accused him of needing to be the center of attention, too. But she'd misjudged what was going on at the time. She hadn't had so much as a clue. Still, he gave a certain weight to words he had heard twice. So he tried them on. But they didn't seem to fit.

He wished briefly that someone would come down the hall and disturb this moment. But no one did.

'No, I don't think it's that,' he said.

'Tell you what . . .' Roger reached into his pocket and pulled out a wad of bills. Peeled off a ten and held it up under Nat's nose. 'Ten dollars for an honest answer.' Then he looked both ways and quickly put the money away again.

It was against the rules for an inmate to have cash while inside. And also very sought-after and valuable. Nat knew he could buy his way out of a lot of trouble with ten bucks. And Roger knew it, too.

'How will you know if it's honest?'

'If it has a ring of truth, I'll give you the benefit of the doubt. No hurry, either. Think about it and get back to me.'

Then he took hold of the shoulder of Nat's jumpsuit, turned him, and marched him back to his cell.

10 August 1978

Weird

In the exercise yard, in the afternoon, Nat purposely dropped out of the game. Left a bunch of guys he didn't like anyway to play basketball without him, pretending to have pulled a muscle in his calf.

He caught Roger's eye as he limped over to a picnic table in the corner of the yard. Four corners, four guards. So of course he headed for Roger's corner.

He had something to say. And Roger seemed to catch that.

Roger leaned on the table with him and they watched the game.

'So, what do you have for me?' Roger asked. 'Anything?'

Nat watched the game a moment longer in silence.

Then he said, 'It's just weird—'

'Ah. Nope. You lost me at weird.'

'No. You didn't let me finish. That isn't what I was going to say. I wasn't going to say *they* were weird. Just that it's weird . . . you know . . . for me. Like, in a few months I'm going to be going back to his house to live. And I was only there for, like, a couple days. So it's all new and strange to me. But I sort of know him now. From all these visits. So I thought it would be OK. But I don't know *her*. So now it's all new and strange again. It's like . . . I guess weird isn't the right word, but I can't think what is.'

'Scary?'

'Maybe. Yeah. I guess.'

A pause, during which Nat wondered how he had done.

Roger spun around suddenly and grabbed Nat by his prison jumpsuit. Brought his face close. Nat winced, and braced himself. He was about to be read the riot act about something. But he had no idea what.

But then, within that private moment he had constructed, Roger winked at him. Slipped a folded bill into the single breast pocket of the jumpsuit.

'Now that has a ring of truth to it,' Roger said.

Then he let him go again, and Nat brushed himself off. Settled his breathing.

Roger pushed off from the table and began to walk away.

'Wait,' Nat said.

Roger stopped and turned around again. Walked back close.

'Why was that worth ten dollars to you?' Nat asked quietly. He knew it was important that none of the other guards heard, or knew.

Roger took a deep breath. 'Because . . . from where I sit, nobody seems to know why the hell they do *anything*. Oh, they have some story for publication. But it always rings like bullshit. Because it *is* bullshit. Way I see it, that's what fills up a place like this. Bunch of scared little idiots running around lying to everybody about why they do what they do. Even themselves. The older I get the more it bothers me. So I just wanted to see if you could do it. You know. Given some time to think and some genuine incentive to get it right. I guess I figured if you could do it, anybody could.'

'Gee, thanks,' Nat said.

27 September 1978

Happy To

Nat slouched into the visiting room as he did every Monday, Wednesday and Friday. He scanned the room for The Man, but saw only some other guy's parents and an old woman.

When he looked more closely at the old woman, she looked up.

It was his grandmother.

Nat looked over at Roger, who glanced away. He wanted to catch Roger's eye. To ask, without words, why Roger hadn't said anything. Why he hadn't favored Nat with a warning. But that appeared to be a game Roger was unwilling to play.

Nat stood in front of her table for quite a long time. Until Roger came up behind him, placed a hand on each of Nat's shoulders, and sat him firmly in the chair.

'Hello, Nat,' the old woman said.

Nat said nothing.

'So. Still not speaking to me after all these years?'

'Where's the man who found me in the woods?' Nat asked. Feeling awkward about the phrasing, but not being sure what else to call him. Nathan? Mr McCann? The guy who, unlike you, is *supposed* to be here?

'He agreed to stay out in the waiting room until we were done talking.'

'If you ask my opinion,' Nat said, 'we *are* done talking.'

'Well, *I* have a few things to say.'

Nat frowned and slumped deeply into his chair. His impulse was to walk away, but he resisted it, knowing Roger would only reseat him.

'First of all,' she said, 'I have a question to ask you. And the question is this: what was I to do? Was I supposed to tell you, when you were just a little slip of a boy, that your mother did such a horrible thing to you? Would that have been the thing to do?'

Nat looked her straight in the eye for the first time, and she predictably averted her gaze.

'Yes,' he said flatly. 'That would have been the thing to do.'

'Why? Would you care to tell me why that would have been a good way to handle things?'

'Sure,' Nat said. 'Happy to. Because then I would have known that my mother was a rotten piece of crap who didn't give a shit about me—' Nat felt her rise to object to his language, but he raised a hand and she retreated again. In his peripheral vision he saw Roger take a step forward, then just freeze and wait. 'No. I'm not done. I would have known all that about *her*. But I would have known I could trust *you*. And then I would have had one person in my life I knew I could trust.'

They both stared at the table for an awkward space of time.

'Well, I'm not sure I agree with you,' she said. 'But let's say you're right. I'm human and we all make mistakes. Right or wrong, I did what I thought best. You can forgive me for that. Right?'

Nat didn't answer. Because he did not forgive her.

'After everything you gave me to forgive?' she asked.

It's news to me if you ever forgave me for anything, Nat thought. But he said nothing.

'And the other thing I came to say to you. I know you're getting out next week. When you turn eighteen. And if you really have learned your lesson now . . . and I can only hope you have . . . if you will absolutely *promise* me that there will be no more violence and no more stealing and lying, and that you'll get a job and walk a straight road . . . you can come back home. And we can try it again.'

Nat had just opened his mouth to tell her where she could stick her patronizing little offer when he remembered that Roger, the rudeness police, was standing within hearing distance.

'No thank you.'

'Excuse me? What did you say?'

'You heard me. I said no thank you.'

'So where are you going to go?'

'Back to Nathan McCann's house.'

'Are you trying to tell me that man has actually welcomed you back? After everything you've done? That sounds like a pipe dream to me. I would think he'd have washed his hands of you long ago.'

'He will never wash his hands of me!' Nat shouted, slamming the table with the heel of one hand. Out of the corner of his eye Nat saw the other guy and his parents jump. Roger gave him a stern look of warning. 'If he washed his hands of me, why is he out in the waiting room right now?' Nat asked, still quite agitated. 'You go ask him if I'm welcome with him. And while you're at it, tell him to come in now. And you go home. And don't ever come back here again. This conversation is over.'

At first, nothing. No movement. No reply.

Then the old woman sighed deeply. Rose heavily to her feet with a grunt.

Nathan purposely did not watch as she walked out of the room.

'Hell of a way to talk to your own grandmother,' Roger said.

'You stay out of this,' Nat snapped back.

Surprisingly, Roger returned no comment.

Nat looked up again to see Nathan McCann lower himself into the chair across from him.

'So,' the old man said. 'Did you and your grand-mother have a good talk?'

'No,' Nat said. 'It sucked. But at least it was our *last* talk. That was the only good thing about it.'

'You know, she calls me. Every week. To see if you're OK.'

'No,' Nat said. 'I didn't know that. You never told me that.'

'I'm telling you now,' the old man said.

Nat stood outside – behind no walls of any kind – in the cool afternoon, next to the old man's station wagon. He waited for the old guy to open the passenger-side door. The guy had gotten a new station wagon, but it was just like the old one. Same make and model of Chevrolet, just a few years more recent. It was even the same dull color of root-beer brown. Nat briefly wondered what it would feel like to enjoy that level of sameness.

Especially today, when everything was changing.

Nat resisted the temptation to squint his eyes against the sun, because, he told himself, the urge was silly and unreal. After all, that same sun had shone into the exercise yard for three years. Yet it seemed different somehow, outside the horrible walls.

Probably only his imagination.

The old man reached over from inside the car and lifted the lock button. Nat opened the door and climbed in. Stared through the windshield of a car for the first time in three years.

It took him a minute to wonder why the old guy wasn't shifting into gear and driving.

Nat glanced over at him.

'As soon as you get your seat belt secured, we'll go home,' the old man said.

Nat had to admit, if only to himself, that the word 'home' had a nice ring to it. Even if he'd only ever lived there for a couple of days. Even if some lady he'd only met once lived there, too.

He put on his seat belt. The man shifted the car into gear and they were off, travelling at a speed Nat had only vaguely remembered in his dreams. In prison you go only as fast as your feet can carry you.

At first, silence.

Then the old guy said, 'How does it feel to be a free man?'

'Hmm,' Nat said. 'I thought it would feel great. And it sort of does. But it also . . . it feels like a lot of things at once.'

In the brief silence that followed, it struck Nat that he had just been called a man. He had only been eighteen for a few days, and no one had taken the time to congratulate him on his new status. It added another whole layer to the complicated web of what he was feeling.

'Most big life events are like that. You think they'll be emotionally one-sided, but when you actually get into them, it's always more complex.'

'I didn't know that,' Nat said. He really meant he hadn't known other people experienced life in a way he would recognize. That his responses were shared by other human beings. But he couldn't find the words for all that, so he didn't elaborate. 'I thought maybe you'd bring Feathers,' Nat said instead, glancing into the back seat as though he might just have missed seeing him.

'I thought of it. But then Maggie would have insisted on coming, and I thought it might be too chaotic.'

'Oh.'

'You'll see him as soon as we get home.'

'OK.'

Silence. For a mile or more.

They were out on the Interstate now, and Nat watched the farmland flash by, and had a sudden vivid memory of seeing the world through a gap in the door of a freight wagon. It wasn't only the world that seemed to match that memory, but the feeling associated with it. Freedom.

When the feeling had faded some and he'd grown tired of watching, Nat said, 'I also thought maybe you'd bring . . . I'm sorry. What's her name again? Your wife.'

'Eleanor.'

'Right. Sorry.'

'She's home making dinner. She thought you might

want a really good home-cooked meal on your first night home. I told her what you said about the food you've been eating. She's making a baked ham with all the trimmings.'

'Really? That was nice of her. Especially after I was such a . . .' He chose not to finish the thought. 'So . . . Um . . . What do I call her?'

'Eleanor will do.'

'OK.' Another long pause. 'Well, then . . . what do I call *you*?'

'How about Nathan? After all, it's my name.'

Another long silence. Two or three miles' worth.

Nat said, 'It's kind of weird. Isn't it? That I've seen you three times a week for the past three years, and I'm going home to live with you, and I just now got around to asking what I'm supposed to call you? It just seems weird.'

The old man mulled that over for a moment, then said, 'There are some differences . . . some . . . complications . . . inherent in our odd situation.'

'I don't know what that word means.'

'Inherent?'

'Yeah.'

'It means built in.'

'Oh. Sorry to sound stupid.'

'You didn't. Not at all. It's a sign of intelligence to ask the meaning of a word if you don't know it.'

'Oh,' Nat said. 'I didn't know that.' Then he

immediately felt stupid again. 'Something I've been meaning to ask you. But I . . .' He stumbled, floundered. Restarted. 'Not that I'm complaining if the answer is yes, but . . . am I going to have to, like, sleep on the couch or something?'

'No, you'll get your same room back.'

'Oh. Good.'

Nat breathed a sigh. Sat back and watched the world some more. It hadn't changed. Long stands of trees. Plowed fields. Black and white cows grazing.

Then he said, 'So you two sleep in the same room.'

The old man didn't answer, but shot Nat a sideways glance that showed he was displeased. It said, as clearly as if in words, 'Go no further.'

'You know what? I really, really, really didn't mean that the way it sounded. I absolutely was not trying to pry into your personal stuff. Really. I didn't mean it that way at all. It's none of my business. All I meant was . . . well, I know I was a real jerk about it when you first told me. But all I'm trying to say is, it sounds like you're happy. That very first day when I came to your house, and you told me about you and your other wife, and how she had her own room, it sounded sad. But this sounds happier. And I was just trying to say . . . if that's true . . . and you're happy . . . then I'm glad. That you're happy.'

'My goodness,' the old man said. 'I think that's more words than you've said to me in the past three years all put together.'

Well, Nat thought, today there's more to say. What was there to talk about day after day in that hole? Besides, he was excited and a little scared. And his excitement was spilling out in words. But he couldn't quite put a voice to that.

So he just said, 'Sorry. I didn't mean to chatter.'

'It wasn't a complaint,' the old man said. 'Thank you for your thoughtful congratulations on my marriage. I *am* happy. And I appreciate that you can be happy for me.'

That seemed like a good opening, but it wasn't. It struck Nat that this unusually successful exchange could be a jumping-off point for almost anything. But the jump felt too hugely intimidating. In fact, that's just what it felt like. A jump. Like standing at the edge of a several-thousand-foot cliff, preparing to take a step.

It alarmed Nat so completely that he clammed up and said nothing more for the rest of the drive.

The old guy opened the dog run and let both dogs out into the yard.

Nat waited for Feathers to run greet him. But he never did. He just circled around and around the old man, jumping straight up into the air, but never hitting him with his paws.

'Hey, Feathers!' Nat called out. 'Feathers, old boy. You're my dog. I'm your person. Come say hi.'

The old man led both dogs over. Maggie licked Nat's

hand enthusiastically, but Feathers just sniffed it once and then stood close to the old man, partly hidden behind his legs.

'He doesn't like me,' Nat said.

'You have to give him time. *I* know he's your dog, and *you* know it, but *he* doesn't know that yet. How can he know? I've been the one taking care of him for three years.'

'So he really isn't my dog.'

'Of course he is.'

'Not according to him.'

'Give him time, Nat. Play with him. Take him for walks. And you should be the one to feed him from this point on. He'll get the idea.'

'Can I bring him inside?'

'Only until dinner is served. And keep a low profile. Eleanor has mixed feelings about dogs in the house. I bring them in at least once every day. But just make sure everybody's on his best behavior.'

Nat wasn't sure if he was part of everybody. And he didn't ask.

It was almost a nice scene, Nat thought. Like you see in a movie or a TV show about a family. The wife in the kitchen, cooking. All those good smells wafting out into the living room. The husband sitting on the couch reading the paper. And the son – who admittedly in the movies had not just been sprung from Juvie after serving a term for armed robbery – playing with the dog, running back and forth from living room to dining room. The dog chasing him and trying to get the toy he held: a short length of rope with a knot on each end that Nat had picked up from the dog run.

He noted on each trip that the table seemed more and more nicely set. First dishes were added on while he was in the living room. Then candles in silver holders.

Then a white porcelain bud vase edged in gold, with a single red flower.

'Please be careful,' Eleanor came into the dining room to say, as Nat chased Feathers in a wide arc around the table.

By the time Nat got back to the living room, the old guy was standing with his arms crossed. Blocking their way.

'Maybe it's time for Feathers to go outside now.'

'Why? We were just playing.'

'I just don't want any problems.'

'It's just a piece of rope,' Nat said. 'It really wouldn't break anything.'

As he said this, Feathers, who couldn't understand not being chased, dropped the rope on to Nat's foot. Nat picked it up, and, as if to prove his point, lofted it into the dining room.

Eleanor stuck her head in from the kitchen. Nat and the old man watched from the living room. Feathers took off after it, skidded on the hardwood floor. Banged into one leg of the table with a solid thunk.

The white porcelain vase teetered once, twice. Time seemed to freeze for one extra moment. Then it fell on to its side and broke into three pieces. The water it had contained seeped into the bone-colored lace tablecloth.

Nat stood frozen, watching Eleanor's face. It seemed to grow whiter with every passing second. At first he thought it was his imagination. But it wasn't. All the blood was draining from her face. Every drop, from the look of it.

Feathers brought the rope back and set it again on Nat's foot.

'Take the dog outside,' the old man said. 'Now.'

Then he went to comfort his wife, who looked for all the world like she was crying. Which might have been Nat's imagination. After all, nobody cries over a little bud vase.

Do they?

By the time Nat got back inside – because he'd purposely taken as much time as he could – the broken vase was gone, and the lace cloth had been replaced by a plain dark blue one.

'Dinner is served,' the old woman said. Her voice sounded unreal. Stiff.

Nat sat at the table and watched Eleanor and the old man carry out platter after platter of food. The baked ham, which looked honey-glazed, and which sizzled on top the way food does in television commercials. Green bean casserole. Yam casserole. Homemade biscuits. Green salad. Some kind of fruit pie.

'I'm really sorry about that little accident,' Nat said.

Eleanor missed a step on her way back to the kitchen.

The old man shot Nat a glance and a little shake of his head. As if to say, no. Don't. It's better not mentioned.

Nat waited quietly for them to sit down.

When they did, a silence fell. A difficult pause. Nat wanted to reach for a slice of ham, but wasn't sure if they were supposed to say grace. Or if the man of the house was supposed to reach first. Or some other rule Nat didn't know, but probably should.

He could hear Feathers whimpering from the dog run, still wanting to play. He wondered if the dog had been complaining the whole time, and he had only just now noticed.

'Well, go ahead and dig in,' Eleanor said.

Nat grabbed the big serving fork and speared three slices of ham all at once.

He started eating the ham without even waiting for side dishes to be passed.

'Salad?' the old man asked.

'No, thanks.'

'Green beans.'

'Not a huge green bean fan.'

'You should try Eleanor's. Don't make up your mind until you try. She makes them with cream of chicken soup and those French-fried onion strips on top.'

'OK. I'll try some.'

Nat wished Eleanor would say something. But she didn't.

The old man put a dab of green beans on Nat's plate, and he poked at them cautiously. Tried a bite.

'Hey. Wow. You're right. These are really good.'

A tiny smile from Eleanor. But no words.

'And I'll have a biscuit, please. And those yams look good.'

The old man passed him the yams. Anything with marshmallows on top had to be OK. He dished a mountain on to his plate and took a bite.

'Mmm. Orange. Tastes like orange. I wouldn't have guessed orange. But it's really good.'

Another tiny smile.

'You know, it was really nice of you to cook all this. I haven't had a meal like this in years. Last really good meal I had was that night we went hunting. Well,' he said, turning to the old man. 'You went hunting. And we had that roast duck and mashed potatoes and apple-sauce. I never forgot that meal. The whole three years I was inside. It's like I could still taste it. Not all the time, but every now and then. If I tried. Or sometimes even if I wasn't trying. When I wasn't even thinking about it. Wasn't even thinking about food. But then I would just taste it. Course, you did bring me that nice half a roast duck every birthday,' he said, looking again at the old man, who was looking down at his plate.

Silence. Either Nat talked or there was silence.

A cold feeling gripped Nat's stomach. How bad was this, really? Worse than he had realized?

'And I guess the only reason I'm not counting that is because I didn't get to heat it up, and there were no mashed potatoes. Or applesauce. But it was still good. But this, this is the best meal I've had in years. Literally. The food in there was so incredibly bad. You just can't believe how bad it was. There were times when I'd fast for three days on just water and apples, because I couldn't stand to eat it. But the apples were terrible, too. All full of spots and bruises. I think the fruit got given to them by farmers because it was too bad to sell. Or maybe they just bought it really cheap. But it was stuff too awful to take to the supermarket. Believe me.'

He paused. Hoping someone else would talk. Silence. So he plunged on.

'Every day at lunch there'd be this box of oranges at the end of the food line. But they weren't even orange. They were almost all green. And I'd be plowing through this box trying to find a good one. But this guard who watched the food line, Gerry, he would always say, "Just take one. They're all the same. Just take one." It was hard for me to believe that was true. Because they looked so bad. But really, he was right. They were all the same. Every day. All completely gross.'

Silence.

In the echo of it, Nat heard his words repeating back to him. As if hearing himself for the first time. As if standing outside of himself, watching and listening.

It struck him hard that he sounded like a fool. Even to himself.

'I'm sorry. I'm talking too much. Aren't I? I never seem to get that right. I either don't talk enough or I talk too much. There must be a right amount to talk. But I can never seem to find it.'

Another tight, tiny smile from the old woman.

Nat looked down at the ham on his plate and realized he could be eating rather than talking. And yet, some-how – no matter how good the food, no matter how much he had missed eating like this – his appetite was running out on him fast.

He began eating slowly. Small, cautious bites.

Little else was said.

Nat lay under the covers, feeling small in the big bed. The girly, flowery quilt had been replaced with one a more boy-suitable plain hunter green. The room had been stripped of wall decorations and most furnishings, as though to invite Nat to fill it with himself.

He was able to absorb the fact that it reflected a great deal of thoughtfulness on his behalf. But it couldn't make him feel any less hopeless.

The old guy came in to say goodnight, and Nat sat up in bed.

'I could buy her another vase,' Nat said. 'I mean, not right now I couldn't. But after I find work. You know, when I get my first paycheck. Whenever that is. Then I could.'

The old man pulled up a plain, cane-back chair and sat by Nat's bed. The way he had on his first night here. So long ago now.

'It belonged to her late grandmother. That's why she got a little emotional. She only has a few things from her grandmother's house, because she has eight brothers and sisters and there was only just so much to go around.'

'Oh. Will you tell her I'm sorry?'

'She knows you're sorry. And she knows anybody can have an accident. She just needs time to feel whatever she's going to feel about it.'

They sat in silence for a few moments.

Then Nat said, 'She doesn't like me.'

'She doesn't know you.'

Nat laughed. 'I got news for you. Lots of people don't like me. And when they get to know me better? Well, that doesn't exactly solve the problem. If you know what I mean.'

The old man smiled sadly. Patted Nat on the knee through the new quilt.

Nat was hoping he would say something. But instead he just rose to let himself out.

As the old man slid the chair back into the corner, Nat asked, 'Do *you* even like me?'

A long silence. Too long.

The old man crossed to the bedroom door. Stood a moment with his hand on the light switch. 'I see value in you,' he said softly.

'Is it inherent?'

The old man laughed, as if Nat had intended the question as a joke. But it had actually been a serious question.

'Yes. It's inherent.'

'Does that mean yes or no?'

Nat watched the old man's face for a moment. It was almost like watching someone think.

'Get some sleep,' the old man said. 'You'll be wanting to go out and look for a job in the morning.'

He snapped off the light and left Nat alone.

4 October 1978

Two Somethings

When Nat came into the kitchen and sat down at the table, the old man seemed to be gone. Eleanor stood looking into the refrigerator. She was already nicely put together in a belted dress and pretty woven shoes. And with her hair up. Perfectly, as though she'd never slept on it.

She glanced at Nat over her shoulder. 'Do you drink coffee?'

'Every chance I get,' he said.

He hadn't had coffee for over three years.

While she poured him a cup at the coffee maker, he noticed that the white bud vase was back in one piece. Sitting on a section of the morning paper on the counter. Freshly glued back together. Even from halfway across the room, Nat could see the fissures that remained as a testament to its accident.

Eleanor set the coffee in front of him. Not in a big sturdy mug, as he would have preferred, but in a dainty china teacup with saucer. He felt as though he would have to drink from it with his pinky finger raised. Or that he would surely damage it just by touching it. But it was coffee, and coffee was good, and he was in no position – or mood – to complain.

'Do you take anything in it?'

'Sugar and milk, please.'

She handed him a napkin and a spoon and indicated a fancy china sugar bowl, the kind with a lid, in the center of the table. While he was scooping three teaspoons of sugar into his cup, he watched her open the refrigerator, take out a small carton of cream, and – rather than simply plunk it on the table in front of him – pour about a third of it into a matching china cream pitcher.

He'd had no idea life could be so complicated.

'So, it looks good as new,' Nat said.

'What does?'

'Your vase. There on the counter. All back together.'

He waited, but she said nothing. Just set the pitcher of cream in front of him. He stared at it for a moment, feeling a light film of ice coat the room, and creep into his gut.

'OK, that's not true,' he continued. 'I'm sorry. It's not good as new. And it never will be. I probably shouldn't have said that.'

Silence. During which Nat wanted to shake her and yell, Like me! Please! Like me! I'm trying so hard here. Can't you see how hard I'm trying?

She never answered.

'I'm really sorry about it.'

'I know you are, Nat.'

More silence. Nat told the part of himself that had wanted more – that was still waiting for more – to sit down and shut up. Because it wasn't going to get it.

Then she said, 'I saved you some pancake batter. If you want pancakes.'

'Thank you. I'd love some pancakes.'

'OK. I'll make you up some fresh.'

'Thank you.'

Nat sipped his coffee and watched her, noticing she seemed more relaxed while puttering. While having something to attend to.

'So. Where's Nathan?'

She glanced over her shoulder as though surprised by the question. 'Why, he's working. Seeing clients. It's after ten, you know.'

'Oh. No. I didn't know it was so late. I don't usually sleep so late. I guess it's just that in Juvie they don't let you. They get you up every morning and make you work or take classes. Even on the weekends. Seven days a week. So I guess I just got carried away. You know. Because it's been so long since I could.'

He stopped himself. Heard the echo of his own

words. Thought, no. I will not have a repeat of last night. I will shut up. Right now. I will not babble like that, like a damn fool, not ever again.

He watched in silence as she poured four big puddles of pancake batter on to the hot griddle. Watched her lift the edges with her spatula to test them. To look at the brownness of their bottoms.

She flipped them carefully. Took down a plate from the cupboard.

'Oh,' she said. 'I just remembered. Nathan asked me to tell you something. If you find a job today . . . or any day while he's at work . . . he said to tell you that they'll give you a tax form to fill out. He told me the number of it, but I've forgotten now. I think it's a W-4, but I might be mistaken. But I think they only give you one. It has some decision about payroll withholding on it. He says you should bring it home. Not fill it out on the spot. He wants to give you some advice about it.'

'OK.' Silence. During which a beautiful steaming stack of pancakes appeared on the table in front of him. 'Thank you.'

'You're welcome, Nat.'

'Do you happen to know where Nathan keeps the dogs' leashes?'

'Hanging inside the garage door.'

'Oh. OK. Thanks. I thought I'd take Feathers downtown with me.'

'*On job interviews?*'

'Oh. Well. No. Not on *interviews*,' he said quickly. Back-pedaling fast. 'I just thought I'd start by seeing who has a "help wanted" sign. You know. If anybody's taking applications. If I'm going to go in and fill out an application I'll leave Feathers tied up outside.'

'Oh. I guess that would be OK. Would you like some homemade raspberry syrup to go with those?'

'Well, yeah,' Nat said. 'Who wouldn't?'

Nat could hear Maggie howling her displeasure as he ran down the driveway with Feathers bounding ahead at the end of the leash.

It was nearly a two-mile walk to downtown. But Nat intended to run it. Though maybe 'intended' was the wrong word. It wasn't a premeditated decision he'd formed in his head. He just needed to run. He just naturally started. And, once he started, he just couldn't seem to stop.

His head felt strangely clear as he ran. No thoughts seemed to cluster there, as they normally did, jostling for position. Instead they seemed to be driven out by the wind that blew into his eyes and nose, and by the slapping of his sneakers on the pavement.

This is freedom.

Those words broke through.

Yesterday, driving home with Nathan, that had not been freedom. It was only going with someone, just as they dictated you should. Dinner sure had not been freedom. And lying in the bed Nathan gave him was a damn sight better than lying in a cot at Juvie listening to Rico snore unevenly and staring at the bars in the dim half-light. But it was not free.

This was free.

No one watching. No one telling him what to do.

His chest ached, and he began to develop a stitch in his side. But he just kept running.

Somewhere along Main Street, a girl sitting on a bus bench smiled shyly at him as he ran by. He smiled back.

Then he stopped. Backtracked a quarter of a block.

Sat down on the bench beside her.

She had scads of long brown hair, thick, with a trace of red highlights where the sun hit it. It reminded him of someone, but he couldn't think who. She had freckles across her nose and cheekbones.

She looked over at him, a little bit defensive.

'Hi,' he said, so out of breath he was barely able to speak.

She said nothing. Just purposely looked away.

'Just needed to rest a minute.' His breathing would surely back him up on that.

Feathers padded over to the girl and licked one of her hands.

'I like your dog,' she said. Her eyes were a rich color of brown, not too dark, like really good-quality honey.

'Thanks. I like him, too.'

'What's his name?'

'Feathers.'

She laughed. A girl laugh. Shy. Like a giggle. 'No, really.'

'Really. That's his name. Feathers.'

'Now why would you go and name your dog an odd name like that? He's not a bird.'

'No. He's a dog.' Nat's breathing was a bit more under control now. He felt more like he could make himself understood.

'Don't you think that's an odd name for a dog?'

'I named him after the only other pet I ever had.'

'And *he* was a bird? Your other pet?'

'Right. He was.'

'So *he* had the feathers.'

'Well, actually . . . no. He didn't have feathers, either.'

'So, let me get this straight. Your only other pet was a bird with no feathers.'

'Right.'

'But you named him Feathers anyway.'

'Right.'

'And then you named your next pet Feathers, even though he was a dog.'

'Right.'

'You're a very strange boy. Did anybody ever tell you that?' She smiled right into his eyes, but then quickly looked away. As though she had embarrassed herself by doing so.

Nat laughed. 'Oh, yeah. Everybody tells me that.'

'Oh. Here comes my bus.'

'No, wait. Don't go yet,' Nat said. Not a very well-thought-out comment, he decided.

'Why not?'

'Well, we were having such a nice time talking . . .'

'I have to go to work.'

'Oh. Can I have your phone number?'

'You certainly may not.'

'Why not?'

Nat watched the bus from the corner of his eye. It was bearing down fast. He would need to hurry.

'Because I'm not that kind of girl.'

The stoplight at the corner turned red, halting the bus on the other side of the intersection. Nat breathed relief.

'What kind of girl is that? You mean you're not the kind of girl who has a phone? You're not the kind of girl who remembers her own phone number?'

'No, silly. I'm not the kind of girl who meets strange boys on the street.'

'Where do you meet strange boys?'

'I don't know. Hopefully I don't meet the strange ones at all. If I met a boy at my junior college. Or at work. Or church. That would be different, I guess.'

The light changed and the bus swooped down.

'Where do you work?'

She stood. Moved a couple of steps closer to the curb. Nat watched and waited without breathing. She seemed to be deciding whether or not to answer him.

The bus pulled level with her, stopped with a sigh of brakes.

'At the Frosty Freeze,' she said, throwing it over her shoulder as the doors squeaked open. Then she climbed on to the bus.

'Wait. You didn't even tell me your name.'

But it was too late. The doors had closed.

She was gone.

Nat tied Feathers's leash to a newspaper dispenser on the street outside the gym. Then he stood a moment, looking at the old place. Jack must be doing better for money, he thought. He had really fixed it up nice.

He opened the door, and froze. Didn't even go in. Just stood there in the open doorway, the wide, cold handle of the door in his hand. Just staring.

No speed bags. No heavy bags. No ratty gloves hanging on the wall. No sparring ring. No Little Manny. No Jack.

Instead Nat saw a man, who surely must have been on steroids, bench-pressing weights with no one to spot or supervise him, and three women in colorful spandex tights working out on stair-climbers and treadmills. Towels around their necks. The woman on the treadmill was reading a magazine positioned on a rack in front of her.

'Excuse me. May I help you?'

Nat glanced over at a young woman behind the counter. The counter that had never been there before. The counter that wasn't supposed to be there now. He stared at it briefly, then back at the women in spandex.

'Excuse me. You're letting the cold in. May I help you?'

'Oh. Sorry.' Nat stepped inside and let the door swing closed behind him. He stepped up to the counter as if in a dream. 'Where's Jack?'

'Jack who?'

'You know. Jack. The guy who . . .' Owned the place? Did he own the place? Nat realized he had no idea. He had never asked. There was a lot he had never really known. 'You know. Jack. The boxer. The guy who trains people to spar.'

'There's no Jack here,' she said. She was blonde, with a turned-up nose, and Nat felt she was looking down on him. And it was beginning to irritate him. And she seemed to know.

'Well, there *was*. I mean, there used to be. There always was before. And I need to know where he is now.'

'I'll get the manager,' she said.

Nat purposely did not look around while he waited. He knew he wouldn't be able to take it. He was right on the edge as it stood. So he just stared down at the counter, and squeezed his eyes shut, intermittently.

In a few moments a big man with a waist-length

blond ponytail came out from behind the curtain. A body-builder. 'Can I help you?' he asked.

Nat wished he hadn't been forced to start over from the beginning.

'I'm looking for Jack.'

'Jack Trudell?'

'Um. Yeah. I think so.'

'The gentleman who used to lease this place?'

'Yeah. That's him.'

'I'm afraid Mr Trudell is deceased.'

Nat stood stupidly, mutely, measuring how much confidence he felt in knowing the meaning of that word. Not enough. He thought he probably knew. But he wasn't sure. The old man found it intelligent to ask if you didn't know. Or so he said. Nat was not at all sure this Mr Muscles would agree.

'As in dead?'

'Yes, I'm afraid so.'

'What did he die of?'

'I wouldn't know that.'

'He wasn't a very old guy.'

'No, from what I heard he wasn't. Anything else we can do for you?'

'Um. No. Thanks.'

Nat walked out with his head down.

Even seeing Feathers waiting for him at the curb, wagging his tail as if he really were Nat's dog – even that couldn't make him feel better.

*　*　*

Nat sat on the freezing concrete in the alley behind the gym. Feathers sat beside him, staring into Nat's face. Cocking his wiry head slightly, as if trying to ask what the trouble might be. Nat scratched him behind the ear, and he straightened out his head and sighed.

'I guess I should go on down the street and look for a help wanted sign,' Nat said out loud to the dog.

Feathers cocked his head again. Nat watched their clouds of frozen breath puffing out and mixing together.

'But I don't think I'm going to.'

Nat had been trying to lift the idea in his head all morning. But it weighed millions of pounds. It was heavier than the world in which he'd have to accept such a job. It would have been impossible enough to imagine, even if Nat had been sure that job applications didn't ask if you'd ever been arrested. But Nat was not sure of that at all. In fact, he figured they probably did ask.

'I wonder if they ask you if you've ever been arrested? You think there's a space for that on a job application?' Nat asked Feathers. 'I bet there is. Maybe I just won't tell them. You think they check?'

A long silence.

His rear end was getting numb from the cold of the pavement, and he could feel the cold seep through his jacket where his back pressed against the brick of the next building. The back wall of the dry cleaners. Nat could smell the chemicals they used. They were making him a little bit queasy.

Well. Something was.

'Maybe I should just go down to the Frosty Freeze instead. That sounds like a better idea. Doesn't it?'

But in the silence that followed, he knew it was not a good idea. Not at all.

Because he had no money in his pocket. Not a dime.

How could he show up at the Frosty Freeze and not even have the money to order a milkshake? Or even a Coke? What kind of a statement would that make about him? And how could he even pretend he had just come in as a customer, like everyone else, like anyone had a perfect right to do? What would he answer, when she asked him why he was even there? Which she obviously would. If he couldn't say, 'Oh, I was just in the mood for a chocolate milkshake,' then what on earth would he say?

'No,' he told Feathers. 'First I have to get a job. Then we can go down to the Frosty Freeze.'

But the instant he said it, the millions of pounds descended on him again. Nat felt that his thoughts had just dragged him on the world's most depressing never-ending loop, dumping him right back at the impossible spot where he'd started.

A voice startled him. 'I know you. You're that kid Jack was gonna train.'

Nat looked up.

'Little Manny!'

'Yup. That's still me, all right. Whatever happened to you, kid? Jack was just starting to like you. Then you up and disappeared.'

'Got myself thrown in Juvie Hall for three years.'

'Oh. That explains it.' Little Manny squatted beside Nat, his back against the brick of the dry cleaners. Patted Feathers on the head. 'Funny-looking dog,' he said, not making it sound like much of an insult.

He'd stopped coloring his hair, Nat noticed. It was now shot through with gray. And much shaggier. No hair cream and neat comb-marks. As if he hadn't the time or the patience any more. Maybe he had just stopped caring.

'Little Manny. What are you doing here?'

'Same thing I always did. Mopping the floor at closing time. Spraying bleach in the showers. Wiping sweat off the machines.'

'So you still work here.'

'Well, they still needed somebody to clean. And I just live right up there. So why not me?' He pointed to a window on the second floor above the gym, and Nat looked up. 'That's how I knew you were down here. I heard you talking. I had my window open. I like the cold. People think I'm crazy, but I like it. Colder it is, the more I like it. So I looked out the window, 'cause I heard you talking. And all I saw was some kid and a dog. So I come all the way down here to see what kind of a kid talks to his dog. And it was you.'

'Yeah,' Nat said. 'That's me. I'm a strange boy.'

'I'll say.'

A long silence. Feathers licked Little Manny's wrist.

Then Nat said, 'What happened to Jack?'

Another silence.

'Jack's dead.'

'Yeah, I heard that much. But why? How? How did he die?'

Nat heard only a long sigh. He thought Little Manny was never going to answer him. Then, 'Let's just call it a series of unfortunate choices and leave it at that.'

'Oh,' Nat said. 'I guess I can relate to bad choices.'

'At least you're still here.'

'Yeah. Great. I'm still here. What terrific news, huh? What good does that do me?'

'What's so bad about not being dead? I mean, when you weigh the alternatives.'

Nat wondered if he could explain. It made him tired to even consider it. But it was Little Manny asking. So he had to at least try.

'I don't know. It's like . . . The whole time I was inside, that whole three years, all I thought about was getting back here. I figured I'd walk in the door, and there Jack would be. Sparring with some old guy in the ring. I pictured it a million times. Really saw it in my head. I figured he'd walk over and ask me where I'd been so long. And I'd tell him. And he'd nod like he totally understood. 'Cause he understood stuff like that. And then he'd say something like, "Well, come on, kid. We wasted three years as it is. Let's not waste any more. Put on a pair of gloves and we'll make up for lost time." '

'Yup. That's probably about what he would've said all right.'

'Now who's going to teach me to box?'

'Well . . .'. Little Manny said. Then he paused for a time. As if trying to decide whether to finish the thought.

'What? You know somebody? You got an idea?'

'Well . . .'

'I'm pretty desperate here. In case you didn't notice. If you got something, I'd really appreciate hearing it.'

'I'm the one trained Jack in the first place.'

'*You* trained Jack?'

'Yup. Taught him everything he knows. I mean, knew. I had the savvy and all. You know, the instincts. I knew how to fight, but I wasn't worth much in the ring. Just not built for it. They got weight classes but not height classes. You know? Where could I hit except below the belt? I couldn't reach much higher. You know the old saying. Those who can't do something, well, then, they just teach it.'

'Teach *me*.'

'I don't know, kid.'

'Please?'

'It's been a long time since I trained anybody.'

'You're my only hope.'

'Aw, don't lay that on me, kid. I couldn't take it. I'm too old and broke-down to be anybody's last hope.'

'You're younger and less broke-down than anybody else who's gonna be willing to train me to fight.'

'Yeah, I guess I see your point about that.'

A long sigh. A long pause.

Nat watched their breath puff out in great clouds of vapor. All three of them. He knew Little Manny would say yes. Because he had to. It just couldn't go any other way. It was too important.

'Aw, hell. Come on upstairs, I guess. Might as well. What better have I got to do? I got a couple bags up there in my room. We'll see if you remember anything at all.'

Nat arrived home a little after five.

The old man was sitting in the living room, watching the evening news.

He looked up and smiled at Nat, then rose and crossed the room to turn down the volume on the TV set.

'How about you don't even bring Feathers in? Maybe just put him straight into his run and then get cleaned up for dinner?'

Nat stood frozen in the foyer, still holding the dog's leash. Not crossing the threshold into the living room.

'Yeah. OK. I mean, good idea.'

'You must have had a successful day.'

'What do you mean?'

'I mean you were gone all day, so I figured you must have found something.'

Oh, yeah. I found something, Nat thought. I finally found something. Finally. Maybe even two somethings.

'Oh. You mean work?'

'Yes. I thought you might have found a job.'

'Oh. No. I didn't find anything.'

'Well, then, what did you do all day?'

'Oh. Well. I was looking.'

A brief, tense moment. Was it tense? It seemed so to Nat. But maybe the tension was only on the inside of Nat. Maybe the old man couldn't see it or hear it at all.

Then the old guy said, 'Maybe you'll have better luck tomorrow.'

'Yeah,' Nat said. 'Maybe tomorrow. Maybe so.'

Nat borrowed an alarm clock from the old man, who seemed more than pleased to lend it.

He set it for six a.m.

Nat arrived at the breakfast table before seven. Showered. Dressed. His hair neatly combed.

He was the third and last to arrive.

The old man was sitting at the kitchen table, reading the morning paper and eating ham and scrambled eggs. Eleanor was standing at the stove, scrambling more. For him? Nat wondered. He hoped so. He had a big day in front of him. He'd need his strength.

Nat glanced at the headline of the paper. For some weird reason it flashed him back, all the way to age twelve. A big, sudden memory that hit him hard. He could almost see the headline of the paper dated just two days after his birth. In his head. Behind his eyes. It seemed to be printed there, but he hadn't known it. It wasn't the actual headline of today's paper itself that set things off. That was nothing. It just said, 'SPECIAL

ELECTION: MEASURE D GOES DOWN TO OVERWHELMING DEFEAT'. Maybe it was the fact that he hadn't seen the morning paper for years. Or maybe because of whose hands held it.

Nat could almost feel the hard, cold boards of his grandmother's bedroom floor against his knees.

He wondered what his grandmother was doing this morning.

He wondered if the old man had sat in this same kitchen eighteen years ago and read the morning paper, just like he was doing now. If he saw that headline and thought, right, I know. You don't have to tell *me*. I was there. I was the hunter whose name they never bothered to mention.

He shook the thoughts away again, but they left a disquieting hangover.

Eleanor set a cup of coffee and a pitcher of cream in front of him.

'Thank you,' he said.

The old guy folded up his paper and set it on the table. 'Nice to see you up and around so early. You look very nice, too. Very professional.'

'Thought I'd get a jump on the old job search.'

'It just so happens that I have a pleasant surprise for you on that score. I called a friend of mine half an hour ago, on your behalf. Marvin LaPlante. He owns a big, thriving dairy on the outskirts of town. Out on the old Hunt Road. I've been doing his books and taxes for years now. Maybe twenty years. And I got you an interview for this morning.'

Nat felt his face go slack and cold. And, he hoped, blank. He tried desperately not to let it fall. He wasn't sure if he'd succeeded.

'An interview?'

'Yes. Marvin said he can always use another able-bodied young man on the loading docks.'

'Loading docks?'

'Yes, you know, loading the milk on to the delivery trucks.'

'Oh. Right. Well . . . Good. Well . . . that's good, then. An interview. This morning. That's great.'

'I thought you'd be pleased. Especially after pounding the pavement all day yesterday and coming up empty-handed.'

'Um. Right. So . . . What time am I supposed to be there?'

'He said anytime this morning would be fine.'

'How do I get out there?'

'The Number 12 bus goes out there. But for this morning, it's really only about fifteen minutes out of my way. Since you're up so early, anyway. If you'd slept in, I was going to leave you bus fare. But you're up and ready. And I have to go out as far as Ellis for my first appointment. So why don't I drop you? And then I'll lend you some bus fare to get home. And if you come home with the job, I'll lend you bus fare for the coming week and the rest of this one, and you can pay me back out of your first paycheck.'

Silence, as Nat's thoughts spun in circles. He didn't have Little Manny's phone number. In fact, he didn't even know if Little Manny had a phone. And even if he did have a phone, and even if he was listed, Nat wouldn't have any change left over for a phone call. He would just have to be late. Really late. Hours late. He had no choice.

Maybe Little Manny would give up on him.

He could take the bus straight to the little apartment over the gym. Straight from the job interview. And then walk home. But maybe Little Manny wouldn't be there by then. Or maybe he would tell Nat to go shove it, if he couldn't do better than hours late. If he didn't care about a valuable offer of free training any more than that.

Eleanor set a plate of scrambled eggs and ham slices in front of him, with a separate small plate of toast and grape jelly.

'Thank you. Very much,' he said to her. Then, to the old man, 'Does he know about my . . . uh . . ?'

'Yes. I told him you had just been released from a three-year incarceration. I thought honesty was the best policy in a case like that.'

'And he still wants to interview me?'

'So he says. Better hurry up and eat your breakfast. We have to go in less than fifteen minutes.'

* * *

'I'm a big believer in frankness,' Mr LaPlante said. 'So I'm going to lay it right on the line.'

Nat hadn't so much as opened his mouth to say a word yet. He hadn't had time. He had just shaken the man's hand. Taken a seat in his office as directed. And now this.

Frankness. On the line.

'You wouldn't even be here if I didn't owe a lot to Nathan McCann. I like to lay everything on the table, so I'm being honest with you right up front.'

Then he allowed a pause. It took Nat a moment to gather it was his turn to talk.

LaPlante wore his hair parted in the middle, which Nat found amusing. So he tried not to look. Because when he looked, it was hard not to crack a smile. Over LaPlante's head was a framed poster of a winged cartoon cow. Wearing a halo. Flying over a cartoon cloud.

The silence extended a beat too long.

'Well, I definitely appreciate your honesty,' Nat said. Hoping it didn't sound like a lie. Because it was.

'Generally, I figure I can tell a lot about a prospective employee from his background. They say the past is the best predictor of the future. But I have a great deal of respect for Nathan McCann, and he asked me to give you a chance. And I would give that man just about anything he asked of me. Within reason. But there's going to be something of a trial period for you. Don't get me wrong. I'm not saying I've made up my mind that you won't make it here. We're not set against you. Nobody's going to judge you unfairly, and if they do they'll answer to me. You'll get the same shot as anybody gets. I guess what I'm saying is, you'll get *one* shot. Is that acceptable to you?'

'Yes, sir. It is. Absolutely. I appreciate the shot. When do you want me to start work?'

'I'll take you out on the loading dock and you can start right now.'

'Now?' Nat asked, reminding himself to close his mouth afterward.

'Someplace you'd rather be?'

'Um. No. No, sir. Now is fine. Now is perfect.'

Nat stood on the loading dock, staring at stack after stack of wooden crates, each containing sixteen milk bottles. Awaiting further instructions.

The foreman, an old but muscular guy named Mr Merino, came around and clapped him on the back. Then he set a printed form on top of the stack right in front of Nat's belt.

'LaPlante wants you to fill this out.'

'What is it?'

'Instructions for withholding. You know, from your paycheck.'

'I can't fill that out here.'

'Why the hell can't you?'

'Because I promised Nathan McCann I'd bring it home and get his advice on it first.'

'I'll have to see what LaPlante thinks about that.'

'He'll think it's fine. Because Nathan McCann said so.'

'OK. Well, I'll just double-check that.'

'Yes, sir. That's fine. Should I be doing something while I'm waiting?'

'Yeah. I'd say so. I'd say you should be picking up those crates that are right under your nose. And loading them into that truck. That's also right under your nose.'

'OK. I just thought maybe there would be instructions.'

Merino stood with hands on hips, his chin raised high. As if to be taller while looking down on the new guy. The one with the huge black mark against him. 'You're unclear on how to pick things up and then put them down again?'

'No, sir. I'm not. Not at all. I can handle that. I'll just get started.'

'Glad to hear it,' Merino said. And turned his back to walk away.

'Mr Merino? What time is quitting?'

Merino whirled back. 'Excuse me?'

'Did I say something wrong?'

'You haven't so much as lifted your first crate, and you already want to know what time you can stop?'

'I didn't mean it like that. Not at all. Just that it's a

weird work day, you know. Not a regular one. Because I started late. And I just have to take the bus home, is all. And I just wanted to be sure it wouldn't be after the buses stopped running.'

Merino continued to eye him harshly. 'Bus runs till ten at night.'

'No problem, then,' Nat said. With a little salute.

He lifted a crate. It was surprising how heavy sixteen quart bottles of milk in a wooden crate could be.

Merino came back around about ten crates later.

'Boss says you can quit at five today. Tomorrow – and every weekday after – get here by six in the morning. And get off at three.'

'Yes, sir.'

'He also said if Nathan McCann told you to take that W-4 form home with you, then you take it home.'

'Yes, sir. That's what I figured he would say.'

'Is that a smart-ass comment?'

'No, sir. Not at all. No disrespect intended at all.'

By the time he got to Little Manny's one-room apartment, it was after six.

He was out of breath from running all the way from the bus stop. The muscles in his lower back and between his shoulder blades had locked into painful spasms. His biceps ached and stung from lifting those heavy crates all day long.

And tomorrow he'd have to start all over again. Six a.m. Six in the morning till three in the afternoon. Imagine how his back and arms would feel by quitting time tomorrow.

He knocked, hearing the dull drone of a *Gilligan's Island* episode from behind the door. Nothing else. No movement. No answer to his knock.

Well, he'd get used to it. He'd get in shape to do the work. Maybe it would even help him in his training. That is, if he still even had an offer of training.

He knocked again.

Little Manny opened the door. His hair looked wildly disheveled, as if he had been asleep. The smell of stale tobacco smoke practically slammed into Nat's face, making him cough.

'You stood me up, kid.' His voice sounded gravelly with sleep.

'I know. I'm sorry. I couldn't help it.'

'I thought you wanted this more than anything.'

'I do. I do want it more than anything.'

'Nope, you just showed me you don't. Obviously you don't. Obviously whatever you were doing all day, you want more.'

'I have to work. I don't have any choice. I have to hold down a job to live where I'm living. I need a roof over my head. I'm off on the weekends. Couldn't I just come over on the weekends?'

'Weekends? I kind of like to keep my weekends free.'

'For *what*?' Nat asked. And then prayed it hadn't sounded as rude to Little Manny as it had to him.

Long silence.

'Well, that's a point, I guess. OK. Saturday morning.'

And he slammed the door shut again.

Nat ran all the way home. Trying to think of a good excuse for being so late.

Nat stood facing Little Manny in his tiny, smoky room, wearing unfamiliar and uncomfortable gloves. Holding them raised, poised, in perfect position. At least, as best he could remember.

Feathers sat between them on the floorboards, panting, little drops of sweat flipping off his tongue and hitting Little Manny's old, filthy wood floor.

Little Manny wore two big padded punch mitts that he held up for Nat to jab at. He was so short he had to hold them above his head. Nat assumed their purpose was to allow his trainer to feel the force of his jabs.

'That dog's drooling on my floor.'

'Sorry. You want me to tie him up outside?'

'Nah. Who cares? Floor's not clean anyway. Only, what's he drooling for? It's cold.'

'I don't know. Maybe from the walk over?'

'What're you waiting for? An engraved invitation to arrive by messenger?'

'Oh. Right.'

He jabbed with his right, glancing off one of Little Manny's training mitts.

'What? Are you joking?'

He jabbed again. Harder this time.

'No, seriously. Is that a joke? Most guys work out in the can. What the hell did *you* do in there for three years? Like I can't guess. Only, even if that's true, your right hand should be in better shape than that.'

'It's just that I'm thrashed from this new job. Geez. You have no idea. My arms feel like they're about to fall off. Thank God I started on a Thursday. If I'd started on Monday I think the week would've just about killed me.'

He tried a couple more jabs, but he knew they were every bit as pathetic.

'You're gonna have to start on Monday next week.'

'Oh. Right. Well, maybe I'll be more used to it by then.'

Little Manny let out a sudden sound, a cross between a sharp laugh and blowing a raspberry. It startled Feathers, who skittered off into the corner. 'Very funny. You're a bundle o' laughs, kid. Heavy labor like that? Eight hours a day? Take you four, five weeks to get used to it. Minimum.'

Nat's gloved hands fell to his sides. *'Four or five weeks?'*

'Don't stop, kid. Keep jabbing. You were doing lousy but at least you were doing.'

A couple more jabs. It was starting to hurt a lot. Not only throwing the punches. That had hurt all along. Just holding his arms in position was getting hard to bear.

'Now, one good thing, though,' Little Manny said. 'When you do get used to it, you'll be in much better shape. They're paying you to work out.'

'That's what I was hoping, yeah. I had to think of something good about that job. The foreman hates me. And it takes me forty-five minutes each way on the bus.'

'What do you think about all that time you're riding the bus?'

'How much better everything's going to be when I go pro.'

'Pro? Who said nothing about going pro? I never said I thought you could go pro.'

'Well, screw you, then. I'm going pro no matter what you think.' And he jabbed again. Harder this time.

'Aha. Now I know how to get something out of you. You're one of those guys has to get mad.'

'Is that why you said it?'

'No. I said it because I never told you I thought you could go pro.'

'Why the hell can't I?'

'I never said you couldn't, either. Just stop getting so ahead of yourself, kid. I can't even get you to hit these mitts so's I can feel it, and you're already accepting the featherweight title in your head.'

'I'm not featherweight.'

Another jab.

'Better. Hell you're not.'

'Welter, maybe.'

'In your dreams, little boy.'

'Don't even do that. It's not funny.'

'Well then, hit me.'

Nat aimed a shot between and well below the mitts. Right at the little man's torso. Little Manny blocked it perfectly. Then he dropped the mitts to his sides and looked Nat in the eye. Nat looked down at the floorboards.

'The anger thing'll help your cause in the ring. Breaking the rules won't. That's what the officials are there for. Make sure you don't get away with nothing. No shit. You know? And don't think they won't be watching you every minute.'

'Sorry.'

'You don't gotta be sorry. You just have to learn to channel what you feel. Use it, you know? Right now it's your worst enemy. It could be your best friend.'

'How?'

'What do you think I'm trying to teach you? Why do you think you gotta show up here every day you don't work?'

'Oh. Right.'

'Now. You gonna hit me, Little Featherweight, or what?'

14 October 1978

Payday

'Yesterday was payday,' Nat said. In-between punches on the heavy bag.

'First payday ever?'

'Yup.'

'How'd it feel?'

'It sucked. I couldn't believe it. They took so much out for taxes. And unemployment. And all this other stuff I never even heard of. And then I had to pay the old guy back for the bus fare. And put aside for bus fare till next payday. So I look at what's left, and I'm like, "I went through all those days of hell for *this*?" I couldn't believe it. If I didn't have a free roof over my head . . . I mean, how do people even do it? I don't get it at all.'

After a couple more good punches Little Manny said, 'Welcome to the real world, kid.'

A few minutes of solid blows. No comments.

Then Nat said, 'What time is it?'

'Five to eleven.'

'I need to take a break.'

'We only just barely started.'

'I need a chocolate milkshake. All of a sudden I'm just in the mood for a chocolate milkshake. How far a walk is the Frosty Freeze from here?'

Nat stepped up to the window with Feathers at his heel. Behind the counter he saw a skinny guy about his own age with glasses, a paper hat, and a red-and-white striped Frosty Freeze shirt.

The other window was still closed, and Nat craned his neck to see if anyone else was working in the back. He could hear someone moving around back there. But when the someone finally moved into view Nat saw a tall, very fat man.

'Welcome to Frosty Freeze. Can I take your order?'

'Oh. Chocolate shake.'

'Yes, sir.'

It felt weird to be called 'sir' by a guy his own age. I guess work'll do that to you, Nat thought. Cut you right down to size.

'So, where's that girl who works here?'

'Which one? Lot of girls work here. Oh, by the way. No dogs on the patio.'

'Oh. Sorry. I couldn't see anyplace to tie him up.'

'Yeah, OK, but just . . . if the boss comes . . . I told you the rule.'

'Right. You did. She has brown hair and brown eyes.'

'That could be about three of 'em.' Then, over his shoulder, 'Freddy? One chocolate shake.'

'And freckles on her nose.'

'Sounds like Carol.'

'OK. Where's Carol?'

'She doesn't come in till two on Saturday.'

'Shit,' Nat said under his breath.

Then, having already ordered the chocolate shake, he had no choice but to pay for it, and walk back to Little Manny's with it, straining to draw the challenging thickness of it up the straw as he walked.

'You got an alarm clock here?' Nat asked Little Manny.

'No, why would I need an alarm clock? I don't gotta be at work till closing time.'

'Kitchen timer?'

'There's one on the stove, but I don't know if it works. I'm not much of a cook. Why? You got someplace better to be?'

'I'm just thinking at two o'clock I might get in the mood for another chocolate shake.'

Little Manny sighed and shook his head. 'I know what you're doing. And it's not gonna work.'

'Why isn't it?'

"Cause it'll just put fat on you. What you want to do

is to bulk up, but with muscle. You wanna gain weight, ask me how. Let me show you how to do it the right way. I'm your trainer. That's what I'm here for.'

'OK. Show me how to gain weight. That would be good. But I'm still going back to the Frosty Freeze at two.'

'So tell me what's at that Frosty place besides the chocolate milkshakes.'

'This girl.'

'That explains a lot.'

'Were you worried it was something dangerous? Like drug deals at the Frosty Freeze?'

'Nothing's more dangerous than a girl,' Little Manny said.

Carol was standing behind the window as Nat stepped up to the counter. She looked cute in her paper hat and red-and-white striped shirt. She had her short sleeves rolled up high, and her upper arms looked smooth and thin. She wore her hair pulled back in a ponytail, then shoved into a hairnet and crowned by the silly hat. Only, it was sillier on the skinny guy. On her it was sort of . . . adorable.

'Welcome to Frosty Freeze. Can I take your order, strange boy with the bird dog? Who, by the way, is not supposed to be on the patio?'

'Who, me or the dog?'

She smiled, though she appeared to be trying not to. 'The dog.'

'If the owner comes, I'll be sure to tell him you told me the rule.'

'You don't follow directions very well, do you?'

'That's putting it mildly.'

'I still think that's a silly name for a dog.'

'Well. I think Frosty Freeze is a silly name for your work. Because Frosty and Freeze both mean the same thing. It's like saying Wet Water.'

'You can think whatever you want about it, Strange Boy, but I didn't name the Frosty Freeze. I just work here. You named that dog yourself.'

'I guess you got a point,' Nat said.

'Can I take your order?'

'Yes. Thank you. I'd like a chocolate shake. I was training. You know. Working out. And I just got in the mood for a chocolate shake.'

'You get in the mood for a chocolate shake a lot, don't you?'

'Now why would you say that?'

'Kenny said you were here about three hours ago getting a chocolate shake—'

'I'm trying to put on weight. Trying to go from . . . To get up to welterweight.'

'. . . and asking about me.'

'Seemed rude to come by your work and not even say hello.'

To his dismay, Nat was unable to force his facial muscles not to smile. They insisted on contracting, like a muscle spasm, into just the type of idiot grin he was hoping to avoid.

'Hey, Freddy. Another chocolate shake for the bottomless pit.'

Nat glanced over his shoulder to see if anyone was waiting in line behind him. If he'd have to step away from the window. Nobody back there. He breathed again.

'So, Strange Boy, are you a boxer?'

'How'd you know that?' Proud and flattered. As if she had seen it just by looking.

'You said you were trying to get up to welterweight.'

'Oh. Right. Yes. I'm a boxer.'

'Is that what you do?'

'Well, it's not the *only* thing I do. But it will be. I mean, in the short run I'm having to hold down a day job. There's a lot involved with going pro. It's a serious business. But that's definitely where I'm going.'

'So, now I know everything about you—'

'Well, not—'

'. . . except your name.'

'Nat.'

'Like Nat King Cole.'

'Yes. Like Nat King Cole.'

'I love Nat King Cole. I know his music probably seems old-fashioned now. I mean, to most people our age. But he's my favorite crooner.'

Not two weeks earlier, if anybody had told Nat they

had a favorite crooner, he would have thought they were from outer space. Now he made a mental note to get a record by Nat King Cole. Or maybe even go to the record store and listen to a few different crooners in that little booth. See if he had a favorite.

No, that wouldn't be necessary. Nat King Cole would definitely be his favorite.

Unfortunately, Fat Freddy waddled by and set the chocolate shake on the counter beside Carol's porcelain arm. And, fortunately, kept waddling. Nat had been hoping he'd work far more slowly.

'What do I owe you for that?' Nat asked her.

'You should know what a chocolate shake costs. After all, it's your second one today.'

'I guess I wasn't paying attention.'

'Shhhh,' she whispered, finger to her lips. 'This one's on me.'

Nat's cheek muscles went crazy.

She likes me. I knew it. I knew she liked me. She really likes me.

He opened his mouth but no words came out.

'You got someone in line behind you,' she said.

Nat looked over his shoulder to see a middle-aged couple, waiting. But they were still peering over Carol's head at the menu. So he had a little time. But maybe not much.

'So, now that you met me at work, can I have your phone number?'

'I didn't meet you at work. I met you on a bus bench.'

'No, you met me here. Just now.'

'How do you figure?'

'You haven't really met someone until you know their name.'

'I guess that's one way to look at it.'

'So, can I have your number?'

'No. I'm not that kind of girl. But if you want to come by here again, that would be OK. Now . . .' She indicated the people behind him with a flip of her head.

Nat grabbed the milkshake and ran all the way back to Little Manny's. Just because he had energy to spare.

Nat lay in bed, the door still open, a spill of soft light pouring in from the hallway.

He figured the old man would come in to say goodnight. He usually did.

He closed his eyes briefly, thinking about Carol. At least, it seemed brief. When he opened them, the old man was pulling up the cane-back chair.

'I thought you might be asleep,' the old man said, seating himself.

'Nope. Just thinking.'

'How do you feel the new job is going?'

'Oh. That. Well. OK, I guess. The foreman doesn't like me. He's just on me all the time. It's like he's got it in for me. When I first got that job, your friend LaPlante said nobody would treat me unfairly, and if they did they'd answer to him. Sometimes I wonder if I should tell him. But then I think maybe that would just make it worse. And besides, sometimes I see Merino talking to some of the other guys on the loading dock, and I think maybe it's not just me. Maybe he hates everybody.'

'Maybe the lesson is to learn not to let him get your goat.'

'I guess.'

'So, then, other than your working relationship with the foreman . . .'

'Well. It's damn hard work. Sorry. Darn hard. My back and arms are just screaming at me all the time. But I think I'll get used to it. And when I do I'll be in much better shape.'

'It's not a bad deal to get paid for staying physically fit.'

'That's what I was thinking.'

An awkward pause. Nat knew there was more the old man wanted to say. In fact, he'd known it all along, he suddenly realized. Since dinner. No, since he'd gotten home.

'I assumed you must be tired. You'd have to be after your first full work-week. That's why I was surprised when you were gone all day today. I thought you'd be home resting most of the weekend.'

'Well, I wanted to take Feathers out. You know. Really be outdoors.'

'Aren't you outdoors all week on that loading dock?'

'Well. That's true.'

Another awkward silence.

Then the old man said, 'You're eighteen years old, Nat. You're a man. A young man, but a man. Not a minor child. You don't owe me all the details of everywhere you go and everything you do. That's on the one hand. But then again, on the other hand, I think the success of this arrangement rests on your willingness to be reasonably forthcoming.'

'I don't know what that word means.'

'Forthcoming?'

'Yeah.'

'It means honest. But it means more than that, too. Being forthcoming is not just telling the truth in a pinch. It's really being willing to let the truth come up into the light. It's not holding anything back.'

'Oh. OK.' Nat paused to gather his thoughts. 'OK. I'll be forthcoming. Down at the Frosty Freeze . . . there's this girl. Her name is Carol. She has freckles on her nose.' An embarrassed pause. 'I'm not sure what else I'm supposed to tell you about her.'

'You don't have to tell me any more about her. That's as much as I need to know.'

'Is it OK?'

'That's an odd question. How could I tell you it's not OK? It's part of being human. I'm just glad it didn't turn out you were mixed up with some kind of lower companions. Something that could lead to trouble.'

The old man rose to go.

'Nathan?'

'Yes, Nat?'

'There's one other thing I wanted to tell you. You know. Just to be forthcoming.'

He sat back down again. 'All right. Go ahead.'

'Remember that first birthday of mine after I got arrested? And you came to see me and brought me roast duck, a cake and a present? And a picture of my dog? And we talked about the presents you'd been leaving for me my whole life, and which ones were really good guesses on what I might like?'

'Yes. I remember. You said the baseball mitt. And the ant farm. But that your grandmother wouldn't let you keep it.'

'I started to tell you something that day. And I don't even know why I stopped myself. It's like it meant too much to me, so I couldn't talk about it. I don't even know if that makes sense. Anyway, what I started to tell you about . . . was the boxing gloves.'

'Oh, yes. Your fourteenth birthday, wasn't it?'

'The boxing gloves changed my whole life.'

'How so?'

'Because I knew then . . . that's what I want to do. That's what I want to be.'

'You want to be a boxer?'

'More than anything.'

'A professional boxer?'

'Yeah. Pro.'

'Do you still have the gloves?'

'No. My grandmother made sure I wouldn't get to keep them.'

A long silence. Nat thought he heard the old man sigh.

'I guess I could keep that in mind come Christmas.'

'That would mean a lot to me if you did.'

The old man rose again. Slid the chair back into its corner. Walked to the bedroom door.

'So you're OK with me being a boxer?'

Silence.

Then, 'It's good to have a dream, Nat.'

'It's not just a dream. It's what I'm really going to do.'

'Until you do it, it's a dream.'

'Oh. OK.' He watched the old man for a moment, standing with one hand on the door. Ready to close it for the night. Back-lit by the light from the hallway. A dark silhouette. 'Did *you* ever have a dream, Nathan?'

In the silence that followed, Nat wished he could see the old man's face.

'Get some sleep, Nat. I'm guessing you'll have a big day ahead of you tomorrow, down at the Frosty Freeze.'

Part Five

Nathan McCann

You Would Think So, Wouldn't You?

It was an hour or more after dinner. Nathan had gone to the trouble of making a wood fire in the fireplace, because it seemed to suit the late autumn mood.

He washed the soot from his hands before sitting on the couch next to Eleanor, who hooked her arm through his.

'I should really be doing the dishes,' she said.

'They're not going anywhere.'

'The food will get stuck on.'

'Just sit with me a minute, and then I'll be happy to help you if you want.'

'You don't have to help me, Nathan, I can—'

Nat stuck his head into the living room. 'I have to ask you a really big favor,' he said.

Nathan felt Eleanor stiffen slightly in anticipation of what he would ask. If called upon to wager, or even just to guess, Nathan would have assumed that cash would be involved.

'You may *ask.*'

'Can I use your record player?'

'Oh. My record player. Yes, I guess that would be all right. But be gentle with the needle, please. Replacement needles are quite expensive. And please close the den door, so we aren't assaulted by the noise.'

'And please keep the volume low,' Eleanor added.

'You got it,' Nat said, and his head disappeared.

Eleanor sighed deeply. 'And it was such a nice, quiet evening, too. Why do I think the peace is about to be shattered? I should have known it couldn't last.'

They waited in silence, tense now, poised to see how dreadful it was really going to be.

A moment later, soft strains of violin leaked under the den door. It was almost the polar opposite of what Nathan had been braced to expect.

'I know this song,' he said. But he hadn't heard enough bars to identify it. 'That's so familiar. What is it?'

'I think that's Nat King Cole.'

They looked at each other for a moment, then burst out laughing.

'My goodness,' Eleanor said. 'I certainly owe Nat an apology for what I've been sitting here thinking. But maybe it's best if I never deliver it, because then he never has to know what I was sitting here thinking.

Now, why on earth would he be listening to Nat King Cole?'

'Maybe he has better taste than we give him credit for.'

'Is this what young people listen to these days?'

'I have no idea what young people listen to these days. But you're looking a gift horse in the mouth. Nat!' he called out in a big voice.

The den door opened. 'Too loud?'

'Turn it up, please, Nat. Eleanor and I can barely hear it.'

'Oh. Up? Oh. OK.'

The volume came up about three notches and the den door closed again.

Nathan stood and reached a hand down to his wife. 'May I have the honor of this dance?'

Eleanor laughed and turned her face away. 'Oh, Nathan. Don't kid.'

'Who's kidding? Dance with me.'

He took her hand and pulled her to her feet.

'I still need to do the dishes.'

'They'll wait.'

'I didn't leave them soaking.'

'Just until the end of this song.' And he pulled her in close. She stopped arguing, set her head against his shoulder and moved with his lead. 'Am I right in thinking we haven't gone out dancing since before we got married?' Nathan asked, his lips close to her ear.

'No, that's not right,' she said. 'We've gone out since

the wedding. We just haven't gone out anywhere since Nat came here to live.'

On that note, the song ended. Nathan waited and held her close, hoping for another slow ballad. But he didn't get it. The next song was up-tempo.

Besides, she pulled away from his arms, complaining that the dishes wouldn't do themselves, and that he was breaking his promise.

The phone rang not two minutes later. Nathan was sitting right beside it, and picked it up on the second ring.

'Nathan?' A familiar man's voice.

'Yes, this is Nathan.'

'Marvin LaPlante.'

'Marvin. How have you been? I owe you an apology. I've really been remiss, I'm afraid. Not calling or writing to thank you for giving the boy a chance. I guess I thought maybe it would be more diplomatic to wait and see how things panned out. I hope that's not being too pessimistic.'

Silence on the line. Then, 'Actually, that's what I was calling about, Nathan. I just wanted to say I was sorry. That things didn't work out better. With your boy.'

'Oh, no. He lost that job?'

'You didn't know?'

'No. When did it happen?'

'Week before last,' Marvin said. 'I had no idea you

didn't know. He started calling in sick on Wednesdays. Always that same day. Seemed a little odd. He didn't seem sick when he came in the next day, but I wanted to give him the benefit of the doubt. But then the third Wednesday he called in, one of the delivery drivers saw him downtown. So, I hope you understand. I had no choice but to let him go.'

'Of course I understand, Marvin. I never meant for you to show him any deferential treatment.'

'I'm just sorry I ended up being the one to break it to you. I figured by now you would know.'

'Yes,' Nathan said. 'You would think so. Wouldn't you?'

A few minutes after Nathan hung up the phone, Eleanor came through to the living room. She took one look at him, sitting on the couch by himself, staring at nothing.

'Nathan, my goodness,' she said. 'What's wrong?'

It surprised and disappointed him. He had made a firm decision to keep his thoughts and reactions to himself. And somehow, in the empty room, before Eleanor had arrived, he had assumed he was succeeding.

'Nothing at all,' he said.

She turned to go without comment.

But Nathan thought better of his words immediately. As soon as they came out of his mouth he knew they were in serious error. No happy marriage was, in his estimation, ever based on thoughtless, automatic untruths and exclusions. And the best way to make someone unhappy, if not downright unbalanced, is to tell her that what she sees with her own eyes is not there at all.

'Eleanor,' he said, and she stopped. 'I'm sorry. I said that without thinking. It's just some trouble with Nat.'

She came closer. Sat beside him on the couch. Put her hand on top of his. 'Do you want to tell me about it?'

'Please don't be offended if I say no. It's just my answer for the moment. It's not that I don't want to share such things with you. It isn't even really to say there's anything at all I *wouldn't* share with you. It's just that I want to hear Nat's version of events before my own theories get blown too far out of proportion.'

'I understand,' she said. And kissed his cheek.

'Do you really?' he asked as she rose to leave.

'Of course.'

'You're a good woman, Eleanor.'

'Oh, nonsense.'

'You are.'

She brushed his words away with a wave of her hand and disappeared back into the kitchen.

Nathan pulled his battered old dictionary down from its resting spot on the living room bookcase.

He sat in his favorite chair, the book open in his lap. Put on his reading glasses.

Taking his good silver pen out of his pocket, he opened the drawer of the end table and found his engraved leather case of notation cards, each card embossed with his name.

He looked up his word, then made a note on a card in his most careful penmanship:

Forthcoming (adjective)
1) Frank. Candid and willing to cooperate.
2) (of a person) Open and willing to talk.

He closed the dictionary, returned it to its rightful place on the shelf, and left the note card in the middle of the pillow on Nat's bed.

Nathan stood at his dresser, emptying his pants pockets before bed. He caught a glimpse of himself in the mirror, and felt dismayed about how angry he still looked. Nathan had never liked anger. It seemed a barbaric and undignified emotion. He knew it always masked fear or hurt, and had often wished everyone could simply be sensible enough to cut out the middleman.

He caught his own eyes again in the mirror.

Was he hurt?

Behind his reflection he saw Eleanor removing the pillow shams and turning down the bed. She looked up and noticed.

'You didn't close the door,' she said. 'You always close the door.'

'I thought Nat might have something to say to me before bed.'

At least, he hoped it would be before bed. He hoped he didn't have to sleep on all of this turmoil all night.

A mere second later Nathan heard a preposterously soft knock. He looked up to see Nat standing respect-fully outside the bedroom doorway with his tail between his legs, figuratively speaking, and the note card quite literally clutched in his hand.

'Yes, Nat?' Nathan asked, in a voice that betrayed his anger.

'Maybe I could talk to you? You know. Alone.'

'All right. We'll take this in the living room.'

'OK,' Nat said. Sounding suitably panicky. 'OK, I'm just gonna say it here. You know, just spit it out. I got fired from that job you got me.'

Nathan regarded the boy's face in the soft glow that spilled in from the streetlamp outside their living room window. Neither had bothered to turn on the light.

'When did that happen?'

'A week ago Thursday LaPlante let me go.'

'And when were you planning on telling me?'

'When I got another job,' he said, fast and obviously prepared. 'I was looking real hard. And really, really hoping I would find something quick. And then I was going to tell you both things at once. Like, "Good news and bad news. The bad news is, I lost that job you got me, but the good news is I already got another one." But it didn't quite pan out. I put in two applications. The only two jobs I could find open. One was over at Watson's market, but the produce manager just told me straight out I didn't have a prayer. Said he had lots of applications from guys who didn't have a record. The guy at the pharmacy said he'd call me back. But now that sign is down, and he never called me. I even went over to the employment development department and looked in their listings. But you have to have experience for what they had.'

'When did you learn that the opening at the pharmacy had been filled?'

'Couple or three days ago the sign came down.'

'So you might as well have come to me two or three days ago.' Long, aching silence. 'What happened at the dairy?'

'It wasn't my fault. I told you, the foreman had it in for me. He said I made a mistake with the numbers on one of the trucks. That I was short. Like I'd just kept some of the milk, or drunk it, or broke some bottles or something, and I was trying to cover it up. It was a total lie, but it was my word against his. Who do you think LaPlante was gonna believe? Nobody ever believes *me*.'

'I'm beginning to see why not,' Nathan said.

Nat glanced up anxiously in the half-dark, then away

again. He did not reply. He apparently did not dare.

'What did you do for those three Wednesdays when you weren't at work? Were you with that girl?'

The boy squeezed his eyes shut. 'You talked to LaPlante. Huh? That's what I was afraid of. When I saw that note you left me.'

'When a young man is your age—'

'That wasn't it. I wasn't with Carol. I was at Little Manny's. My trainer. Training two days a week just wasn't getting it. It's just not enough. I was never gonna get where I was going. If I could train full-time I'd be ready in six or seven months. Maybe eight. But just weekends . . . It's like spinning your wheels. You might as well not be doing it at all.'

A silence followed, a silence so complete that the sound of the refrigerator motor cycling on in the kitchen seemed startlingly loud.

Nathan pulled a long, deep breath before speaking.

'I'll need a little time to think how I want to handle this situation. But one thing I do want to tell you right now. If you ever lie to me again . . . No. Wait. Let me start that sentence all over again, from the beginning. Don't ever lie to me again. Are we clear?'

'Very clear, sir.'

'My name is not sir.'

'Very clear, Nathan.'

* * *

Eleanor had already turned off the bedroom light. Nathan closed the door behind him and found his way to bed by feel.

He was surprised that Eleanor had not closed the door. She always closed the door.

Then again, he supposed she might have wanted to hear.

'Are you awake?' Nathan asked quietly.

'What kind of training? Training for what?'

'Nat wants to be a professional boxer.'

'God help us all,' Eleanor said.

'I started to tell him that if he ever lied to me again . . . See, I can't even finish the sentence now. If he lied to me again, then I would react how? Do what? Wash my hands of him? I promised him I never would. Throw him away? That would make three out of three.'

'Maybe there's a reason everybody throws him away.'

'I find it hard to believe that he irreparably offended his mother in the first four or five hours of his life.'

She didn't answer immediately. In the dark, he felt himself unclear as to whether the conversation was over. It didn't feel over.

Then she said, 'Are you trying to say that no matter what that boy does he will continue to have your support?'

'Why . . . yes. That's exactly what I'm saying.'

'So whatever kind of trouble he brings into our lives, we just have to sit here and accept it?'

'I wish you hadn't already made up your mind that he'll be nothing but trouble.'

'Goodnight, Nathan.'

'Please try to have an open mind about the boy.'

'Goodnight, Nathan.'

A pause, while he weighed the potential benefits of saying more. Then a sigh, which he tried to keep silent.

'Goodnight,' he said.

A World Without Boundaries

Nathan awoke to discover that the first good, deep snow of the season had fallen overnight.

He stood a few moments at the bedroom window, surveying the yard. All the boundaries of the world disappeared after a good snow. Nathan had always noticed that. The seemingly sturdy, dependable dividing lines between his yard and his neighbor's yard, or the sidewalk and the street, simply disappeared. Erased by white.

As if the world were advising him not to put too much faith in such markings. That perhaps these lines had never been entirely real to begin with.

This morning, though, Nathan's appreciation of the pristine scene was dulled by a graininess in his eyes and a slightly unsettled digestion, the reminders of a spotty and unsuccessful night's sleep.

He looked down at Eleanor, still sleeping.

It was early. Barely after five.

It's a happy turn of events that this is a Sunday, he thought. Everyone can have a good, hot breakfast, read the Sunday paper, and wake up slowly before tackling the big shoveling jobs.

Nathan put on his robe and made his way to the kitchen for coffee.

He found Nat already sitting at the table in the half-dark, wrapped in the hunter green quilt from his bed.

'Nat?' Nathan turned on the kitchen light and the boy winced and blinked miserably, but said nothing. 'Are you cold?'

'I'm always cold.'

'You can turn up the heat if you're cold.'

'I can?'

'Of course. That's what the heat is for.'

Nathan sat in the chair next to the boy's. Leaned in a bit closer. 'I was awake a long time last night . . .'

'Yeah, I was awake all of it.'

'. . . thinking what would be the most appropriate action to take regarding our situation.'

Nat's face grew whiter. More miserable, if such a thing were even possible. 'I think I'm going to be sick,' he said.

Nathan could tell he meant it quite literally.

'The sink, Nat.'

The boy jumped up and stumbled toward the sink,

tripping over the quilt and catching himself against the kitchen counter. When he had made it to the sink, he stood a moment, frozen, hands gripping the edge. Blessedly, nothing happened.

Nathan walked over and put his hand on the boy's back through the quilt.

'Are you OK, Nat?'

'OK, maybe I was wrong. Maybe I'm not going to be sick,' Nat said. 'Oh. Uh-oh. Maybe I am.'

'I've decided to give you your six to eight months to train.'

A ringing silence. Over Nat's head, another view of the white, boundary-free world of the side yard.

'What?'

'That's how I've decided to handle our situation.'

'You're giving me . . . giving me how? What does that mean?'

'The way I see it is this: I wasn't planning on charging you for your room and board anyway. I insisted that you hold a job on principle. I didn't want you lying around the house playing with your dog all day. It's not a healthy way to live, in my opinion. I wanted to insist that you be working hard. Accomplishing something. Putting your energy into a good direction, to build something. But I was up last night thinking. And I decided, that's exactly what you're trying to do with your training. You're trying to work hard to accomplish something that's important to you. So I withdraw my insistence that you be employed while living under my roof. For as long as eight months.'

'I can't believe you would do that for me.' Nat still faced away, over the sink and looking out the window.

'I know it means a great deal to you.'

'I . . . That's . . . I don't know what to say.'

'One thing will be challenging, though. I'm not going to give you any money. No allowance, no nickel-and-dime loans. I expect you to handle your own life, so your finances are your responsibility. You'll have no money at all. Not even bus fare.'

'I can walk to Little Manny's.'

'No money to take a girl on a date.'

'Oh,' Nat said. Deflating even as the word passed through him.

'Unless you find some way to earn a little. For example, when I was your age, I saw a morning like this one as a prime financial opportunity. I'd shovel our driveway, then sling the shovel over my shoulder and begin knocking on neighbors' doors. Shoveling is a big job, and nobody really likes it. If an able-bodied young person is standing on your doorstep offering to take it off your hands for a few dollars, the temptation can be overwhelming.'

No movement. No reply.

Then the boy spun quite suddenly. Turned to face Nathan and threw his arms around him, startling the older man. The quilt fell to the kitchen floor, forgotten.

Nathan stood with his arms still at his sides, unable to react quickly. Before he could even decide whether or not to return the embrace, Nat had picked up the quilt and scrambled away.

'I'll go get dressed,' the boy said.

'Nat. Wait. You can't knock on anybody's door at this hour.'

But it was too late. He was already gone.

No matter, Nathan thought. He would catch the boy on his way out the door.

He made a quick trip to the living room, where he turned up the thermostat by five degrees. Then he went back into the kitchen to start a much-needed pot of coffee.

Nat stuck his head back into the kitchen. 'I thought you were going to tell me to get out,' he said.

'I can understand how you would be gun-shy on that score,' Nathan replied.

He looked up, prepared to say more, but Nat had gone.

'Oh, *that's* telling him,' Eleanor said.

Nathan had been somewhat prepared for her reaction. He knew she would take exception to his thinking on the matter. But he had not expected sarcasm to come out of her mouth. So far as he could remember, she had never spoken sarcastically to him.

He sat on the edge of the bed and watched her brush

her hair in front of the mirror at the dresser. He had never seen her brush it quite so viciously before.

'It's his dream.'

'To hit people for a living? To go around with black eyes and stitches in his lip and butterfly bandages holding the skin under his eyebrow together? To hang out in seedy places with seedy people? To take bets on whether he can knock some big bruiser down before he's put in the hospital himself? That's the dream you want to support in him?'

Nathan took a deep breath and considered his words carefully.

'Every word you just said adds up to one thing and one thing only. In my mind, anyway. That it's Nat's dream, not yours. You can't tell someone to pursue their dream only if it's a good match for your own. You can't dictate *what* dream he should pursue.'

She dropped her hands to her sides and turned to face him directly.

'You went back on your word,' she said, pointing the hairbrush at him. 'Your one absolute condition for his living here was that he had to hold a job.'

'I know,' Nathan said. 'I know that.' He paused again, to gather his thoughts. It seemed that the careful selection of words had never been more crucial. 'I seem to remember that Gandhi once said his commitment was to truth, not consistency. Not that I'm comparing myself to the man in any way. Just borrowing some of his wisdom.'

Eleanor looked to the bedroom window, as if something had caught her eye. 'I thought you said he was shoveling snow for the neighbors.'

Nathan looked out the window and saw that Nat had shoveled almost to the garage in their own driveway. 'Maybe because I told him it was too early to knock on doors.'

'Maybe because it's easier to ask *you* for money than it is to ask a stranger. I always taught my son that a certain amount of work around the house was part of what it meant to live there. Especially after age eighteen.'

'I would tend to agree with that.'

'I never had these problems with my own son.'

'You had the advantage of influencing his behavior from day one.'

'So what will you say when he comes back in and tells you that will be twenty dollars?'

'Maybe that's an "if" and not a "when". Eleanor. Please don't take this the wrong way. I really don't say this in criticism of you. But I feel that I need to say it, because I believe it's true. I think the fact that you have this chip on your shoulder against Nat is what's causing the bulk of the unrest around here.'

She didn't answer.

She set her brush down on the dresser and walked out of the room.

Nathan found her in the kitchen, pouring herself a cup of coffee.

'So,' she said. 'The problem is not that I have this big nail sticking into my foot. Digging in every time I take a step. The problem is that I mind it.'

Nathan sighed. 'How is he hurting you, Eleanor? How does it even affect you? Can you please explain to me how it directly injures you if Nat goes to his trainer's every day instead of to a job on a loading dock?'

Before she could even answer, Nat appeared in the kitchen doorway, still bundled against the cold, and very much out of breath.

'Nat,' Eleanor said. 'You're dripping all over my clean floor.'

'Oh. Sorry. I did our driveway. No charge for that, of course. Now I'm going to go out and see if I can earn some money.'

He hurried out again.

Eleanor simply turned back to her coffee, and Nathan wisely decided not to say it. Not only would he avoid saying 'I told you so,' but he would avoid saying any more on the subject at all.

He tore a few paper towels off the roll and mopped up the melted snow that had dripped off Nat's winter boots.

4 March 1979

Like, Pretty Much Any Minute Now

'Oh, my goodness,' Eleanor said when she heard the front door slam. 'Nat's home for dinner. Nat hasn't been home for dinner in months.'

'I think it will be good to see him,' Nathan said. Carefully laying out his view that Nat's presence was a *welcome* surprise.

Nearly every day since last November, Nat had been gone by the time they got to the breakfast table, leaving only a dirty cereal bowl in the sink as evidence that he lived in the house at all. Eleanor always left a dinner plate in the refrigerator for him, covered in plastic wrap. Nathan often heard the boy come in as late as midnight.

He'd initially thought it was the sign of an active social life, but Nat had re-educated him. Carol always needed to be home by nine. House rules. The reason Nat stayed out so late was because his trainer, the man

Nat called Little Manny, had to wait until after closing time to let them both into the downstairs gym with his key. Training involved more than just hitting punching bags, he was told. It was an overall system of fitness, and required a lot of professional equipment.

Nathan hated to admit it, but things had finally settled down at his home, and in his marriage. Much as he wished it didn't have to be that way, the more Nat stayed gone, the more Eleanor found her way back to happiness.

'I'll set an extra place,' she said.

Nat appeared in the dining room doorway. Holding the hand of a young woman.

Nathan knew Carol was Nat's age, but she looked younger. She seemed slight and shy. Pretty. Very pretty, with her thick brown hair and freckled nose. Physically, she was much as Nat had described her. Yet somehow Nathan had expected her to be a tough girl. More fitting to Nat's element. More worldly.

Then he wondered why he would make an assumption like that. And what exactly was Nat's element, anyway?

'Nat,' Eleanor said. 'What happened to your eye?'

Nat's hand came up to touch a dark, swollen bruise. 'Oh. Nothing. I mean, it was just sparring. Little Manny's been taking me to a gym across town where I can spar with some decent fighters. Nathan? Eleanor? This is Carol.'

Nathan crossed the dining room to shake her hand.

'Pleased to meet you,' Carol muttered, so quietly that Nathan almost had to guess by context what she must have said.

'We need to talk to you both,' Nat said.

'Don't make it sound terrible,' Carol told him. Nathan noticed that her voice gained more confidence – not to mention volume – when she spoke to Nat.

'No, no, it's not,' Nat said. 'It's not a bad thing. Not at all. It's good news. And a favor. Maybe we could go sit down in the living room?'

'We were just sitting down to dinner,' Eleanor said. 'I was just setting an extra place for you, Nat. Are you both hungry? I could set two extra places.'

Nat wore a look on his face that said dinner might be an entirely foreign concept to him. At least, at this moment. As if someone had unexpectedly asked him if he wanted to go on an elephant ride or fly to Greenland.

'Um. Is there enough?'

'I guess there could be,' Eleanor said. 'I could whip up a green salad. And we could have some bread and butter on the side.'

'Carol eats like a bird, anyway,' Nat said. 'And I'm not even very hungry.'

'My goodness,' Eleanor said. 'Since when are you not hungry after a long day of training?'

When he's nervous, Nathan thought. He loses his

appetite when he's nervous, or excited, or both. But of course he did not share that thought out loud.

'We're getting married.'

'Way to blurt it out, Nat.'

'Well, how am I supposed to say it if I don't just say it?'

They had not even finished passing around the tuna casserole and dishing it on to their plates.

Nathan set down his fork. 'That *is* good news.'

'See?' Nat said, obviously to Carol, though he wasn't looking at her. 'I told you he'd be OK.'

Then Nat looked at Eleanor, who glanced up and caught him watching.

'I think it's wonderful, Nat,' she said.

Nathan had no doubt, judging from her voice, that she spoke sincerely. He only hoped she was genuinely happy for Nat, rather than simply relieved to see him forging out on his own.

'How long have you two known each other now?' Nathan asked.

'About five months.'

'That's a reasonable enough time to start making your plans, I suppose. When were you thinking of setting the date?'

'Soon,' Nat said.

'How soon?'

'Very soon.'

'Months? Weeks?'

'Pretty much right away.'

Nathan dabbed at his mouth with the cloth napkin, then set it thoughtlessly beside his plate, rather than back in his lap. As if he had finished eating. 'I'm not sure that's ideal planning, Nat.'

'I knew you'd say that. But we'll be OK.'

Carol nibbled at her casserole in the tiniest bites imaginable. Head down.

'Where will you live?'

'Well, that's the other good news. You know those little apartments over the gym? Where my trainer lives? We think there's one coming open at the end of this month. We're about seventy-five per cent sure one's coming open.'

'Sixty per cent sure,' Carol said.

'Seventy-five. Little Manny is pretty sure. He usually has the inside line on stuff like that. And they're really cheap.'

'If you saw them you'd know why,' Carol said.

'Yeah, it'll take us for ever to clean it up. And it's just one room. But we'll find a way to make it livable. And then I'll be right where I need to be to train.'

'But how will you afford any rent at all? You have no job.'

'Carol has a job. We can get by on that for a little bit. It'll be tight. But we'll manage.'

'I don't understand. Why not wait and make a solid, reasonable plan?'

'We like *this* plan,' Nat said.

They ate in silence for several minutes.

Nathan noticed that Carol glanced up every few seconds, as if taking the emotional temperature of the room.

Then Nathan remembered something he had briefly forgotten. When Nat first came in, he'd said he had good news, and also a favor. But he hadn't asked any favors. Yet.

'What was the favor you wanted to ask?'

'Carol's father wants to meet you. You know. Meet my family.'

'We want his blessing,' Carol added.

'We don't need it,' Nat said. 'She's eighteen. So we don't need it.'

'But we want it,' Carol added.

Nathan breathed an inward sigh of relief. Looming requests for favors tended to make him edgy. 'Why, of course. That's no problem at all.'

'We'll invite them over to dinner,' Eleanor said.

'Well, it's not really a *them*,' Nat said. 'It's more just a him. Carol just lives with her father.'

'We'll ask him to come to dinner,' Nathan said. 'That's no problem at all. We're happy to do it. We'll be happy to meet him. Just ask him what night he'd like to come, and then let us know. All right?'

'There's one other thing,' Nat added cautiously.

Nathan noticed that he didn't feel at all surprised. Of

course there was one other thing. Wasn't there always one other thing? Not only with Nat specifically, but with life in general.

He said nothing. Just waited for Nat to elaborate.

'He thinks you're my grandfather.'

'Because you told him I was?'

'Well. Um, yeah. Pretty much. Yeah.'

'I'm not going to lie to him.'

'But you don't have to, like, jump up and say I'm a liar and you're no blood relation. Right?'

'I suppose not. I think it's unlikely that he'll look straight into my face and say, "You really are Nat's grandfather, aren't you?"'

'Thanks,' Nat said. 'I knew I could count on you.'

After Eleanor and Carol cleared the table – Carol had insisted on helping – the women surprised Nathan by remaining in the kitchen, tackling the dishes together. The sound of running water seemed a good enough screen for a private conversation.

'She seems like a very nice girl.'

'She's great. She's one of the best things that's ever happened to me.'

'You can tell me this is none of my business if you want to, Nat. But I'm going to ask you anyway. I'm going to risk being unconscionably rude. Is Carol pregnant?'

Nat's head jerked up. He looked truly stunned.

Nathan knew, just by the look on the boy's face, that she was not.

'No. God, no. Why would you think a thing like that?'

'I just wondered why the big hurry.'

Maybe just young love, he thought. Heaven knows Nat was impetuous enough even when he wasn't in love.

'No. If she was, it would only be the second time in history that ever happened,' Nat said. 'Carol isn't like that. She's not that kind of girl. She goes to church. She was— She's going to be pure on her wedding night. You know?'

'Oh. I see,' Nathan said. Still processing how much that really explained. 'I apologize. I didn't mean to pry.'

As soon as they had gone, Eleanor said, 'We had the nicest talk. She is just a delightful girl.'

'I'm glad you like her.'

They stood in the foyer, having just closed the door behind the young pair. They hadn't even gone back into the living room to sit.

'I know it would sound terrible if I said I wonder what she sees in our Nat.'

'Actually, yes,' Nathan said. 'It would. It would be a highly uncharitable comment.'

'I know. I feel guilty for saying it. I feel guilty for *thinking* it. But, really . . . doesn't it have just a tiny ring of truth to you?'

'I hope not,' Nathan replied. 'If there's some hidden part of me that thinks like that, I'd rather not go searching for it. Maybe she sees some value in Nat that you don't.'

'She definitely loves him. There's no doubt in my mind about that. I think she has this idea that her love will be the missing piece in his life. That she's that one needed addition that will change everything for him.'

'Hmm,' Nathan said. 'That's always problematical.'

'My thought exactly,' Eleanor said.

Or Did You Used to Be Like Me?

'Just go right ahead and dig in, everybody,' Eleanor said. 'Please. Don't stand on ceremony.'

But Carol didn't move. And neither did Reginald Farrelly, her father.

'Without even saying grace?' Farrelly asked.

A moment transpired during which no one seemed to know what to say. Nathan decided he had best be the one to salvage the situation.

'All right,' he said. 'Fair enough. In honor of our guests, we'll say grace tonight. Mr Farrelly, would you care to do the honors?'

Farrelly reached out his hands in both directions. One to Eleanor. One to Nat. Nat looked at it for several beats, as though it might be poisoned, or on fire. Meanwhile Carol took Nat's hand, and also Nathan's, and Nathan held hands with his wife.

Finally, reluctantly – very reluctantly – Nat joined hands.

'Heavenly Father, we thank you for giving us your only Son, to be our savior and our Lord. Bless us all as we take this food. Hear our prayer, oh Father, for we ask you this in Jesus's name. Amen.'

'Amen,' Carol said.

A brief pause while Farrelly waited in vain for additional amens.

Eleanor broke the silence. 'OK. Now. As I was saying. Please don't stand on ceremony. Please dig in.'

Farrelly seemed to accept the invitation as though it extended to information as well as dinner. 'So. Mr McCann,' he said. 'Tell me something about your young man here. Tell me why I want him in my family. Why he's good enough to marry my daughter. See if you can make the sale.'

Nathan, who had been trying for the better part of an hour to like this huge, beefy man with the booming voice, wordlessly surrendered that goal.

Eleanor passed the gravy without comment, but in his peripheral vision Nathan could see her toss him a glance.

He looked across the table at Nat and Carol. Carol stared intensely at her plate as though she hoped she could melt right through it, creating an escape route. Nathan had not seen anyone look so genuinely miserable in quite some time. Not even Nat. Nat was becoming visibly angry. And it was not like Nat to hold his anger inside.

'This is not a sales call, Mr Farrelly. I do people's books and taxes. I don't sell young men. Nat is a grown man. He can speak for himself. If you want to know more about him, why not ask him directly? He's sitting right over there.'

A long silence. Farrelly sat back in his chair. Nathan knew he was offended. That was not a point in question. He had known, even as he spoke, that Farrelly would be. The only remaining question was whether he would cover it over or state it out loud.

Farrelly's next move was unexpected. He turned his attention to Eleanor instead. 'What about you, Mrs McCann? Do you want to tell me anything about your grandson?'

'Oh, Nat's not my grandson,' she said. Quite automatically.

Nathan knew her well enough to know she would pull her words back in and swallow them if only she could. She had spoken without thinking first, a habit of hers.

Nathan stepped in to save the moment. Again.

'This is a second marriage for Eleanor and myself. We've only been married for a little under a year.'

'Oh? You were divorcees?'

Nathan opened his mouth while still sorely tempted to say, what a brash, discourteous man you are. No wonder your poor daughter wants to get married and get out of your house. Of course, he stopped himself in time. The anxiety in the room felt genuinely palpable. Something Nathan could almost imagine spearing with his fork.

'Eleanor had been a widow for more than seventeen years when we married. I had been a widower for more than five.'

'Oops. Sorry,' Farrelly said. 'I guess I shouldn't make assumptions. You know what they say. When you assume, you make an *ass* of *you* and *me*.'

'Yes,' Nathan said. 'Quite.'

'Well, anyway, back to the question. Mrs McCann the Second? Anything you care to share about your step-grandson here?'

'No, sir, Mr Farrelly. There is not. I agree with my husband. Nat can talk. He can tell you about himself.'

Good God, Nathan thought. How on earth had things gotten so out of hand in such a short space of time? But the answer was quite simple, he realized. Carol's father was an ass. An uncharitable thought, but a thought too true to be avoided.

'Nat talks? You couldn't prove it by me.'

'Daddy,' Carol said. Her voice pitifully strained. 'Please don't embarrass me.'

'Embarrass you how, bunny? By wanting only the best for you? What part of my taking good care of you do you find embarrassing?'

'Daddy—'

'OK. Nat. Tell me about yourself. What's your church? Where did you go to high school? Any plans for college? What do you want to be when you grow up?'

Silence. Painful silence. Nat squeezed his eyes shut and kept them that way for a time. Nathan waited for him to blow. To burst under the strain like an old steam boiler or pressure cooker. He knew Nat had been getting more and more angry for some time. He also knew there was not one of Farrelly's questions that Nat would want to answer – would dare to answer. Not a simple, unloaded bit of small talk in the pack.

'I thought you talked,' Farrelly said. 'They claimed you talked.'

Did he *want* Nat to blow? Was that it?

'I'm already grown up,' Nat said. Surprisingly calmly. Though perhaps an artificial calm. No 'um' or 'uh', Nathan noticed. No 'well', followed by a comma. He spoke like someone else entirely.

Nathan felt his shoulders ease. Good boy, he thought. He wished Nat would meet his gaze so he could communicate that praise with his eyes. But Nat continued to stare at the tablecloth.

'And I went to high school at North Park,' he added.

Technically true. Until the week of his fifteenth birthday, he had attended North Park High School, ten blocks from his grandmother's home.

'Graduated, I assume?'

'Well . . . I'm not a drop-out. If that's what you mean.'

'What I mean is, did you graduate North Park?'

'No. After that I . . . studied somewhere else.'

'But you graduated.'

'I have my GED,' Nat said quietly.

'Now why would you get a General Educational Development test when you could just finish high school?'

Nathan was just about to step in. To rescue the boy. Who, he felt, was holding up remarkably well. But he never got the chance.

Nat leaped to his feet, hitting the table hard with his thighs, and knocking into his plate, sending a wash of beef gravy spilling off on to the tablecloth. In fact, the plate flew several inches. Nathan was left unclear as to whether Nat had purposely pushed or flipped the plate. It had all happened so fast.

'None of your damn business why I do what I do,' he shouted. 'Why are you asking me questions like that? Why don't you ask me if we love each other? If I'll take good care of her? Why don't you ask me about something that matters? That stuff you asked me is none of your damn business. And it's none of your damn business if I marry your daughter—'

'Now you—'

'I'm not finished yet. You've been talking all night, old man. Now it's my turn. Carol's eighteen. She can do what she wants. You can't stop us. As a matter of fact—'

'Nat, don't,' Carol said. Tugging violently at his sleeve.

'I'm telling him.'

'Don't, Nat. Please.'

'Telling me what?' Farrelly asked.

The room went deadly quiet again. Nat stood in front of his place at the table, looking awkward and uncomfortable now that his rant seemed to have abandoned him.

'Carol and I are already married,' he said. 'We went down to city hall the day before yesterday.'

Farrelly looked at his daughter, who refused to meet his eyes. 'Is that true, bunny? Is what he said true?'

Nothing at all for a time. She looked as though she might be about to cry. Or maybe she was crying already, but just trying hard to hide it.

Then she nodded almost imperceptibly.

Farrelly rose. Wiped his mouth on his napkin. Threw it down on the table. Half of it landed on his gravy-soaked beef.

He took a step closer to Nat, and they stood nose to nose, quite literally, for an awkward length of time. It might only have been two or three seconds, but to Nathan it seemed long. Nat was a few inches shorter, but he rose to his toes to face the big man, and stood his ground unswervingly.

In the painful silence, Nathan noticed how much Nat had bulked up. He was wearing a short-sleeved tee, and his chest and arms had changed so much that Nathan worried the boy might be using steroids. Or, more immediately, that he might be just about to use some of what he had been learning.

'I knew you were nothing but trouble,' Farrelly said quietly.

Nathan saw the boy's hands clench into fists.

He jumped to his feet. 'Nat!' he said sharply. And it seemed to interrupt the immediate danger of the moment. 'Nat. Think very carefully before acting.'

He watched the boy's fists turn back into hands again, and he let out a long breath of relief.

Farrelly peeled away from the confrontation. 'Don't come home tonight,' he said, pointing roughly at his daughter. 'In fact, don't come home. Period.'

'What about my things?' She was now crying openly.

'I'll have them boxed up and sent over here. Don't bother walking me to the door, anyone. I'll see myself out.'

'I'll get your coat,' Nathan said.

Nathan found the young man in the kitchen, sitting at the table alone, head in hands. He didn't know where Carol and Eleanor had gone, and he didn't ask.

He sat across from Nat and waited. Waited for Nat to choose his moment to speak.

'He's such an asshole,' Nat said miserably, his head still in his hands.

'That's not the exact choice of phrasing I would have

used. But he is a horrible man. No one is disputing that.'

'He was trying to make a fool of me. He thinks I'm not good enough for her. And he was trying to get me to say the things that would prove it.'

'Oh. So you think he's right.'

'No! I don't. Why would you say that?'

'You just said that if you had answered his questions, you would have proved it.'

'I didn't mean it like that. Stop putting words in my mouth. He was trying to make me look like a jerk. I don't care what you say. I don't care if you think I'm wrong. I know him. I know what he was doing.'

'I don't think you're wrong. I agree. He was trying to make you look bad. I just think, if you had been civil, he would have failed.'

Nat looked up at him for the first time. 'Why shouldn't I tell him off? Somebody has to. Somebody should have a long time ago. He deserves it. Why should I have been civil?'

'Because if you had been civil, *he* would have been the one to look bad. Not you. This way you appear to validate him. You give him all the ammunition he needs. And you hurt Carol with the way you handled things, too. When are you going to learn to act in your own best interests? In spite of what your emotions tell you to do?'

No answer. Nat just stared at him for several seconds. But the look on his face was not what Nathan might have expected. Nathan found it hard to put words to the look. Curiosity, maybe. Genuine interest.

'Were you always like this?' Nat asked. With no derogatory note in his voice.

'I'm not sure I understand the question.'

'Did you always handle things right, and act reasonable? Or did you used to get mad like me, but you learned to control it?'

Nathan thought a moment before answering. It was a question no one had ever asked, and he had never considered. So he didn't answer off the top of his head. He wanted to be careful to get it right the first time.

'I think it's just part of who I am,' he said, in time.

'Well, maybe this is just part of who *I* am. And maybe we just don't change.'

'We *can* change,' Nathan said. 'We just have to want to. First we have to believe we need to. And that it's time.' Silence. 'Now maybe you'd better go comfort your wife.'

'I think we'll have to stay the night.'

'I think you'll have to stay the month. Let's be honest with each other.'

'Is it OK?'

'I suppose it's going to have to be,' Nathan said.

A Very Good Question, Actually

Nathan sat at the breakfast table with Eleanor and Carol. Nat, of course, was long gone, as always. The topic of conversation was the weather. The heat, which was already quite pronounced at only eight o'clock in the morning.

Nathan was explaining to Carol why, in the nearly fifty years he'd lived in this house, he'd never bothered to have air conditioning installed. After all, the number of days per year the house felt uncomfortably warm could usually be counted on one hand. And he could only remember a handful of times it had ever gotten as hot as this.

'Boy,' Carol said, gazing down into her cornflakes. 'Who would have thought . . . when we moved in . . . that we'd still be here by August?'

Nathan saw a missed beat in Eleanor's movements as

she raised her cereal spoon to her lips. It looked something like a flaw in the playback of an old film.

'Oh, I'm not sure it's so surprising,' she said.

It seemed like a moment of tension, but it passed on its own, and Nathan picked up his paper again. Began looking for a letter to the editor that a colleague had written, and had asked Nathan to read. It didn't seem to be in that morning's edition. But, while looking for it, Nathan immediately got caught up in one of the other letters.

'I know you must be sick to death of us by now,' Carol said, breaking the silence, and Nathan's concentration. It was clear to Nathan that Carol had directed her comment toward Eleanor, and not him.

'Oh, now, honey, you know I don't mind having you here.'

'No, I know you don't,' she replied, quite sincerely. 'I know you don't get sick of me. Just Nat.'

Silence, which hung over the table. Nathan tried to get back to his reading, but couldn't seem to absorb the words. He had to keep reading the same paragraph over again, a pattern he found annoying. At least, on the rare occasions it happened.

In time Carol got up, washed her bowl at the sink, and left the room to get ready for school.

Eleanor looked up at Nathan immediately. 'I never said a word against Nat in front of Carol.'

'I doubt you needed to.'

'What is that supposed to mean?'

'It means your feelings come through loud and clear whether you express them in words or not.'

'Maybe Nat's been complaining to her that I'm not patient enough with him.'

'Maybe. But whether he's said anything or not, I'm sure she can't help noticing.'

Eleanor stood, cleared the breakfast dishes into the sink, and began to run the sink full of hot, soapy water.

'You know his eight months are up,' she said.

'Are they? No, actually, I hadn't realized that.'

'On November twenty-fifth you told him he could have *as long as* eight months. Less would have been better, of course. That took us to July twenty-fifth. *Last* month. This is August sixth. I've been wanting to bring it up, but it's such a sore subject with us.'

'Oh, so that's what you've been wanting to bring up. I sensed there was something. You're awfully exacting. Did you write down the date?'

'I didn't have to. It was important to me, so I remembered it. Don't you think it's time he got a job?'

'He's actually gone from the house a lot more this way than he would be if he were working a forty-hour week.'

'Yes, but the forty-hour week would *pay*. And then they could get their own place.'

'Well, in any case,' Nathan said, giving up and setting down his paper with a sigh, 'he's not going to quit his training and get a job. Then the whole thing would have been for nothing. He's going to wrap up his training and get a fight. A professional fight. And he'll try to make some money that way.'

'Well, then why *doesn't* he?' she said, her voice rising alarmingly. 'He was so anxious to finish his training and go pro. What is he waiting for?'

Nathan thought the question over briefly before answering. 'That's actually a very valid question. I'll have a talk with him and see what I can find out.'

After breakfast, Nathan knocked gently on Nat and Carol's bedroom door. No answer. He called Carol's name, then cautiously stuck his head in. But apparently Carol had already left for school.

He made his way to the living room, where he wrote a note for Nat on one of his name-embossed cards.

Nat,
Please come in and wake me tonight, even if it's late,
so we can talk.
Nathan

He left the note in the middle of Nat and Carol's bed, not knowing whose pillow was whose.

'What? What did I do?'

'You didn't do anything, Nat. I just wanted to ask

about the progress of your training. Is it taking longer than you expected?'

They sat at the dining room table, Nat slumped defensively in his chair. The only illumination was a spill of light from the kitchen. Nathan had carefully closed both bedroom doors. To avoid disturbing Carol and Eleanor, and for privacy. He wondered briefly if he would return to his own bedroom to find that Eleanor had opened the door again to listen.

It still felt warm in the house, though it was well after midnight. All the windows had been left open a crack, but the breeze they allowed in barely felt cool.

'No. It's going great. I'm in great shape. I'm totally ready. I could get in the ring on a moment's notice.'

'That's good. I'm glad to hear that. Now, as far as time goes, we had estimated—'

'I know, Nathan. I know. You think I don't know? I know my eight months is up. I knew on the day it was up. I knew every day before it was up that it was about to be up. You don't have to tell me I'm out of time. I know.'

A long pause that felt oddly comfortable to Nathan. He had grown to enjoy conversations in the half-dark, though he was not sure why. Also, he was comfortable in knowing that he would probably not need to say much more. The lid had been pried off the jar, and Nat would now do most of the work on his own.

'You know what's holding me back,' Nat said. 'Don't you?'

'No. I don't.'

'Really? You can't even imagine? You can't even guess?'

'Fear?'

Nat snorted laughter. 'Fear? Are you kidding me? I *dream* of getting in that ring for a real fight. I think about it every minute of every day. I'm not afraid of it. I want it more than anything.'

'OK. Tell me what's holding you back.'

'Money.' Another wordless, half-dark space to breathe. 'Look. I swear I didn't know this when I said I needed eight months. I swear to you. I thought I could just train and then get a pro fight. But Little Manny wants me to fight amateur for a year. We've already been doing some sparring across town with some guys he knows, and I thought that would be enough, but he says it's not. He says most guys he'd say three years, but because I work so hard . . . Anyway, so I need money to stay afloat while I'm doing the amateur thing. And then after that Little Manny could get me a fight any time. All I have to do is say the word. Only it'd probably be in New York or Atlantic City. How are we supposed to get there? Everything costs money. It takes money to launch a career in the ring. Damn it,' he said, and put his head in his hands briefly. It looked to Nathan as though he were trying to wring out his own head. 'I'm just kicking myself because I knew this was coming. I feel like that idiot who's painting his floor and ends up getting himself stuck in the corner. I guess I just kept thinking something would happen between then and now. Like some big miracle or something. I don't know what I was thinking.'

'We should calmly look at possible solutions,' Nathan said.

'You're better at that calmly thing than I am.'

'Could you get a job for a few months and earn enough money?'

'Sure. Only after a few months off from my training I wouldn't be in shape to fight any more.'

'Hmm. That's true, I suppose. Could you get somebody to invest in you?'

'It would have to be somebody who really believes in me. And let's face it. The only people who believe in me are you and Carol. But you don't believe in loaning money, and she doesn't have any. The only time you ever loaned me money was for bus fare when I got a job. A couple nights ago I was lying awake thinking about it. Thinking maybe this was the same sort of situation. But I know you can't do that now. First of all, it's a lot more than bus fare. Second of all, Eleanor would shoot you.'

'Let's just keep this to you and me for the moment. Now, this is not to say that I intend to invest in you. But anytime anybody comes to me with a potential investment, I ask a lot of questions.'

'OK. Go ahead and ask.'

'How much money are we talking about?'

'I really have no idea.'

'That's not the ideal investment pitch.'

'I didn't know I'd be pitching tonight! I thought I'd just go home and go to sleep, like any other night.'

'That's true. I'm sorry.'

'I could talk to Little Manny and we could try to figure it out. It's hard, though. I mean, we don't know exactly how many out-of-town fights we want to schedule right away. As many as we can afford. If we have more money we'll get more good equipment, if not we'll get by on what we got. I'm not sure there's any magic number.'

'OK. We'll put the number aside for now, too. How would you pay me back if you didn't win?'

'I'm going to win.'

'Wrong answer. I'm not asking what you think will happen. I'm asking what kind of Plan B you've formulated, in case you're wrong for any reason.'

'Oh. Plan B. I hate Plan B. Because it makes it sound like you don't believe in your own Plan A. I put everything into Plan A. I think you get more of what you want that way.'

'But your potential investor might be more cautious.'

'Yeah, right. OK. You know, what difference does this make, anyway? You can't loan me the money and you know you can't. Eleanor would bust a gut.'

'So, what is your Plan B?'

In the pause, Nathan could hear the young man breathing. As if every breath were a sigh.

'If my career didn't work out the way I planned for some reason, then I would get a job and pay my investor back a little bit at a time. I mean, if it was you. If it was a professional investor, I'd just say, "Oh, well, you know. You took your chances." But nobody's gonna invest in me right now but you, because I'm unproven. If I could get in there and win, and look good, I might get offers.'

'OK. Let's get some sleep and we'll let these ideas mellow a bit. I'll need some time to think.'

'Oh. Yeah. Right. Of course.'

'How would you feel about my talking to your trainer?'

'Little Manny? Sure. He could tell you a lot about what we need.'

'I meant more for an analysis of what I would be investing in. I was just thinking, if I invested in any other boxer, I'd want to know that he was good.'

'Fine with me.'

A silence. And – was it only Nathan's imagination? – a spreading sense of peace. As if something heavy had been set down at last. As if the whole room breathed a sigh of relief.

'Nathan? Now that we've talked all this out . . . maybe I could take a couple days off? I really need a couple days off. I haven't had a break in months.'

'Of course. If you need to take a break, you just take a break.'

'*Now* you tell me,' Nat said.

* * *

When Nathan returned to his bedroom, the door had been opened.

Nathan closed it behind him, and found his way to bed in the dark.

'I trust you heard all of that,' he said, not even trying to keep his voice down.

'I have a say in this. It's our retirement. Not just yours. I know I don't work, and I know you've been putting aside for retirement for years, since long before we got married. But still, in a marriage, what's mine is yours and vice versa. And it will affect my quality of life when you retire. Just as much as it will affect yours. I'd hate to think you'd make a decision like that without my input.' Her voice sounded strained, Nathan thought, yet not exactly angry. At least, not in the way he expected. In fact, she sounded like she might be about to cry.

'It would only be a small percentage of what we've saved,' he said.

'That doesn't address what I just said to you.'

'Of course I'll discuss it with you. I discuss everything with you. I'm not going to commit money without considering your thoughts and feelings on the matter. And I would certainly hope you wouldn't decide to try to stop me without considering mine. Now, you're borrowing trouble here, Eleanor, because I haven't even decided what I'm going to do yet. Let's just get some sleep, and let the matter rest for now.'

But Nathan didn't sense a lot of sleep, or even rest, in his immediate future.

'It's always going to be like this, isn't it?' she asked, startling him.

It might have been as little as five minutes later. Or half an hour might have transpired. Nathan found it significant that she spoke at full volume, as though the conversation had never lagged. As if it had never occurred to her that he might be asleep.

Of course, she was right.

He noticed something else about her voice. She seemed to speak without energy now. As if all the fight had gone out of her.

'Nat will always be part of my life, if that's what you mean. What do you really want in this situation, Eleanor?'

While he was waiting for her reply, Nathan watched the shadow on the wall cast by the tree outside their bedroom window. Watched it sway the tiniest bit in the warm breeze.

'I want what I thought I was getting when I married you.'

'You knew about Nat before we were married.'

'I guess I thought your relationship with Nat would be more like my relationship with my grown son.'

'Your son wasn't incarcerated, so you must have known there would be some differences.'

'I just want my life back the way it was before.'

'He'll move out in a couple of months.'

'I doubt it. But even if he does, some disaster will drop him back here. And even if it doesn't, he'll have some disaster wherever he is, and he'll manage to involve you. And you'll jump right in and get involved. And nothing I say will stop you.'

'I'll ask you again, Eleanor. What do you really want in this situation? What would fix this for you?'

'That's the problem,' she said. 'I'm just not sure any more. I'm losing hope that it's fixable, Nathan.'

The Debatable Value of Arguing with Life

Nathan crossed the parking lot to the little apartment over the gym, already wilting in the heat. The sun baked the back of his neck, making him wish he had worn a hat. He had always prided himself on being able to gauge the temperature within a degree or two of accuracy. Ninety-two, he decided. Maybe even ninety-three.

The stairwell felt airless and stifling as he climbed.

He stood in front of Manny Schultz's apartment, listening to the soft, muffled sound of television dialogue filtering through the door.

Then he knocked.

A call from inside. 'Yeah? Who's there?'

'Nathan McCann.'

'Meaning what? I don't know no Nathan whatever-you-said.'

'Nat's . . . guardian.'

Silence. Then the door opened a crack. Nathan was startled to see the man's head appear at about the level of an average man's chest. At almost the exact same moment, Nathan's sinuses caught the assault of stale smoke. Cigar and cigarette both, from the odor of it. He tried not to twist his face into an insulting mask of judgment.

'Oh. Nathan. Yeah. That Nathan. Nat's Nathan. So. What? Are you pissed at me about something?'

'No. I just want your advice.'

The tiny man snorted rudely. It took Nathan a moment to realize that the sharp, offensive sound was actually a type of laughter.

'Sorry. Didn't mean to laugh in your face. Just that, people don't come to me asking for advice. Not much, anyway. 'Cept about boxing.'

'This *is* about boxing, actually.'

Nathan had always found it hard to stand in the baking heat. Not even so much to walk in the heat, but to stand still. A circulation issue, he assumed. It always made him feel slightly woozy. Today was no exception.

'Aren't you kind of on the old side?' the little man asked.

'*Nat's* boxing. I was hoping you'd give me some advice on my role in Nat's boxing career.'

'Ah,' Manny said. Still speaking through a several-inch

opening in the door. 'Now you're starting to make some sense.'

'No, I was making sense all along. It's just that you're only now beginning to understand me.'

'Yeah, yeah, yeah. Come on in.'

He opened the door wide. Nathan did not step in.

Inside he saw beer cans lying on their sides. A torn couch which must have doubled as the only bed in the place, still made up with a pillow and blankets. An empty pizza box lying open on the floor, grease-stained and littered with crumbs. Two punching bags of different varieties, one hanging from the ceiling, one suspended from a metal stand.

An air conditioner strained and blew from its jury-rigged place in the window.

And, in spite of it, that horrible tobacco stench.

'Maybe we could talk outside.'

'You're kidding, right? It's like a hundred degrees out there. At least in here we got the air conditioner going. It's crap, but it's better than nothing. I mean, at least in here it's not a hundred. Ninety, maybe. But not a hundred.'

Nathan did not answer. And he still did not move.

'Oh, wait,' Little Manny said. 'I get it. You're a neat freak.'

'More of a non-smoker,' Nathan said.

'OK, have it your own way. We can sit out on the fire escape. At least that way we'll be in the shade.'

* * *

'Nat didn't seem to be able to provide what you might call a comprehensive summary of how much money he's going to need.'

'Yeah, well, it's not an exact science. I mean, you work with what you got.'

Nathan felt the warm grating of the fire escape under his buttocks and the heels of his hands. He looked down at the parking lot. At his own car. He had never thought to appreciate the joys of a neighborhood with lawns and hedges and trees. It had seemed so automatic. As if everyone lived the way he did.

He wondered briefly what it would feel like to look out over the urban decay of downtown every day of your life. Would it change a person?

'How can I know whether I'm willing to lend him the money if I don't even know how much money we're talking about?'

'I guess I could work you up a rough estimate. Like, if we had this much we could do just these basics, but if we had this much more we could do this much more. That type of a thing. Like I say, you work with what you got. But you gotta have something. I mean, right now he doesn't even have enough for decent trunks and a robe and good shoes and stuff. Without that, he's gonna look like somebody's poor relation walking into the ring. They'll laugh at him. The handicap'll be too much for him. You know. To his psyche.'

Nathan was surprised to hear the word 'psyche' come out of Little Manny's mouth. It seemed out of keeping with the rest of his vocabulary. Then he chided himself for being judgmental.

He looked at the little man's hands during the pause in the conversation. Trying to decide if he was actually suffering from some type of dwarfism. But his fingers, stained orange from tobacco, looked perfectly proportioned.

'I can't imagine that trunks and a robe would be too expensive.'

'That ain't the half of it. It's the transportation. Plus meals and lodging on the road. Most of these fights'll be out of town. New York, especially for the amateurs. Atlantic City mostly after he goes pro. Or even Vegas. And it costs more to get to Vegas.'

'Here's what I really want you to tell me. We can worry later about what it will cost. Right now I need to ask you if he's good enough.'

'No,' Little Manny said.

'No, I may not ask you that?'

'No, he's not good enough.'

'You don't think he's good enough to win?'

'Not really, no.'

They sat in silence for a beat or two. Nathan could feel perspiration trickle down under his collar. He wasn't sure how to respond.

'I mean, don't get me wrong,' the little man said. 'I'm

not saying he's bad. I'm not even saying he's not good. Only, you didn't ask me if he was good. You asked me if he was good *enough*.'

'What about him is good? And what about him is not good enough?'

'His attitude is great. Just what it needs to be. It'd be the wrong attitude for just about anything else. But for a fighter, he's really got the frame-of-mind thing nailed. He has a lot of passion, you know? Anger, really. But he's learning to use it right. Plus, he's not afraid of hard work. Some guys, they got all the talent in the world. But they just won't buckle down to the training. It's like they just don't have the discipline. But Nat, boy, he works like a Trojan. I tell him, "You can knock off now," and he just wants to keep going. Now, here's the thing, though. He doesn't have enough of that natural talent. A lot of it is about instincts, you know? The competition is real stiff. Real high. You really gotta have both. Oh, he could win a pro fight or two on sheer stubbornness. But he's not a natural. And he never will be.'

Nathan took a minute to absorb the little man's words.

'I'm surprised,' he said.

'Why? You figured he'd be great?'

'Not necessarily. But I suppose I didn't expect you to be so candid with me. And I'm surprised that Nat would even let me come over here and talk to you if he knew that's what you were going to say.'

'Oh, Nat doesn't know I feel that way.'

'You never told him you don't think he's good enough?'

'Nope. I never told him that. Probably never will. One, he never asked. And he probably never will. Two, he wouldn't never hear me anyway. He hears what he wants to hear, just like anybody else that wants something real bad. There's two things you can do with a kid like that. Way I see it. You can burst his bubble. Or you can wait and let life burst it. Let life do the dirty work for you. If you burst it he'll hate you for ever. And he'll never really believe he couldn't have made it. He'll always think it's your fault for standing in his way. For not having more faith in him. Now, life. When life bursts your bubble, well. It's a little harder to argue with life.'

'I see people argue with life all the time,' Nathan said.

'Betcha never see 'em win, though.'

Nathan breathed deeply and rose to his feet. He could feel the dampness of his shirt as he moved. It would be good to get back in the car and turn on the fan.

'Thank you, Manny. That was just the advice I needed.'

'Yeah, hey. Don't tell the kid I talked you out of backing him, huh?'

'You didn't talk me out of backing him. You talked me into it.'

'I did? Huh. Well, what do you know?'

*   *   *

The little man accompanied Nathan to the top of the sweltering stairwell.

As he was walking down the stairs, he heard Little Manny call after him. 'Hey. I bet you were the guy gave him those sweet gloves. That was you, wasn't it? That first time, I mean. Way back when.'

Nathan stopped and turned back. 'Yes,' he said. 'That was me.'

'Yeah. I knew it. I knew that kid didn't have two people in his life that would treat him so good.'

Also Literally Terrible

'What would you say if I asked you to choose?' Eleanor asked upon waking.

'Oh. That would be a terrible thing to ask of me.'

'Hypothetically.'

'It would even be hypothetically terrible.'

Nathan lay in bed with his hands interlocked behind his head. Thinking that the ceiling needed paint much more urgently that he had realized.

He knew better than to speak of paint out loud. He knew how it might be construed. As if he weren't listening to his wife, or didn't care. Or didn't find her dissatisfaction important and troubling.

In reality, it was quite the opposite. The more troubling an emotional situation became, the more Nathan found himself tempted to focus on the condition of the paint on the bedroom ceiling.

'That's what I thought,' she said.

'What's what you thought?'

'That there's no clear indication you would put me first. A wife needs to feel she comes first. Just the fact that you didn't answer right away says so much.'

'Are you sure you want me to answer the question at all?'

'I think so. I'll hate it, I know. But I guess it's time to hear it, anyway.'

'My grandfather had two brothers,' Nathan said. With very little pause. Very little preparation. It turned out he had been more prepared than he realized. 'My two great-uncles. Christopher and Daniel. They got along very well when they were younger. But then they tried to go into business together. And it didn't go well. So they ended up feuding. And this was very hard for my grand-father, because he liked to have the whole family over for Thanksgiving and Christmas. Everybody thought it would be the hardest thing in the world to decide. But he had no trouble with it at all. He said, "Christopher can come to Thanksgiving. Daniel will have to stay home." Just like that. Everyone was shocked. But I think I might have been the only one to ask why. He said it was because Christopher was willing to share the day with Daniel, but Daniel wasn't willing to share the day with Christopher.

'Nat would never ask me to choose between the two of you, Eleanor. Not even hypothetically. He never had anything against you. Never said so much as a bad word about you. He tried so hard to make you like him. He tried so hard to coexist.'

Eleanor didn't answer. Then again, Nathan hadn't expected her to.

Part Six

Nathan Bates

9 August 1979

Fragile

'So, how long has that been sitting in your window?' Nat asked the tiny, elderly woman in the antique store.

'How long?' A thick accent, but he wasn't sure what kind. Russian or Polish, or whatever accent you have if you're from Yugoslavia or Romania or some such place as that. 'What matters how long?'

'I'm just trying to figure out why I never saw it before. I run by here every day. Did you just put it in the window today?'

'No. Not today. Many days.'

'But I run by here every day. With my dog.' He pointed through the window to the spot where Feathers was sitting, tied to a parking meter.

'You just don't see,' the old woman said.

Nat gingerly set the little white, gold-edged china bud

vase on the counter between them. As if it were a raw egg.

'Very fragile,' the old woman said.

'You're telling me.'

Nat examined it more closely under the light. His heart was pounding. He couldn't be sure it was exactly the same. Not from memory. Not unless he could actually hold the two side by side. And he didn't figure he ever could, because the broken one had disappeared. Whether it had been thrown away or just buried away, Nat didn't know. But it seemed clear that Eleanor did not care to look at it again.

What if it wasn't exactly the same? Just close? It seemed to him it would be close enough, anyway. It would fill the gaping hole left open in her bud vase department. Unless she had so completely memorized the look of the original one that she would only see the differences.

Besides, even if this *was* exactly the same, it still wasn't the same. It wasn't from her grandmother's house.

But it looked to be such a perfect twin. It was like some kind of resurrection. Like that mythical do-over you always want from life and never get. And everybody is so quick to assure you that you never will.

Trying to decide was literally giving him a headache.

'How much?'

'Seventeen dollar fifty cent.'

'Ouch.'

So far he'd only managed to earn twenty dollars doing odd jobs before and after his training. And every bit of that had gone into the ring fund. He was saving up to buy Carol a real ring.

'Would you hold it for me?'

'Only with deposit.'

Nat frowned.

'Will you hold it just till the end of today?'

'Yeah, yeah. All right. One day I hold.'

'I think you should cash out the ring fund,' Carol said.

They sat on the patio of the Frosty Freeze, sharing the burger that Carol was allowed to have for free on her lunch break. She had pushed all the fries over to his side of the white paper.

Nat could hear Feathers whimpering all the way from the stop sign on the corner, frustrated at always having to be tied up so far from French fries.

'I can't do that.'

'Why can't you?'

'It's not a piggy bank. That money is for one thing only. It goes in and it doesn't come out until we have enough for a ring.'

'Look. Nat. By the time you win your first fight you're only going to have about fifty dollars in the ring fund. But then, with your prize money, you can afford a whole ring and then some. So what was the point of the fifty dollars?'

'I guess. But I still feel funny doing it.'

'I'd rather have a ring you buy me with your first big prize money. Besides, I think doing something for Eleanor would be really important. She is *so* not happy.'

'Right,' Nat said. 'I noticed that.'

He arrived home that afternoon at nearly five, carrying his precious little parcel.

Nathan should have been home by then. And Eleanor should have been making dinner in the kitchen. It was hard for Nat's brain to process the scene. What did it even mean, if it was nearly five o'clock and no food was being prepared?

The den door was closed, which it never was, not even when Nathan was in there reading.

Somehow the quiet in the house felt weirdly exaggerated. Not that Nat could ever have explained – to himself or anyone else – how one quiet could seem quieter than another. Still, this silence was different in a way he couldn't quite bring into focus.

'Eleanor?' he called.

A long enough pause to convince him that nobody was home. Had there been some kind of emergency?

Then, 'I'm in the bedroom, Nat.'

Nat walked to Nathan and Eleanor's open bedroom doorway and stood with his shoulder leaning against the jamb.

She had a suitcase open on the bed, and was

meticulously folding dresses and packing them. Two more suitcases sat on the rug near the window. He watched her in silence for a time, not knowing what question to ask first. She had been crying. That much was obvious just from her face. But he couldn't ask about that. Her emotions were surely none of his business.

'Are you going somewhere?'

She looked up at him and smiled sadly. 'Yes. My son is coming to pick me up.'

'I didn't know you had a son.'

'Really? Didn't you, really? I guess we don't know each other all that well. Yes, I have a grown son.'

'How old is he?'

'Forty-one.'

A long silence.

Nat felt as though he were taking steps in shifting sand. He wanted to ask no more questions, but there were so many more at hand, just screaming to be asked. Where's Nathan? When are you coming back? Did somebody die? Should I feel any less scared than I already do?

'I brought you a present,' he said.

'Me?' she asked distractedly. As if she hadn't understood.

He crossed the room and handed her the box. The old woman in the antique store had wrapped the vase in cotton padding and placed it in a sturdy box for him.

Because he had been afraid he couldn't get it home in one piece.

'I don't understand,' she said. 'There's no occasion.'

'I know.'

'Thank you. That's very sweet. I'll take it with me.'

'No, open it,' Nat said. 'Open it now.'

He couldn't imagine spending so much money and making such a difficult decision only to miss the look on her face, that priceless evidence of how his gift had been received.

'Well. All right. If you think that's best.'

She took the lid off the box, moved the cotton padding aside, and burst into tears.

'I'm sorry,' Nat said. 'I didn't mean for it to make you cry. Is it exactly like the other one? Or is it just close?'

He wished he had a handkerchief, or even a tissue to offer her. He also wished he were somewhere else. It was hard for him to hold still while someone cried.

'It's a very close relative,' she said, her voice breaking. She turned it over and examined its bottom. 'It's made by the same manufacturer, and it's the same design. It's just a slightly smaller one.'

'Do you like it?'

Before she could answer, they heard a car horn honk in the driveway.

'Oh,' she said. 'My son is here. I have to go.'

'When are you coming back?'

She turned her back to him and hurried to the bed,

where she tucked the little vase safely between dresses, and snapped the last suitcase shut. Her back still to him, she said, 'You might want to ask Nathan about that.'

'Where *is* Nathan?'

'In the den, I think.'

'I'll help you carry your bags,' he said.

Just as he was lifting them off the rug, straightening himself with a heavy bag in each hand, he looked up to see Eleanor suddenly right in front of him. Not even a step away. He tried to hide the fact that her closeness alarmed him. He held very still.

She reached out and held his head in both of her hands, then leaned in and gave him a firm kiss on the forehead. Her lips felt dry and cool.

Before he could even close his jaw again, she had turned and hurried out of the room.

Nat sat on the window seat in the living room for nearly four hours, watching the light fade and waiting for Carol to come home from school. Now and then he would glance at the den door, hoping for some kind of change. Even if Nathan would just turn on a light or make a noise, he would feel so much better.

But nothing changed.

'Did you knock?' Carol asked. First thing.

'Well . . . no. Of course not.'

'Why not?'

'Well, I don't know. Maybe he wants to be alone. Maybe he doesn't *want* anybody to knock.'

'Oh, Nat. Don't be silly. I've never seen you like this.'

'Like what?'

'Like *this*,' she said. As though it should be obvious to him. But it wasn't. Not at all.

She charged over to the den door and rapped softly. 'Nathan? Are you all right?'

'Yes, I'm fine,' his muffled voice replied. 'I'll be out in just a few minutes.'

'There,' she said to Nat. 'See? Is that so hard? Come on. I'll make us scrambled eggs for dinner. It's the only thing I know how to cook.'

Nat sat at the kitchen table with Nathan, watching him stare at the plate of scrambled eggs and toast that Carol had left for him. It seemed clear that he was not hungry. But he had accepted the dinner when Carol offered it. Maybe because it would have seemed rude to refuse such a thoughtful gesture.

Carol had gone off to take a shower and go to bed. She had an early morning facing her. Nat actually felt relieved, because of a strange sense that he could talk to either Carol or Nathan individually, but not both at the same time.

'Is this about me?' Nat asked, when he finally got up the nerve.

'No. It's not. It's about her.'

'Oh. OK. Good. I mean, not good, but . . . You know what I mean.'

A silence, during which Nathan ate a bite of toast.

Then, 'She couldn't accept you for yourself. Somehow her resentments were more important. She wasn't willing to be separated from them.'

'So, it *was* about me.'

'No,' Nathan said. 'It was about her.'

'I don't get it.'

'I suppose most people wouldn't,' Nathan said with a sigh. 'Most people prefer to think that their resentment is entirely the fault of the person they resent, and that twisted logic seems to make sense in their minds. But it makes no sense to me at all. It's like saying it's your fault if I shoot you, because the gun is aiming at you. It completely disregards who's doing the aiming. But it's a popular point of view. Probably because it's so much easier. It relieves you of the burden of any and all self-examination. You don't have to understand it now, Nat. Just file it away with everything else I've said that sounds like a foreign language to you. Maybe you'll learn a new language some day. Some people do. It depends how important it is to them to see things differently. I thought Eleanor was . . . I'm not sure how to finish that sentence. I don't know what I thought Eleanor was. But in any case, I was wrong.'

'I'm sorry, Nathan.'

'Yes,' Nathan said. 'I'm sorry, too.'

'We'll be out soon.'

Nathan looked up from his plate. Suddenly. And maybe for the first time. 'What do you mean, Nat?'

'I mean, I'll get a job or something. Maybe part-time, I don't know. But we'll find someplace to live. Like we should have a long time ago.'

In the silence that followed he felt the old man's hand rest on his arm.

'Nat. Eleanor is gone. You may stay as long as you like.'

'Seriously?'

'I enjoy your company,' Nathan said.

What he didn't say, Nat thought, is that if they moved out it would leave him completely alone. Then again, he really didn't need to say it.

'So, what was with you back there?' Carol asked.

He had just barely climbed into bed beside her, and it startled him. He hadn't known she was awake.

'I don't know. What do you mean?'

'I've never seen you like that.'

'Like what?'

'I don't know. Like . . . paralyzed or something. Usually you just know what to do. Even if you do the wrong thing. Usually you just go ahead and do it.'

He rolled up behind her, his chest against her back. Lay close to her in silence, hearing and feeling her breathing. He put one hand on her heart for further evidence that he was not alone.

'It's *Nathan*,' he said in time.

'Meaning what?'

'Meaning, like . . . It's like, if somebody said, "OK, here's the ground we all walk around on, and now all of a sudden it's your job to hold it up." You know what I mean?'

'Maybe. I'm not sure.'

'It's *Nathan*.'

'Yeah,' she said. 'I guess I see your point.'

'So, how'd you enjoy your big vacation, Little Featherweight?'

Nat looked up to see Little Manny standing over him in the mostly-dark.

It was after midnight, and Nat had let himself into the downstairs gym with the key Little Manny had quietly copied and passed along. He was on his back on a weight bench, bench-pressing without anyone to spot him, which Little Manny had many times told him not to do. He tried not to feel guilty over being caught disobeying.

'I hate it when you call me that.'

'I know. I thought you weren't coming back to train till tomorrow.'

'I got tired of waiting. I'm not featherweight, and you know it. I used to be lightweight. Now I'm welter. I've been gaining weight, and I'm welter now.'

'Light welter. And you think that's a good thing.'

Little Manny took a spotter position, his hands guiding but barely touching the bottom of the bar as Nat pumped it up and down.

'Yes, I do.'

'Well, you're wrong.' Silence except for the grunting rush of Nat's breathing. 'Don't you even want to know why you're wrong?'

'Not really, but I know you're gonna tell me anyway.'

'Because you just earned the honor of smallest guy in your weight class. You gotta eat about fourteen bananas the day before the fight just to weigh in light welter, and even then you're barely two ounces into the class. You'd be better off being the heaviest lightweight in the ring. Besides, if you miss the weigh-in by even an ounce or two—'

'You always got something negative to say.'

'And you always got your head in the clouds. I speak reality, kid. If you know it all, feel free to go on without me. Besides. I got something positive to say. I got a check from your friend Nathan the elder today.'

Nat carefully set the weight bar back in its cradle and sat up. 'Really? How much?'

'None of your business.'

'How can that not be my business?'

'Because I'm your manager. So just let me manage. I'll keep my accounting real good with him, but you get to stay out of it. If I tell you, I know you'll get carried away with all the different ways we can spend it. I know you pretty good. So, now, listen. Friday the twenty-fourth we're taking the bus down to Philly for your first amateur match. That is, if we can get your license mailed back in time. Anyway, we'll think positive. Hope the mail doesn't let us down. We'll fill out the form in the morning. And you'll need to get some pictures taken. Like the kind they use for passports. I'll take care of mailing it all in. Then all you gotta do is cut the six-mile morning runs down to two or three miles of wind sprints, and do all speed work on the bags for a few days. And leave the numbers and the money and the planning and all that other crap up to me. We'll have to get you a bunch of equipment. Mouth guards and a head guard and stuff. And hand wraps and a belt, and they gotta be real boxing shoes. No sneakers.'

'I don't want a head guard.'

'You got no choice.'

'I can't see in those things! I tried that. You were there. You know how bad it worked out. I can't see the punches coming. And then when it gets hit it sort of slides around, and then I really can't see.'

'Look, how many times do I gotta tell you, kid? You don't get a choice. So just get used to it. Focus on what's important. Oh, and another thing you gotta do. Go to a doctor and get examined.'

'For the boxing license?'

'For Nathan's insurance company. He won't back you unless you're insured.'

'God. He's so . . .'

'So what? So what's wrong with a little insurance?'

'I'm not going to get hurt.'

'Oh. I see. Good to know. I didn't realize I was working with the only unbreakable boxer in the US of A. Just go to the damn doctor. If we hurry this up I think we'll be in time to get in on the Golden Gloves schedule after the first of next year. Lot of bus trips to New York, but it's worth it.'

'I don't care about the damn Golden Gloves.'

'Well, start caring. 'Cause they're like the fashion show of amateur boxing. People turn out to see who's coming up. You need to get seen.'

'Why? I already got an investor.'

'Well, if he's the only investor you got, then you better hope he's got a shitload of money, kid.'

'I don't want to do a bunch of two-bit amateur fights with that head thing on. And a tank top and shit. And do that thing where they're scoring you on how many punches, and they stop the fight before you can even knock a guy down. I just want to put on trunks, and get in the ring with my regular bare head, so I can see what I'm hitting, and then just show everybody what I can do. That's what I want.'

Little Manny crossed his arms in the near-darkness, leaving Nat wishing he could see the older man's face.

'Oh, is *that* what you want? Well, here's what I want. I want to be six-foot-two and look like a young John Wayne. So we'll just keep track of how far our wanting gets us. You know what your problem is, kid? You think passion is enough. That it's all you really need. You think if something's just really, really important to you, it'll magically appear. Well, passion is all well and good. You won't get nowhere without it. But it's not the whole enchilada. You still gotta go step by step like everybody else. Now, I'm going back to bed. You work out all night if you want. It still ain't gonna magically turn you pro.'

'Good. Go to bed. Leave me alone.'

'What's with you tonight, kid? You're even snarkier than usual.'

'I'm fine.'

'No, you're not.'

For one brief, fleeting instant, Nat almost thought he might tell him. That Eleanor was gone, and it was probably his fault, and Nathan was inconsolable in that steely way that only Nathan could manage; and that Nat was scared, a kind of scared he'd never known existed, because he had always thought Nathan would be there, feeling nothing out of the ordinary and steering the ship.

'I'm fine.'

'OK, fine. You're fine. Got it. Lie to me. See if I care. I don't care. I'm used to it by now.'

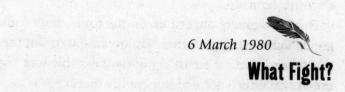

6 March 1980

What Fight?

Nat stood with his back against the wall of the enormous gym, biting on the cuticle of his right thumb and trying to block out the din of the crowd. Or even just to tolerate it. He hated to be in rooms where a huge crowd of people all talked at once. It hurt the inside of his head.

If only the next event would start. Then at least people would quiet down a little, because there would be a fight to watch.

If you could call this amateur crap a fight.

Nat watched the next two boxers getting their gloves checked and their minds brainwashed by their trainers. He could see them both nod every couple of seconds, so he knew a lot of last-minute advice was being pushed into their heads.

He thought they both looked ridiculous in their

Golden Gloves tank tops and matching head protectors. Nat always thought head protectors were a lot like training wheels. Like the kindergarten of the boxing world. Like the bunny slopes instead of real skiing.

And he would have to put one on himself soon. Right after this fight.

The two fighters ducked under the ropes, both looking panicky. Which irritated Nat, because it meant they took their amateur status seriously. Like this was big-time stuff. Which seemed impossibly dumb.

He wouldn't even be here if Little Manny would listen to reason and train him by any other system.

Nat felt grudgingly aware that the real drive behind his nervousness was having Nathan and Carol along. He had tried every possible tack to convince them to stay home. It wasn't a big deal, after all. It was just the damn quarterfinals. I mean, if they had wanted to come to the grand championship, that at least he could see. But even at the grand championship, Nat didn't figure he could get around the humiliation he would feel putting on that stupid padded head guard in front of Carol.

That was so not the way he wanted to be seen by her.

He chewed more aggressively on the cuticle, causing it to bleed.

The announcer's loudspeaker was turned up too high, and the sound quality was bad, which wasn't helping.

He tried to focus on the fight. One guy was already dominating. Really outclassing his opponent. He was a tall, light-skinned black guy who looked a little on the skinny side. But Nat could see his punches had a lot of power behind them, plus his timing was perfect. There's a guy who must be on the fast track to pro, he thought.

For the first time that day, he doubted himself slightly.

Just at that moment, the better fighter landed his last punch. His opponent fell on to the ropes and didn't bounce back again, and the official got between them, counted, and waved his arms to call the fight. Took the black kid's arm and held it high.

It was still hard for Nat to believe that they didn't even let you go on and knock a guy down. What kind of fighting is that, when nobody even ends up on the mat? It seemed pathetic.

He winced against the noise of the cheering, and the applause.

The minute the fight was over, the din of the crowd bored into Nat's head again.

Nathan appeared suddenly before his face, camera at the ready.

Well, Nat thought, it could be worse. At least he wants the photo now, before I have to put the damn training wheels on my head.

'Stand over here under the sign,' Nathan said, raising his voice to be heard above the crowd noise. He took hold of Nat's arm and pulled him over to stand under the Golden Gloves 1980 Quarterfinals banner.

He smiled, but it was all an acting job.

'Come on,' Nathan said when he had his shot. 'You're up next.'

Like Nat hadn't known that already.

Little Manny re-examined the tape on Nat's gloves ringside, a nervous habit. 'I ain't gonna give you a bunch of advice, because I told it all to you before, and I know you were listening.'

'Thank you,' Nat said.

Carol raced up and kissed Nat on the cheek. At least, as much of his cheek as she could find through the stupid head guard. The kiss ended up landing more on the side of his nose instead. It made his face feel hot. Then she ran back to her seat.

'Just make that wife of yours proud. That's all I got to say.'

Now, how was he going to make Carol proud wearing that stupid-looking thing on his head, and a tank top instead of a proud, bare fighter's chest? But then he decided. In a rush, just like that. He would look so good out there that no one would have time to think about head guards or tank tops. He would outclass his own amateur status and look like a pro. He would rise above it all.

For her.

He smiled at her as he stepped into the ring, and she beamed back at him.

*   *   *

Nat's very first blow landed perfectly. It was a right to the guy's body, and it felt great. He could hear a grunt as the air rushed out of the kid. Nat had been thinking of him as a kid, for psychological advantage. He had a baby face, so Nat tried to think of him as a baby.

That first punch had been so fast, so perfectly timed, that it just beat the baby's defenses.

After that Nat could do nothing wrong. And the baby could do nothing right.

Nat stayed a step ahead at all times, listening to the roar of the crowd in his ears. It felt good. Now that same din felt good, because it was for him. Every move the baby made was defensive, because Nat wasn't giving him time to do anything but guard.

He could hear the announcer over the loudspeaker, but somehow he couldn't focus on the words. It was all a background muddle of sound. Just 'Bates' came through. He heard his last name each time it was said. Which was a lot.

He watched the punches come in through that weird window created by the head guard. It was like watching a movie on a small screen. But even with that handicap, he blocked almost every one perfectly.

He was on fire.

The baby came in too close and clinched with him, trying to avoid the pummeling to his head. He followed Nat for five or six steps, too close to hit. Then the official pulled him off again.

The minute he came free, the baby aimed a powerful swing at Nat's head. If it had connected, it might have been a knockout punch. But Nat ducked it successfully. And then, in the split second that followed, Nat knew the baby had put so much into that one punch that he was now completely off-balance. And completely unguarded.

Nat capitalized. With a knockout punch of his own.

He drove a hard right to the baby's head. It connected with a satisfying thud.

The baby did not fall. But he staggered. He took three or four steps back and forth, as if to try to balance himself, his legs looking like rubber. Like a drunkard on a swaying ship.

In a real fight Nat would have thrown one more great punch and finished him off. In a real fight the baby would be down on the mat, the ref counting over him while the crowd cheered.

But this was the amateurs.

The official stepped between them, held up one, then two, then three fingers in front of the drunken baby. Nat turned his head to look for Carol in the crowd. Just as he saw her, he heard the official call the fight.

Nat felt a hand grasp his wrist and raise his gloved hand in the air. The crowd cheered. He felt a little cheated, because he'd wanted to fight for a lot longer than a minute and a half. It felt good, and he wasn't ready to stop.

He found Carol's face again in the crowd. She was on her feet. Clapping. Cheering. She threw her arms around Nathan and hugged him from the side, jumping up and down while he stood still and applauded.

She was proud of him. He'd made his wife proud of him. Just like Little Manny said he should. The rest didn't seem to matter.

Nat stepped up to the urinal, careful, as always, to keep his eyes straight ahead. A guy no older than him stepped up beside him. Nathan could see in the mirror, in his peripheral vision, that it was another fighter. He could tell by the brightly colored flash of his Golden Gloves tank top.

The guy looked over at him.

No, no, no, Nat thought. Eyes front. Always eyes front at the urinals. He did not return the glance.

'So,' the guy said. 'You gonna take that fight? Awful lot of money.'

Nat looked over. It was the guy who had won the fight right before his. The light-skinned black guy who had fought so well.

He quickly looked away again.

'I don't know what fight you're talking about.'

'The one in the Bronx.'

'I didn't hear about it.'

'Really? That guy was talking to your trainer. Isn't that your trainer, that real short little guy? That guy with the beard and the wild hair was talking to him. Right after he talked to my father. Right after my father said no.'

'And he offered you a fight? What kind of a fight?'

'Pro. Hundred bucks for every round you can stay in. But it's unregulated, so my father won't let me do it. I just wondered if you were gonna do it. Awful lot of money.'

Nat shook off and zipped up. Stepped back away from the urinal. 'Yeah. I am. I'm gonna do it.'

'You're lucky,' he said. 'Good fight, by the way.'

'Thanks,' Nat said. 'You looked good out there, too.'

He found Little Manny right where he had left him, sitting with Nathan and Carol, watching total strangers fight. If you could call it fighting.

Carol looked over her shoulder at Nat and smiled in a way that made his stomach feel warm and runny. He wanted to smile back properly, but he couldn't shake being mad. Not on such short notice.

'Little Manny,' he said, speaking up slightly to be heard over the noise of the crowd. 'Can I have a word with you?'

'Sure, kid. You wanna take it outside?'

'Yeah,' Nat said. 'I do.'

'So when were you planning on telling me?'

'Never. I was planning on telling you never. Because we're not gonna do it.'

'Well, maybe *you're* not. But *I* am.'

They stood with their backs against the brick of the building. Nat nursed the silence briefly while a siren went by. Fire engine. There was always some disaster in New York City. But at least here something happened.

He shivered slightly in his tank top and trunks, but refused to let on that he was cold.

'Look. Kid. It's my job to protect you—'

'From what? From fights?'

'From fights like this. Yeah. Look. You still don't know the boxing world so good. So lemme give you a crash course. This is a fight nobody regulates. That means if a guy fights you dirty, maybe the official says something, maybe not. Probably not. No regulation means no weigh-in. This guy tells me his boy is a welterweight, but we don't know. We're just taking his word. For all we know the guy could outweigh you by forty pounds. Plus it's tomorrow night, and I never trust a fight that comes together last-minute like that. And he's trying to get four, five guys to go up against his boy in one night. Offering big money to whoever can stay in. But did you stop to ask yourself what he's doing recruiting a bunch of amateurs? Plus it's too much money.'

Nat snorted laughter. 'Too much money? *Too much?* You gotta be kidding me. There's no such thing as too much money. Too much for who?'

'How do I explain it to you, kid? So's you get it? It's like, if you see all-you-can-eat pancakes for about a dollar, you think it's a good deal. You think you'll put one over on 'em. Get something for nothing. Only, turns out you can only eat three or four pancakes anyway, and they know it. This guy's got no intention of shelling out a thousand bucks to four or five fighters. If he's offering that kind of bucks it's because he knows he'll never have to pay it. He's just putting on a show. It's like a gladiator sport. You know? It's a chance to make his boy look good in front of a crowd that pays to watch you bleed.'

'I don't care. I'm doing it.'

For one wonderful moment, Little Manny said nothing. A woman in a startlingly short skirt walked by and gave Nat a suggestive glance over her shoulder.

'You don't care about much of anything, do you?'

'You want to know what I care about?' Nat said, raising his voice in a way he never had with Little Manny before. 'I'll tell you what I care about. My wife. I care about my wife. Who, by the way, still doesn't even have a decent wedding ring. If I can hold my ground even three rounds with this guy, I could buy her a nice ring. That's what I care about. So don't tell me I don't care about anything. If you really believe that, you don't know me at all. Now when is this fight? And where?'

Little Manny shook his head five or six times before answering. 'Oh, no. No, no. Maybe I can't stop you from doing this fool thing, kid, but I ain't about to draw you a map.'

Little Manny turned on his heel and went back inside.

Nat stood a moment, breathing the bitingly cold city air. Then he followed Little Manny back into the gym.

He scanned the room for a guy with a beard and wild hair. He wasn't hard to find. A guy with hair like that – like he'd grabbed hold of a live electrical wire – was as easy to pick out of a crowd as a car in a parking lot with a balloon tied to its antenna.

Nat elbowed his way through the crowd to try to reach him. But it was between events, and the spectators were all on their feet and milling. The guy with the hair was talking to another fighter, which made Nat feel he had to hurry. That an opportunity was just about to slip away.

He felt the presence of someone on his heels, and turned around to see Little Manny following barely a step behind.

'What are you doing here? Are you stupid enough to try to stop me?'

'No. No, kid, I ain't nearly that stupid. I just figure if you're gonna do this fool thing, you're better to do it with me than without me.'

'Um. We're going to send you guys home without us,' Nat said.

'Is everything all right?' Nathan asked.

'Oh. Yeah. Yeah. Everything's good. Little Manny just ran into some friends of his and we have this chance to do some sparring. You know. Like, on a different level than I could do at home.'

But to Nat's own ears it sounded like the lie it was. And he was sure everyone else must have heard the lie in it, too. Plus Little Manny kept looking away, at the floor, and that didn't help one bit. Nat felt a strong jolt to his stomach, remembering Nathan's voice when he said 'Don't ever lie to me again.' He had done it, and it was too late to undo it now.

'So, Carol and I will drive home and you'll . . .' Nathan trailed off. Let Nat finish the sentence.

'Take the bus. Or the train. Probably day after tomorrow.'

'OK,' Nathan said.

So Nathan did not have super powers after all. He could not see right through Nat, as feared.

Just before they left the gym, Nathan pulled him aside.

'I just want you to know I'm proud of you tonight,' he said.

'You are?'

'Very.'

'You never said that to me before.'

'I never claimed to be easily impressed.'

'As a matter of fact I'm trying to think if *anybody* ever said that to me before. But I don't really think so.' The pause felt awkward, so he rushed on. 'Because I won?'

'No, not because you won. Partly because you've

worked so hard, but mostly because you did this thing right. I know you wanted to rush, and I know there are parts of your trainer's schedule that you don't like, but you exercised patience. Along with everything else you exercised.'

Nat looked away. Down at the gym floor. 'Thanks,' he said.

When he looked up, Nathan was already walking away.

For one long, struggling, balancing-act of a moment, Nat almost ran after him. Almost said, Never mind. We'll catch the ride home with you after all.

Carol tipped it for him. She tossed a glance over her shoulder at him. Smiled. Blew him a kiss. Then she turned and ran back to him. Threw her arms around him and kissed him on the lips. 'You were so great. I love you so much.'

'I love you, too,' he said.

'Have a good time sparring. Be as good as you were tonight.'

He looked down at her left hand, resting on his bare forearm. At the impossibly cheap silver band they were using as a sort of placeholder for the real thing.

'I'll try,' he said.

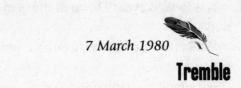

7 March 1980

Tremble

'This can't be it,' Nat said.

'Oh, this is it, all right,' Little Manny said. 'What'd you expect? Madison Square Garden?'

They stood in front of a dark equipment yard, surrounded by high-chain link topped with loops of razor wire. A good city block back into the yard, Nat could see a few dark shapes of people moving into and out of a huge sheet-metal warehouse.

'Not too late to back out, kid,' Little Manny said.

'I don't back out,' Nat said. 'I'm not a guy who backs out.'

The words seemed to tremble slightly as they rose up from his lungs, making him feel like a layered being with his steel only on the outermost skin.

'Yeah. Tell me all about it. I noticed that about you. I'll be sure to carve that on your gravestone.'

'Thanks heaps,' Nat said.

* * *

'*That's a welterweight?*' It came out of Nat's mouth before he could stop it. He hoped the crowd noise had swallowed his words. That Little Manny had never received them. He looked down at the little man, who was just opening his mouth to speak. 'Yeah, yeah. I know. I know. Don't even bother to say it. You warned me. I know.'

The first fight was already in progress. No announcer, which seemed weird to Nat. The seats consisted of a bunch of folding chairs scattered at random. Maybe a hundred guys sat around the ring, cheering and booing and drinking beer and hard liquor out of translucent plastic cups, the bottles sitting on the concrete floor at their feet.

The dominating boxer had a smaller fighter on the ropes, pummeling him. Nat waited for a bell to ring, or an official to pull the big guy off. Then he reminded himself. At least he hadn't said it out loud, to Little Manny, and opened up another opportunity to be reminded that he'd been warned. Because the smaller fighter was pinned on the ropes, it was hard for him to fall. And as long as he wasn't on the mat, the fight would go on. But it looked like nothing more than a bloodbath to Nat. The kid on the ropes had completely given up fighting, and just held both gloves in front of his face while his big opponent landed blows to the head on either side of them. It got clearer by the second that only the ropes held the poor guy up at all. The crowd went crazy. Really ate it up. I guess I was warned about that, too, Nat thought.

He felt a deep and growing sensation of heat, melting heat. It started in his lower gut and groin and poured down through his thighs, making them feel wobbly and weak.

The poor kid on the ropes finally went down by the quickest route possible. His knees buckled, folded up, and he just sank away from his opponent, as though a trap door had blessedly opened under his feet to swallow him, leaving nothing left for his opponent to strike.

Nat watched the count, but couldn't hear it over the wild noise of the crowd.

He looked around and saw, with a jolt of panic, that Little Manny had disappeared.

It had never felt so important to him to keep someone he knew standing by his side. Someone he trusted to be solidly on his team. His mind shifted back to last night's amateur fight. Looking up to see Nathan and Carol in the audience cheering for him. He wished he could transport himself back there, somehow.

Little Manny appeared suddenly in front of him, and he sighed with relief.

'You wanna go next? Get this over with? The next fighter didn't show.'

'Wonder what happened to him.'

'Prob'ly had a brain left in his head, unlike you, and backed out.'

'Yeah, OK,' Nat said. 'I'll go next. Get this over with.'

'OK, go change into your trunks.'

'Where?' Nat asked, looking around.

'Men's room, I guess.'

Nat stood a moment in front of the filthy mirror in the tiny, filthy toilet. The bare light bulb over his head seemed to show everything for what it really was. Nothing hidden. No lies.

He took himself in. The boxing trunks and belt. The six-pack abs. The biceps. The pecs. No head guard. No tank top. Just him, and his months of hard work.

I look like a fighter, he thought. You look like Jack, his head said back to him.

Nathan had said boxing was a dream, until Nat did it. So, tonight was the night. Tonight the dream was real.

The door pushed open a crack and Little Manny stuck his head in.

'Enough with admiring yourself, Cinderella. It's time to roll.'

Little Manny hovered over Nat in their corner of the ring, holding out Nat's mouth guard. Nat opened up to receive it. He barely felt himself doing it. He couldn't hear himself think over the noise of the crowd. Every movement felt like a walk through a vivid dream.

Ironic, he thought. Tonight it's not a dream, but it's never felt more like one.

'OK, here's what I'm thinking for a strategy. Just guard. Just keep your guard up. Don't try to get fancy, because I don't think you're going to throw a punch that'll faze him much anyway. So don't even leave yourself open. The idea is to hold in a few rounds, so just stay away from him and keep your guard up.'

Nat wanted to say something like, thanks for all your confidence in me. But he settled for a weak nod instead.

'On your feet, kid.'

Nat stepped into the center of the ring and touched gloves with his opponent. A white guy with his wiry black hair shaved short, who Nat had sized up as a good two weight-classes too big. Maybe even light heavyweight.

The guy sneered at him. It was a sarcastic smile that seemed to say, this will be easy.

The warm, melty feeling in his groin intensified. It felt more liquid this time, and he glanced down to be sure he hadn't literally urinated on himself. Thank God he had not. Thank God it was only a sensation.

He returned to his corner as instructed. Found Little Manny's face, because it was something familiar. The only thing familiar. Then he looked away again, because he didn't like what he saw on that face.

The bell in his vivid dream rang.

Nat stepped in boldly, but the monster fighter of this

dream stepped in faster, and threw a punch. Nat felt as though he'd seen first the monster, then the monster's fist, approaching in slow motion. He blocked the punch, but was surprised by the force of it hitting his gloves.

Three more landed, each equally surprising.

He heard Little Manny shout something about footwork.

A sudden flash of a memory. The old gym. Little Manny's voice. 'Watch Jack's footwork. When it comes to footwork, he's the king.' It woke him up, and he began to dance away from the punches. At least make himself harder to hit, a moving target. Minimize the number of blows that would land.

Jack would want me to fight this one, Nat thought.

He threw a punch, but it bounced off the monster's gloves.

After that, it seemed he had no choice but to dance, evade and protect. He was able to kill well over a minute just by being hard to pin down.

Each second seemed to last minutes, but the bell was coming. It was right around the corner. He knew it by feel. Every cell in his body knew the length of two minutes in the ring. It should come . . . right about . . . here.

No bell.

Nat continued to dance, taking blows to his gloved fists and occasionally his head, thinking his timing had been off by a few seconds.

Still no bell.

That's when it dawned on him. This was an unregulated fight. No one was keeping watch. They could ring that damn bell any time they wanted. Or not. And every time they did, it would cost somebody a hundred bucks. So why should they?

The thought moved down from his head and through his body as a distracting moment of shock.

Before he could regroup, the monster landed a body blow to Nat's right side that broke several of his ribs. Or cracked them at least. He heard himself involuntarily release a big sound. A cross between a grunt and crying out loud. It ashamed him, but he couldn't help it. It just all happened so fast.

The crowd noise intensified, if such a thing were possible, inside Nat's skull.

He raised his gloves again to defend himself, but the right didn't come up as high as he expected it to, as he told it to. As if the pain tied it down closer to his waist.

The final blow hit him in the right temple.

He heard the crowd suck in its collective breath.

His head whipped around, painfully wrenching his neck and sending his mouth guard flying. Time dealt a weird, uneven wrinkle. First he hovered too long, out of balance and destined to go down, hanging at an impossible angle for an impossible length of time. Then the mat smacked him without any intervening fall.

The jolt to his ribs felt searing, but he found himself unable to express anything about it.

He lay with his eyes open. He vacantly saw the crowd on its feet now, cheering and sloshing beer. The scene in front of his eyes moved from crowd, to dim, to dark, then back to crowd again. Back to dark. Back to crowd. It felt surprisingly satisfying to lie entirely still. Appropriate. The ceiling lights at the far end of the building glowed with light haloes. He heard the counting but it sounded muted, muffled. Drawn out and far away.

He might possibly have lost a few brief segments of time, but he wasn't sure.

He felt a hand on his shoulder. 'You OK, kid? Can you get up?' Little Manny.

'I'm fine, yeah.'

'Can you get up?'

'Yeah.'

'Here, I'll help you.'

'I don't need help. I'm fine.'

Nat placed both gloved fists on the mat and raised himself to his knees. The haloed ceiling lights began to spin in a broad circle around him, making him feel as though he might throw up. The crowd was booing. Booing *him*? That was too hard to figure out. But he knew they'd been doing it for some time. It just hadn't quite broken through.

Little Manny stuck a hand under each of Nat's armpits and tried to help him to his feet.

'I'm fine. I told you.' He knocked the hands away. 'I'll get up on my own.'

He rose partway to his feet in the wildly spinning ring, then had to brace himself on the mat again to keep from falling.

He made it on the second try.

He ducked carefully through the ropes and followed Little Manny toward the door.

The crowd booed him. A guy threw a cup of freezing cold liquid on him, and he felt bits of ice slide down his back and chest. Another guy aimed a beer bottle at him and he dodged it, causing the room to spin even more violently. Again he worried he might vomit.

He ducked after Little Manny out into the cold, quiet night of the equipment yard. The noise from inside sounded blessedly muffled and far away. Unreal.

'Why did they boo me?' Nat asked, his voice not sounding like his own to him.

'Why not?'

'It's not like they had money on me to win.'

'I think they wanted a better show. More than two minutes.'

'That *was* more than two minutes. They should've rung the bell. They owe me a hundred bucks.'

'Good luck collecting. You sure you're OK?' Little Manny pried open one of Nat's eyelids and peered in at close range.

Nat reflexively shook him off again. Pushed him away. 'Stop it. What are you doing?'

'Doesn't matter. I can't see in this light, anyway. Ready to go home, kid?'

'Oh, yeah. Definitely. I definitely want to go home.' He began to walk toward the street.

'Hey. Cinderella. Forgetting something?'

Nat turned back to face his trainer, still not clear on what he was forgetting. Little Manny glanced down to a spot below Nat's face, so Nat looked down, too. He was wearing only his boxing trunks. He hadn't even taken his gloves off.

'I'll go get your clothes,' Little Manny said, and ducked back inside.

Nat lowered himself gingerly on to a stack of three or four wooden pallets. He looked down at his gloves and felt suddenly desperate to have them off. So he tore at the tape with his teeth, which he knew from the start was pointless, then gave up and wedged his wrists between his bare thighs.

He looked up at the sky, and saw stars. It seemed so out of place. How could the stars be shining over a place like this one?

The heat of exertion began to wear off, leaving him shivering in the cold. To his great humiliation, Nat found himself blinking back hot tears. To be seen that way by Little Manny felt unimaginable. It even embarrassed Nat to cry in front of himself.

He fought desperately to beat them back again, but was only partially successful.

He looked up to see Little Manny standing over him. Was it pity Nat saw in his eyes? Or was he just reading his worst fear into the scene before his eyes?

'Come on, kid. Let's get you home.' He turned and walked toward the street.

'Little Manny,' Nat called. And Little Manny turned around. 'Thanks for coming here with me.'

Little Manny passed the words off with a wave of his hand. 'You coming? Or do you like it here?'

'I'm coming,' Nat said.

8 March 1980

Seconds

'What time is it?' Nat asked again.

'Four thirty.'

Nat could feel the slight rocking of the train as he sat with his eyes squeezed shut. He wished for the hundredth time that they had taken the bus instead. Smoother ride. He opened his eyes and looked out the window. Watched the occasional lights of some little farming village flash by. But it hurt too much, so he closed them again. Even though it didn't seem to help.

Every second seemed an hour long, and he ached to be home. Even knowing that home wouldn't make the pain stop. And yet he felt that if he could simply lie curled up on his side on his own bed in the dark, everything would somehow be all right, in a way that it wasn't now.

Especially if Carol would curl up against him.

'You got any more of those aspirin?' he asked Little Manny.

'You already took six.'

'Just another two or three.'

'They're gonna make you throw up.'

'So, go get me something to put in my stomach.'

'Café car's not even open at this hour.'

'Coffee with a whole bunch of cream. You could go up to business class and get it.'

'Yeah. All right.'

'My neck is so stiff.'

'Not surprising. Is that what's bothering you? Or is it your head?'

'My head. But my neck is so stiff.'

'Get used to the headaches.'

'I *am* used to them. This one is special.'

'Get used to the special ones, too.'

The lights came up inside the train car and Nat, who had no idea he'd fallen asleep, lurched awake with a cry of pain. He shielded his eyes with one arm.

He'd been dreaming of flashes of colored light in front of his closed eyes. If they could be considered dreams.

'Why'd they turn the lights on?'

'We're at a station I guess. Might be Albany. Anyway, we stopped. Told you not to fall asleep,' Little Manny said. 'Not good to fall asleep when you've got a concussion. Here.'

He picked up his hat from his lap and placed it over Nat's face. An old-fashioned hat like men used to wear on the street in the fifties. It hurt where it touched his temple, but the light hurt more, so Nat left it in place.

'How do you know I have a concussion?'

'What? I can't hear you under the hat.'

Nat lifted it a few inches. 'How do you know I have a concussion?'

'Because I saw the freight train that hit you. That's how.'

'Oh.'

He gently set the hat back in place, and stared into its light-ringed darkness, surviving the pain of each second individually. What was the point, though, really, of surviving an hour-long second if another waited right behind it, also needing to be survived? But it made him feel panicky to think about that, so he returned to the one-second-at-a-time plan.

The train began to move again. Nat breathed carefully until the light leaking in through the edges of the hat went dark again. Then he gave the hat back to Little Manny.

'That was the most humiliating thing that ever happened to me,' he said quietly.

'There'll be more.'

'Thanks loads.'

'What'd you expect? To win without breaking a sweat every time?'

'No, but I thought I'd do better than that. Can you tell if my ribs are broken by feel?'

'I dunno. Raise your arm.'

'It hurts to raise my arm. That's how I got in this trouble to begin with.'

'No, you got in this trouble when you said yes to that fight. Against my advice. Raise it anyway.'

Nat slowly, gently coaxed his right arm to about shoulder height. He felt Little Manny's hands run over his side.

'Ow! Gently, please.'

'That's as gentle as I can be and still feel. I dunno. They're not out of place as far as I can tell. So prob'ly just cracked. But first thing Monday morning, go to the doctor, get an X-ray. And tell him you took a mean one to the head. Let him give you one of them neuro exams.'

'Yeah. Whatever.'

'No. Not whatever. Promise.'

Long pause. Nat figured he probably wouldn't bother to go. 'OK.'

They rode the rest of the way home in silence.

Nat sat on a bench at the station, shivering miserably in the morning cold, his head in his hands to block out the light.

Several paces behind him, he could hear Little Manny talking on the pay phone.

'Yeah, he don't feel so good. Got a mean headache.

Otherwise I'd just tell him to walk home. But he feels so lousy, that's why I'm asking. Hate to make him walk all that way.'

A pause. Then, 'Yeah. OK. Good. Thanks, Nathan.'

Little Manny came back and sat next to him on the bench. Patted him on the back. Which hurt. Not because his back hurt. Just because it moved everything slightly.

'He's coming to pick you up.'

'Promise me you won't tell him,' Nat said. 'Promise me you won't tell anybody. Ever.'

'Don't worry,' Little Manny said.

'Meaning what?'

'Meaning I don't come off too good in the story, either.'

Carol came into their bedroom about seven p.m.

'What are you doing in bed? It's like seven o'clock.' She flipped on the light.

Nat yelped out loud. 'Turn it off, OK? Ow. Jeez.'

'Wow. Sorry. You OK?'

'I have a headache.'

She flipped off the light again and crossed over to the bed, where Nat lay curled in a fetal position.

'Want me to get you some aspirin?'

'I already had eight. They didn't help much.'

'Poor Nat. Is there anything I can get you?'

'How 'bout a morphine drip?' He reached a hand up to her. 'Come lie down with me.'

She kicked off her shoes and settled next to him on the bed. In front of him. He uncurled slightly to make room for her. Then he threw an arm over her and tucked in close.

'That's better,' he said.

'Than what?'

'Than anything.'

'How was your sparring match? Were you as good as in Golden Gloves?'

'Not quite that good, no.'

They lay together in silence for several minutes.

So, this was the brass ring, the great finish line that he had promised himself all the way home. Lying on his own bed, with her.

He still hurt like hell. But if you have to hurt, he figured, there are worse places to do it.

'I've been dreaming about this,' he said.

'What?'

'This.'

'Just this?'

'Yeah. Just this.'

'But we do this every night.'

'No. We didn't do it last night. And I could have used it, too. I just wanted to get home and hold you. That's all. Is that so weird?'

'Yes and no. I mean, no. It's not weird. Not exactly. It's just that . . . you don't usually talk like this.'

'Like what?'

'I don't know. Almost like . . . like you need me. I'm not saying you don't. Just that you don't usually talk like you do. That must be some headache.'

Worse

Nat eased himself down at the breakfast table, using all of his scant energy to squash what could easily have blossomed into a full-on state of panic. He couldn't believe he'd wakened up to find the headache had gotten worse. He wouldn't have believed, if anyone had tried to tell him, that there was such a thing as worse.

He tried to smile at Nathan, but was pretty sure it came out as a grimace.

'Do you still have a headache?' Nathan asked. 'You look terrible.'

Nat nodded ever so slightly. His neck felt locked into place. As if with steel braces. He had to move his whole upper body to give the appearance of a nod.

'Is Carol coming to breakfast?'

Nat shook his head as best he could.

'Already gone to see her grandparents?'

Nat nodded.

'I hope she had some breakfast.'

Damn. This did not seem to be a yes or no question.

'I think she had cereal,' he said. But something went wrong. Something happened to the words. They slurred and blended at the edges. As if he were drunk.

Nathan looked up briefly. Curiously.

They both held still for a split second. Then the moment seemed to pass on its own. He had just wakened up and he had a headache. The perception was dismissed.

It must have been nothing.

Nat put his head in his hands, shielding his eyes from the light.

He heard a small noise in front of him, and opened his eyes to see that Nathan had set a plate of poached eggs on toast in front of him. The smell made him a little bit nauseous. The last thing he wanted was food, but he had to get something in his stomach. So he could take another fistful of aspirin.

He reached to the middle of the table for the salt.

His fingertips touched down a good ten inches to the right of it.

He stared at the hand for a moment, detached. As if it must belong to someone else entirely.

He tried again. This time it landed three or four inches left.

When he tried to pick up the hand for a third try, he

failed. It just didn't pick up. As though it had never received a signal. As though the lines were down.

He looked up to see Nathan watching him, a shocked look on his face.

'Nat,' Nathan said. 'Are you drunk?'

'No!' he said, or tried to say, but it came out sounding spastic. Like the retarded boy in his fourth-grade class. The one everybody made fun of. Like a person who had been born deaf learning to talk for the first time.

'Nat,' Nathan said again. Clearly alarmed. 'What's the matter? What's wrong?'

'I don't know,' he tried to say. But this time it didn't sound nearly so good. This time it sounded like the howl of some wounded animal.

His stomach suddenly revolted in response to the pain, and Nat knew he was about to throw up. He lurched up from the table and turned toward the sink, but the first step opened a whole new category of trouble. His legs felt rubbery and weak, as if his muscles had turned to rubber bands, and they refused to follow the simplest instructions.

He felt himself pitch forward. He braced for the pain of landing.

But he never felt himself land.

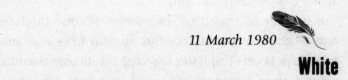

11 March 1980

White

Nat opened his eyes.

He saw white walls in front of him, and on either side. White sheets beneath his direct field of vision. A television set hung suspended high on the wall. It was the only thing he saw that was not white.

The headache was gone.

He let his eyes drift closed again, experiencing and blessing that relief.

When he opened them again, a pretty young black woman stood over him. Wearing a white uniform.

'Well, look who's awake,' she said. She spoke with an accent. It was lilting and songlike. Probably from one of those islands where you go on vacation to snorkel and drink rum. 'That's a lovely thing now, to see those eyes open. Are you in much pain, darlin'?'

Nat shook his head slightly.

'OK, well, if you feel a lot of pain, you can ring me with this button. Can you reach this button on your own, do ya think? Try it now, so we see.'

She held up a power cord with a red push-button device on the end. Then she set it down on the bed again, beside his right hand.

Nat gathered up all of his powers of concentration and reached for the button. But his arm felt weak, and his aim was off. The hand wavered on its way into the air and never quite touched down anywhere different.

'Don't worry, darlin', I'll be checkin' in on ya. If you need your morphine adjusted, you just give me a nod or a blink. 'Kay?'

Nat nodded hazily.

She disappeared from his field of vision, leaving mostly white.

Nat's eyes closed again, and he drifted back to wherever he had been before.

Nat opened his eyes. Let them close. Willed them open again.

He saw Nathan fill up nearly his entire field of vision. Leaning over his bed.

'There you are. Good to see you back with us. Carol will kick herself. She just went down to the cafeteria, and it's all my fault. I twisted her arm, because she hadn't eaten in more than two days. She had to eat something. How do you feel?'

He felt great, actually. Maybe it was just the morphine. But he wasn't convinced that even morphine could have cured a headache like that one. Not completely, anyway. So he figured it was really, blissfully gone.

'Better,' he said. But it came out sounding like the same mess. The vowels twisted into spastic, howly nonsense, and the consonants seemed not to have been found at all. 'Huh?' Nat asked reflexively. Alarmed at his own voice. But even that was barely intelligible. It was only the inflection, the way he raised his voice at the end of the word to suggest a question, that allowed it to make any sense at all. 'What?' He tried again. He felt, even through the haze of drugs, the beginnings of a rising panic.

'It's OK,' Nathan said. 'Relax. It's normal. The doctor says it's normal. You'll have trouble with speech for a while. We'll probably need to get you a speech therapist. And a physical therapist. There'll be some muscle weakness. And—'

'What? No!'

He wanted to ask how much muscle weakness, and for how long. But he wasn't even sure his last two syllables had come through. He couldn't have muscle weakness. He was a boxer. Boxers can't have muscle weakness.

He had to ask the important question. He had to make those words come out right.

He gathered his inner resources together, much the way he would if someone had asked him to lift up a car.

'When can I box?'

It was pathetic. Maybe the 'when' came through well enough to guess at. The 'I' sounded like 'a' and the other words never made it out of the gate in one piece.

'When . . .' Nathan said. 'When what?'

Frustrated, Nat raised his right hand and tried to imitate writing. But the loops came out looking shaky, and bigger than he had intended.

'I'm not sure what you're trying to tell me.'

A flash of silver caught Nat's eye. In Nathan's shirt pocket. It was the clip end of a good silver pen. He pointed to it.

Nathan looked down. 'Oh. You want to write something.'

Nathan took the pen out of his pocket. Twisted it open. Then he produced a leather case of index-card-sized note cards. He pulled out a blank card and set it on top of the case, then laid it on the bed within Nat's reach. He handed Nat the pen, helping him wrap his fingers around it.

Nat knew this wasn't going to be much easier. So he set the bar low. Just three letters.

They came out looking as though he had written them with his left hand. Or foot. But they could be read.

B – O – X.

Nathan's face fell. 'Nat . . .'

Nat turned his face away. Squeezed his eyes closed. As if that would close his ears as well, and then he wouldn't have to hear.

It didn't work. He heard.

'Nat . . . You've just survived a craniotomy. And you were lucky to survive it. Do you know what that is? It's a procedure that involves peeling back a huge crescent of scalp and removing a square window of bone out of your skull. So the surgeon could flush out a very large hematoma that was putting pressure on your brain. They replaced the piece of skull, but right now you have steel plates holding it in place. Not for ever. But you'll have other problems, and they're not going away overnight. Muscle weakness . . .'

There it was again. Nat shook his head, as if he could deny it and thereby avoid it.

'. . . speech difficulties. Motor-skill difficulties. You may even have seizures, but they can be controlled with—'

Nathan stopped speaking. Because Nat had raised a hand and was moving it, carefully, inexactly, toward Nathan's face. The hand, much as he tried to direct it accurately, landed gently on Nathan's forehead. Nathan remained tensely silent, as though straining to understand.

Nat tried again. This time the hand found its mark. It pressed firmly over the older man's mouth.

They remained that way for a beat or two.

Then Nathan gently took hold of Nat's wrist, removed the hand, and placed it on the sheet near Nat's hip.

'I guess we can talk about that some other time,' he said.

Nat held very still, his eyes closed. Hoping he appeared to be doing something other than what he was doing. Trying desperately not to cry.

'Nat,' Nathan said. His voice low. Almost reverent. 'What happened? What happened to you on your last night in New York?' A silence. 'How do you sign on for some practice sparring and come home with a traumatic brain injury?'

The tears gained the upper hand. Nat concentrated all his effort, all his strength, into his eyelids. But apparently they were suffering from muscle weakness, too. Or maybe the tears were stronger than he had realized. Stronger than he had ever been. Anyway, it was too late. A couple of tears had made it past the guards. Out where Nathan could see.

'Never mind,' Nathan said. 'I guess we can talk about that some other time, too.'

Part Seven

Nathan McCann

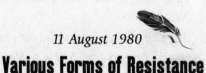

11 August 1980

Various Forms of Resistance

At a little after seven in the evening, Nathan set down his newspaper and turned off the light in the den. The darkness surprised him, because both Nat and Carol were home. Then he corrected himself. Carol was home, in addition to Nat. When was Nat ever not home?

In any case, he expected lights to be on in some other part of the house.

He stepped out into the darkness of the living room and heard sobbing. He switched on a lamp. Carol did not look up or respond. She continued to cry, curled in a fetal position, on her side on the sofa.

Nathan resisted the temptation to ask foolish questions, such as, what's wrong? From the point of view of Carol's world, what *wasn't* wrong?

He sat down beside her on the couch. Put a hand on her shoulder. She sat up and tucked under his arm, still crying. Though it made him uncomfortable to play such a role, Nathan sat still with his arm around her while she cried it out.

After a time he said, 'I take it he still won't talk to you.'

'Right.'

'Anything worse than usual going on?'

'Yes.'

But she didn't immediately elaborate. And he opted for declining to pry. A few seconds of silence. Her sobs seemed to be calming some.

Then she said, 'He said one word to me tonight. One word. Guess what it was?'

'I can't imagine.'

'Nathan.'

'Nathan what?'

'He wants to do his physical therapy with you. Not me.'

'How do you get all that from the one word: Nathan?'

'Because I asked him. I said, "Nathan what? What about Nathan?" And he pointed to what I was doing with his leg. And I said, "What? You want Nathan to do your PT with you?" And he nodded.' On that last sentence, she began again to cry softly.

'Why would he want that?'

'Your guess is as good as mine. I don't understand him at all these days. I don't understand why five months later he suddenly doesn't want me for the exercises any more. I don't understand why he talks to you, but not to me.'

'Barely. He barely talks to me.'

'Well, it's a pile of words compared to how much he says to me.'

'Have you ever asked him why? Oh. Never mind. That was a foolish question. I forgot. He doesn't talk to you, so what good would it do to ask questions? I'll go in and see if I can find out what's going on with him.'

'Thanks, Nathan.'

Nathan found Nat lying on his back on the bed, in just a pair of boxer shorts, listening to the irritating drone of some kind of raucous cartoon comedy show on TV. The TV he'd insisted on having placed in his and Carol's bedroom. He did not look up as Nathan came through the door.

Feathers lay on the bed beside Nat, snoring audibly, his chin on Nat's belly. Nat stroked the dog's head absent-mindedly while he gazed at the TV screen.

Nathan stood over the bed for a moment, expecting the young man's eyes to meet his eventually.

It was hard not to notice that Nat's body was changing.

Nathan's mind filled with the image of Nat's last night in the Golden Gloves in New York. In the remembered image, his chest was so fully developed. Carved, almost. Visible right through his tank top. The muscles in his calves looked like thick ropes. The circumference of his upper arms was so remarkably impressive.

Now he looked as if he'd gained twenty pounds and lost twenty pounds of muscle, all at the same time.

Nat's eyes finally came up. Questioning.

Nathan turned off the TV.

'Hey!' Nat said. Just that one word, exiting Nat's mouth all by itself, sounded almost normal.

'You need to do your physical therapy,' Nathan said.

The young man turned his face away.

Nathan picked up one of Nat's bare feet. Raised Nat's leg so that his knee bent, and his calf paralleled the bed. He waited for Nat to push against his hand. And waited. He shouldn't have needed to say, 'Push against my hand.' After five months of physical therapy, both the professional and the homework variety, Nathan figured he must have caught on to the routine by now.

'What's going on with you tonight?' Nathan asked.

Nat only shrugged.

'Would you like to start by pushing against my hand?' Light pressure from Nat's bare heel. Very light. 'I can't imagine that's all you've got.'

First only silence. Then Nat spoke. 'Don't you know . . . I'm a cripple?'

The words twisted in the usual way as they made their way through Nat's mouth, sounding like the words of a deaf person guessing at speech. But Nathan was able to understand each one.

'Your speech is getting better.'

Nat snorted bitter laughter. 'I sound like . . . a retard,' he said.

Much as Nathan hated to admit it, and unlikely as he was to say it out loud, Nat did speak as though he suffered from a serious learning disability.

A thought struck him for the first time. 'Is that why you won't talk to Carol?'

Nat turned his face away again, and did not reply.

'Carol loves you, Nat. That young woman genuinely loves you. You have to trust that. You have to trust that it's really you she loves. Not the speech patterns or the biceps.' The minute the words left his mouth, Nathan realized that the comment about Nat's muscles would have been better left unsaid.

A long silence, during which Nat did not bother to push against Nathan's hand.

Then Nat moved his right hand in a way that suggested writing. Asking Nathan to give him something to write with, and on.

'No,' Nathan said. 'I promised your speech therapist I would not let you write things out any more. She says it's a lazy habit. You need to keep practicing your speech, Nat. You won't get it back without practise.'

More silence. Nathan watched the young man move his jaw in some indecipherable, repetitious pattern. Finally, Nat took his leg back from Nathan and let it fall on to the bed.

'Tell me what's wrong tonight,' Nathan said. 'I know a

lot has been wrong for a long time. I know this is a hard adjustment for you. But something changed tonight. And I'm hoping you'll tell me what it is.'

Nathan sat down on the edge of the bed and waited.

A split second before he gave up and left Nat to his solitude, the young man spoke. His words formed slowly, with long breaks in between. A pattern that suggested great concentration and stress on his part.

'Finally . . . figured out . . .' He trailed off.

'What? You figured out what, Nat?'

'I won't . . .' He trailed off again, as if refusing to finish.

'What, Nat? You won't do what?'

'Make the doctors eat their words.'

A long, sad silence. I should have known, Nathan thought. Whatever the doctors told him to expect, I should have known he wouldn't believe it. Not Nat. He'd think those rules applied to everybody else except him.

'Nat—'

'I'm disappearing.'

'You're still here, Nat.'

'Look.' He raised his right arm, somewhat unsteadily, and tried to flex his bicep. With less than dramatic results.

'I really don't think a big bicep is the heart of the issue here, Nat. But if you want your muscle tone to improve, you need to throw yourself much harder into your physical therapy.'

'Tired,' Nat said.

Nathan sighed. 'I understand. I can imagine you would be. But I've never known you to give up before. So I know you'll keep up with the exercises.'

Long silence.

'With you,' Nat said.

'You don't want Carol to help you with your therapy any more?'

Nat shook his head.

'Because you don't want her to see you like this?'

Nathan waited. But Nat never answered.

After a time, Nathan rose, turned the TV back on, and left Nat alone.

Almost Any idea Will Do

'Yeah? Who is it?' Manny Schultz's voice, calling through his battered and poorly painted apartment door. It was like a flashback for Nathan, who had stood in this spot on one previous occasion. Only the weather had changed. It was now a lovely, cool spring afternoon.

'It's Nathan McCann, Manny.'

The door opened a crack, as it had two summers earlier. Again Nathan's sinuses recoiled from the assault of thick, stale tobacco smoke.

The tiny man's face appeared.

'Oh. Nathan. Yeah. How are you? I feel bad. I oughta come visit the kid more. I know I oughta. It's not just because it's depressing. Even though it is. But I think it's hard for him, too. It seemed to bring him down those few times I visited. Did you notice that, too?'

'I'm not sure,' Nathan said. 'That's not exactly why I'm here, though.'

'Oh. OK. Come in.' Manny brushed his hair roughly back into place with one hand and held the door wide for Nathan, who did not step in. 'Oh. Right. I forgot. You're a non-smoker. OK. I'll come out.'

'I notice the gym downstairs is for lease,' Nathan said, leaning against the fire escape rail. He looked out over the declining downtown neighborhood, amazed at how much further it had decayed in just a couple of years.

'Yeah. I told 'em. I told 'em they were making a mistake. You know, putting in an upscale gym and all. This is downtown. You don't go upscale downtown. The people here, they come up hard. They don't want to put on them silly tights and bounce up and down on a stair-climber. I could just kick myself for letting the place go when Jack died. That was such a great boxing gym. He was doing good, too. All I had to do was take the wheel. But I just couldn't bring myself to do it. It just cut the heart out of me when Jack died.'

'I don't know anything about a Jack,' Nathan said. 'I don't know who he was.'

'A story better left untold.'

A long silence as Nathan sorted through his thoughts. He supposed Manny was waiting to hear what he wanted, why he had come. But Nathan was still organizing and framing those thoughts in his mind. It was unlike him to enter into a conversation without first putting his thoughts in order. But these thoughts seemed particularly hard to tame.

'You know it's been almost a year,' Nathan said.

'Don't think I don't know it. Don't think I don't got those dates burned into my brain. March ninth was the date he landed in the hospital. I got it memorized. March seventh was the day . . .' But the little man never finished the thought.

'Please finish your sentence, Manny. What happened the night of March the seventh?'

'I can't. I promised Nat I'd never say nothing, never, to nobody. I'm not an angel, and I'm not a saint, and I don't do everything right. But I don't look somebody in the eye and promise 'em I won't tell a story, and then turn around and tell it. That bad I'm not.'

'All right,' Nathan said. And then listened to the straining awkwardness of the silence that followed. 'So, does the new gym going out of business put you out of a job?'

'Not sure. If it does, it puts me out on the street, too. These little apartments go with the lease and they might wanta use 'em for something else. Or maybe they'll still want somebody to clean up at night. Depends on who moves in.'

'How many square feet?'

'I got no idea. I'm no good at stuff like that. Why? You thinking of setting up some kind of shop?'

'I just wondered.'

'You wanna see it? Till somebody leases it and changes the locks, I still got the key.'

'Yes,' Nathan said. 'I would like to see it.'

'I'd put a boxing ring right here,' Manny said. 'And over there is where we used to hang the heavy bags.' Nathan watched dust swirl in the late afternoon light through the storefront windows as the little man paced the empty, dusty space. 'I'd probably put some workout equipment over there in the corner. Just real basic stuff. Slant board, weight bench, free weights. Nothing fancy. What kills me is it wouldn't cost much to get it going. You don't need that much equipment, and anyway you can get it second-hand. And the rent is cheap because the whole neighborhood is falling apart. But it's about a thousand times more than what I got. I shoulda kept it going when Jack died. I just didn't have the heart to do it back then.'

'How much would you need?'

The little man stopped moving. He did not immediately speak.

'Why do you ask that?' he said after a time.

'Just a question.'

Manny shook his head. 'Seems to me we took enough from you already. Every time I went and saw that kid since the . . . since he got hurt, he said the same thing to me. "Good thing Nathan made us get insurance." He kicked about it at the time. Thought he was invincible. Now he figures the insurance solves everything. But I know better. It covers eighty per cent. Right? So twenty per cent of all that's happened to him is a shitload of money. Pardon my French.'

Nathan shrugged slightly. Gathered his thoughts before answering. 'It just means an extra year or two of doing people's financial records before I retire. It's not like I'm having to work as a coal miner or a heavy-equipment operator. I think an old man my age can still lift those heavy books. If I made an additional invest-ment, maybe one more year beyond that.'

'Now why would you wanna do a thing like that for me? You haven't already made enough bad invest-ments?'

'Would this be a bad investment?'

'Actually, no. I might not make a fortune, but I bet I could make enough to pay back a small business loan. I still wanna know why you'd do a thing like that for me.'

'It wouldn't really be for you. Quite truthfully. It would be for Nat.'

'Oh. Oh! I get it. You think if he could go to work in a boxing gym, it might get him out of the house. Yeah. Yeah, he might be good here. He could pay back what me and Jack gave him for free. You know, find some other kids and help them come up. I'd pay him some-thing, of course. Only . . . I just hope he wouldn't scare the new guys away. You know, remind 'em how bad you can get hurt.' Manny seemed to chew that thought over for a beat or two. Then he said, 'Well, one good thing, anyway. They won't gimme a hard time when I tell 'em to put on that head guard.'

'So he wasn't wearing a head guard that night?'

No reply.

'I guess he couldn't have been.'

Little Manny stared at the floor. 'I promised him,' he said.

Nathan nodded and moved the conversation in another direction. 'I keep telling him he needs to find another dream. But he says he can't. He says he only ever had that one. So, I thought, if he can't fight any more, at least he can be involved with the sport in some other way.'

'I think I get it now, why you came over here. How long have you known this place was for lease?'

'I didn't know until I parked my car just now.'

'Really? So what did you come over here to say?'

'I'm not sure, actually. I just knew I needed an idea. I thought you might have one. I didn't expect one to be dropped into my lap. But I guess life is like that sometimes.'

'Much of the time as you let it be,' Manny said.

'So how much would you need?'

When Nathan arrived home, Nat was lying on the couch wearing just a pair of sweatpants. Watching the living room TV. An old *I Love Lucy* rerun. Lucy and Superman. One of Nat's hands trailed down to where Feathers lay on the carpet.

'Where's Carol?' Nathan asked, raising his voice to be heard over the canned laughter.

Nat only shrugged.

'Is she coming home for dinner?'

Nat shrugged again.

Nathan chose not to force the issue. But he couldn't help being curious. Because she hadn't been home for dinner last night, either. And he had missed her at breakfast.

He walked down the hall to his bedroom, loosening his tie as he went.

The door to Nat and Carol's room stood partway open.

He stopped in front of it. Pushed it open a bit more.

The doors of the closet had been flung open and left that way. All of Carol's clothes were gone, leaving only dozens of empty hangers to testify that she had ever lived in that room at all.

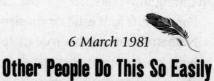

6 March 1981

Other People Do This So Easily

Before Nathan could even park his car in front of Carol's grandparents' house, he saw Carol step out on to the porch and lock the front door behind her. She strode down the steps and along the neatly-tended walkway, then turned and walked quickly toward the bus stop.

Nathan cruised along beside her, slowed, and reached over to crank down the passenger window. She spun nervously, defensively. Then she seemed to register who he was.

He stopped his car, and she walked up to the open window and leaned in, looking sad.

'Hello, Nathan,' she said.

'Would you like a ride to work?'

'Sure. Thanks.'

She climbed in and they sat a moment in silence. Nathan did not drive away.

After a time she looked over at him.

'As soon as you get your seat belt secured, we'll be going.'

'Oh, right,' she said.

Nathan heard the reassuring click of the belt latch snapping into place. He put the car into gear and drove.

For the first half mile or so, silence.

Nathan felt it was his role to speak. After all, he had sought her out, not vice versa.

'The main reason I came by is to see if you're OK.'

'Depends on what you mean by OK.'

'Physically. Psychologically. Financially.'

'I guess I will be,' she said. 'Sounds like a tall order for right now.'

'I guess it is,' Nathan said.

'How did you know where I was? Did he tell you?'

'Eventually.' Nathan allowed a medium-length silence. 'You don't have to tell me this if you don't want to. It's none of my business. I just wondered why you left.'

'Why? *Why*? He didn't tell you why?'

'No. He didn't.'

'Because he told me to go. That's why.'

'Nat told you to go? Are you sure you didn't misunderstand him?'

'He wrote it out in a note, Nathan. There was no misunderstanding. He said this was not what I signed on for.'

'You signed on for better or for worse. In sickness and in health.'

'Don't tell *me*. Tell *him*. He also said he wanted my admiration, not my pity. And I would never say this to him, Nathan, because he'd take it all wrong, but how can I admire him the way he is now? If I said that, he'd think I mean because he talks funny, and his arms and legs don't work right. But that's not why. It's because he's not fighting any more. And I don't mean in the ring.'

'No, I know you don't,' Nathan said. 'I know what you mean.'

'Whatever used to get in his way in life, he always fought like hell. But he won't fight this any more. It's like he just gave up.'

'I know,' Nathan said.

'Any ideas on what to do for him?'

'Maybe. Give me time.'

He pulled up in front of the Frosty Freeze and shifted into park in a passenger-loading zone, sorry the conversation couldn't have lasted longer.

Carol looked at the shabby white building and sighed. 'I need a better job.'

Nathan said nothing.

'He'll come around,' she said. 'We'll get back together. We were meant to be together. I just need a way to convince him that I love him for him. You know, the actual him.'

Nathan shook his head. 'No. It's not your job to convince him. It's his job to believe it. This is his short-coming, not yours. He needs to think well enough of himself to believe it. And that's always been a problem for him.'

Carol sat a moment with her mouth open before answering. 'But . . . I can't do anything about *that*.'

'That's right,' Nathan said. 'You can't.'

A long silence. Nathan glanced at his watch to see if he was making her late for her shift.

'Promise me something, Nathan?'

'I will if I honestly can.'

'Promise me that no matter what happens with Nat and me, you and I will always be friends.'

It took Nathan completely by surprise, and he found it hard to answer.

Carol raced on. 'You've been such a steady thing in my life, ever since I met you. I don't want to lose that. Whatever Nat does.'

Silence. Nathan wished he were better at emotional situations like this. He berated himself for making it to age seventy without mastering exchanges that everyone else found so simple. At least, he assumed they did.

'All right,' Nathan said. 'I promise.'

A Semi-Voluntary Occasion

'I'm not going,' Nat said.

He sat at the breakfast table, stirring the honey and cinnamon into his oatmeal. And stirring. And stirring. And stirring. He looked as though he were trying to guard the bowl, the way he hunched his upper body over it. But unfortunately his posture was nothing out of the ordinary. Nathan had noticed that the young man never went to the trouble of sitting up straight any more.

Nathan sighed deeply. 'I was sincerely hoping it wouldn't come to this,' he said. 'But I guess it has. I've been supporting you for several years now. I financed your boxing career—'

'What there was of it.'

'. . . I paid all the medical bills your insurance didn't cover. I've driven you back and forth to physical therapy for the better part of two years. I didn't do it for thanks, and I never thought I would throw it up at you like this. But the truth remains that I have done a great deal for you, and asked very little in return. I asked you to go hunting once, because I thought you might enjoy it, and this morning I'm asking you to go see the new boxing gym with me.'

'Not even really that new,' Nat said. Still stirring.

'All the more reason it's high time for you to go.'

'So that's it. I got no choice.'

'No. You do have a choice. We always have choices in life. I'm not forcing you to go. I'm asking you to. And reminding you that I ask very little of you.'

Nat dropped his forehead into his left hand, still stirring. It was only when Nat sighed dramatically that Nathan knew he had prevailed.

'Hey, it's Nat!' Manny practically shouted. 'Look everybody. It's Nat.'

'Everybody' consisted of nine young men, working out on bags, weight-lifting, or sparring with each other in the ring. And none of them could possibly have known Nat. So it seemed an odd bit of theatrics to Nathan.

And he knew Nat did not like the attention. Not one bit.

As they stood just inside the doorway, Manny began to applaud. Eight out of nine of the young men followed suit, for no apparent reason. As if someone had turned on an applause sign. People tend to do as they're told, Nathan thought.

The ninth young man, the non-applauder, said, 'Who the hell is Nat?'

Manny strode three steps across the gym floor and cuffed him on the ear. 'Show a little respect. This place wouldn't even exist without Nat.'

Nathan winced inwardly. He had been hoping to avoid that direct connection.

The applause had withered and died now, leaving Nathan and the reluctant Nat standing awkwardly, all eyes fixed on them.

'Besides,' Manny said. 'Nat used to be a hell of a fighter in his day.'

A second strong flinch reaction in Nathan's gut. *In his day?*

'Not that his day was so long ago,' Manny said quickly. Awkwardly attempting to mop up the mistake. 'Not like he's old or anything. I just mean, he was. A hell of a fighter.'

'So what happened to him?' the non-applauder asked.

Nat turned his head toward Nathan and spoke quietly. 'I'll just wait outside,' he said.

The door swung closed behind him, with an audible whoosh and a blast of frigid air.

When Nathan looked around again, Manny was standing right in front of him.

'Guess that didn't go so good,' the little man said.

'Or we could look on the bright side. I got him in here. Finally. After all this time. Even if I only made it stick for about thirty seconds.'

'That Tony kid's not what you might call long on diplomacy. Then again, I gave him the opening. So I guess I'm not the big expert, either.'

'I'd better go see how Nat's doing,' Nathan said.

He found the young man out back, sitting on the snowy bottom of the fire escape stairway, his knees drawn up, his head resting in the cradle of his arms.

Nathan approached slowly, and sat down beside him.

For a time, neither spoke.

Then Nat said, 'What did he mean when he said there wouldn't be a gym without me?'

Nathan didn't answer, because he could not think of an answer that seemed either useful or constructive.

'So, the whole point of this place was to get me out of the house. Right? Get me working again? What am I supposed to do? Mop the sweat off the floor at closing time?'

'We thought you could use your knowledge of the sport to advantage.'

'To *whose* advantage? A bunch of guys who are going to go on and do what I can't? And how am I supposed to get down here? You want me to ride the bus to this place every day? You think I'm going out in public, talking like I do? Walking like this?'

'Yes,' Nathan said. 'I do.'

'Well, that's easy for you to say.'

'You have to have some kind of life, Nat. I feel like I'm not helping you any more by allowing you to lie in front of the TV all day. I'm starting to feel like I'm hurting you by supporting that. Whatever you think your short-comings are . . . you can't just lock yourself in the house so no one can notice or comment. We all have to take ourselves out into the world, flaws and all. And find a way to make the adjustment.'

'Could you take me home?'

Nathan sighed. 'All right. We'll go home for now.'

About halfway through the drive, Nat startled him by speaking.

'Maybe one of these days we could go hunting,' he said.

The comment surprised Nathan so much that it took him several beats to answer.

'What brought that idea on?'

'Well, you mentioned it earlier. You said the only other thing you asked of me was to try hunting. But I really didn't try it that day.'

'You don't have to go hunting with me just because—'

'No, I want to,' Nat said. 'Really. I'll give it a try.'

No more was said for a time, and it struck Nathan that too many more questions might qualify as looking the proverbial gift horse in its proverbial mouth.

'It's true,' Nat said. 'You don't ask much of me. I never really thought about it like that. Until you said it. But it's true.'

Nathan cleared his throat before speaking. 'Unfortunately, the season is over now. And it won't open again until the fall.'

'Oh,' Nat said. 'Well. I guess that's OK. I guess we'll both still be here in the fall.'

'Yes,' Nathan said. 'I suppose we will.'

Mandatory Emotional Responses

Nathan stood outside the door of the shabby little apartment over the gym. The one right next door to Manny Schultz's. Before he could even raise his hand to knock, the door swung open and Nat stuck his head out.

'I'm all ready,' he said, sounding uncharacteristically eager. 'I got a little bag packed right here. Just let me get it. And let me get a leash on Feathers. And then I'm all ready to go.'

'How is it working out living over the gym?' Nathan asked on the drive home.

'OK, I guess. Nice short commute time. There's never any food, though, like there was at your house. If I want something to eat I gotta go out for it. And the dog drives me nuts. I'm used to just opening the back door for him. Now every time he needs to go out I gotta put on my shoes and my coat and put a leash on him and take him out for a walk. Even if he gets the bright idea in the middle of the night. But it's OK, I guess. If it wasn't for him I'd probably never breathe any fresh air. Not that the air downtown is all that fresh.'

'Your speech sounds good.'

'Slow, though.'

'It doesn't even sound that slow to me.'

'Sounds slow from in here. It's so much work. I say that much and I need a nap.'

They drove for a while without speaking. Nathan found himself inwardly gearing up for his next state-ment. He was surprised to notice a trace of butterflies. He was not usually given to butterflies.

'I saw Carol yesterday,' Nathan said.

Nat's head snapped around, but then he caught himself and looked out the window again. He didn't answer for a time. Then he said, 'You just happened to run into her?'

'No. We had lunch. We have lunch about once a month or so.'

'So you can talk about me?'

'No. Because she felt she had a friendship with me, and she didn't want to lose that. But it occurred to both of us that you might take it that way. Which is why I haven't said anything up until now. Carol didn't want me to say anything at all. But I didn't feel comfortable with that. I like to be . . .'

'Forthcoming?'

'Yes,' Nathan said. 'Exactly. I like to be forthcoming.'

'Well. I guess I can't tell either one of you who to be friends with.' Nat looked out the window in silence for a block or two. Then he said, 'Is she seeing somebody?'

Nathan opened his mouth to speak but never got the chance.

'Never mind. Don't answer that. I'm sorry. I guess that was none of my business. Let's talk about something else.'

So Nathan was simultaneously spared from, and deprived of having to say, no. She isn't. Rightly or wrongly, she's waiting for you to come to your senses.

Nat supplied the something else. 'Anybody else you talk to behind my back?'

'Well, your grandmother still calls me. Once a month or so. After all these years.'

He glanced over at Nat in the ensuing silence. Watched him reclaim and close his open lower jaw.

'I'm surprised.'

'Once a grandmother, always a grandmother, I suppose.'

'And what do you tell her? Do you tell her private things about me?'

'Now how would I even know private things about you?' Nathan asked.

It was a question that never received an answer.

* * *

Just as he was turning out the light for bed, Nathan heard Nat call to him from his old bedroom.

'Nathan?'

He put on a robe and went into the young man's room.

'Yes, Nat?'

'I was just wondering if you were going to come in and pull up a chair like you used to always do before bed. I mean, before I got married, that is.'

'Do you want me to?'

'Yeah. Sure.'

Nathan pulled the straight-backed cane chair around to face the bed, and settled himself into it.

'So, what time do we have to get up?' Nat asked. 'Like four?'

'Maybe I'll go easy on you and let you sleep until four fifteen or four thirty.'

'Gee, thanks.'

An awkward silence. They hadn't talked like this for so long. In the old days, Nathan seemed to recall that he would ask various questions about the young man's life. But he couldn't seem to produce anything now.

'Anything in particular on your mind, Nat?'

'Just the job, I guess.'

'Are you physically up to it?'

'Oh, yeah. Physically, it's fine.'

'What part of it isn't fine?'

'I don't know. I'm not sure I can explain it. It's like I

know how everybody thinks I should feel. Like Little Manny. He always wanted to be a fighter. But he wasn't built for it. So he taught other people how to fight. And it seems like that's OK with him. Like he gets some kind of satisfaction out of watching somebody else get what he wanted. And I know everybody wants me to feel that way.'

'But you don't.'

'No. I don't. I hate it. I'm jealous of those guys. Every day. Even the ones that aren't good. At least they get their shot. I try not to show it. But it just chews at me. All the time.'

'Hmm. All I know is that you can't force yourself to feel something you don't.'

'Is there something wrong with me, Nathan?'

'I doubt it. I think you just need more time.'

'Yeah. Maybe so. Maybe that's it. I just need more time.'

12 October 1982

But How Can i When They're So Beautiful?

'Feathers is gonna freak out if Maggie goes and he can't go,' Nat said as Nathan parked the car off the roadway in the dirt.

'I still think we should leave him in the car. He's not a trained hunting dog. He'll scare the ducks away.'

'He'll probably bark or howl the whole time.'

'It hardly matters. No one lives within miles of here.'

'OK,' Nat said, and reached into the back seat to pat the dog's head. 'You heard him, boy. Maggie comes, you stay.'

Nathan stepped out of the car and took both shot-guns from the floor of the back seat. He looked up to see Nat standing beside him in the pre-dawn dark.

'I know,' Nat said. 'Check the safety. Plus carry the gun so it's not pointing at anything. Like ahead and down at the ground. Just to be double-safe.'

'That's some pretty good remembering,' Nathan said, handing him one of the shotguns.

'Depends on whether I'm trying.'

They set off down the trail to the lake together, by flashlight, Maggie bounding ahead. Nathan could hear the plaintive howls of Feathers, abandoned in the car.

He waited to see if Nat would stop at the spot, or respond to passing it in any way.

He saw Nat miss one step as they passed the tree in question. But that was all.

They crouched behind the blind together, in the freezing morning, perfectly silent and perfectly still. Nathan was aware of Maggie nearly trembling in her readiness.

He listened until he heard the sound of beating wings in the distance.

'Hear that?' he whispered near Nat's ear.

Nat nodded.

'When they come in and land on the lake, I'm going to fire on one. When I do, they'll all rise up into the air again. I'll take one more if I can. That's the time for you to try a shot.'

The mallards came into view, nearly filling the dawn sky. Maybe seventy-five of them touched down on the water, their wings open for landing. It was just light enough to see the full color on the bright teal-green heads of the drakes.

Nathan rose slightly, steadied himself, and squeezed

off a shot, feeling the familiar kick of the shotgun butt against his right shoulder.

The ducks rose from the water as if they were one huge, multi-faceted body. Nathan could hear their webbed feet beating the surface of the lake as they took a running step or two before achieving flight. He aimed one more time. Squeezed off another shot.

He heard Maggie hit the water.

He did not hear Nat fire his shotgun.

They stood watching as Maggie swam to retrieve the first duck.

'She's old for this,' Nat said. 'Huh?'

'Very. She's nearly fourteen. I should have retired her years ago. But she's still in good shape. And she loves her work so much. I can't bring myself to break her heart.'

Nathan vacillated over whether or not to mention Nat's absence of a shot. Was Nat concerned about his motor skills? But they had practiced how Nat would hold the gun. And the practise session had appeared to go well enough.

He decided against mentioning it.

Maggie brought the first duck ashore, a big drake, and gently laid it at Nathan's feet. Then she dove back into the water for the second bird.

Nat squatted over the dead animal. Stroked the bright green feathers of its neck and head.

'It's so beautiful,' he said.

'Yes,' Nathan said. 'They're a lovely bird.'

'Is it OK if I can't bring myself to shoot one?'

'Of course it is.'

'I'm not saying it's wrong that you do. And I know it's stupid to get you to bring me all the way out here. But I didn't know how I'd feel about it. You know. Until I tried.'

'Pulling the trigger on a living being is a very personal decision. If you're not a hundred per cent right with it, I don't suggest you do.'

'I'm sorry, Nathan.'

'You don't have to be sorry.'

Maggie laid the second duck on Nathan's foot, a more subtly colored hen, and Nat stroked it as he had the first.

'I'm still glad we got to go hunting together,' Nat said.

'Yes,' Nathan replied. 'That would be the more important thing.'

'Is that the shotgun?' Nat asked as they walked along the trail back to the car. 'The one your grandfather gave you?'

Nat carried the canvas sack of ducks slung over his shoulder, and his borrowed shotgun, leaving Nathan to carry only his own gun.

'It is.'

'So you finally got it back from evidence.'

'Finally. It took me nearly a year and more than half a dozen requests. But it's back.'

'If I had known that one was more important, I'd have taken one of the other ones.'

Nathan did not reply. How exactly would one reply to a statement like that, about which of your guns someone should have stolen to commit armed robbery?

'I can't believe I put you through all that crap,' Nat said.

'You put yourself through a lot more.'

'Yeah. But I can see how I could do all that crap to myself. I just have no idea why I would do it to you.'

Nat pushed back from the table and wiped his mouth on his napkin.

'I don't know what it is about a duck dinner, but it hits the spot every time.'

'I think it's because it's so fresh,' Nathan said. 'When's the last time you had a good home-cooked meal?'

'Last time I ate at your house.' He smiled as he said it. Then the smile faded. No, more than faded. Fell. 'I guess I kind of wish I didn't have to go back to that tiny little hole.'

'You can stay tonight, if you want.'

Nat seemed to mull that over for a moment. He pursed his lips, as if it would help him think harder. Then he shook his head.

'Your house is so comfortable,' he said. 'But that's the problem. It's too comfortable. It's like that magic dream land where you never have to do anything. No responsibility. Like being a little kid. It's addictive. Now that I tore myself out of that, and kind of pushed myself into the whole life thing . . . well . . . I can feel how easy it would be to slide right back again. Now that I'm started, I better keep going. Easier than starting all over again.'

'All right,' Nathan said. 'Good decision, then. Grab your coat. And your dog. And I'll take you home.'

The Code You Don't Ever Break

Nathan watched out the den window, waiting for Manny Schultz to arrive. When Manny finally appeared, he came in a car. A fairly late-model car. Drove right up and parked, as if he'd been an automobile owner all his life. He must be doing well, Nathan thought.

Ever since Manny had phoned, Nathan had felt restless to hear the news. Manny had indicated good news. Nathan just hoped it had something to do with Nat. There hadn't been much good news regarding Nat lately. Nathan had been waiting so long to hear something positive about Nat.

He met the little man at the front door and ushered him in.

He looks so old, Nathan thought. But then it hit him. We *are* old. He's an old man, and I'm an even older one.

Nathan sat on the couch and indicated a place beside

him. Before even sitting down, Manny took an envelope out of his pocket and extended it to Nathan.

'My good news,' he said. 'The last payment.'

'Really. The loan wasn't supposed to be paid off until August.'

'What can I say? Things are going good.'

He sat down on the sofa beside Nathan, the smell of tobacco, both old and new, wafting up from his hair and clothes.

'What about Nat? How are things going with Nat?'

Manny's face fell, and Nathan wished he could grab the words by the tail and pull them back inside again.

'Ah, Nathan. Not so good. I wasn't even gonna say this. He did this thing but I wasn't even gonna repeat it. But you asked, and I gotta get this off my chest. 'Cause it just cut the heart outta me, what happened. The other day, this kid come in. No more than twelve. Right off the bat, reminded me so much of Nat the first day he walked in. Even though they don't look nothing alike. This kid is black, and real big. Could even grow into a heavyweight. But I mean, in other ways he reminded me. I guess you don't know the story about how Nat met Jack.'

'No. I don't. You said it was a story better left untold.'

'I meant the end of Jack's story, actually. But the day Nat walked into that gym. He was thirteen, fourteen years old. Had these new gloves and didn't even know how to put 'em on or lace 'em up. Didn't even know what to hit or how. Didn't have probably a nickel in his jeans. So I says to Jack, "Hey, Jack, you got time for a kid who don't know nothing about nothing?" Jack comes over, sizes him up. Nat looked a little bit like this kid Jack was working with who went and got himself killed, so I think that's why Jack took a liking to him, you know? Anyway, he took him on.

'Some people'll do that and some won't. Personal decision, I guess. But it seems to me that the people who do, it's because they had it done for *them*. You know? I took Jack on. He didn't have no money, either. So Jack took on Nat. And then I took on Nat. I must be boring the crap out of you. I didn't mean to make a short story long.'

'No, it's OK. But I am a little anxious to hear what Nat did that was so bad.'

'So this kid walks in. 'Bout the same age as Nat was. No money. Even lives with his grandmother, if you can believe that. 'Course these days that's not so un-common. Anyway, it just felt so made in heaven. Like God was smiling right down on our heads, and that's coming from me, who most of the time don't even believe in the son of a bitch, pardon my French. And even when I do believe, we're hardly on speaking terms. So, anyway, it was the perfect setup. Just picture perfect, made in heaven. So I says to Nat, "Hey, Nat. You got time for a kid who don't know nothing from nothing and don't have two nickels to rub together?" '

Nathan waited anxiously for him to continue. Still wanting to get the bad news over with. 'What did he say?'

'He said no.'

'Oh. I'm sorry to hear that.'

'It's like the law, you know? It's like this code you don't break. Not ever.'

'Did he say why?'

'Yeah, I took him over in a corner where this poor kid wouldn't have to hear. And I told him Jack would roll over in his grave to hear him say that. And he knew what I meant all right. He remembered the deal. He said Jack had it to spare. He said, "I don't have anything for this kid. Jack had something, so he gave it. I got nothing to spare."'

They sat in silence for a moment or two. The weight of the moment seemed to further bend Nathan's shoulders.

'What happened to the boy?'

'Oh, he's still around. I put him on a bag and gave him some pointers.'

'Maybe Nat just needs more time.'

Manny laughed his odd laugh. That spitting, spewing sound. 'It's been eight years, Nathan. Eight years since he got hurt. I just kind of think that maybe if you don't come back in eight years it's because you can't. And I used to think everybody got over everything. We always say we never will. But then we do. Because, really, what choice do we have? But I don't know about Nat any more. I think he packed it in.'

'I never like to make absolute predictions,' Nathan said. But he noticed his own words sounded considerably less than confident.

'Yeah, I guess. If we're not dead yet, who knows? Well, anyway, I didn't mean to take up your whole day here. I just had to get that off my chest.'

The little man rose suddenly to his feet, and Nathan walked him to the door.

'One thing I'll say for sure,' Manny said on his way out. 'If he never comes around, it's not for lack of trying on your part. You did everything for that kid.'

'Everything I could.'

'And him not even any kin to you. Why'd you do all that for him, anyway? All that above and beyond stuff?'

He peered up into Nathan's face, waiting for his answer. Suddenly, intensely serious.

'Why not?' Nathan asked. 'What else have I done with my life that's above and beyond?'

Part Eight

Nathan Bates

Nat sprinted, somewhat awkwardly, down the third-floor hallway of the hospital, until he literally ran into a nurse. A short, round, older woman who brushed herself off, scolded him with her face, and crossed her arms stubbornly.

'Young man,' she said. 'This is a hospital.'

Nat sighed and inwardly counted to ten. Or began, anyway. Somewhere around three it became his turn to speak.

'First off, ma'am, I'm going to be thirty this year, so I think I've finally outgrown the "young man" bull, thank you very much. And not a moment too soon. Secondly, I *know* this is a hospital, which is why I'm in a hurry. When you all of a sudden find out someone you love is in the hospital, it makes you impatient to know . . .' He cranked up the volume at this juncture,

'. . . what the hell is going on!'

He waited to be chastised for raising his voice to her. Instead she just said, 'Patient name, please?'

'Nathan McCann.'

'Second door on your right. He's probably in there right now, listening to you shout at me.'

'Good,' Nat said. 'That's how he'll know it's me.'

She shook her head and walked off down the hall.

Nat stuck his head into the second door on his right.

'Nathan?'

'Yes, Nat,' he said quietly. 'I sensed you had arrived.'

Nat stepped inside and up to Nathan's hospital bed.

Nat had never seen Nathan with his hair uncombed. Or looking helpless. Or looking so old. He'd seen Nathan just about six days ago. They'd had lunch. But he hadn't looked like this. Six days ago he'd been a fairly healthy-looking old guy in his late seventies. Now he was visually ninety, leaving Nat scrambling to keep up.

'Nathan. How could you have surgery and not tell me?'

'I didn't want to worry you,' Nathan said, his voice small.

'Whatever happened to all that truth you were always preaching? How the truth is the truth, even if we don't like it, and we're not doing the person any favors to lie?'

'I didn't lie to you,' Nathan said. 'I didn't say I *wasn't* having surgery.'

Nat threw his head back and sighed deeply, looking

at the white acoustic ceiling. Then he pulled up a hard plastic chair and sat backwards on it, folding his arms on the top of the chair back and staring into Nathan's face.

For the first time in all the years Nat had known him, Nathan cut his eyes away.

'That's not exactly what you might call forthcoming, Nathan.'

Long silence.

Then Nathan said, 'I know. I'm sorry. I thought they were going to go in and remove this tumor that was sitting on my kidney. And I was hoping they would say they were confident they'd gotten it all. And then I could tell you the good news and the bad news all at one time. I had cancer, but they're sure the surgery was successful. They're sure they got it all.'

A pause, as the word 'cancer' ricocheted around in Nat's head and gut, leaving a weak, trembly feeling behind it.

'So. Are they sure they got it all?'

'No,' Nathan said.

'So, maybe there's this tiny bit they didn't get, and then maybe they'll do radiation and chemo, and everything'll be fine?'

'No,' Nathan said.

Unable to bring himself to ask any more questions, Nat just waited, silently, staring at a spot on Nathan's bed sheet.

'When they got inside, it was everywhere. So they just closed me back up again.'

'They didn't even try to get it out?'

'There wasn't much point.'

'But they'll still do radiation and chemo.' Still staring at the spot on the sheet.

'They gave me the option. But it would only have potentially doubled the time I have. And it would have completely destroyed any quality of life I might enjoy during that time.'

Nat looked at Nathan's face again. An effort. 'Yeah, but double? Double the time you have left? That's gotta be worth it, right?'

He forced himself to hold his gaze on Nathan's face. Nathan did not return the look.

'Double would only represent about another month or six weeks.'

Back to the spot on the sheet.

A literal two or three minutes ticked by. Nat nursed an odd feeling in his stomach. A buzzing. Like the humming of a high-voltage electrical wire. As if he had just suffered a mild electrocution. He knew he had to say something, sometime. He just couldn't imagine what it might be. He searched desperately in his mind, and finally found something that he thought would be OK.

'What can I do to help you, Nathan?'

He realized, after the fact, that he'd arrived at those

words by imagining what Nathan would say if the shoe were on the other foot.

'You can take me home.'

'Home?'

'Yes. I want to be in my own home.'

'Don't you have to be here?'

'No. I don't *have* to do anything any more. I can do whatever I damn well please. And I want to be in my own home.'

Nat briefly scanned his mind to see if Nathan had ever used the word 'damn' in his presence before. No matches.

'But they know what to do for you here.'

'There's nothing they *can* do, Nat. Please just call a cab and take me home.'

Another minute of the buzzing, which seemed almost to have an accompanying sound. Then Nat realized it was just a ringing in his ears.

'OK. I'll go get a cab.'

Nat stood. His legs worked just as he expected them to.

He stepped out into the hall. And almost ran smack into Carol.

'Oh. Nat,' she said. As if she'd seen him last month sometime. Or the month before. Definitely not as though they hadn't spoken in almost nine years. 'Isn't it awful about Nathan?'

She looked so much older, but in a good way. Less

like a girl, and more like a grown woman. Had he grown up that much, too? It didn't feel like it from the inside of him.

'When did he call you?'

'Just now. I left work and came right over.'

'So he didn't tell you he was having surgery, either.'

'No.'

Thank God, Nat thought. That would have been just about the final insult in all of this. If everyone had known except him.

Unable to add the whole Carol issue to the weight he already carried, he simply walked around her and tried to be gone.

'I have to call a cab,' he said over his shoulder. 'Nathan wants to go home.'

'I could drive you,' she said.

Nat stopped. He did not immediately answer. He closed his eyes, as if he could transport himself to someplace easier. But when he opened them again, he was still in the hospital. And Carol was still standing in the hall staring at him.

'You have a car, now?'

'Yes. I do. I got my license. And I got a better job and I bought a second-hand Toyota.'

'You know . . . a cab'll be fine. He asked me to call a cab.'

'You want me to go ask him? If he'd rather have a ride?'

Nat inwardly sighed, and gave it all up for lost. Sometimes it's easier to fall deeply into the worst day imaginable. At least save yourself the trouble of trying to fight.

'I guess it should be up to Nathan,' he said. 'I'll go with whatever Nathan says.'

'Where's Carol?' Nathan asked. 'Did she go home?'

'No. She's in the kitchen making dinner.'

Nat sat on one of the straight-backed wooden chairs by Nathan's bed. Sitting on his hands, quite literally. Leaning forward and watching Nathan as if he might be about to blow away. He'd never spent any time in Nathan's bedroom, and it felt awkward to be here now.

Nathan did not reply. And the silence made Nat nervous.

So he said, 'Scrambled eggs, most likely.'

'Oh, I doubt it,' Nathan said. 'Carol is a wonderful cook.' Nat cocked an eyebrow but said nothing. 'She had me over to dinner just before the holidays.'

'I thought she only knew how to make scrambled eggs.'

'That was a long time ago, Nat.'

'Thanks for reminding me.'

'I'm sorry. I didn't mean it the way it came out.'

Nat rocked back and forth slightly on his hands. Not knowing what to say. Or what to feel. Or where to be.

This didn't feel like the place to be, but he was oddly sure that moving wouldn't fix it.

'Tell me,' Nathan said, startling him. 'Are you sitting there out of complete devotion to me, and utter shock that it's come time for me to get my affairs in order? Or are you hiding out here to avoid seeing Carol?'

'Yes,' Nat said.

They both smiled, which Nat suspected came as a surprise to both of them. It certainly surprised Nat.

'Why don't you go out and help her with dinner?'

'Because it scares the crap out of me.'

'Fear of cooking?'

'Very funny. Talking to her. Looking at her. Being in the same room with her. It all scares the crap out of me.'

'What would you say to her if she didn't scare the . . . crap out of you?'

'Nathan. You said crap!' Nat announced this almost proudly.

'I'm definitely feeling a lifting of the rules. But you're ducking the question.'

'Oh. Right. I guess I would say I was an idiot. And that I'm really, seriously sorry. Even though sorry probably doesn't help at all.'

'Sounds like a good start.'

'You want me to *start* with that?'

'What if you never see her again? You might not have much time.'

Nat sighed. Rose, and pushed the chair back into the corner.

'OK. Wish me luck. I'm going in.'

'Nathan thinks I should help you with dinner.'

Nat stood with his shoulder leaned against the kitchen door jamb. As if crossing the threshold might prove too dangerous.

'I don't really need help, actually. It's all under control. But thank you.' A split second before Nat could slink away in utter defeat, she said, 'You can keep me company while I cook, if you like.'

So he didn't slink away. But neither did he cross the dangerous threshold.

Say it, he thought. Just open your mouth and say it.

'Carol,' he said, because he thought after saying that much he'd be obligated to finish.

'Yes, Nat?'

She turned away from the stove and stood facing him. Put down her wooden spoon on the Coney Island spoon-rest on the stove, and pushed back a wisp of hair that had come down from its barrette. She looked right into his face, freezing everything. Even time.

'Thanks for making dinner,' he said.

'It's no problem. I want to do something for Nathan. I can't believe this. Oh, that's a stupid thing to say, I guess. I mean, he's almost seventy-nine. I don't see why I should be shocked. But I guess I still am. Are you going to take care of him all by yourself? Or are you going to have a nurse or a hospice person come in?'

Nat tried to force his brain into some kind of action, but he still felt as though she'd asked him to solve a complex algebra equation.

'I don't know. We haven't really worked out a plan. I'll have to see what Nathan wants to do.'

'Would you like me to stay?'

A shocked silence, one that was probably fairly short, but felt endless and impenetrable to Nat. He offered no response. Because he had none. He had nothing.

'I'd have to go to work on the weekdays. But I could make breakfast and dinner. And run errands in my car. And maybe just help out if you got tired and needed a rest. I could sleep in the den. Or on the couch.'

'No, you can sleep in the bed. I'm going to sleep in Nathan's room. On the floor, or whatever. In case he needs anything in the night.'

'It's all set, then. Will you tell him I'll bring his dinner in twenty minutes?'

Say it, he thought. Say something. Say anything. Open your mouth and speak.

'Carol?'

'Yes, Nat?'

'Thanks.'

'I think I'll have to start someplace easier. Oh, and dinner's coming in twenty minutes.'

Nathan set down the book he had been reading. The biography of one of those old political guys from colonial times, but Nat couldn't read the name from across the room and didn't recognize the picture. Nathan took off his reading glasses. Sighed. Shook his head.

'You might have just forfeited your last chance to apologize.'

'I doubt it,' Nat said. 'She's staying.'

4 January 1990

Exceptions

'All of this is such a shock to me,' Nat said. 'I just can't seem to get my head around it all.'

He lay on a rollaway cot in Nathan's room, wondering what time it was. Not dawn. That's all he knew for sure. That and the fact that Nathan was also awake.

'I'm going to be seventy-nine years old, Nat. If I make it until the fourth of next month, that is. I was born in 1911. People born in 1911 have average lifespans of less than seventy-nine years.'

'Yeah, all right. But I'm not talking about stuff like that, anyway. I'm talking about shock. Shock doesn't live in the part of your brain that does math. You know?'

Nat noticed that they spoke more easily in the dark. Maybe he should try this with everybody. Maybe he should turn out the lights and tell Carol he was an idiot and he was sorry.

'You must have known I'd have to die someday.'

'Not really, no.' Then he realized how stupid it must have sounded. 'I'm not saying I thought you never would. Just that I never thought about it. No. You know what? That's not really the truth. The truth is, I really thought you never would. I mean, not literally, but . . . I know everybody dies. I just think there was this weird little part of me that sort of . . . not literally, but . . . I thought you'd be the exception to the rule.'

'I'm sorry I can't be immortal for you.'

'That makes two of us,' Nat said.

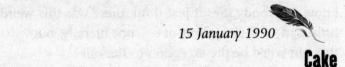

15 January 1990

Cake

'Carol had to leave for work early this morning, Nathan.' Nat sat on the edge of his little cot, pulling off his pajama top and pulling on a sweatshirt. He reflexively turned his back to Nathan because he was ashamed of his chest. Its lack of any noticeable development. 'So I'll be making breakfast. What would you like?'

'I know Carol prides herself on always doing something fancy. But lately I've had a taste for Cream of Wheat.'

'Good. Because fancy is not my department. And Cream of Wheat has directions on the box.' Nat stood, and pulled sweatpants on over his boxer shorts. 'Do you need me to bring you the bed pan before I go?'

'No, thank you. After breakfast will be fine.'

'OK. One Cream of Wheat. Coming up.'

'With a little butter, please. And some milk.'

'Check.'

Just as Nat was leaving the room, Nathan said, 'Nat?' Nat turned back and leaned in the open doorway, waiting. 'Make that a lot of butter. And cream. It just suddenly hit me. I can stop watching my weight now.'

'I'll go along with that,' Nat said. Trying to sound bright. Trying to cover the mood crash that hit him every time he had to be reminded. 'Oh. I've been meaning to ask you. What's your favorite kind of cake, Nathan?'

'For breakfast?'

'In general.'

'Hmm.' He gingerly sat up a little more in bed, propping an extra feather pillow behind his back. 'I'd say lemon cake.'

'Really? Lemon?'

'What's wrong with lemon?'

'I don't know. Nothing, I guess. But I'd never have thought lemon. If it were me I'd have gone with something like chocolate with chocolate frosting. Or even German chocolate.'

'We're all different. That's the beauty of diversity. Why are you asking me about cake?'

'Carol wants to make you a cake for your birthday.'

'Tell her not to buy the ingredients just yet.'

'I wish you wouldn't say things like that, Nathan. It's only, like, three weeks from now.'

'You're right. I apologize.'

'I'll go make some Cream of Wheat.'

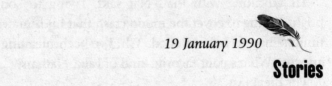

19 January 1990

Stories

'I need another sponge bath,' Nathan said.

'No problem.'

'If you have a hard time with things like this, we could get a nurse to come in for a few hours a week.'

'Stop it, Nathan. I said I'd take care of you. And I'm taking care of you.'

'I'm just thinking it might get harder. In certain ways. When things like this come up.'

'I'm taking care of you, Nathan.'

'Let me know if you change your mind.'

'I won't change my mind.'

Nat ran the water in Nathan's bathroom until it was good and hot. Not burning hot, but hot enough to stay comfortable for the whole bath. He gathered up three big bath sheets. A clean washcloth. A bar of soap.

He helped Nathan turn on to his side, and laid out a

towel for him to roll back on to, careful not to leave any creases that would make him uncomfortable. Then he helped him roll to the other side and did the same again.

'I'll have to wash your back,' Nat said.

'All right.'

He unbuttoned Nathan's pajama top and helped him sit up so he could take it off. He dipped the washcloth into the hot water and squeezed it out. Then he sat down at the very head of the bed, behind Nathan. It always shocked Nat to see the surgery scar. He'd had no idea such a huge piece of Nathan's back had been sliced open. Just so some surgeon could give up trying.

'Is it OK to wash over this now?' he asked, touching the raised scar lightly.

'Yes. It's healed enough.'

Nat began to gently work with the cloth, seeing and feeling every knob of Nathan's curved spine.

'Does that hurt?'

'No, it's fine.'

'Is the water too hot?'

'No, it feels good.'

He rinsed the back carefully, and gently blotted it with the clean towel. Then he helped Nathan lie back down again.

'I'm going to pull this part of the sheet over the middle of you,' Nat said. 'And then we'll pull the pajamas off from underneath. That way you'll have your privacy.'

Nat put a hand under Nathan's waist and helped him raise up. It was hard, because Nat's left arm was his weakest limb. But together they managed. He pulled at the thin flannel pajamas with his right, and Nathan held the sheet to keep it from being pulled away at the same time. Then he eased Nathan down again, and pulled the pajamas off by the bottom of their legs. Nathan lay naked on his bed with a sheet over his privates, and Nat tried to keep his glance averted. But even in his peripheral vision, Nat was surprised by the increased swelling of Nathan's stomach. Does cancer do that to a person? he wondered.

It shocked him enough that he looked directly. For just a split second, he took Nathan in. Just as he was now. Then he quickly looked away again.

A long silence while Nat moved the cloth and the basin to a safe spot where Nathan could reach them. He set the soap on a towel on Nathan's night stand, moving aside the dozen bottles of prescription pain medication.

'Penny for your thoughts,' Nathan said. 'Even though I know I won't like them.'

'I was just thinking . . .' Nat realized he really was about to say what he was thinking. Which surprised him. 'I was thinking . . . how the way we come into the world, and the way we go out of it are sort of the same.

How helpless we are. You know. At both ends of things. And how . . . sort of . . . fragile.'

'Yes,' Nathan said. 'I still remember your coming in very clearly. Fragile is the word.'

'I'll be over here by the window,' Nat said. 'If you need me for anything.'

He walked to Nathan's bedroom window. The blinds had been left up, because it only looked out on to the private back yard, anyway. It was snowing. Hard. He worried briefly about Carol, driving home from work. Hoped the roads would be plowed by then.

'I'll have to shovel the driveway,' Nat said. 'So Carol can get back in.'

'I have a snowblower now.'

'Ah. Good to know.' He watched the big, wet flakes swirl for a bit. Heard the sound of water pouring back into the basin each time Nathan wrung out the cloth. Then he said, 'Nathan? Will you tell me the story of the day you found me in the woods?'

'Of course I will. I'd be happy to. I wish I'd had more chances to tell it in my life. Everybody wanted to talk about it, but nobody really wanted to hear my experience with it. They just jumped right off into how a thing like that could happen, and why, and then immediately they would begin to relate it to their own children, trying to imagine someone they loved in such a position. And it became about their own shock and horror, then. So, yes. I'll tell you.

'It was the same hour of morning as the two times we went hunting. So not even quite light yet. I was walking to the lake by flashlight, with my shotgun up over my shoulder—'

'The one your grandfather gave you?'

'Yes. All of a sudden, I realized Sadie wasn't with me. And that had never happened before. Sadie was a bred and trained hunting dog, and there was no distracting her on the way to a hunt. So I knew already that something was very wrong. I called her name. Three times. But she didn't respond. I think at the time I was cross with her, which seems strange in retrospect, because I should have known she had a monumental reason. I held still and listened, and I could hear her scratching in the leaves. So I shone the flashlight on her. There was something in her face. In her eyes. She was begging me to come see what she saw. Asking in the only way a dog is able to ask. So I went to her. And I shone the light on the pile of leaves. And what do you think I saw? Which part of you do you think I saw first?'

Swirling snow. Coming faster. Piling up more deeply in Nathan's yard. Nat stood with his hands clasped behind his back. 'The little knit cap?'

'No. It was your foot.'

'Which one?'

'Your left. I picked you up. And I just held you like that for a long time. I was wondering how a thing like that could happen. Who would do it. I didn't jump up and rush you to the hospital because I had no idea you were alive. It never occurred to me that you could be. Your eyes were closed. You weren't moving. Your skin felt cold.'

'How did you finally figure it out?'

'I set you back down and shone the flashlight on you. And you moved. Just your mouth. Just a little. A very sluggish little bit of movement. This is the moment I remember the most clearly, but it's probably the hardest one to describe. I was so certain I had found a tiny corpse of a baby. I was so sure that was what you were. And then you moved. And it changed everything, so suddenly and so drastically. I was truly shocked. I don't know how to describe it any better than that.'

'So then you rushed me to the hospital.'

'Yes. I left the shotgun right where it was—'

'Your good shotgun?'

'I couldn't hold both. I had to support your head. And the gun was less important. I ran all the way back to the car. And it was still just barely dawn. Hardly light. I was so afraid I'd trip and go flying. I had no idea how I would protect you if I fell. But I didn't fall. Thank God I knew that trail so well.'

'Where was I while you were driving? On the seat?'

'Oh, no. I didn't dare leave you on the seat. What if I'd had to stop suddenly? No, you rode on my lap. But even on my lap, I was afraid you'd fly forward if I had to slam on the brakes. I was driving awfully fast. So I held you with your bottom half resting on my lap, but with your head and shoulders in the crook of my left arm. And I drove with my right. Fortunately the transmission was an automatic. I never had a child but I know it's important to support a baby's head. You know what's odd? I never thought about it until just now, as I'm telling the story. But even at first, when I thought you were dead . . . when I thought I was holding only the remains of a newborn . . . I still supported your head. And I'm not even sure why.

'But one thing I definitely remember. It was the clearest feeling I can ever remember having. I don't know if you're familiar with the saying "you can't unring the bell". But it was a feeling similar to that. I knew that our paths had crossed in that moment, and that they would never uncross again. I wasn't used to knowing things like that. But I was sure.'

'And you were right.'

Silence. Flakes of wet snow ticking against the window and melting there.

Then Nathan said, 'I'm about done here. If you'll help me get dressed again.'

Nat returned to the bed and helped Nathan dry off his feet, put on his pajama top. Helped him keep himself covered with the sheet while Nat struggled to get the pajama bottoms back on underneath it. Then he gathered up all the wet towels. Left them on top of the hamper to dry. Emptied the basin in the bathroom sink.

He felt genuinely tired when he was done, so he laid down on the cot beside Nathan's bed.

'It feels good to be clean,' Nathan said. 'Thank you.'

'The first day I met you . . . I mean, not the first day. Not the one you just told me about.'

'I know what day you mean. The day your grand-mother left you here.'

'I said you hadn't done me any big favor. But that wasn't true.'

'I know,' Nathan said. 'I knew it then, too.'

They lay in silence for a time. Three minutes, maybe four. Nat expected Nathan to drop straight into a nap. Nathan had been sleeping a lot lately, often without notice.

So it startled him when Nathan said, 'Now I'd like *you* to tell *me* a story. I'd like you to tell me about the night of March seventh, 1980. The night you stayed on in New York and came home with a devastating brain injury.'

Nat squeezed his eyes more tightly shut. Gathered his strength before speaking. Noticed his left hand trembled slightly. 'I really screwed up, Nathan.'

'I sensed that much.'

'I took a pro fight. An unregulated fight. There was a lot of money in it. Little Manny tried to talk me out of it. Well, he did more than talk. He refused to tell me where it was, or how to do it without him. But the guy was still there. The fight promoter. And I was just about to find him on my own. That's the only reason Little Manny went along. Just to protect me. Because I was gonna do it on my own, anyway. With him or without him.'

'So when you said you were staying to do some sparring, you already knew you were going to take this fight.'

'Yes.'

'So that was a lie.'

'Yes. The minute it came out of my mouth, I remembered how you said never to lie to you again. But it was out by then. I felt terrible. But I did it, anyway.'

'Did you lie to me about anything else after I asked you not to?'

'No. Just that fight. I'm sorry, Nathan. It was so stupid.'

'Why, Nat? Can you just give me something to help me see why?'

'I wanted to buy Carol a real wedding ring. I hated that cheap silver one. She deserved better. I didn't even think I'd win that damn fight. I thought I'd just hold my own for two or three rounds and then I could come home with a real ring for Carol.'

No reply. No sound. Nat looked up to see Nathan nodding slowly to himself.

'Love,' Nathan said. 'Love explains a lot.'

'Can you forgive me for lying about it, Nathan? I mean, I don't know why you should. I'm not even saying I expect it. I'm just wondering. If it's the kind of thing you could forgive.'

Half a minute or more, during which Nat listened carefully to the sound of Nathan's audible breathing.

'I'll make a deal with you,' Nathan said. 'I'll forgive you for lying about the fight, if you'll forgive me for not telling you I had cancer.'

Nat rose, walked to Nathan's bed. Sat down next to him. He held out his right hand and Nathan shook it. Then he rose and headed for the door.

'Nat. Before you go . . .'

'Yes?'

'Did you ever try to find your father?'

'No.' He waited to see if Nathan would ask why not. He didn't. But Nat felt compelled to say anyway. 'Because you said I should be ready for a disappointment. For him to let me down. I knew you were right about that. And I wasn't. Ready. I never got ready. I just knew I couldn't take that. So I decided to stick with you.'

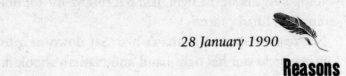

28 January 1990

Reasons

'Are you awake, Nat?' Nathan's voice seemed to lose volume every day. He barely sounded like Nathan any more. The strength of that voice, the sureness of it, the way it had seemed to project up from the depths of his chest . . . all that was gone now. It sounded as though it lived in his throat and barely succeeded in making the short journey.

Nat glanced at the new glow-in-the-dark clock. Two thirty.

'Oh, yes.'

'Why didn't you help that boy?'

'What boy?'

'The one Little Manny wanted you to help.'

'Oh. Danny?'

'Big boy. Lives with his grandmother.'

'Danny.'

'Why wouldn't you help him? Are you still jealous of those boys?'

'Yes.'

'But you work with them every day. It's your job.'

'But they pay.'

'They pay Manny. You get paid either way.'

'I just don't like Danny.'

'Why not?'

'I don't know. I just don't. Just something about him I don't like.'

Silence. Nat listened to the clock ticking. The wind whistling outside.

Nathan didn't say anything.

'Didn't you ever meet someone you didn't like?'

'Often. But I could usually state my reasons.'

'Well, I don't know mine.'

'See if you can figure it out and get back to me. OK?'

'Why? Because you really want to know? Or because you really want *me* to know?'

'Yes,' Nathan said.

In spite of himself, Nat laughed slightly.

'You know,' Nathan said, 'your grandmother still calls me. To ask after you. Once a month or so. After all these years.'

'No. I didn't know she still did. You didn't tell me she still did.'

'I'm telling you now,' Nathan said.

'She must be quite an old woman by now.'

'I thought when I met her that she was my age. But she's actually four years younger. So she's just about in her mid-seventies. So she's getting up in years, yes.'

'Meaning if I'm going to call her, I should do it soon.'

'I didn't say that. I'm merely telling you.'

'Why now? All of a sudden? Why tell me now?'

'How many more chances do you suppose I'll get?' Nathan asked.

3 February 1990

Still

Carol came in at six thirty.

Nat sat in the living room, in the dark. On the window seat. Watching the snow fly in the light from the street lamp out front.

At the corner of his eye he saw the lights come on in the foyer. Carol stuck her head into the living room. Reached for the overhead light switch.

'Nat?'

'Don't turn on the light, please.'

'Are you OK?'

'I want to tell you something.'

She walked into the middle of the living room and froze there in the near-dark, a paper grocery sack clutched in both arms.

'I was an idiot. And I'm sorry. I know sorry doesn't help. But I really mean it. I'm really sorry for being such a complete idiot. I just couldn't do it. I couldn't believe you would love me if I wasn't in shape. If I wasn't a fighter. You know. If I wasn't everything I was when you met me.'

'You might be overestimating what you were when I met you.'

'What's that supposed to mean?'

'Never mind. Sorry. Do you believe it now?'

'Not entirely, no.'

'Sorry to hear that. But thanks for the apology. And thanks for snowblowing the driveway. I have to go make Nathan's cake. So it'll be ready in the morning.'

'I don't think he's really going to eat cake for breakfast.'

'He can eat it whenever he wants. But I still think it would be funny to serve it for breakfast.'

She disappeared into the kitchen, leaving Nat alone in the dark.

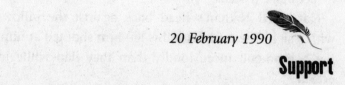

20 February 1990

Support

Nat's left arm trembled with the exertion of supporting Nathan's head while he spoon-fed him his afternoon clear broth. Not that Nathan's head was all that heavy. But Nat's left arm was still weak. And Nathan could only take about half a teaspoonful at a time. So he'd been holding the position for some time.

'Hospice woman is coming next week,' Nathan whispered between sips.

'Why? I can take care of you.'

'Different system of pain management.'

'Oh.'

'But I could have her take over some of the feeding.'

'No. I can feed you.'

'It's too hard for you to support my head.'

'It's fine, Nathan.'

'I can feel your arm trembling.'

'Nathan. You made sure my head was supported. Even when you thought I was dead, you made sure my head was supported. And all the way to the hospital. Did your arm get tired? I bet it did. Now just finish your soup, OK?'

'Let's take a break.'

Nat eased Nathan's head back against the pillows with a sigh. The muscles in his left arm shouted at him. For a moment, more loudly than they had while in action.

They sat for a minute, quietly. Resting from the ordeal of clear broth.

Then Nat said, 'It's because he's better than I was.'

'Who?'

'Danny.'

'Oh. Danny.'

'He's better than I ever was and he'll be better than I ever would have been. Plus if he keeps growing at this rate, he'll go heavyweight. And the heavyweights get all the glory.'

'So that's why you don't like him.'

'Yes.'

'Aren't you glad to know that?'

'Not really, no.'

'You'll thank me for it some day.'

'I doubt it,' Nat said.

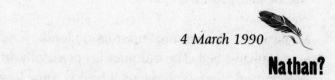

4 March 1990

Nathan?

The light poured into Nathan's bedroom, causing Nat to wince and blink when he opened his eyes. He knew he'd slept much later than usual. Nathan must have been awake for hours. He must have stayed quiet to let Nat sleep.

He slowly adjusted his eyes to the light and then clasped his hands behind his head. Looking up and out the window to clear, blue-white winter sky.

'Nathan?' he asked after a time. 'Why did you do everything you did for me? I mean, I know why you rushed me to the hospital when you found me. Hell, anybody would have. Even *I* would do that much. But I mean . . . taking me into your house. Visiting me three times a week in Juvie. Financing my boxing career. And the gym. And all that time I was being such a dick. Sorry about the language, but if you can think of a better description feel free to jump in. Why did you do all of it?'

Nat lay still, waiting for his answer. It didn't surprise him to have to wait. Nathan took more and more time to speak these days. And it was a hard question, anyway.

But the pause just kept going.

'Nathan?'

No answer. Nat scrambled up from under the covers. Ran to Nathan's bed. The old man lay peacefully with his eyes closed. As if napping. As if having some lovely dream.

'Nathan?'

Nat backed up two steps.

A knock at the front door startled him. Even though the sound was muffled from all the way in the back bedroom. Nat sprinted to the door, still only in pajamas, praying it would be Wilma, the hospice lady. Wilma would know what to do.

He threw the door wide.

'My goodness,' Wilma said. 'Everything all right?'

'Nathan's . . . I don't know what he is, Wilma, but he doesn't answer me.'

'Did you check his pulse?'

'No, it was just now. Just when you knocked.'

'Well, let's go see what's what, then.'

She followed him back down the carpeted hallway. Nat's heart beat so violently that he could feel it in his chest and hear it in his ears.

He watched Wilma silently, calmly, lean over Nathan and hold her fingertips on his wrist.

She nodded at Nat. 'He's still with us,' she said. 'Still in there. Somewhere. Very weak pulse. I think he's down below the place where you're going to see him conscious. I don't think he'll wake up and talk much from here on. Then again, you never know.'

'So what do I do, Wilma?'

'Nothing much *to* do, really. Just stay with him. Try to see the beauty in it, if such a thing is possible for you.'

Without even waiting for Wilma to finish up and go, Nat lay on the bed beside Nathan. Moved in close and threw one arm over Nathan's shoulders.

'It's nice to see a young man so devoted to his grand-father,' Wilma said. 'I don't see a thing like that every day.'

Call

'Nat?' He heard Carol's voice from the doorway. 'Are you OK?'

'Yeah.'

'Is Nathan OK?'

'I think so. I hope so. He's not still in there, though.'

'Oh, Nat.'

'He left sometime in the night.'

'We should call somebody.'

'Who?'

'The lady from the hospice, maybe. She'll tell us what to do.'

'You call her. OK?'

'OK. I'll call right now.' She moved toward the bedroom phone.

'From the kitchen, please.'

She stood frozen. Leveled him with a confused look.

'I just need a little more time with him,' Nat said. 'Please?'

7 March 1990

Why

Nat squinted his eyes when the bedroom door opened, letting in light from the hall. Carol stuck her head in and watched Nat for a moment, curled in a fetal position on Nathan's otherwise empty bed. He watched back, blinking into the light. She looked like an angel, haloed from behind.

'I'm worried about you,' she said.

'I'm OK.'

'Can I come in?'

'Yes.'

She came in and stood over the bed, looking down on him. Nat patted a spot beside him, Nathan's side, and she lay down facing him.

'Now that Nathan's gone, do you want me to go home?'

'Not if you don't want to.'

'There's nothing to help with any more.'

'I'll take that as a compliment. So, you're saying I don't need any help.'

'Are you going to stay on here at the house?'

'Yeah, he didn't have any relatives. I mean, not living. So he left everything to me.'

'You're lucky. You have a house and a little money.'

'I'd rather have Nathan.'

'I know. I know you would, Nat.'

An awkward silence.

Then Nat said, 'Why do you think he did everything he did for me?'

'I wish you'd had a chance to ask him.'

'I did. Actually. But my timing was a little bit off.'

They lay in silence for a few moments. Nat tried to shake off the feeling of awkwardness caused by her closeness. But it was stubborn. Or maybe he wasn't trying hard enough.

Carol said, 'I have a couple of theories. Want to hear them?'

'Sure. Why not?'

'First off, I think part of it was how much his grandfather did for him. You know his grandfather pretty much raised him after his father died?'

Nat blinked once or twice. 'No. I didn't know that. His father died? When?'

'When he was twelve.'

'How did you know that? I knew Nathan so much

better than you. I mean longer. I knew him for so much longer. And I didn't know that. How did you know that?'

A pause. As if she were waiting for him to figure it out on his own. 'I asked him.' Then, rushing past the awkward spot, she said, 'So maybe he was doing that thing people do. That thing where they know how it feels to really need help and get it, so they do the same for somebody. Plus . . . I'm not saying this to criticize him, Nat, you know I'd never do that. But Nathan was an accountant all his life. His first marriage was unhappy. The second ended in divorce. He was nearly fifty when he found you in the woods. Right around that age when people start to wonder if their lives are turning out the way they want them to. I think maybe he just wanted his life to be more.'

'I can understand that. But I can't understand how I could be the more.'

'Lots of people use helping somebody to make their life feel like more. Look at Mother Theresa. Look how happy she is.'

Nat pulled in a deep, noisy breath of preparation. As if oxygen would soften the sudden jump in his heart rate. 'Wait a while and think about what you want to do now. OK? Think whether you want to stay or go.'

'OK. Sure.' A pause. 'You have to get up, you know. Sometime.'

'I'll get up. I just need a little more time.'

'Really? You'll really get up all on your own? Pretty soon?'

'Yeah. I will. He would have wanted me to, so I will. Pretty soon here I'll get up and do something that would make him proud.'

'That's nice. Do you know what it's going to be yet?'

'I'm thinking.'

'OK. I'll leave you to think.'

'Thank you,' Nat said.

Ten minutes may have gone by, or it may have been half an hour. It was hard for Nat to judge. But in time he reached for the phone. Pulled the receiver off its cradle on the bedside table without getting up. Without moving much.

He dialed a number he still knew by heart.

'Hello?' An old woman's voice. Startlingly old. Did it even sound familiar to him?

'Gamma?'

A long, weighted silence. She couldn't very well ask who was calling. She had to know. That one word said it all. Maybe she was just too taken aback to answer.

'Gamma, it's me. Nat.'

8 March 1990

Mad

Nat stepped into the gym around eight o'clock in the evening. Everybody had gone home except Danny. Which was hardly a surprise. Nat had planned it that way quite purposely.

Danny was pounding a heavy bag, his back to Nat. Nat knew Danny must have heard the door swing shut. But he did not turn around. Man, he was one big kid. Working out with just his trunks on, he looked close to a heavyweight already. And probably no more than fourteen. Not much more, anyway.

'Danny.'

'What you want, Nat?' Still without turning around. Without missing a punch. No wonder Little Manny kept saying Danny reminded him of Nat.

'My name is Nathan, actually.'

Danny stopped punching. Held the bag a moment

and looked over his shoulder. 'Well, I know that,' he said. 'But you go by Nat.'

'Not any more. Now I go by Nathan.'

'Oh, so now I lose points because I didn't know that, when how could I know?'

'I'm not upset. I'm just telling you.'

'Doesn't that make it more confusing with the older Nathan?'

'The older Nathan is gone now. He died.'

'Oh. I'm sorry, Nat. I mean, Nathan. That's too bad.'

'Yeah,' Nat said. 'I'm sorry, too. Come on, get in the ring with me. I want to see what you can do.'

Nat walked over to the equipment shelves and took down a pair of mitts. When he turned back, Danny hadn't moved. He just stood there next to the bag, gloved fists hanging at his sides. Staring at Nat.

'What?' Nat asked.

'I been hanging around here the better part of two years and you ain't wanted to see what I can do.'

'Well, tonight I do.' Nat stepped through the ropes and into the ring.

Danny seemed to chew that over for another few seconds. Then he shrugged and ducked through the ropes. He waited patiently while Nat put the mitts on, raised them to position and gave the word.

'OK. Hit me.'

Danny began sparring gently. Too gently. Technically, his punches looked good. But they felt too easy on Nat's mitts. As if Danny were treating him like fine bone china.

'Know what your problem is?' Nat asked.

Danny stopped punching. Stood still in the ring, hands frozen in position. As though someone had punched *him*. His face soft. Too nice, Nat thought. Too sweet a kid. At least, for this business.

'As a fighter?'

'Yeah. As a fighter.'

'Didn't think I *had* a problem. Little Manny thinks I'm good.'

'You want to hear my opinion or not?'

Danny's arms fell to his sides. 'OK. What's my problem?'

'Passion.'

'Passion?'

'Yes. Passion. As in, where's yours?'

'I thought passion was like . . . a thing between a guy and his girlfriend.'

'That's just one kind of passion and it's not the kind I'm talking about. I'm talking about emotion. Fire. Anger. That's it!' Nat shouted, and Danny jumped as if someone had fired off a gun next to his ear. 'That's what's missing. Anger.'

'Who'm I supposed to be mad at?'

'Has to be somebody. What about me? I refused to train you.'

'That's up to you. You don't gotta work for free.'

'It didn't make you mad?'

'No. I just don't like you much.'

'OK, let's try this another way. Who would you be mad at if you *were* the kind of guy to get mad?'

Danny tried to scratch his nose with one glove, but gave up quickly. 'My dad, I guess. For taking off before I was born. And my mom. 'Cause when she left me at my grandma's she said she'd be back in just a few weeks, and we'd live together again. But she only came back one summer and a couple weekends, and we ain't lived together since.'

'Ha. You call that a sad story? My mother could have dumped me at my grandmother's house, but instead she left me in the woods under a pile of leaves. To die. In October.'

Danny rocked his head back in disbelief. 'Why you standing here, then?'

'Just luck. Nathan was out hunting with his dog, and the dog sniffed me out before I could freeze all the way to death.'

'You feeding me shit?'

Nat raised his right mitt as if in a court of law. 'God's honest truth. I've got the newspaper clipping to prove it.'

Danny stared down at the mat for a beat or two. Then he looked Nat right in the eye. 'OK. So your story sadder'n mine. OK. But my story still my story. I mean . . . even if somebody else got it worse. What I got was bad enough. You know?'

Nat took two steps in. Stood almost nose to nose with the boy. Raised his mitts again. 'Then why don't you . . . get . . .' He geared up every ounce of volume he had in him. 'Mad!'

Danny hit him with a powerful shot to the right mitt. Nat, who still wasn't a hundred per cent steady on his feet, ended up on his back, his head thumping hard on the mat.

He looked up into Danny's terrified face.

'Nat! You OK? Did I hurt you?'

'I'm fine, kid. I'm not a raw egg.'

'Little Manny said you gotta be careful with your head.'

'That's just the right side here. Back of my head is just as hard as anybody's. Harder than most. You want to back off a little so I can get up?'

Danny took a step back and held out an arm to Nat.

'I know how to get up on my own,' Nat said.

He rolled over and rose to his feet.

'You sure you're OK? I'm sorry, Nat. I mean, Nathan.'

'Do *not* be sorry. *Never* be sorry for your anger in the ring. Now, that was good just then. Show me some more of that.'

31 December 1999

Epilogue

The minute Nat stepped out of the elevator and into the hotel lobby, he spotted Danny in the crowd. It wasn't difficult. First of all, he was a good head taller than anybody around him. Secondly, he had sighted Nat and was hopping up and down like a little kid, waving his arms wildly.

'I want to go with *you*, Nathan,' Danny said the minute Nat caught up to him. He stood in a pack of trainers and managers and promoters, all of whom turned their eyes on Nat when Danny spoke.

'What? We're not all going in one limo?'

Vick, one of Danny's two managers, said, 'They sent two limos. There're nine of us, so they sent two. I thought we could've squeezed in . . .'

'Or we could have gotten reservations at the Mandalay,' Nat said, 'and not bothered with limos at all.'

'Yeah, yeah, sure,' Vick said. 'And if things were different they wouldn't be the same.'

He herded them through the front doors of the hotel, held open for them by uniformed doormen. Out on to the pavement, where two black stretches waited at the valet curb, their doors also held open by uniformed employees.

Mike, one of the trainers, said, 'So we'll split into four and five. And Nathan can go in Danny's limo.'

'No,' Danny said. All eyes turned to him. 'I want to go in a limo with Nathan. Just Nathan.'

Vick rolled his eyes.

Nat said, 'You should go with your trainers, Danny.'

Danny put a hand on Nat's chest and pushed him back a few steps, away from the ears of the crowd.

'Thing is,' he said quietly, his face close to Nat's, 'I still sort of think of you as my trainer.'

'Oh, come on. Don't make me laugh. You're in such a different league now. We're not even orbiting the same planets.'

'I don't mean it like that. Just that we go way back.'

Nat sighed. Walked around Danny and up to where Vick was waiting, tapping his foot on the curb.

'He's just nervous,' Nat said.

'Fine. Whatever. Who cares? Both cars go to the same place.' Then, more loudly, to Danny, 'We'll see you there, kid.'

'I'm not a kid!' Danny shouted back. 'I'm twenty-four years old.'

'Twenty-four years old *is* a kid,' Vick said, and ducked inside the first limo.

'I want to sit on this backwards side,' Danny said, settling on the seat facing the rear of the limo, his back to the driver. 'I like to watch the world go by backwards.'

'Now why is that?'

'I dunno. Just do. How often do you get to see the world go by backwards?'

Nat shifted from his forward-facing seat and sat beside Danny, watching the Las Vegas strip flash by in reverse. 'Yeah. I guess I see what you mean,' he said.

'This sure is one lit-up town.'

'Never been to Vegas before?'

'Now how would I've ever been to Vegas?'

'I don't know. Maybe your grandmother was a gambler.'

'My grandma wasn't no gambler.'

'No offense intended.'

'No offense taken. But she wasn't.' He leaned his head back and watched the lights stream by. Looking nearly hypnotized. Then he said, 'Wish she was still here to see this.'

'Yeah. I know what you mean. I wish Nathan were still here.'

'And Little Manny.'

'Yeah. And Little Manny.'

'Is Carol gonna watch from home?'

'Are you kidding? She wouldn't miss it. She's watching *and* taping.'

'If my grandma and your Nathan and Little Manny had lived to see this, even if they was too old and sick to come, they coulda watched it on the TV.'

'If they had cable, yeah.'

'If my grandma was alive, she'd *get* cable. She'd *buy* her some HBO to see this.'

'Maybe she'll still see,' Nat said. 'Even so.'

'Think so?'

'I don't know. Truthfully, I got no idea. But why not think the best in a situation? Since we don't know.'

'Yeah. Maybe. I hope so. Speaking of which. Speaking of what we don't know. What you think gonna happen come midnight tonight? Think planes'll fall out of the sky, and shit? And there won't be no lights, and no water, and all the nuclear plants'll melt down or something? Think the whole world'll fall apart over that computer Y2K shit?'

Nat smiled inwardly to himself. He knew this was a month's worth of words for Danny. And he also knew it meant Danny was nervous.

'No,' he said. 'I don't.'

'Why not?'

'I don't know. I just don't. I just don't think it'll be that big a deal.'

'You don't think people'll go to their ATM money machines and find 'em all screwed up and shut down? You be willing to bet that won't happen?'

'I'm not a betting man, Danny.'

'What? You don't have some dollars on me to win tonight?'

'Well. Yeah. Sure I do. Of course I do. But that's not the same. That's not really gambling. That's a sure thing.'

Danny grinned widely.

Then something caught his eye out the window, and he pitched forward, his fingers marking the glass with his nervous perspiration.

'Look at that, Nathan! Look!'

Nat leaned over and tried to see around him. Just before the driver turned into the circular hotel driveway, Nat caught a glimpse of what Danny had seen.

Danny had his name up in neon on the hotel sign. It said:

MANDALAY BAY RESORT AND CASINO PRESENTS
LIVE TONIGHT
DIEGO GARCIA vs DANIEL LATHROP

There was another line underneath, but the limo was circling the fountain now, and the sign spun out of Nat's view.

'Holy shit,' Danny said. Sounding truly scared. 'That

makes my legs feel all gooey inside. You believe what we just saw?'

'What? You didn't think they'd put it on the sign?'

'No. I knew they would. But do you *believe* it?'

'Yup. This is the big time, Danny. You're going to the show.'

'You got any last words for me, Nathan?'

'You're not dying, Danny. But, yeah. I do.'

He took Danny by the elbow and pulled him off into the corner of the huge dressing room. Away from the entourage crowd.

'First of all, I'm so freaking jealous of you I could die right here on the spot. And also I'm so happy for you I could die all over again. That's twice in one night. But not necessarily in that order. But the main thing I want to tell you is that I'm proud of you tonight.'

Danny furrowed his brow, frowning. 'What if I don't win?'

'It's not contingent on your winning.'

'I don't know what that word means.'

'Contingent? It just means it doesn't depend on it. That's why I'm telling you now. Because I'm proud of you now. I'm proud of you for getting this far. And for who you are. And how you did this.'

A rapping on the door.

A voice on the other side called, 'Two minutes.'

They both stared at the door for another moment. As if expecting it to do something.

Then Danny said, 'Thanks, Nathan. Wish you could be in that corner with me.'

'But you know I can't. But I'll be right behind you. The whole time. But I don't want you to think about that. Just know I'm back there, but give all your attention to Mike. In-between rounds, when you're in your corner, there's nobody else in the world except Mike. When the bell rings again, there's nobody else in the world except Garcia. I'm right behind you. But don't split your focus.'

'OK, Nathan. I won't. Nathan? Is it OK if I'm really scared?'

'If you weren't, I'd figure you didn't know the half of what was going on here. But you'll be good. I'm going out there now. And I'm going to watch you walk out. You walk into that place like you own it. You hear me?'

Nat reached out his fists and Danny bumped them lightly with his own, like fighters in the middle of the ring.

'Thanks, Nathan. I still don't got no idea why you did everything you did for me. But thanks.'

Even Danny's back looked scared, Nat thought.

He watched from behind as Danny opened up to accept his mouth guard from Mike.

Then he watched as Danny nodded. And nodded. And nodded.

What could Mike possibly have to say to him that hadn't been said a hundred times before?

A few seconds later, Danny broke the rules. He glanced over his shoulder and made eye contact with Nat.

Nat winked at him, and smiled. Then he pointed back to Mike. To say, 'Back to your focus.'

Danny's head and eyes shifted forward again.

Nat pulled his wallet out of his front pocket. He always kept it in his front pocket at any sort of boxing event. Not the most dependable crowd in the world. If he lost a few bucks, that wouldn't have been the end of the world. And he didn't have a driver's license anyway.

But the good-luck charm. That was one of a kind. And it was not about to go anywhere, if he could help it.

He pulled the photo out of the wallet. He'd had it laminated, so he could run his thumb over the face in the picture without fading or smearing it. Even if his hands were sweating just a little bit.

Like they were tonight.

He felt a presence behind him and whipped his head around. Vick was looking over his shoulder.

'Who's that, your grandfather?'

'Something like that, yeah.' When Vick didn't comment further, Nat said, 'It's my good-luck charm.

I've had it with me at every single match Danny ever fought. Amateur and pro both.'

'Yeah? Well, generally speaking I don't put much stock in luck. But if it got the kid this far, I say have at it.'

He moved away again. Which was good.

It allowed Nat to say what he always said before one of Danny's fights. Quietly. Under his breath. But always out loud.

'If you've got any kind of influence where you are, Nathan, this would be a good moment to use it.'

He slid the photo back into his pocket when the bell rang.

THE END

CATHERINE RYAN HYDE

CHASING WINDMILLS

It says a lot about someone when they don't get off at the end of the line. When they just sit there with the doors open until the train starts back the other way.

Sebastian, at 17, has never eaten pizza, never been to school, never even hung out with other kids. He rides the subway at night to escape his father's strict, possessive parenting.

Maria, 22 and mother to two young children, has just lost her job. Afraid to confess to her violent boyfriend, Maria resorts to riding the subway when he thinks she's at work.

And then one night, on an empty train, Sebastian and Maria make eye contact . . .

'This gritty love story is compelling reading'
Sun

'Surprisingly wonderful'
Mirror

The opening chapter follows here . . .

Sebastian | *One*
Chemistry

This is the part that's going to be hard to explain: How can I tell you why two people who were afraid of everything—other people, open places, noise, confusion, life itself—wound up riding the subways alone under Manhattan late at night?

Okay, it's like this: When everything is unfamiliar and scary, your heart pounds just getting change from the grocery cashier. That feels like enough to kill you right there. So the danger of the subways at night can't be much worse. All danger begins to fall into the same category. You have no way to sink any deeper into fear.

Besides, consider the alternative. Staying home.

That's enough about that for now. I need to tell you about her.

She got on the Lexington Avenue local at . . . what was it? . . . I think Union Square. Funny how a thing like that can be so damned important, but you don't know it's important until an instant later in the big scheme of time. Then you go back and try to retrieve it. You tell yourself it's in there somewhere. But it's really in that no-man's-land of the moment before you woke up and started paying attention to your own life.

I'm pretty sure it was Union Square.

At first we looked at each other for a split second, but of course we looked away immediately. It's part of what makes us like the animals, I suppose. Ever seen two dogs circling to fight? They look right into each other's eyes. It's a challenge. So when a dog doesn't want to challenge anybody, he looks away. In case I haven't made it clear by now, we were two dogs who weren't looking for a fight.

But then, after we both looked away, we weren't afraid of each other anymore. We knew we didn't have to be. I mean, except to the extent that we were afraid of everything.

There was no one else in the car. It rumbled along again, with that special rocking, and the clacking noise, the lights flashing off now and then. And the heat. It was only May, but the heat had started early. It was after midnight, so I guess you'd think it was all cooled off by then, but it wasn't. A little bit cooler up on the street. Not so much down there. It was stuffy, like more air would be nice.

Every now and then we'd hear a noise that could

have been somebody opening the door from another car. And we'd jump in unison, and look up. But it was never anybody. Just the two of us all the way to the end of the line.

Once I looked over at her while she was looking away. Her hair was dark and thick and about down to her shoulders. Her face was thin, like the rest of her. I couldn't figure out if there was something angular about her face, or something almost delicate. Maybe both.

I was trying to get a bead on how old she was. Older than me, that's for sure. I mean, she was a full-grown woman. But young enough, I guess. But maybe old compared to me. Early twenties.

Every inch of her was covered. Except her face. Jeans, boots, some kind of shawl thing wrapped around her. Seemed like too much to wear in that heat.

And a hat. She was wearing a hat over all that dark hair. A gray felt thing with a big brim. So all she had to do was dip her head an inch or two, and she was gone again. She could break off eye contact just like that. It seemed like such a great plan. I wondered why I'd never thought of it myself.

And on one cheek, a dark spot. Not exactly a bruise, but something like one. Like a shadow. Like she'd had some sort of an accident.

I think I remember feeling that it was a lovely face, but maybe I'm adding that in after the fact. It's hard to go back and describe what you thought of such an important face the first time you saw it. The memory gets colored with all those other things you felt later on. It's hard to separate them out again. But whatever I thought about her face, I noticed it. And it held me.

Then she looked up and I quickly looked away.

At the end of the line, we both waited. And neither one of us got off the train.

You see, it says a lot about someone when they don't get off at the end of the line. When they just sit there with the doors open until the train starts back the other way. Right back to—or past—where they started out in the first place. That says a lot.

After the train started back up again, she looked right into my eyes. She didn't look away and neither did I.

Something happened in me. I'm not sure how good I'll be at explaining what it was. But it was an actual physical something. Something in my body. And I'm not going to go into any personal information about certain body reactions, because some things I'm just not comfortable discussing. Some things a gentleman doesn't talk about. Or, anyway, that's what I believe. But something happened in my gut. Like all of a sudden something that used to be solid in there turned to water. Hot water. In my arms, too, around my elbows. And a little bit down my legs. Especially around my knees. I remembered hearing an expression about being weak in the knees, and I guess I understood it for the first time.

And there was a tingling associated with all this. A kind of all-over tingling, but mostly in my face. Which felt a little hot, like it might be turning red.

Then it was too much and we both looked away again. But not the same way we had before.

We rode like that for another hour or so, and never looked at each other after that. I wanted to look, but I couldn't bring myself to do it.

Then I woke up—which was weird, because I'd never felt myself go to sleep—and I was on that subway car by myself, and she was gone. I looked at my watch, and it was after three.

All I could think was that I wanted to talk to Delilah about this. About what had just happened. But, what had just happened? What was I supposed to say? There was this woman on the subway, and she looked at me. But in the few weeks I'd been talking to Delilah, every time I told her something I'd been feeling, she seemed to know what that feeling was. It made me seem almost . . . normal.

WHEN I GOT HOME, the apartment was dark and quiet, and of course my father was asleep. I came in on my tip-toes, even though it's pretty hard to wake him after he's taken his sleeping pill. You'd almost have to be trying. But I was careful all the same.

I looked at myself in my bathroom mirror. I wanted

to look at myself the way someone else would look at me. I wanted to see what she saw.

I discovered something strange about myself in that moment. The moment I caught my own eyes in the mirror, I looked away. It was hard to force myself to look at myself. I wasn't bad to look at. It wasn't that. I wasn't the handsomest guy in the world, but I wasn't ugly. I guess I thought I looked fine. But it was almost as though I'd never really looked into my own eyes before. Like it was as hard to look at myself as it was to look at somebody else. And I wasn't sure what that meant. Unless it meant I was the kind of dog who didn't even want to challenge myself.

IN THE MORNING, I came to the breakfast table, and my father was staring at me. Taking my emotional temperature, as I like to put it. He only looked away once, to glance at his watch. That was his way of telling me I'd slept too long. If he only knew.

Then he went back to scrutinizing me again.

I hate that. It makes me feel like I guess a worm must feel when some fisherman is about to stick him on a hook. Like you want to get away, but there's no way to get away, so you just squirm. It's no use, but you do it anyway.

He said, "Good morning, Sebastian."

I said, "Good morning, Father."

I know how weird that sounds, but that's what I have to call him. He's not into any of that "Dad" or "Pop" stuff. I'm Sebastian, all three syllables every time, and he's Father. And that's not negotiable. That is one of any number of things that are not negotiable.

He was wearing his glasses at the table, his weird little round, wire-rimmed glasses. All the better to stare at me, I suppose. And some of his hair was spilling down over his forehead. His hair was curly and a little unruly, like mine, but gray. Suddenly, it seemed. Almost as if every morning you could see how much grayer it was than the day before.

And he was still studying me. It was as if he could see that something had changed in me. It was horrifying.

"What?" I said, finally, when I couldn't take it anymore.

"You seem different."

"I don't feel different," I said. Lying.

"You seem different."

"Different how?"

"I'm not sure. Like you were happy or excited about something."

Ah, yes. That. The sin of being happy or excited. According to my father, we must guard carefully against such things. According to my father, these emotions are the equivalent of dancing on our fifth-floor window ledge. Clearly inviting a nasty fall.

"Well, I'm not," I said. Hoping that would be the end of it.

It wasn't.

"I think you're taking too much sleep," he said.

"Sleep is good for you. You can tell because I've been so healthy. Think how long it's been since I've been sick. It's the running, if you ask me, and plenty of sleep."

"There's still such a thing as too much."

I shifted tactics in midstream. "I was up late last night. I couldn't sleep. Didn't get to sleep until after three. That's why I slept in."

At first he said nothing. But I could tell by his mood that he wasn't done. You could feel it shifting around in him. You can always tell when he's mixing up another batch of something. But for a while he just stirred his bowl of cereal with a spoon. I remember thinking it must be getting really soggy.

Then he said, "What do you do? When you can't sleep?"

"I don't know. Just lie there."

"And do what?"

"I don't know. Think, I guess."

"What do you think about?"

I wanted to jump into that. I always want to jump him when he does that. It makes me want to attack. Not physically; I'm not like that. Attack verbally, the way he does with me. It makes me crazy when he tries to get inside my head. The only place I have left. But it never helps to rise up against him like that. It just never does any good.

"I don't remember," I said.

The face of the woman on the subway came into my head, fully formed, perfect. A perfect recollection. I wondered if I would ever see her again. I couldn't have imagined at that moment that I would.

I FINISHED MY LESSONS by one p.m. and went out for my run. My father frowned, the way he always did when I left the apartment to run. But he said nothing anymore. This point, at least, I had permanently won.

The whole time I was running, mostly in the park, I thought, *Please let Delilah be there today. Please.* It was like a chant that kept me going.

As I turned the final corner, I looked up at our building and there she was. Three floors up, hanging half out her window, waving at me. I smiled without even meaning to. Out loud but quietly, I said, "Thank you," and then realized I didn't even know who I was talking to.

I waited by the outside door, panting, for a few minutes, and then she hobbled down, and I held the door for her. She said what she always said.

"Thank you, child."

It's hard for her to get through the door without

help. She has a bad hip, or maybe it's both of them, and she's very big, and walks with a cane. So getting through the door is hard unless somebody else holds it. Something about her hips or her back pushes the top of her body forward, so she looks like some kind of punctuation mark, though I'm not sure which one. Maybe a question mark that doesn't really curve around all the way on top. And she walks with her huge back end kind of trailing in a noticeable way. But I'm not criticizing. She's the best friend I have. She's the best friend I've ever had. Maybe it seems weird we could be friends when she's over fifty and I'm under eighteen. But we manage just fine.

We started off on our walk together. I had to remember to walk about twelve times slower than I would on my own.

Delilah took her little portable fan out of her pocket. A little plastic rocket of a fan, bright blue, with little blades like a miniature helicopter. She had to turn it on with her left hand, because she needed to lean on the cane with her right. The blades opened up like a flower and I could hear the buzz as they started to spin, and she trained the breeze onto her face and sighed.

"This weather, child," she said. "Good Lord, this heat."

She had a wonderful face, Delilah. Light-skinned black with freckles on her cheeks, and eyes the color of walnut shells, and the biggest teeth you ever saw in your life, so that when she smiled it seemed to take up her whole face. It was fun to make her smile, just to see it again. And it wasn't hard, either. Lots of things made Delilah smile.

"So," she said. "Where does that father of yours think you are right now?"

I looked down at the sidewalk and didn't answer.

"So you still haven't seen fit to tell him you made a friend."

"You don't know how he is," I said. "You don't know him."

"Not sure I got a yen to. Not sure what I think of a man doesn't want his own boy to have a single friend."

I looked up from the sidewalk and gave her a pleading look. Like, *Please. Not now. Not again.* And she caught it, and nodded, and waved it away with the hand that held the little plastic fan.

"Okay, okay, never you mind," she said.

Imagine such a thing. Being able to tell somebody what you want with your eyes. And get it. See why I loved Delilah so much? Even though I'd only known her for a few weeks.

"Something happened last night," I said.

"'Bout time," she said.

"I'm afraid it'll sound silly. Like it was nothing."

"If it's something to you, then it's something to me."

So I told her about the woman on the subway, and

the way she looked at me, and the way it made me feel inside. She listened with a little closed-mouth smile getting wider and wider on her face. Not like she was making fun of me, though. More like she knew what I was talking about even if I didn't.

When she was sure I was done she said, "Oooooh-weeee."

"Meaning what?"

"Your first dose of electricity."

"What does that mean?"

It's not that I didn't know what it meant, exactly. I'm not a complete idiot. I meant . . . what did I mean? I meant, why *that* woman? And why not ever before? At least, not quite like that ever before.

"Means you're a boy. And you're not dead yet. And you're not a little child no more."

But those were the parts I already knew.

We walked without talking for a couple of minutes. But it was still okay.

Then her fan slowed down. I could hear the sound of the blades change, and get low and sluggish. She rapped it hard on the top of her cane, and it seemed to pick up again. But a minute later, it slowed even more.

She stopped walking, so I stopped, too. She looked down at the fan like she was looking under the hood of a broken-down car. Like she would see the problem and know how to fix it.

"Bat-tries are dead. I wore the darn bat-tries down. Can't believe I didn't charge the darn bat-tries." She turned it off, sighed a very different kind of sigh from when she'd turned it on, and slipped it into the pocket of her enormous linen pants.

"I didn't even know her," I said. "I'd never even seen her before."

"That won't matter," she said. "Chemistry won't care. Two people either have it or they don't. Have it first time they set eyes on each other. Across a crowded room. Like the song says."

I didn't know what song, but I didn't ask.

A minute later, we passed by one of those stores that sell cheap souvenirs to the tourists. Electronics and postcards and little plastic Statues of Liberty. And in the window I saw they had fans. The old-fashioned, low-tech kind. The kind that fold up into a little stick, but unfolded they look like an accordion and have Chinese or Japanese art on them.

"Wait here," I said.

She looked like she could use a minute to rest, anyway. I ran inside to buy one for Delilah. Yes, ran inside. Risked the horrors of people I'd never even met. Walked right through the heart pounding. All for my friend.

It only cost me $1.99, about ten percent of my weekly allowance, but from the look in her eyes you'd have thought I bought her a new car or a mink coat. She unfolded it and hid the bottom half of her face behind it, pretend coy like a Japanese geisha girl. Then she lowered it and laughed so loud I bet they could hear her inside the store.

"Child, if you aren't just the sweetest thing," she said, when she was all through laughing. And she put her hand on the top of my head and brought it down to her level and kissed me right on the forehead.

Then we walked on, and she fanned herself with her left hand and seemed to feel better.

"Congratulations," she said.

"For what?"

"For being alive. Hope something like last night happens to you again real soon."

Buy CHASING WINDMILLS online
at www.rbooks.co.uk

Love in the Present Tense

Catherine Ryan Hyde

'So much of how it started was when that cop got out and came up to me. But I didn't know all this when it first happened. I didn't know there would ever be a Leonard, or that this man would be his father, or that anyone would have to die . . .'

Leonard is an eerily wise five-year-old boy with asthma, terrible eyesight, and the ability to captivate everyone he meets.

Pearl is Leonard's devoted teenage mother, desperately trying to hide a violent secret from her past.

Mitch is Leonard's twenty-five-year-old next-door neighbour, busy running his own company and entertaining the Mayor's wife.

Then one day Pearl drops Leonard off with Mitch, and never returns.

How do you go on loving someone who isn't there? As truth and fiction, memory and dreams collide, Mitch finds himself learning from a surprising source the true, magical definition of love.

'A sweet and honest look at the pains and pleasures of love, and who could not fall in love with leonard – what a beautifully drawn character'
JANE GREEN

'A work of art . . . Enchanting'
SAN FRANCISCO CHRONICLE

'Haunting'
WASHINGTON POST

'A remarkable story of the magic of love'
DAILY EXPRESS

'A work of art'
SAN FRANCISCO CHRONICLE

9780552773645

Pay It Forward

Catherine Ryan Hyde

It all started with the social studies teacher's
extra-credit project:

Think of an idea for world change, and put it into action

WHILST THIS PROVED a little ambitious for most of his classmates, twelve-year-old Trevor thought he would start by doing something good for three people. But instead of paying *him* back, he would ask them to 'pay it forward' by doing a favour for three more people. If it all went to plan, Trevor thought, it would be the start of a long chain of human kindness . . .

Sound unlikely? Well a lot of other people had their doubts too – Trevor's teacher, his classmates, his mother, in fact everyone in his small California town. It could never really work . . . could it?

'Hyde's book delivers a profound vision:
the simple magic of the human heart'
SAN FRANCISCO CHRONICLE

HAVE YOU HEARD?
www.payitforwardmovement.org
www.payitforwardfoundation.org

9780552774253